Reap the Whirlwind

Reap the Whirlwind

Josh Aterovis

P.D. Publishing, Inc.
Clayton, North Carolina

ISBN-13: 978-1-933720-35-7
ISBN-10: 1-933720-35-2

9 8 7 6 5 4 3 2

Cover design by Josh Aterovis
Edited by: Medora MacDougall

Published by:

P.D. Publishing, Inc.
P.O. Box 70
Clayton, NC 27528

http://www.pdpublishing.com

Acknowledgements:

I'd like to thank everyone who had a part in the development of this book, from my readers and fans to the editors and critics. Thank you to Barb and Linda for giving *Reap the Whirlwind* a second chance. Finally, thank you to Jonathan Hernandez for modeling for the cover.

Prologue

I opened the door and stepped into the well-appointed office, closing the door behind me. The room was intimately lit by incandescent table lamps instead of institutional fluorescent overhead lighting. An oriental design rug covered the floor, and two upholstered armchairs sat facing a massive dark-colored wooden desk. Glass-fronted oak bookcases lined the walls. Behind the desk sat a small man, slightly balding, wearing a dark brown, high quality suit, and glasses.

"Hello, Will," he said. "It's been a while."

"Yes," I said simply.

"Sit down, please," he motioned toward the chairs and smiled encouragingly. I sat down on the closest one. "What's on your mind?" he prompted.

"You said when I was ready to talk to call you."

"And you're ready to talk now?"

I nodded.

"Why now and not before?"

I shrugged.

"Just ready? Or did something happen that made you change your mind?"

"Something happened..."

He sat, waiting for me to elaborate.

"I don't even know where to begin," I said. "So much has happened since I saw you last. I need to talk to someone. I feel like I'm going crazy."

"Will," he said softly, "you are not going crazy. Instead of starting at the end and working back, why don't we start at the beginning? Pretend we've never talked before. Tell me everything."

The beginning. It seemed like so long ago now. Could it really have been only a few months? "That could take a while," I said.

He shrugged and pushed a button on his intercom.

"Yes?" the receptionist answered.

"Linda, cancel the rest of my afternoon appointments, please."

"Yes, sir," she answered.

He looked up and smiled, his kind eyes radiating understanding. "Now we've got plenty of time," he said to me.

I took a deep breath.

Chapter 1

Nothing can stay the same forever. We get in trouble in life when we think it can and will. Everything changes, or as King Solomon said in the Bible and The Byrds sang in the '60s, to everything there is a season and a time for every purpose under heaven. It's not a particularly easy lesson to learn or a fun one for that matter. I learned it the summer between high school and college, and my life would never be the same.

We burst into the house, laughing and shoving each other playfully. We were both sweaty from playing basketball on the driveway. The black macadam drew heat like a magnet. For what must have been the millionth time I looked at Joey and thought about how different we were. We were a study in contrasts, a true testament to the old adage that opposites attract. We'd been best friends since we were toddlers, but we couldn't have been more different. Joey was tall, a little over six feet, and I was...well, short. If I wore my Airwalks with the thick soles I just managed to eke out five foot six. He had poker-straight pale blond hair that he wore cut off bluntly just above his shoulders. Today he had pulled it back into a ponytail, but half of it had fallen down and was stuck now to his face. My black hair was so curly I had to keep it cut short or it sprung out into an afro. Joey had a year-round tan that darkened to a golden brown on the first day of summer. I had pale white skin that burned over and over, never tanned, turned an unflattering shade of red if you even looked at me funny, and broke into freckles across my nose at the first hint of sunlight. Joey had these huge puppy-dog brown eyes while mine were a deep blue.

Actually, my eyes are my favorite feature. They are so dark they are almost violet, and these incredibly long black lashes frame them. My other best friend, Laura, is always saying that she would kill to have my eyes.

The differences didn't end at the physical, however. Even our personalities were polar opposites. Joey was gregarious, while I was shy. He was caught up in popularity games, while I was content to hide in the background. Joey took everything at face value and rarely looked deeper, while I tended to be introspective, always looking for a deeper meaning.

Laura, Joey, and I were almost inseparable all through high school. We'd grown up in the same neighborhood and played together since we were old enough to walk. Everyone at school had called us the three musketeers.

Since we'd graduated though, things had started to change. We didn't see each other nearly as much as we used to. Laura had met Gabriel, or Gabe as he preferred, and they had started dating. Over the summer, they had grown closer and closer. I had been dating Beth on and off all through high school and I guess you could say things were semi-serious between us. Beth was from the neighborhood, too, and while she had never really been a part of our little clique she'd been around enough that when we had started dating no one was really surprised. She was a year younger than the rest of us, but she was always the most serious one in the bunch.

The latest blow to the three musketeers had taken place two weeks earlier when Joey and Laura started college at Pemberton University, a local school here in town. Both had been accepted at other schools, but picked Pemberton when I decided to take a year off to work before going to college. My main reasoning behind this decision was that I hated school and really couldn't see jumping right into more studying just as soon as I was finished with high school. Actually, my intense dislike of school had less to do with the academics — I'd always gotten above average grades with very little effort — and much more to do with the fact that I'd never done well in the complex social environment that was the public school system. So Joey and Laura had stayed in order to keep the musketeers intact. The only problem was I had hardly seen them since classes took up. Today was the first day Joey and I had really been able to spend together. I was surprised how much I missed him, and without thinking, I suddenly grabbed him in a tight hug.

"Dude!" he said, pushing me away roughly. "What the hell was that for?"

"Language!" my mother called from the next room.

Joey rolled his eyes, and I shrugged. "I dunno," I answered, choosing to ignore my mother. "I guess I just miss you."

"Yeah, well, I miss you, too, but you know I don't like all that touchy-feely stuff."

That was another difference between Joey and me. I was from a very affectionate family, and I wasn't afraid to show my affection; Joey was very reserved emotionally, the typical macho man who never showed his feelings.

"Let's get something to drink," he said as he headed for the kitchen, dribbling the ball as he went.

"Don't bounce the ball in the house," Mom called.

I trailed after him, mentally kicking myself all the while.

"God! When are you going to get out of here?" he said as soon as we were in the kitchen. "It's like we're still twelve. You make enough at your job that you could get an apartment, especially if you had a roommate."

"I would definitely need a roommate," I told him. "I don't make that much. So that means it's pretty much out of the question."

"Why?"

"Because I don't really know anybody."

"Well, it just so happens that I do."

My eyes lit up. "You?"

"No, not me, dumbass. You know every penny I make goes right to ye olde tuition fund." I felt my face heating up and knew I was turning red. Thankfully, Joey had his back toward me as he hunted in the fridge for something cold. He came out with a carton of orange juice, grabbed two glasses out of cabinet, and proceeded to pour OJ all over the counter as he tried to get it in both glasses at once.

"Jeez, Joey, wreck the kitchen, why don't you," I complained.

"You sound just like your mom," Joey grumbled as he mopped up his mess with a towel. "Anyway, as I was saying, there's this guy at school, his name's Aidan, and he has this two-bedroom apartment so he's looking for a roommate. I told him I'd ask you."

"Why'd he get a two bedroom if it's just him?"

"I don't know, Will, what difference does it make? Are you interested or not?"

"I don't even know this guy...what's his name? Adam?"

"Aidan. And I do know him. He's a really nice guy. I think you two would get along. Look, he just moved in and he's having a kind of housewarming party tonight. I'm supposed to go; why don't you go with me? That way you can meet him, see the apartment, see if you like him...the whole nine yards."

He handed me my glass of OJ and started gulping his down.

"I won't know anyone there," I protested.

"Yes, you will. Laura and Gabe will be there. Gabe knows him from last year; they had some classes together or something. There'll only be a couple other people there, so you don't have to worry about your terminal shyness."

"I don't want to crash his party, especially if there aren't even that many people going." I was getting weaker, and Joey knew it.

"He said I could bring a friend." I hesitated, and he moved in for the kill. "There's going to be someone there I want you to meet besides Aidan."

"Who?"

"Come and you'll find out."

I played my last ace. "I'm supposed to go out with Beth tonight."

"So cancel!" he yelled, throwing his hands up. "Come on, Will. You just said you missed me. Here's your chance to spend some time with me plus meet some new people and maybe find some new digs. Live a little. Bethie will get over it."

I sighed and Joey grinned. He knew he'd won. Why he still got any pleasure from it was beyond me since he always won. You'd think he'd be used to it by now, the manipulative bastard.

"What should I wear?"

"Whatever you want. It's just a party, not a debutante ball."

"A what?"

"Look it up."

"Oh, so you don't know either."

"Shut up." He laughed and punched me in the arm.

"Ow!" I shoved him back, and soon we were wrestling around the kitchen, crashing into the table and knocking over a chair.

"No roughhousing inside!" Mom called.

We froze and looked at each other, then collapsed into a giggling heap on the floor...just like old times.

An hour later, I stood in my room with a towel around my waist as a puddle of water collected at my feet. I stared at the phone, wondering if there was any way I could avoid picking it up. I had been getting out of the shower when

Mom called up that Beth was on the phone. I dreaded the inevitable confrontation when I broke off our date tonight...for the third time in a row.

As I said earlier, Beth is my on-again-off-again girlfriend — more off than on. Not because of Beth; she would have us engaged if she had her way. I was always the one who put things on hold, and Beth was always the one who talked me into going out again. I was content just to hang out with Joey and Laura. In fact, Beth was the only girl I had ever dated. Going to dances with Laura because she didn't have a date doesn't count. Laura says I have a problem with commitment and maybe I do, but I really think I've just watched too many romantic movies. I want that kind of romance where you light up when you hear their name and melt down when they walk into the room. That just wasn't there with Beth. We got along fine; she was comfortable — but there was just no...spark.

I sighed and knew I couldn't put it off any longer.

"Hello?" I answered.

"Well, it's about time," my mother joked as she hung up. My parents loved Beth to no end.

"What happened? You fall down getting out of the shower?" Beth said.

"No, I guess I got lost in thought," I said lamely.

"Oh? And you were thinking about me, of course," she teased.

"Actually, yes."

"Don't sound so excited."

"Listen, Beth, about tonight..."

"No! Will!" she interrupted. "Don't do this to me again. Tonight was going to be special. You promised. Just you and me."

"Something came up." I was dying, and I knew it.

"Let me guess, it has something to do with Joey, right?"

"What does Joey have to do with anything?"

"Everything with you has something to do with Joey. Joey always comes first with you. When is it my turn? You treat me like you treat Laura."

"What's that supposed to mean? What's wrong with how I treat Laura? She's one of my closest friends."

"That's just it, Will." She sighed. "Laura's your friend. But I'm supposed to be your girlfriend. And what's wrong with how you treat both of us is that anytime Joey wants to do something, we both get shoved aside. At least Laura has found someone who knows how to treat her."

"Did she...did Laura tell you this?"

"She didn't have to. Look, Will, this obviously isn't working. You aren't committed to us. I think we should take a break until you figure out what you want."

"Wait a minute; you're breaking up with me?"

"You can call it that. Just don't call me until you've figured things out. It's your move this time."

"Figured things out? What's to figure out? What I want is that...that spark of chemistry. That feeling that everything is all right when you're with them, that you're finally home. Don't you want that?"

"Yes, Will, I do," she said quietly, "but the thing is, I thought I had it — with you. I'm sorry you don't feel the same way. I hope you find it. I really do. Goodbye."

"Beth..." I tried, but she'd already hung up.

I stood there with the phone in my hand for several minutes replaying my conversation with Beth in my head. She had said so much it took a while for it all to sink in, and when it did, I didn't know whether to be angry, laugh, or cry. Maybe all three would suffice.

The car horn sounded, letting me know that Joey had arrived to pick me up for the big shindig at Aidan's. I checked myself in the mirror and was somewhat surprised to see that I was wearing jeans and a short-sleeved dark blue pull-over shirt and leather sandals. I didn't remember choosing that particular out-fit, but then I had been kind of preoccupied with my thoughts since Beth's phone call. At any rate, it would do. At least the blue brought out my eyes.

"Hey," I said as I slid into Joey's Jetta.

"Hey," he gave me a close look, then threw the car into reverse and backed onto the road. "Ok, what's wrong?" he asked as soon as we were moving forward.

"What do you mean?" I tried for the dumb approach.

"Give it up, Will. We both know you're a terrible liar and I know you well enough to know when something is bothering you. Is it this whole apartment thing? 'Cause if it is, I'll back off. It's not that big a deal. Your parents are just a drag sometimes..."

"It's not that," I cut him off. "Beth and I broke up tonight."

"So? You guys break up like every other week. It's a tradition. You'll be dating again next week."

"I don't think so. This time was different. She broke up with me."

"Whoa!" He looked over at me to gauge my reaction.

"Look at the road, please," I said automatically. Having driven with Joey before, I knew we needed all the help we could get.

"So, what happened?"

"I don't want to talk about it."

"You? Mr. Let's-talk-about-our-feelings?"

"It's just...I need some time to think about stuff. She said some things that...I don't know. I just need to think about it."

"She really upset you, huh?"

"Yeah."

The rest of the short ride was spent in silence. The apartment building turned out to be a renovated turn-of-the-century brick warehouse down by the newly rejuvenated river district. It looked like it once served an industrial function of some sort. The renovation project had included installing an eleva-tor that was cleverly designed to look like a grain lift, complete with a wrought iron gate. I was thankful for the elevator considering the building was four stories and Aidan's apartment was on the top floor.

We knocked, and after a moment, a young guy around our age opened the door. He had wavy dark blond hair and the greenest eyes I had ever seen. I wondered if they were contacts. He was taller than I was, of course, but shorter than Joey, so that would put him at about five foot ten.

"Hey, you made it!" he said, breaking into a wide grin bordered by twin dimples.

"Aidan, this is my best friend, Will Keegan," Joey said.

We shook hands as Aidan said, "Hi Will. I'm Aidan Scott. I've heard a lot about you."

I forced a smile. "Well, you're ahead of me."

He laughed and stepped back to allow us in. We entered a large and airy room with high ceilings and rough brick walls. Enormous floor-to-ceiling multi-paned windows with the original wavy glass still intact lined the outside wall. Sparse furnishings made the room look even larger: The overstuffed sofa and recliner's only company was a large entertainment center that housed a state-of-the-art system including a TV, VCR, CD player, and DVD player. The latest R&B dance groove blasted from the surround sound speakers. Laura and Gabe occupied the sofa, sitting so close a sheet of paper couldn't have slipped between them. A leggy blonde had draped herself over the recliner like a carefully positioned model in a La-Z-Boy commercial. Laura waved to acknowledge our arrival then went back to her conversation with the blonde.

"It's not much, but I guess it's home for now. At least for one year according to the lease," Aidan said.

"Are you kidding? It's awesome," I said sincerely. "This place must cost a fortune."

"It's not that bad. You want to see the rest of the place?"

"Sure. You coming, Joey?"

"Nah. You go ahead. I'm gonna go say hi," he said as he headed toward the living area.

I shrugged and turned toward Aidan.

"Now, for the grand tour," he said. "On your right you will notice the lavishly furnished living area. If you turn to your left, you will enter the large and spacious kitchen complete with all the gourmet accoutrements one could ever desire. Julia Child, eat your heart out."

I laughed since the kitchen was barely large enough for the both of us. A built-in table and the three chairs around it took up most of the space.

"Small, but functional," I said helpfully.

Aidan narrowed his eyes. "Have you been talking to my real estate agent?"

I laughed again, and Aidan motioned me back into the living room.

"As we continue with the guided tour, we will now be going through the door just to the right of the kitchen door which, as you will see, leads to this marvelous hallway." He switched now to a game show host voice. "Well, Will, what will it be? Door Number One? Or maybe you'd like to try Door Number Two? Or how about trying your luck with Door Number Three?"

Three doors opened off the hallway, one straight ahead, and one each on the left and right.

"Can I use a lifeline?" I ventured.

"Do I look like Regis?"

"Um...no...let's try for Door Number Two."

"Oh, jeez, Will. I'm sorry, but you chose the bathroom. But we have some lovely parting gifts, don't we, Jimmy?" He dropped his voice an octave and boomed, "That's right, Aidan. We'll be sending Will home with a lifetime supply of Charmin. It's squeezably soft."

I laughed so hard I snorted, which of course caused my face to begin to burn. I imagined I must have been pretty close to the color of a tomato. Aidan acted as if I hadn't just made a rude porcine noise and went on with his game show host shtick.

"But the game's not over yet. Try again, Will."

"Door Number Three."

"Excellent choice," he said as he swung open the door, "and may I just say that is a lovely shade of red you are wearing. Very flattering."

The room we walked into now was apparently Aidan's bedroom, and it was huge. It held a double bed, two dressers, a computer desk outfitted with a brand new computer, and an open closet full of clothes...and there was still room to spare.

"If you decide to be my roomie, your room will be across the hall," Aidan said in his normal voice. He opened that door, and I stepped in expecting a copy of the room I had just seen. I was surprised to find it was half the size and stacked to the ceiling with boxes.

"I, uh, haven't finished unpacking yet," he said sheepishly. "I know this room is smaller, but I needed the extra space for my computer desk. And to make it fair you would only have to pay a third of the rent instead of half."

"Are you sure you can afford that?" I asked automatically.

"Oh, money's not really a problem. That's not why I wanted a roommate. It's more for company. I'm from a big family, and it's weird going from that to living by myself. I thought I could offset the culture shock some by having someone else live here. I mean I have the extra room so it made sense. Not that I'm expecting you, or whoever moves in, to be my best bud or anything. I know you and Joey are really tight, but it'll just be nice having someone else here. Oh yeah, I almost forgot, there is a bonus to having the smaller room. Check this out."

He shoved boxes aside until he had cleared a path to the window. I followed him and looked out. I had to give it to him; the view was spectacular. The window overlooked the river, the lights from the apartment building sparkling and dancing across its black surface. An iron fire escape just outside the window formed a sort of balcony that would be awesome on a summer night.

"I guess we should get back to the party before they think we ditched them," Aidan said after a moment.

"Do you have a boat?" I asked him, still looking out the window. I was reluctant to leave the scene and even more reluctant to return to the group. I wasn't in a party mood even though Aidan's good humor had lifted my dark mood somewhat.

"No. I wish I did, but that's a little out of reach right now. Especially with rent and tuition."

"Too bad," I said. I pulled myself away from the window and followed Aidan back to the living area.

The music had moved on to something a little softer, and the mood seemed to be as mellow as the music. Laura and Gabe were still sitting closely on the couch with plenty of room for another person, but Joey had perched himself on the arm of the recliner. The leggy blonde was resting her hand rather possessively on his thigh.

"Hi, I'm Will," I said pointedly, since no one seemed to be planning on introducing us anytime soon.

"Nice to meet you, Will. I'm Shelley," she said. "I've heard a lot about you from Joe here," she added, giving his leg a little squeeze to punctuate her pronouncement.

I lifted one eyebrow and tried to make eye contact with Joey, but he seemed to suddenly find the carpet pattern extremely fascinating.

"Joe seems to have been doing a lot more talking about me than to me, because I'm afraid I've never heard anything about you."

For a moment, everyone froze; a very awkward silence followed. I forced a laugh in an attempt to undo the damage, and everyone smiled uncertainly. Joey was still busy trying not to look at me.

"Sorry," I said. "I didn't mean that the way it came out. I've had a bad day."

"It's ok, I understand," she said graciously. She had a rather pronounced southern drawl that I couldn't quite place. I guess she was pretty if you liked the type: long white-blonde hair, big blue eyes, pouty lips, and big boobs — she had the whole package.

Personally, I thought Laura was much prettier. Her father is black, and her mother is a full-blooded Cherokee. The results were quite stunning. Her flawless skin was the color of caramel, and her large almond-shaped eyes were a dark chocolate brown. She had high cheekbones and her jet-black hair hung almost to her waist. She and Gabe made a striking couple. Gabe was Hispanic and quite handsome. He was only a year older than Joey, Laura, and I, but he seemed much more sophisticated. Maybe that was just because I hadn't known him all his life as I had Joey and Laura. I didn't have any milk-shooting-from-the-nose memories about him. He seemed to be good for Laura; he complemented her in every way. He wore his straight black hair short and spiky, and his dark good looks matched hers perfectly.

"So you had a bad day?" Laura asked after a brief but loaded pause. Leave it to Laura to pick up the one thing that I didn't want to talk about.

I waved my hand dismissively. "I don't want to talk about it. So, Shelley, do you go to school with Joey...er, Joe?"

I ignored the looks on everyone's faces: the dirty look Laura shot me, the curious ones from Gabe and Aidan, and the uncomfortable expression on Joey's face. I kept my focus carefully on Shelley's pointy little face.

"Yes, we're both in Professor Strauss' American History class. That's where we met on the first day of school. He asked me out the next day, and we've been going out ever since. But it's only been two weeks, so I guess that's why you haven't heard of me," she added quickly. She cast Joey a look that clearly said, "Help me out here!", but he was still engrossed in plush pile.

Well, that explained why Joey had been so busy the last two weeks. I was surprised how hurt I was.

"Yeah, you're right," I said with venom in my voice. "Two weeks is not really long enough for a best friend to tell someone they have a new girl-friend." I stood up and almost had to sit back down as my knees buckled. "If you'll excuse me, I think I need some fresh air."

"Will!" Laura said sharply.

"I'm...I'm sorry. I'm going to...go take a walk...or something," I mumbled haltingly as I stumbled toward the door. Tears were threatening to spill over before I could make my escape. I paused at the door long enough to say, "I've had a bad day, really."

I found my way out of the building and wandered into the back yard. The wooden bulkhead edging the river made a great seat. I had just about gotten myself under control when I felt someone come up behind me. I didn't have to look up to know it was Laura.

"Ok, that was appalling. What the hell was that all about?"

"I've had a bad day," I repeated softly.

"So you keep saying. Wanna tell me about it?"

"No."

"How 'bout you do it anyway." She sat down next to me and swung her long legs out over the water.

"Beth and I broke up today."

"So? You're always breaking up or getting back together. Call her tomor-row, and tell her you're sorry."

"It's not like that this time. She broke up with me."

"Oh...oh, my gosh."

"Yeah, I got the feeling it was pretty permanent this time."

"Will, I don't know how to say this tactfully..."

I snorted. "Since when have you been tactful?"

"Point made. Ok then, have it your way. Why are you so beat up about Beth dumping you for a change? You've dumped her enough times. You don't like being on the receiving end?"

"It's not that. Actually, I don't really care about Beth that much. She was comfortable, familiar...I mean we've been together for years...but..."

"A 'but' is never a good sign, sweetie, and there was always a 'but' with Beth."

"Yeah."

"So what's really bothering you?"

"Something she said. She said that I always put you and her second."

"How did I get into this?"

"She said that I always put Joey first. Do you feel that way too?" I looked over at Laura for the first time. She was looking out over the river, the reflected light playing softly over her even features. For a moment she didn't answer. When she began to talk, I had to lean in closer to catch what she was saying.

"You never knew this," she said. "I never told anyone really, but I've had a huge crush on you for the longest time."

I opened my mouth, but she shook her head before I could speak. "Let me finish. I used to get so hurt whenever I would call you to do something and the answer was always 'Joey and I are doing this' or 'Joey and I are doing that.' It was even worse when it was 'Joey and I *might* be doing this or that.' I wasn't even competition with a possibility. After awhile, I guess I just accepted the fact that Joey would always get top billing when it came to you, but I still wanted to be close to you, so I infiltrated your little club. We became the three musketeers, and we lived platonically ever after. All for one, right? As long as Joey was 'the one'. I got over you eventually. Now I wouldn't trade your friendship for anything. Gabe knows I exist. He treats me right, and I love him. But to answer your question, yeah, I do feel as if I always came second to Joey."

"Why...why didn't you ever say anything?"

"Like what? Hey, Will, I'm in love with you but you treat me like dirt? Hey, Will, why is Joey so great? What's wrong with me? Hey, Will, acknowledge that I exist, dammit? What was I supposed to say?" She swiped angrily at the tears that were rolling down her cheeks. I had only seen Laura cry a few times as long as I had known her. It unnerved me worse than anything she had said.

"I'm sorry," I whispered, "I'm so sorry, Laura."

"It's ancient history," she said taking a deep breath. "I moved on. Like I said, Gabe is the greatest. I really do love him. Maybe I'm not as over you as I thought, but I am moving on."

We sat in silence for a few minutes.

"Did you know Joey and Shelley were dating?" I said at last.

Laura sighed. "He still comes first doesn't he?"

"I didn't...it's just..."

"It's ok. I should be used to it by now. Yeah, I knew."

"Why didn't he tell me?" I tried to keep the whine out of my voice, but I still came out sounding like a petulant five-year-old.

"Maybe because he knew this would happen."

"What do you mean?"

"Will, every time Joey has ever had a girlfriend, you've been jealous. You do nothing but pick them apart and criticize their every move. Maybe Joey wanted a little grace period with Shelley before you started in on her."

"I'm not jealous," I said defensively.

"Oh, please, then what was that whole scene up there?"

"I was just surprised. I mean, you saw the way she was all over him. 'Joe has told me all about you,'" I mocked.

"See, there you go."

I opened my mouth to argue, but Laura hurried on, "Look, Will, I have a very serious question I need to ask you. I want you to be honest with me. Please, I've never asked anything of you. And I don't want you to answer until you can give me a one hundred percent sure answer."

"Of course, Laura," I said indignantly. "You know I would never lie to you."

"Not on purpose, maybe."

"What's that mean?"

"Never mind. Here's my question." She took a deep breath. "Are you in love with Joey? I mean romantically — 'in love' in love. Because if you are, you need to face it and deal with it and figure out what it means. You can't just keep on hurting everyone around you. You know I'll always love you no matter what."

"Are you...are you asking if I'm *gay*?" I asked in amazement.

"Will?" We both turned toward the voice. It was Joey up by the parking lot. "Hey, Will? Laura? Are you guys out here?"

"We're down by the water," Laura called back. She turned back to me, reached out, and touched my cheek for just the briefest moment. I almost didn't feel it. "Think about what I said, and remember I love you."

She jumped up and ducked into the shadows as Joey approached.

"I, uh, didn't interrupt anything, did I?" he asked.

"No, we were finished," I said slowly.

"So, uh...what did you think of the apartment?"

"It was great — airy and light with a great sense of the original integrity of the building. Great color schemes and tastefully decorated. Everything a guy could want," I said sarcastically. "Why'd you come here, Joey? It wasn't to talk about the apartment. Or are you that eager to foist me off on Aidan?"

"Will, it's not like that, and you know it. Shelley thought I should go see..."

"And when were you going to tell me about her? Was I going to be invited to the wedding?"

"We've only been dating two weeks! I was going to tell you tonight. I told you there was someone I wanted you to meet. Do you think I'd be that stupid as to invite you to a party she was going to be at if I wasn't going to tell you about her? I would have told you sooner but...I guess I needed some time with her just to myself first."

I looked out across the river. "We're growing apart," I said softly. "Laura and Gabe, you and Shelley...me with nobody."

"We're not growing apart, we're growing up. You're my best friend, Will, and you'll always be my best friend. Nothing will ever change that. But we're not fourteen anymore. We can't spend all our lives together. We're all going to have families and careers. It can't be just the three of us forever."

"I don't want things to change."

"Everything changes. If you don't change, then you're dead. Make the most of it. Now that Beth is out of the picture, date new people. Try some new things. Get out there and live. You can start by moving in with Aidan. He's a great guy; you won't find a better roommate. I think it would be good for you to be more independent."

I sat for a few minutes thinking about everything that had happened today, especially what Joey had just said. Finally, I stood up, dusted the dirt off my bottom, and started for the building.

"Where're you going?" Joey asked, trotting to catch up.

"To see if that roommate position has been filled."

Chapter 2

I lay awake in my bed that night, staring at the ceiling lit only by moonlight. I'd been awake for hours watching the minutes tick by on my alarm clock, unable to sleep. My mind refused to turn off. So much had happened today — too much for my brain to absorb so quickly. My mind replayed snippets of conversation from the day over and over, like a slide show on constant rotation.

Joey: You should move out...
Beth: Joey always comes first...
Shelley: We've only been going out for two weeks...
Laura: Why wasn't I ever good enough for you...
Joey: We're growing up...things change...

Things changed all right. I knew that logically. But I didn't have to like it. And I especially didn't have to like the way things were changing for me. Didn't I get any say in any of this?

There were two conversations that I wasn't sure what to think of. The first was with Aidan when I asked if he still wanted me to be his roommate. In my mind at least that had become not so certain after my horrible behavior, but he'd acted as if nothing had happened and had actually seemed pretty excited.

I knew my parents wouldn't be at all excited when I told them. They tended to be a little over-protective. I was an only child, and my father was a rather conservative pastor. Although I hardly ever saw him when I was growing up, his child-rearing philosophies tended to be a bit old fashioned and Mom was more than capable of carrying them out to the letter of the law. I could just imagine their reaction when I told them; "You're doing what? We don't even know this young man! Does he do drugs?"

And the truth was I really didn't know Aidan. But Joey had said he was a good guy, and I instinctively liked him. I generally trusted my instincts. He was funny, nice and he had seemed genuinely happy that I was moving in. We were supposed to start moving some time later that week. Now all I had to do was figure out how to tell my parents.

The other thing that I was very uncertain about was Laura's question down by the river and all that it implied. I'd been trying to avoid thinking about it all night, but my mind kept going back to it anyway. It was like having an ulcer in your mouth and even though it hurts, you just can't keep your tongue away from it. No matter how I tried to distract myself I always ended up in the same place — was I in love with Joey?

The idea was preposterous, the implication being that I might be gay. That, of course, was impossible. Right?

No one jumped to my defense; no one rushed to reassure me of my heterosexuality. It was just me and my thoughts, and they refused to leave me alone.

I'd practically been raised in the church. All my life I'd heard that homosexuality was wrong, that it was unnatural and against God's law. I couldn't be gay, I just couldn't! I worked at the church, my dad was the pastor, there was just no way I could be gay!

Then why wouldn't Laura's question stop haunting me?

Finally, in frustration I threw back the sheets and jumped out of bed. If I couldn't fall asleep, then I'd find something to physically distract myself. I turned on the light and rummaged through my closet until I found what I was looking for. I flipped through my old sketchbook until I came to a charcoal sketch that I had started for a painting but never finished. For some reason, it had been on my mind all night. It had started out as a school art project, but I had abandoned it in favor of another project I'd been working on at the time. Now seemed like a good time to come back to this one. We were supposed to have drawn a landscape that was symbolic of where we were in our lives at that time. I had sketched out the rough shape of a beach scene from one of my favorite places on earth, Assateague Island. The beautiful barrier island is home to small, shaggy wild ponies, imported Asian sika deer, and loads of other wildlife. It even boasts its own scenic lighthouse on the Virginia side of the island. The scene I had drawn was simple, though, just a small dune complete with dune fence and grass, and a wave breaking on the beach. Footprints disappeared into the distance.

I cleared off the top surface of the worktable and turned on the overhead adjustable lamp. I dropped the sketchbook into the pool of warm light created by the 100-watt incandescent bulb. The table was arranged under the wide double windows to catch as much natural light as possible, but natural light wasn't an option at two in the morning. I stared at the sketch for a few minutes. It may have represented where I was a few months ago, but it sure didn't represent where I was tonight. I picked up a stick of charcoal and started changing a few small details. I darkened the sky, starting at the top and slowly getting lighter as I neared the horizon. Then I made the grass look as if it were being blown violently in the wind. I lifted out a streak of lightning over the waves. The foreboding storm definitely matched my mood, I thought, but it still needed something. I sketched in a funnel cloud dropping down from the sky to touch down where the footprints and the horizon converged.

I sat back and looked at the drawing. It was almost perfect, but something was still missing. The storm suited my situation perfectly. I was beginning to feel like I was caught up in a tornado and everything in my life was veering out of control. With a sudden flash of inspiration, I knew what it needed. There was nothing affected by the storm, just an empty beach. It needed life. Now what kind of life? I thought of several ideas and discarded each almost as quickly as it came to me. The sturdy ponies were too tough to represent how I felt. The diminutive sika deer were too delicate and exotic. A bird was too free. I needed something inconsequential, something most people never thought twice about. I glanced over at the window and froze. Hanging on the windowpane was a small, bright green tree frog. It was the perfect touch.

I quickly added the little frog into the sketch, drawing him clinging tightly to a stalk of the coarse beach grass. With a contented sigh, I sat back and admired my work. I was happy with it, but I was still wide-awake. I decided the sketch would make a great painting and there was no better time than the present to get started. My painting supplies were already set out, so I began the tedious process of transferring the drawing onto watercolor paper. I carefully outlined my pencil drawing on tracing paper so that the end product looked like a coloring book outline. Then, using graphite transfer paper, I copied the lines I had traced onto the watercolor paper. A long process, but one that I felt necessary for a good, clean image with no eraser marks or mistakes on my finished painting. When that was done, I began the actual painting. By the time I was done, the sun was just starting to break over the horizon. I stepped back to admire it and had to admit that it was probably one of my best pieces ever. It had accomplished its purpose as well. I was completely exhausted. I cleaned my brushes and dropped into bed, where I fell asleep almost immediately.

My alarm went off less than an hour later. With a groan, I rolled over and turned it off. I wanted more than anything to just go back to sleep, but it was Sunday. The last thing I wanted to do right then was go to church, but when your dad is the pastor it's not exactly an option, at least not as long as I lived at home.

I dragged myself out of bed and into the bathroom. Maybe I'd feel better after a shower. I turned the water on, and as I turned to get a towel, I caught my reflection in the full-length mirror on the back of the door. There I was in all my glory, wearing only my boxers — short, skinny, and pale with a charcoal smudge across my nose and matching circles around my eyes. I looked like I was fourteen at the most, and a sick fourteen-year-old at that. I stuck my tongue out at myself and turned away from the disappointing reflection.

If I had thought the shower would make me feel better, I was wrong. And I didn't feel better after I ate breakfast, or after I drank three cups of coffee, which I hate and usually never drink, or even after I got to church. I somehow managed to get through the morning, although I'm pretty sure I dozed off a few times during the sermon. I was feeling pretty self-satisfied as I drove home, but it turned out to be the afternoon that I should have been worried about.

It never would have happened if I hadn't been so tired, if I'd had all my wits about me. But I *was* tired and I *didn't* have all my wits about me, and when Dad started in on me about leaving my room in a such a mess this morning I snapped.

"You won't have to worry about it after this week," I said before I could stop myself.

"What's that supposed to mean?" he asked as Mom froze on her way out of the room.

I tried to think of a plausible lie, but I was so tired I just wasn't up to the effort. I always was a lousy liar anyway. "I'm moving out this week," I mumbled finally.

Mom slowly turned around with an odd, fixed expression on her face. Meanwhile, Dad looked as if I'd kicked him.

"What did you say?" Mom asked in a falsely cheery voice, as if she must have misunderstood and thought that it was going to be a funny story to tell the deacon chairman's wife the next time she talked to her.

What could I say? Just kidding? It was too late to turn back now. I took a deep breath. "I'm moving out this week," I said firmly.

For a long time no one spoke. I realized I was holding my breath and let it out in a loud whoosh.

"And where are you planning on living?" Dad said slowly.

"With a friend of Joey's, from college."

"Do we know him?" Mom asked, then a panicked look crossed her face. "He is a boy, isn't he? Oh, Will, don't tell me you're moving in with a girl!"

"No, it's a boy, and you don't know him, but I met him last night and he seems like a really nice guy. He said I'll only have to pay a third of the rent, and it's a really nice apartment. It's down by the river in this renovated warehouse..." I faded out under Dad's disapproving glare.

"Will, I don't approve," he said ominously.

Big surprise, I thought, but caught myself just in time from saying. "I'm eighteen," I said instead, in what I hoped was a reasonable tone of voice. "It's time I moved out. If I'd gone to college I would have left already. At least I'll be in the same town."

"What is this boy's name?" Mom asked.

"Aidan..." I realized I couldn't remember his last name. "Aidan...Aidan." I finished lamely.

"Aidan Aidan?"

"No, Aidan something, I can't remember his last name," I admitted sheepishly.

"You're not moving anywhere," Dad said, as if that settled everything. I clenched my jaw and counted to ten.

"Actually, Dad, I am," I said decisively. "Aidan is going to help me move later this week. I'll still be working at the church, so it's not like you'll never see me. It's just time for me to start growing up."

Dad threw up his hands and stood up. "I think you're making a huge mistake. The real world is a different place from living here at home. If you do this, you're on your own. You want to grow up? Fine. But mark my word, you'll be back." He stalked angrily out of the room.

Mom stared after him for a minute, then turned back to me. "Just know this will always be your home and you can come back whenever you want," she said before rushing out after him.

Over my dead body, I thought. I would never give him the satisfaction of crawling back. I went upstairs to my room and slept for the rest of the afternoon. When I woke up that evening, I started packing. It kept my mind out of areas I wasn't ready for it to go and reinforced my decision. Putting things into boxes made it all seem more real. Everywhere I looked, though, something made my thoughts skitter right back to the forbidden place: a love note from Beth, one of Joey's T-shirts in my closet, a picture of Joey, Laura, and me with our arms thrown around each other's necks.

Joey called once, but I told Mom to tell him I was busy packing. When Laura called, I tried the same ploy, but I should have known she wouldn't be put off so easily. I'd barely had time to hang up before she appeared in my doorway.

"Hey," she said softly as her eyes swept over the mess in my room. I had pulled everything out of my closet, and it sat in haphazard piles all around me.

"I'm busy," I said, keeping my eyes carefully averted to avoid her probing look.

"So I see. You wouldn't talk to me on the phone and I know what that means. It means you're avoiding me. I figured I could corner you in your lair. You need a hand?"

"I've got it," I said.

"Are you ok, Will?"

"I'm fine. I just have a lot to do."

"Are you really ok? Look at me and tell me you're ok."

"I said I was fine, didn't I?" I snapped, still not looking at her.

"I know what you said, but I also know you well enough to know when you are lying to me."

"Everyone thinks they know me so well."

"Not as well as I'd like. For someone who is so transparent with their emotions you do a pretty damn good job of keeping people away. What are you so scared of, Will?"

"I'm not scared of anything. Look, I've got a lot of packing to do. If you're not going to help, why don't you just go home? And standing in the door psychoanalyzing me is not helping. All you are doing is pissing me off."

"I noticed. I'm sorry. I'm also sorry if what I said last night upset you. It just seemed like it needed to be said."

I didn't answer, just kept on packing things into the box in front of me. She waited a few beats, then sighed and moved behind me to the bed.

"Wow, this is really good, Will," she said after a moment. "Does it represent something or what?"

She had picked up the painting I had done the night before. "Sort of," I said.

"It's beautiful and, I don't know, strangely disturbing somehow."

"Gee, thanks."

"No, it's a compliment. What's it mean?"

"It's my life right now; dark, stormy and out of control."

"So you're the frog?"

"I guess you could say that."

She suddenly went quiet. I sensed that her attention had shifted from the painting to something else. I heard the bed creak as she sat down on the edge. Still she didn't say a word. Finally, I couldn't stand it anymore so I turned to see what she was doing. She was holding the picture of the three of us that I had found earlier.

"Do you remember when this was taken?" she asked quietly.

"Yeah, that's the summer we all went to Busch Gardens. We were what? Fourteen?"

"Yeah, that was the summer I realized that you'd never love me the way I wanted you to. You spent the whole vacation following Joey around like a puppy dog, and I followed you. I might as well have not even been there."

And here we were back here again, come full circle. Why did everything have to be so complicated?

"What do you see?" she said, holding the picture out to me.

"What do you mean?" I asked.

"Look at it."

"I am...what am I looking for?"

"Look at us. What do you see?"

I looked closer. In the picture I was in the center with Joey on my right and Laura on my left. Joey's head was thrown back slightly as he laughed at some joke. His eyes were locked with the camera in a typical Joey expression of challenge. He was always challenging something. At first, I couldn't figure out what Laura was talking about. And then I saw it.

"You know now, don't you?" she whispered. I nodded. "You have to deal with it, Will, for your own sake."

She handed me the photo, then stood up and left.

I sat looking at the picture for a long time before I turned the lights out and went to bed. As I drifted off to sleep, the image in the photo seemed to be burned into my retina; I could still see it on the inside of my eyelids. In it, Laura looked longingly at me, completely ignoring the camera. But all my attention was focused on Joey, a look of complete adoration in my eyes. Joey was the only one who seemed conscious of the camera, oblivious to everything else but his own posing. The rest of us lesser beings were too caught up in our objects of desire.

I avoided so much as even thinking about Laura and Joey for the rest of the week. It wasn't that hard. They were in school, and I was at work during the day and busy moving at night. Aidan came over several times in his beat-up Ford pick-up and, under Dad's disapproving gaze, we moved most of my stuff out by that Friday night. I drove the last few odds and ends over in my car.

Aidan threw open the door dramatically before I could even knock.

"Welcome home!" he said with a grin, complete with dimples.

I smiled back and pushed past him; the box was starting to get heavy. "I guess this *is* home now, huh?" I said and laughed. I couldn't believe how excited I was and a little nervous.

"Yep. Home is where the heart is or something like that," he said as he followed me down the hall to my room.

"Does that mean my heart is here now?" We'd cleared out his remaining boxes during the week and replaced them with mine.

"I hope so; the rest of you is here. But sometimes I get the impression that your heart is somewhere else."

I looked up sharply, but he was busy opening up one of my boxes. We spent the next hour or so unpacking enough of my stuff so I could at least sleep there that night.

"Hey, Will?" Aidan asked hesitantly after a while.

Something in his voice made me put down the box I was poking in and give him my full attention. A slightly concerned expression clouded his green eyes. "Yeah?" I asked carefully.

"I have something I need to tell you and I guess I should have said something sooner, like before you moved in and all, but..."

"Please tell me it's just that you wear colored contact lenses," I said with a forced smile.

"Huh?" Now he just looked confused.

"It's just that your eyes are so green...oh never mind..."

"My eyes? They're natural." He still seemed confused as if he couldn't figure out how we had started talking about his eyes. "Look, can we maybe sit down to talk?"

Oh no, you never had to sit down to talk about something good. My feeling of unease heightened. What was he going to tell me? Was he from a mob family? Was that why he could afford this apartment? He had said he was from a big family. I sat down heavily on the bed.

Aidan looked around uncomfortably. "Uh, I was thinking of more like the living room."

"Oh," I said weakly and followed him down the hall. I sat on the couch, and Aidan sat on the chair closest to me. He blinked at me for several minutes, then stood up and began to pace. I was getting more and more nervous with every second that passed.

"I don't know how to say this," he said finally, "so I'm just going to say it and let happen whatever happens. Will...I'm gay." He stopped pacing and looked at me anxiously. I waited for the punch line. When it became apparent that it wasn't coming, I stood up and walked to the windows.

"Did Laura set you up for this?" I asked with my back to him.

"What? Laura? What does she have to do with this?"

"Did she?"

"No, she doesn't even know."

"Does Joey know?"

"No, no one down here knows yet. You're the first person I've told since I moved. Well, my cousin knows, but he doesn't live in town and he's still in high school. I only told you because, well...I thought you should know since we're going to be living together and all."

"You should have told me before," I said. I was desperately trying to stay calm, but my delicate façade was dangerously close to crumbling. I couldn't believe this was happening right now, when I was so confused about myself. I had avoided thinking about it all week, and now here I was slapped upside the head with the same issue from a direction I'd never even suspected. My head was reeling.

"I know I should have told you earlier, and I'm really sorry. You've got to believe me; it's really hard to tell people. But it's not going to change anything, right? I mean I'm not going to hit on you or anything, and I don't dress in women's clothing or anything. I'm still the same person I was before; it's just now you know a little more about me."

"A little more than I wanted to know," I snapped. Immediately I regretted it. I could see the hurt written all over his face. "I'm sorry, Aidan." I sighed. "I didn't mean that. It just...it just caught me by surprise. You must be regretting that you even asked me to move in. The first time you meet me I act like a jerk and storm out like some spoiled brat, and now, my first night here, I freak out because you try to be honest with me."

He gave me a lopsided grin, a weak shadow of his usual luminous grins but more than I could have managed in his place. "Hey, you were having a bad day that first night, remember? And as far as tonight goes, well...I would have to go through something like this with whoever moved in, and I have to say that you've handled it better than most of the people I've told."

I sat back down, "I thought you said I was the only person you've told besides your cousin."

"Down here. Back home I came out to pretty much everyone at one time. I didn't know that it's better to come out gradually. Most people didn't take it very well, and I didn't have a support system built up yet so it was pretty rough. The people who would have supported me were too shocked to be much comfort when I needed it. That was what made up my mind to transfer down here. I would have never got through the rest of last year if it hadn't been for my Aunt Meg. She was my rock through everything."

"What happened?"

"Well, some people just stopped having anything to do with me, but those were the best-case scenarios. Others felt it was their duty to go out of their way to tell me how they felt about alternative lifestyles. But my cousin that lives down here, he's Aunt Meg's son, is gay and he's been pretty much accepted since he came out, so I thought that maybe this would be a better area for me. I was already looking at Pemberton; that just cemented the decision. Does it bother you?"

"That you're gay?" I thought a moment. "No, it doesn't really bother me," I said, and I meant it. "It just adds to something I was already dealing with."

"You want to explain that?"

"No, not really. Not yet anyway. I've still got a lot to figure out."

He gave me a suspicious look but didn't push the issue. "Well, if you change your mind I'm here for you."

"So, uh...how did you know?" I asked, partly to divert his attention back to himself and partly because I honestly wanted to know.

"Actually, my cousin helped me. He figured out he was gay about a year ago, and he just seemed to have everything together. He has a boyfriend that he's crazy about and who's crazy about him, and he's two years younger than I am. When I came down for Thanksgiving and saw them together, I saw how happy they were, and I realized that I desperately wanted that, too. I'd had a few girlfriends, but it just never felt right. So I asked him the same thing you just asked me. He may be younger than me, but the kid's really sharp. He said, 'Either you are or you aren't. You just know. You either like girls or you like guys.' When you boil it down like that it was pretty obvious, for me, anyway."

I nodded thoughtfully. I didn't like where I was going with that train of thought. He said something else, but I didn't catch it since I was so lost in my own thoughts. I realized he was waiting for me to say something.

"Huh?" I said wittily.

"I said, 'Do you want to see a picture of my cousin and his boyfriend.' You know, you actually remind me an awful lot of his boyfriend."

"Sure," I said absently.

Aidan went back to his room and came back out a minute later with a small, framed photo, which he handed to me. I looked down and felt my mouth drop open.

"That's Asher!" I gasped.

Chapter 3

"You know Asher?" Aidan said in surprise.

"You know Asher?" I repeated in equal surprise.

"He's dating my cousin Killian!"

"Asher's my cousin!" I was dumbfounded.

"Whoa! What are the chances? That's freaky."

"No kidding. I didn't even know Asher is gay."

"You didn't? He's not like a closet case or anything; he's really open about it. Their whole school knows. I can't believe you didn't see it on TV."

"TV? Why would it be on TV? Do they televise coming out parties now? Is there a GAY TV — All Gay All Day?"

Aidan laughed. "Not that I know of, although it wouldn't surprise me. You don't recognize Killian?"

"Should I?" I asked as I took a closer look at the photo. At first glance, all I had been able to see was Asher and, as Aidan had already said, there was a strong family resemblance between Asher and me. We both had inherited that same curly dark-brown, almost black hair and fair skin that blushes too easily. And we both have those same eternally rosy cheeks that Asher had once told me made him feel like one of Raphael's angels. Now that I looked again, I realized that there were two other people in the picture posing in front of a Christmas tree. Aidan was one of them and the other one I assumed to be Killian. He had lightly curling blond hair and was very cute. It was hard to tell in the picture, but it looked like he might have eyes almost as blue as mine. I looked closely, but I still didn't recognize him.

"I don't think I know him."

"To hear him and Asher tell it, you'd think he was some kind of minor celebrity around here. I've caught bits and pieces of the story, but I don't know if I've ever heard the whole thing. From what I've gathered, Killian's friend, Seth, was murdered, and Killian investigated it."

"Oh, wait — I think I do remember that now. Didn't the murderer end up killing a bunch of other people, too? But then Killian caught him or something."

"Yeah, he was on the national news and was like some kind of hero or something."

"I remember now, but I didn't know Asher was involved."

"Involved? He was almost killed. Man, you guys don't talk much do you?"

"Actually, no. My dad and Asher's mom are brother and sister, but they were never particularly close, so I only really see them on big holidays and at family reunions. Besides, I'm probably not the first person Asher would rush to tell that he's gay."

"Why's that?"

"My dad's a preacher and a pretty conservative one at that. Asher and I used to be pretty tight when we were little, but Dad can be kind of overbearing at times, so we're not the most popular branch of the family tree."

"Oh, does this have something to do with the problem you mentioned earlier?"

"No...well, yeah, I guess it does in a way."

"Is it going to cause more problems for you to live with me?"

"Not as far as I'm concerned. Now as for my dad...well, what he doesn't know won't hurt me, right?"

Aidan grinned, "Gotcha! So tell me some more about yourself, any brothers or sisters? What do you do? How come you're not in school like Laura and Joey?"

"Whoa, slow down!" I laughed. "I can only answer one question at a time. I'm an only child, a spoiled brat if you listen to Laura and Joey. I work at the church as I guess what you'd call a secretary, but I really do just about anything and everything that you can imagine. And before you ask, no, it's not what I want to do with the rest of my life. That's the thing: I don't know what I want to do with the rest of my life. I know my dad wants me to be involved with the church, but I don't know what I want. That's the main reason I haven't gone to college. I decided to wait a year, and hopefully I'll figure something out between now and then."

"What about a girlfriend? Didn't Joey mention you had a girlfriend? Becky or something?"

"Beth and we broke up. That was part of the reason I was having such a bad day last Saturday."

"So you were heartbroken?"

"Not exactly."

"So you broke up with her?"

"No, she broke up with me."

"I see, said the blind man."

I laughed. "It's complicated. It's just as well that she broke it off; I would have just let things drag on forever. At least now it's over and done with. See, I didn't feel the same way for her as she apparently felt for me. She wanted more from me than I felt like I could give her, and I don't think I ever would have been able to. It's hard to explain. There just wasn't...it wasn't...I just didn't feel anything with Beth."

"I understand what you're saying. I went through the same thing." He seemed to realize what he was saying at the same time I did. He rushed on, "Not that it means anything as far as, you know, you or anything. I was just saying that for me..." He trailed off into an uncomfortable silence. I rushed to fill it.

"So tell me about you." I didn't want to lose our growing rapport, but I did want to get the attention off of me. This seemed like a safe enough topic.

"Well, I come from a pretty big family. There're six of us altogether and I'm the oldest. My dad died three years ago from cancer, so it's just been our mom and us since then."

"I'm sorry."

"Yeah, well, it was rough, especially at first. My mom had to go back to work, and I had to help a lot with my brothers and sister. I have one sister who is only two years younger than I am so she helped, too, but with four boys under twelve, it was still a lot of work. Then, last year, my Aunt Meg moved in with us and that freed me up to be able to go to college. That was about the same time I started realizing I was gay, so when things got ugly up there I was able to just pick up and transfer down here. Like I said, though, Aunt Meg was a huge support for me when I was coming out. I don't think I could have made it without her. She'd already gone through the whole gay thing with Killian, you know, learning about what it meant and coming to terms with it and all, so she was really supportive of me and helped my mom a lot, too."

"So are you planning on coming out down here?"

"Eventually, when I'm ready. Not right now. I'd rather people got to know me for who I am rather than through a preconception of what a stereotypical gay guy is supposed to be like. Not that I'm lying either, though. If someone comes right out and asks me, I'll be honest."

I nodded. I was ashamed to admit how relieved I was that he wasn't going to don rainbow T-shirts and announce his sexual orientation to the entire Eastern Shore. "So, uh, what are you majoring in?"

"I just changed my major to psychology, so we'll see how that goes. I was doing criminal justice and some psych courses are part of that, and I really found them interesting so I switched over."

"Ok, wait, I'm confused about something."

"What's that?"

"Well, earlier you said that your mom had to go back to work to support the family but — I don't mean to be rude — I was under the impression that money wasn't an object. I mean with the rent and all this..." I trailed off as I gestured around the apartment.

"Oh, yeah, I guess that would be confusing. If it was up to my mom and me to pay for my college, I'd be living at home and going to a local school still. But thank God for rich relatives," he laughed. "My grandmother on Dad's side is stinking loaded. We only see her once a year at Christmas cuz she lives in Belgium or something like that. Dad was her only son, and we're her only grandchildren, so she is paying for all of us to go to college. She has trust funds set up in case she kicks the bucket."

"Must be nice!"

"Yeah, I guess it is, now that you mention it. It's funny the things you take for granted. I don't even think about it. It's just something I've always known. God knows, she reminds us of it every time we see her."

"You don't sound like you like her very much."

He thought for a moment, then slowly said, "I'm grateful to her for what she's doing for me. I mean I wouldn't be here if it weren't for her, but I always get the impression that she does it out of a sense of duty rather than any real affection. So no, I don't really like her. She's always treated us like the poor relatives. I guess Dad was kind of a disappointment becoming a professor at a small college instead of some jet-setting socialite. You know, she didn't even come to Dad's funeral. She just sent flowers. Can you believe that?"

"No. Even with my family's strained relations, I think we'd still show up for a family member's funeral."

"You'd think. My dad was like her in a lot of ways, except he didn't have the money to throw around. He was always distant, as if he didn't know how to show affection. I don't know what his dad was like. He never talked about him, and he was dead long before I was born. My mom was very affectionate, though, so I guess that made up for it."

"My family's always been pretty affectionate." I looked down at the photo I was still holding and noticed that Asher and Killian were holding hands. "They look really happy together," I said almost without thought. I was surprised to hear a wistful note in my voice.

"They are," Aidan said matter-of-factly. He either hadn't noticed my tone of voice or had chosen to ignore it. Either way I was grateful. "I've never seen any two people be more completely in love. Hey, I have an idea! Why don't we invite them over this weekend? I promised them I would once I got settled in, and now that you're here it's even better!"

"Sounds good! But don't tell them who your new roommate is, I want to surprise Asher."

Aidan laughed. "I love it! I'll call them now."

He flipped through an address book he kept by the phone and dialed the phone. After a brief conversation, he hung up and turned toward me, a huge smile lighting up his face. "It's all set. Asher was there, as usual, so they talked it over and got permission. They're coming over tomorrow night around six and spending the night."

"Cool! Our first slumber party!"

We both laughed as I thought how much I was going to enjoy living here.

The next day passed by in a flurry of activity as Aidan and I actually went about setting up house. For two guys on their own for the first time we had a surprising amount of stuff. Most of mine consisted of my art supplies, and most of Aidan's was either hi-fi or weight equipment. The weights at least explained Aidan's physique, which was nicely toned, to say the least.

We chose a large section of the living room closest to the huge windows to be my studio. We placed Aidan's in-home gym next to me so we could talk while I painted and he worked out. Setting up all my crap just the way I wanted it took up a large chunk of the afternoon, but Aidan seemed content to watch me while he did sit-ups, push-ups, and reps or whatever you call them. I'm not really up on my exercise lingo since as Garfield — the cat, not the president — once said: My idea of exercise is a good brisk sit. Actually, I like to roller blade, too, but that just about sums up the extent of my physical exertion.

Aidan seemed fascinated by all my paraphernalia, occasionally asking what something was and what I did with it. The last thing I pulled out of its protective cover was the painting I had completed last Saturday night. I was very self-conscious about my artwork; for the most part only Joey and Laura had seen much of my work. My parents had seen some, enough to know I had talent, so they'd sent me to a few art classes when I was younger. They seemed to think of my interest in art as a phase that I would outgrow — like my rock collection or my chemistry set.

"You did that?" Aidan exclaimed when I pulled out the painting.

"Yeah," I said shyly. "You didn't think all this was just for show, did you?"

"No, but...I mean that's really good, Will. You're really talented."

I felt a blush begin to creep up my neck. "Thanks," I mumbled.

"You just do this as a hobby?"

"Yeah."

"Have you ever sold anything?"

"Are you kidding? I'm not good enough to sell this stuff. I've never even had any real art classes, just school stuff and some kiddie classes."

"Who says you have to have art classes? Haven't you ever heard of natural talent? If your other stuff is this good, then you're a heck of a lot better than a lot of people I've seen showing in galleries."

"You know art?"

"Some. Like I was telling you last night, my dad was a bit of a snob. He made sure us kids were exposed to 'culture'. Most of the stuff he dragged us to see was modern crap that looked like something my youngest brother did the day before in Pre-K. Worse, one time he took us to see a toilet. I'm not kidding. It was just a regular toilet that the guy had bought at your average hardware store and stuck in the middle of the museum. And it was art. What a joke. But some of the stuff I fell in love with: the old Masters, the Impressionists, and the surrealistic stuff."

"At least you had the opportunity to see that stuff. The Eastern Shore's idea of culture is the Delmarva Chicken Festival. I envy you for that."

"Well, I envy you for your talent. I love art, but I can't even draw a straight line."

"I guess that makes us even then, huh? We can agree to envy each other."

Aidan laughed, then asked, "Do you have any more paintings here?"

"Um...I think I left most of them at home...well, Mom and Dad's because I didn't know what I'd do with them here."

"Next time you go by there, pick them up; I'd really like to see them. This is really good; it's kind of different. It reminds me of some stuff I saw one time at this show by some guy who was being called the next big thing. That was actually how they billed the showing. Maybe that could be you, Will. You could be the next big thing!"

I felt a blush coming on again. I really hated having both fair skin and a predisposition to blushing.

"You don't like getting compliments or talking about yourself, do you?" Aidan asked, noticing my discomfort.

"No, not really. It makes me uncomfortable."

"Why?"

"I dunno. I guess I feel like I don't deserve the compliments, like they aren't true."

"But you have to know how talented you are," he persisted.

"You're just saying that to be nice. I mean what else could you say, 'Man, Will, that sucks'?"

"I wouldn't say I liked it if I didn't. First thing you need to know about me is I'm always straight...well, bad choice of words, but you know what I mean."

I laughed as he grinned at me.

"Just accept the compliments for what they are and say thank you," he went on.

"That's easy for you to say, you're confident and outgoing."

"And you have low self-esteem."

"Thank you for your diagnosis, Dr. Scott, but I could have told you that."

"Why do you think you have low self-esteem? I mean you're cute, talented, funny..."

"Do you think we could continue this session at another time," I interrupted loudly as I felt my face blaze with color. "Killian and Asher will be here in an hour, and we still have shit all over the place."

"Hmm...aggression, change of subject...the subject is exhibiting signs of classic avoidance," he said in a phony Freudian accent.

"I'll show you avoidance," I growled playfully as I tackled him. We rolled into a laughing heap on the floor where we wrestled for several minutes. I wrestled with Joey all the time, but I was no match for Aidan; he had me outweighed and out-muscled. There was really no contest, but I suspected that he was giving me a lot more openings than I would have ever gotten if this were a serious fight.

We were so caught up in our wrestling match that we didn't even hear the knocking or the door swinging open. The first we knew of our visitors was when someone called, "Hello? Aidan?"

Aidan let go of me so quickly that my head bounced off the hardwood floor. "Ugh," I grunted and stayed still while I waited for the stars to stop spinning. Aidan scrambled to his feet above me. His shirt was pulled halfway over his head, and he hastily tugged it back into place. For the first time I saw him blush for a change. I heard giggles from the door, but from my spot on the floor I couldn't see who it was.

"Are we interrupting something?" the same voice asked.

"No, I mean...uh...we were just playing around," Aidan stammered. It was the first time I had seen him really flustered, and I was definitely enjoying seeing the usually unflappable Aidan come unflapped. Uncharacteristically, I decided to push things a little farther. I ran my hand up his leg to his thigh. Aidan yelped and danced away to a safer distance and glared at me.

"We have guests, *darling*," he said deliberately, then turned back toward the door. "Come on in, *Asher* and Killian."

At the mention of Asher's name I sat bolt upright. Asher's mouth dropped open, and a very satisfied grin spread across Aidan's face. The boy I assumed to be Killian just looked confused as he looked from Aidan to Asher to me. His eyes grew wide as he looked back and forth from me to Asher.

"Will?" Asher gasped.

"Uh, hi, Asher. Long time no see, cuz," I said as I turned what I could only guess to be approximately the same color as a stop sign.

"Cuz? As in cousin?" Killian asked, his blue eyes bright with amusement. I had to say one thing for Asher; he had good taste in his men.

"Yeah, this is my cousin Will. What are you doing here?" he asked me.

"I live here."

"You're Aidan's roommate?" Killian asked.

"Surprise."

He looked from me to Aidan. "And you two are..."

"No!" I gasped. Aidan started laughing.

"But when we walked in you two were..."

"We were wrestling! That's all. Right, Aidan?"

He laughed for another minute before he managed to choke out, "That's what I tried to tell them from the beginning, before you decided to feel me up."

"I didn't...I was just...I'm not..." I sputtered.

Aidan was bent double laughing, while Killian and Asher still stood uncertainly in the doorway. Aidan waved them in as I pulled myself up off the floor and attempted to salvage what little dignity I still had left.

"You should have seen your face!" Aidan crowed.

I chose to ignore him. "Just put your stuff over here by the wall for now," I said, playing the host. "The couch opens up into a bed so you can share that. Sorry about all the boxes; we weren't expecting you to be here this early."

"Obviously," Killian said with a grin. "We'll help you clean up."

Aidan managed to stop laughing in time to help straighten up the living room and carry the empty boxes out to the dumpster. By the time we were done, Killian had visibly relaxed, but Asher still seemed tense. Then I remembered that Asher didn't know that I knew he was gay. He must have been worried about what I would think if I figured it out. As soon as I saw a chance to speak to him privately, I sat down next to him. Killian and Aidan were busy hooking up my N64, arguing about which wire connected where.

"Asher," I said quietly, "I know about you and Killian, and it's ok. I'm cool with it."

Relief flooded his eyes, "What about Uncle Lowell?"

"Dad doesn't know, and he won't find out from me," I assured him. "I just found out last night. While we're on the subject, Dad doesn't know that Aidan is gay either, and I'd like to keep it that way."

"Well, you don't have to worry about me telling him. It's not like I talk to him anyway. No offense but I usually try to avoid Uncle Lowell at family reunions. I always feel guilty around him. Not for anything in particular...just guilty in general."

I laughed. "Yeah, he does have that effect on people."

Killian wandered over and peered closely at both of us.

"Quit that!" Asher said testily.

"It's just that you guys look so much alike it's freaky. The only difference is that Will's eyes are blue."

"Stand up," I ordered Asher as I stood up myself. He complied, and Killian laughed.

"Ok, so there's also about six inches of difference."

"Seven," Asher said smugly, "I grew an inch." I stuck my tongue out at him, showing that what I lacked in height I made up for in maturity.

"I didn't think anyone could be cuter than you, Ashke, but I think you might have some competition with Will on the scene."

Once again, I blushed as Asher punched Killian in the arm. Then he punched me in mine.

"Hey! What did I do?" I yelled.

"I dunno, but I'm sure you deserved it for some reason."

"The 64's hooked up," Aidan called, and Asher darted to his side; he was quite the video game addict. I turned to Killian.

"You just called Asher 'Ashke'. Is that just a nickname or are you a Mercedes Lackey fan, too?"

"You know Mercedes Lackey?"

"Oh yeah, we had coffee just last week."

"You know what I meant; you've read her books?"

"Yeah, she's one of my favorite authors."

"Me, too! I just discovered her a few months ago, but I think I've read everything she's written. I started calling Asher 'Ashke' after reading the *Last Herald Mage Trilogy* — the ones with Vanyel?"

"I've read them. In fact, I haven't unpacked them yet, but I own a bunch of the Valdemar series."

"Wow, that's so cool."

"What's cool?" Aidan yelled from his spot in front of the TV.

"None of your business, Mr. Nosy!" I called back.

"How about me? Will you tell me?" Asher piped up.

"Yeah, I'll tell you. Killian and I are both Mercedes Lackey fans."

"You'll tell him but not me?" Aidan pretended to pout.

"He's family," I shot back.

"Aidan's my family," Killian said protectively.

"Not another Lackey fan," Asher moaned over the friendly banter.

"What's wrong with Mercedes Lackey?" Aidan said defensively.

"Not you, too?"

"You really don't like her?" I asked.

"She's ok; I just didn't get as excited about her as Killian. I like mysteries better than fantasy."

"Did you read many of them?" I persisted.

"No, he only read one! And it was the middle of one of the trilogies, so he didn't even know what was going on," Killian inserted indignantly.

"You didn't give them a chance," Aidan said. "There's mystery, action, romance...everything you want in a good book."

"Jeez, what is this? A meeting of the official Mercedes Lackey Fan Club?"

"She has one, you know," I pointed out, and we all laughed.

The playful bickering went on all night. It was as if we'd all been friends forever. We played Clue and a marathon game of Monopoly that Killian eventually won in the wee hours of the morning. Asher was looking very droopy by then, and I knew I was just as tired, so I suggested we all hit the sack. Aidan and I helped Asher and Killian make up the sofa bed, then we retired to our respective rooms.

Maybe change doesn't have to be so bad after all, I thought as I undressed. Who needs Joey and Laura when you have friends like Aidan, Asher, and Killian?

Chapter 4

I brushed my teeth and went through all my evening rituals, then just before I got into bed, I decided I was thirsty. I didn't want to disturb anyone else if they were trying to fall asleep so I eased open my door and padded softly down the hall to the kitchen. As I passed through the living room, I overheard Asher and Killian talking quietly. Even though I knew I shouldn't, I stopped and listened.

"Will seems really nice," Killian was saying.

I felt horrible for eavesdropping, but I didn't move.

"Yeah, he is. He's always been one of my favorite relatives, maybe because we look so much alike. One of our great aunts always got us backwards. One time he even got blamed for something I did at a family reunion. I never did tell them I did it." They giggled, and Asher was quiet for a moment. Then he said, "Do you really think he's cuter than me?"

I saw movement under the blankets as Killian turned to face Asher.

"What do you think, silly?"

"I think he has prettier eyes. His are blue, and mine are this stupid blah gray."

"They're silver, and they are beautiful. You are beautiful. You're the most beautiful thing I've ever seen. Asher, you have to know by now that I love you more than life itself. I love being with you. When we're apart, I feel like part of me is missing. I think about you all the time. I want to spend the rest of my life with you. After all we've been through together, how can you doubt my love for even a single second?"

"It's not that I doubt it. I mean I love you too, and I know you love me. It's just...you're so incredible; I keep wondering why you are with me. Never mind, I'm just being silly."

"Yes...you...are..." Each word was separated by a kiss and was punctuated emphatically at the end with a passionate embrace.

I backed slowly out of the room and returned to my own. I hadn't gotten my drink, but suddenly I wasn't thirsty anymore. My thirst had been swallowed by a sharp pang of...was it jealousy? Maybe, but it was definitely longing. I wanted what they had so badly that I could hardly breathe. I'd never even come close to having that depth of relationship with Beth. Would I ever have that?

Unbidden, an image of Joey suddenly leapt into my mind. I mentally swatted it away in annoyance.

"Stop it!" I hissed out loud at myself. "I am not in love with Joey. It's just because Laura put the idea in my head. I can't be gay."

But this time it wouldn't go away. It was suddenly like there were two people arguing inside my head.

Why can't I be gay?

Because...

Because why?

Because...

Ok. So it wasn't as simple as that. With a growl of frustration I threw myself backwards onto my bed. Well, maybe it was time to settle this once and for all. Then at least I could stop avoiding Laura. She was getting harder and harder to dodge.

I decided to do this logically. I started making a mental list of all the things that I never felt for Beth that I saw in Killian and Asher. One, Beth was never my top priority. I never loved her more than life itself as Killian had said. Two, I didn't want to be with her all the time; in fact, I hardly ever thought about her when we were apart. Three, I definitely didn't want to spend the rest of my life with her.

Ok, so it was obvious that I did not love Beth, but that didn't mean that I was in love with Joey. I took the same list and measured my feelings for Joey against them. One, everyone said Joey was my top priority so maybe he was. I had to admit his decisions were usually set in concrete where my life was concerned. Strike one. Two, Joey and I were almost always together. Well, at least we had been before he'd started college. And when we weren't, I missed him terribly. Hmm...strike two. Three, did I want to spend the rest of my life with Joey?

I sat up. I didn't like what I was thinking. It went against everything I'd ever been taught. Could I be in love with Joey? It was getting harder and harder to come up with reasonable excuses as to why I wasn't. The idea really shook me.

I felt a sudden need for the comfort of light, so I crawled across the bed and reached for the lamp on my bedside table. My hand was shaking so hard, however, that I couldn't twist the little knob that turned it on. In frustration, I threw my hands up, knocking off the clip-on shade in the process and toppling the lamp onto the floor where I heard the light bulb smash. I cursed and fumbled in the darkness. I found the shade and was feeling for the lamp when a soft knock came at my door.

I heaved a sigh, crawled back to the foot of the bed, and went to open it. It was Aidan. He eyed the shade still in my hand and gave me a curious look.

"The party's over, dude," he said in a hushed voice.

To my utter embarrassment, I burst into tears. I threw the shade across the floor and threw myself face down on the bed.

"Will! What's wrong?" he asked, his voice filled with concern. I heard the door close and a few seconds later felt his hand on my back. "Look, Will, I know we really don't know each other that well yet, but I already feel close to you and I consider you my friend. So I'm going to make the same offer to you that applies to all my friends. If you want to talk about anything, I mean anything at all, I'll always be here to listen. I'm a good listener, and I won't judge or repeat anything you tell me. You have my word."

I cried all the harder. I felt the hand leave my back, quickly followed by the sound of the window opening. Cool air washed over me.

"Let's step out for some fresh air, shall we?" he said formally.

I looked up to find Aidan straddling the window sash with one leg flung out on the fire escape. He held out a hand and smiled. I was so surprised I simply got up and let him help me through the window, sniffling like a little kid the whole time.

We sat down Indian style next to each other, our knees almost but not quite touching. We sat in silence broken only by my continued sniveling. Finally, he said, "Do you want to talk about it?"

"I think I'm in love with Joey!" I blurted out and started crying again.

"Wow...um...that's not what I expected," he said in a stunned voice.

"Does that mean I'm gay? I don't wanna be gay. I can't be gay!" I wailed.

"Shh, shh, shh," Aidan hissed. He sounded so much like a snake with a lisp that I started giggling through my tears, then I hiccupped. "People are trying to sleep," he said seriously. He was eying me as if he were afraid I was losing it. Maybe I was. He went on, "I don't know if it means you're gay or not. Maybe you're bi. Or maybe you just love Joey, you know like a fluke. But if you are gay, then you need to face it and accept it. It's not that bad, you know."

"Yes, it is! You don't understand; I'm a Christian."

"So? I didn't realize the two were mutually exclusive."

"They are according to my dad."

"Well, no offense, I mean I've never even met your dad, but I'm pretty sure he's not God."

"But the Bible..."

"Christianity is based on the teachings of Jesus, right?"

"Yeah, but..."

"Show me where Jesus ever once even mentions homosexuality."

"It..." I thought for a minute. "He doesn't."

"Exactly. And it doesn't really say anything about homosexuality as we know it anywhere else either."

"But it does, I've read it!"

"No, you've read a modern interpretation of an ancient language; an interpretation that's been made to say what the religious leaders of the time wanted it to say. The original languages of the Bible didn't even have a word for homosexual, not as we think of it today. In most cases, wherever you see anything that's been translated as gay or homosexual, the original texts are talking about male prostitutes or pedophiles."

"How do you know so much about the Bible?"

"Well, when someone takes such pains to condemn you based on the teachings of a book, I thought it would be best if I knew that book as well as they did. So I did some studying on my own. It just seemed that from what I know about myself and everyone else I've ever met that was gay, no one chooses to be gay. Either you are or you aren't. There's nothing you can do about it except accept it and try to live your life the best way you know how. It didn't make sense to me that God would create something that he hated. So I studied a lot of books on the subject and even talked to some people who had translated the original Aramaic; you'd be amazed at how different it is from the scriptures we have today. Those are the conclusions that I came to. I'm not saying that they are the absolute truth. God knows I'm no expert, but I came to a peace of mind with this...and a peace with God."

"How...how will I know if I'm gay?"

"I think you'll know, Will. But like I said before, if you are, you need to face it and deal with it."

"Now you sound like Laura. Why does everyone keep trying to be my shrink?"

"Maybe because we care about you and we want to help you," Aidan said softly.

I looked over at him and saw nothing but sincerity. A sudden shiver went through me.

"Jeez, you're going to get sick! Here we are sitting out here on this cold metal half-naked."

I realized that we were both sitting on the metal grill of the fire escape in nothing but our thin cotton boxers. We were experiencing unseasonably cool weather for September, and I noticed the goose bumps on my arms.

"Let's get back inside," Aidan said as he stood up and pulled me to my feet. We climbed back into my bedroom, and Aidan shut the window while I crawled into bed.

"Think you can sleep now?" he asked me. I nodded. "You've got a lot to think about." I nodded again. "If you need me, I'm right across the hall." He let himself out, closing the door behind him. For a moment, I felt a sense of panic, afraid to be alone with my thoughts, afraid I wouldn't be able to fall asleep. I shouldn't have worried, though; I was exhausted, and my last thought before falling asleep was that I was very lucky to have moved in with a guy like Aidan.

I was rudely awakened the next morning when 160 pounds of Asher landed in the middle of my bed. I came up kicking and flailing, much to his amusement.

"Time to wake up, Lil' Cuz!" he screamed at the top of his lungs.

I flopped back down. "Who you callin' little?" I grumbled sleepily.

"You, silly-head!"

"Humph, well, haven't you ever heard that big things come in small packages?"

Asher peeked under my sheets. "So much for that myth," he teased.

I laughed and shoved him off the bed. He climbed back on amidst giggles, and I finally got up. I started pulling open drawers in my dresser trying to remember where I had put what.

"So...?" he said from behind me.

"So what?"

"So, are you and Aidan an item or what?"

"I told you last night that we weren't."

"Yeah, but there was that very interesting scene when we got here yesterday, and then last night I got up to pee and ran into Aidan in the hallway. He was sneaking out of your room. He just looked embarrassed and hurried into his room."

"I told you, we were just wrestling when you got here, and he wasn't sneaking anywhere. He was probably just trying not to wake you guys up." Asher arched an eyebrow. "Neat trick. Really, we were just talking. He's my friend. That's it."

"Ok, if you say so. So I guess that means you're still straight?"

I sat down on the bed and tried to decide how to answer that. I wasn't even sure myself.

"Earth to Will," Asher said after a minute. "Are you ok?"

"Huh?" I said stupidly. I had almost forgotten he was there.

"I asked if you were straight and you spaced out."

I stood up and walked a few feet away. "Am I straight?"

"That's what I'm asking you."

"As opposed to what? Crooked?"

"You know perfectly well what I mean; straight as opposed to gay, queer, homosexual. It's a simple yes or no question." He eyed me critically.

"Maybe it's not so simple for me."

His eyes widened. "You mean..."

"I don't know what I mean." I sighed. "It used to be so clear cut, then Laura had to go and get me all confused."

"Laura? How did she confuse you?"

"It's a long story. How did you know you were gay?"

"I guess I've always known on some level, but I was afraid to tell anyone. I mean, as soon as I was old enough to understand that only girls were supposed to have crushes on guys I knew I was different. I've been in love with Killian almost as long as I can remember, even back when he was a shy, awkward kid. We've been best friends since we were little."

"Oh great!" I moaned. I sat down on a box that was still in the room and to my surprise found myself going right through the top. With my feet in the air, I struggled to pull myself out of the empty box while Asher laughed hysterically. I finally succeeded only in splitting it open, but at least I was out.

"I'm going to take a shower," I said with as much dignity as I could muster and, grabbing my clothes, I made my exit. I left Asher rolling on the bed in tears, gasping for breath in between uncontrolled fits of laughter.

When I got out, we had cold cereal for breakfast, the extent of our culinary talents that early in the morning. After eating, we set to unpacking the rest of the boxes. With extra sets of hands, the work went quickly, and by lunchtime, the apartment looked like we'd always lived here.

We were making a large pizza with everything disappear when someone knocked on our door. Aidan and I raced the short distance to the door, but he got there first and pulled the door open with one hand while holding a slice of pizza in the other. A woman I didn't know stood in the doorway. I would have guessed her to be in her early- to mid-twenties. She had short, spiky dark hair with the tips bleached white-blonde and wore black horn-rimmed glasses, a white halter under faded bib overalls, and funky faux leopard-skin fuzzy sandals. These last items caught and held my attention.

"Hiya! I'm Nikki Avanti. I live right across the hall. I just thought I'd stick my head in and say welcome to the neighborhood. I was going to bring a fruit basket, but then I thought who the hell brings fruit these days?"

We stood blinking at her for a moment; neither of us knew quite what to say. Aidan recovered first. "Uh, thanks. I'm Aidan Scott, and this is my roommate, Will Keegan," Aidan said. My attention wandered back to her feet, or actually her sandals, which she now waggled in greeting. I quickly looked up and held out my hand as my face turned red.

She took my proffered hand in a firm grasp with an amused smile on her not-quite-attractive face. "Like my shoes?" she said. "I kinda have my own style. I like to dress with flair! I think certain other residents of the building have betting pools on just how bizarre I can get. I'm always trying to top myself. You know, do my part to keep their lives interesting."

I grinned back. I liked her already. She had an easy manner that put me at ease. "This is Killian and Asher, they're our cousins," I told her as they came into the hall to see who we were talking to, each carrying his own slice of pizza. "Would you like a slice of pizza?" I offered.

"No thanks, I'm a health food freak. You know, organic foods only, lots of herbs, almost a vegetarian." She looked around the apartment while she talked. Her eyes lit up when she spotted my drawing table. "Oh, wow! Who's the artist?"

"That would be me," I said, making an effort not to blush.

"Nifty! Can I?" She made a motion toward the table.

"Help yourself."

She looked over my supplies for a few minutes. "Quite a professional set up you got here, Will. Nice quality, no junk. You must be a serious artist."

I lost my battle against the blush. "No, it's just a hobby."

"Don't listen to him," Aidan said as he walked over. "He's really good. Look at this." He pulled out the frog painting with a dramatic flourish.

Nikki's eyebrows shot up above her glasses. "You did this?" she said, leaning in for a closer look.

"Yeah," I said. I wondered how much blood could rush to my face before it exploded. I was actually starting to feel a little lightheaded.

"Nice, very dramatic. I like the symbolism here. Are you represented?" she asked.

"I guess you could say the frog."

She gave me a blank look. "Come again?"

I blushed. "Well, the frog kind of represents me because I've been feeling like I'm caught in a storm..." I stopped abruptly as she began to laugh.

"That's not quite what I meant. I meant, are you represented by a gallery? Do you show anywhere?"

"Oh God, no!"

She looked at me over the top of her glasses. "You should be."

"I'm not good enough..."

"Bullshit. Pardon my French. I'm an artist; I know what I'm talking about here. Actually, I own my own gallery, and I'm always looking for new talent. Are you from around here?"

"Yeah," I said with my head spinning.

"I'd like to see some of your other work. Do you have it here?"

"No, it's at home...I mean my parents' home."

"Can you get it for me to see? If I like it as much as what I see here, I might be interested in exhibiting a few of your pieces. We could see what kind of reaction we get, maybe do a show. You know, after we see what kind of vibes we get."

I had to sit down. So I did. Without checking to see if there was a chair there first. There wasn't. Aidan snorted, and I heard laughter from the kitchen where Killian and Asher had quickly ducked.

"Am I going too fast for you?" Nikki asked.

I nodded mutely.

"You have your own gallery?" Killian asked as he came back out of the kitchen.

"Yes, well, my brother and I own it. My father started it, and he left it to us when he died. It's called Avant Guard, and it's on the old downtown plaza."

"Cool. You look pretty young to have your own gallery."

"I didn't know there was an age limit, and actually I'm thirty."

"The health food must work," Aidan quipped.

Nikki laughed and turned her attention back to me. "So what do you say, Will? Can I see your work? You interested in maybe taking a shot at being a professional artiste?"

"I don't know," I said slowly.

"Come on, Will," Asher said. "How often do you get an offer like that?"

"Why don't you think about it for a while?" Nikki suggested.

"I don't mean to sound rude, but can I ask you a question?" I said hesitantly.

"Hey, you can ask me anything you want. I don't insult easily. You have to have pretty thick skin to dress like I do."

"Well, what do you get out of this?"

She threw her head back and laughed loudly. "A shrewd business man! I love it! Ok, let's see, what do I get out of it? Well, I'm assuming you mean besides the altruistic pleasure of helping out a fellow artist?"

I heard Asher mutter to Killian, "Quick, get a dictionary." Nikki winked at me.

"Yeah, besides that," I agreed.

"Well, it's standard procedure for the gallery to get a commission on anything we sell, usually between thirty and fifty percent. I'd only ask thirty from you since you're just getting started. More importantly, though, I get the pleasure and credit, keyword 'credit', of discovering an up-and-coming artist. If you make a splash, then Avant Guard gets exposure and publicity, and I can really start building a reputation of my own instead of riding on Daddy's coattails."

I nodded. "I need to think about it."

"Sure. Why don't you and Aidan come over to my apartment for dinner tomorrow night? You can meet my new boyfriend and see some of my work."

I looked over to Aidan, who nodded encouragingly. "Ok," I said.

"Great! It's a date! Toodles." And with that she let herself out, leaving behind the slightest hint of incense.

"Wow! Will, a real live artist!" Asher exclaimed.

"I dunno, it seems too good to be true," I said.

"Don't be so negative," Aidan scolded. "She's like a force of nature, isn't she? I bet if anyone can make this work she can."

"She seemed cool to me," Killian added helpfully.

"I have an idea," Aidan said. "How 'bout the four of us drive downtown to the plaza and check out the gallery for ourselves. That way we'll know what we're looking at."

"What if it's not open on Sunday?" Asher asked.

"Oh, shit!" I gasped.

"What?"

"Today is Sunday!"

"And..."

"I missed church!"

"Too late to worry about it now," Aidan said philosophically. "Let's go see if this gallery is open right now, and you can worry about that later."

Chapter 5

We piled into Killian's black Volkswagen Bug and drove to the downtown area.
The Plaza, as it is known, is a brick courtyard in the middle of the city with tall
Victorian-era brick buildings lining it and fountains, sculptures, and flowerbeds scattered about the middle. The buildings mostly house upscale bou-
tiques, lawyers' offices, and antique stores. It didn't take long to find Avant
Guard once we were there. It stood out a bit since it was the only place with a
life-sized sculpture in the window of a man and a woman caught in the act of
making love. The people depicted in this particular work actually had wings,
and something that looked like horns coming out of their heads. Not your typical couple. It looked like it was made of bronze, and it must have weighed a
ton. We all stood in a kind of silent awe for several minutes before anyone
spoke.

"Well...isn't that...amazingly accurate?" Aidan said.

"I wouldn't know. I'm still a virgin," Asher said with a giggle.

"You two might have to wait outside," I said, only half joking.

"Why?" Killian asked.

"It might be over twenty-one only!"

"That eliminates you guys, too," Killian pointed out reasonably.

We finally managed to tear ourselves away from the amorous couple and
entered the gallery, which was indeed open.

There were no other pornographic statues in view, but everything I did
see looked terribly expensive and elegant. I felt very out of place in my cargo-
pocket shorts and surf T-shirt. I was having some trouble picturing Nikki here
as well.

I was just about to suggest we leave when a stuffy looking man in an
Armani suit suddenly appeared out of thin air. "Hello, this is Avant Guard.
Can I help you with something?" His tone of voice clearly said that he seri-
ously doubted that this would be the case.

Before I could say no, Aidan stepped forward and offered his hand. Mr.
Armani looked at it disdainfully for a moment before reluctantly shaking it.
He casually wiped it on his pant leg as if it had possibly become contaminated
by Aidan's touch.

"I'm Aidan Scott," Aidan said in a cool, cultured voice that was so unlike
his usual voice that I almost did a double take. "This is my client, Will Keegan;
perhaps you've heard of him." He managed to make it sound like he was a fool
if he hadn't.

The suit began to look a bit flustered. Meanwhile I turned a lovely shade
of crimson.

"He's being called the next big thing. We met earlier today with Ms.
Avanti," Aidan swept on, "and she expressed an interest in perhaps representing Mr. Keegan in this area. We thought we'd stop by unannounced and have a
look around. You know we can't be represented by just anyone."

"Of course," Mr. Armani gushed. "I think you'll be very pleased with Avant Guard. We may be a small gallery, but we've had some wonderful success on the international market. As you can see, we cater to a very specific clientele."

"Yes, so I see," Aidan said, allowing just a hint of disapproval to enter his voice. "I just hope the scope isn't too narrow."

"I'm afraid I don't understand."

"I'm afraid you don't," Aidan agreed. "We'll look around now. Thank you." It was clearly a dismissal but the man seemed hesitant to leave us alone in the gallery.

"Please let me know if I can help you with anything..." he tried.

"I doubt that very seriously, but thank you ever so much once again."

The man now looked completely unnerved and began to back away with a slight bow that would have been laughable if I wasn't so nervous myself.

"That was freaking awesome!" Killian whispered as soon as he was out of sight.

"Shh!" I hissed, then reeled to face Aidan. "What was that?" I growled as quietly as possible while still letting him know exactly how I felt about his little performance.

"What was what?" he asked innocently.

"The next big thing?"

"What? I called you that, didn't I?"

"Your client?"

"Will, calm down. You're gonna pop a vein."

"What if Nikki finds out about this?"

"Relax. I know his type. He won't dare breathe a word of this to Nikki and make himself look bad. He'll wait and see if we say anything, see what take we give her, then he'll try to spin it to make himself look better. Trust me. I'm telling you I grew up in places like this."

I threw my hands up in defeat and started to look around. The work displayed was an eclectic mix of modern, abstract, and traditional art, complete with everything from sculptures to paintings to collages. They really seemed to have something for everyone, although I couldn't help but wonder if the athletic couple in the window might not put off the more conservative folks. We did find one more statue on a platform in the back of the gallery. Once again, it was life-sized and erotic, but this one was of two men. One was standing facing the viewer, and the other stood behind him with his arms around him in an intimate and touching embrace as he kissed his neck.

Once again, we were all struck silent at first. Asher was the first to break the mood. "My God, he's hung like a horse," he whispered loudly.

We all cracked up. I thought for sure Mr. Armani would come running, but we actually made it out of the gallery without running into His Stuffiness again.

"Well, what did you think?" Aidan asked as we walked back to the car.

"I think I wanna try that!" Asher said with a leer directed at Killian.

"Not about that, you perv." Aidan laughed. "About the gallery."

"I thought it was really cool but kinda stuffy," Killian volunteered.

"I think that sums it up pretty well," I agreed, "especially that stuffed suit."

"Stuffed Armani suit," Aidan corrected me, "and I agree, too."

We all turned to look at Asher.

"I'm horny!" he announced happily.

When we got back to the apartment, Asher and Killian came in only long enough to grab their bags before they had to leave to get home.

"So how are you doing? I've been thinking a lot about what we talked about last night," Aidan asked as soon as they were gone.

"You and me both," I said with a sigh. "I'm ok, I guess."

"Have you come to any conclusions?"

"No, and I don't think I will. Not right now anyway. I'm just going to let it slide for now. There's no reason I have to make up my mind right this second."

"Ignoring it isn't going to make it go away."

"Thank you, Dr. Ruth."

"No, really. I mean it's your decision, but for your own sake I don't think you should put it off too long."

"Or what? I'll self-destruct?"

Aidan looked thoughtful. "Maybe. It wouldn't be the first time it's happened."

Before I could pursue that intriguing line of thought further, a knock came at the door. I was closer so I answered it. It was Joey.

"Hey, Will," he said. "I haven't been able to get up with you all week. What's up?"

"I, uh...you know, with moving and work and stuff..."

"Can I come in?"

"Oh, yeah, sure." I stepped back to allow him in, shutting the door behind him.

"Hey, Aidan!" he said.

"Hiya, Joey. Hey, I'll be in my room on the computer if anyone needs me," he said as he left the room.

"I came by earlier, but no one answered the door," Joey said somewhat accusingly.

"We weren't here," I said.

"Yeah, I figured that. Will, are you avoiding me?"

"Why would you think that?" I said evasively.

"You don't answer my calls, you don't call me back, and now you're acting like you can't wait to get rid of me."

"I told you I've been busy."

"Too busy to call your best friend?"

"Yeah, well, my best friend was too busy to tell me about his new girlfriend, so it's a little like the pot calling the kettle black."

"Are you still mad about that? I said I was sorry. I made a mistake. Will, I really am sorry. I missed you this week."

"You did?"

"Yes. You're my best friend. Who else am I going to talk to about everything?"

"What about Shelley?"

"We've been going out three weeks; I've known you for eighteen years."

I sighed. "I missed you, too."

"I thought you were busy."

I grinned, and he playfully punched me in the arm. We moved over to the furniture and sat down to continue talking. He ended up staying until about eleven that night. After a while, Aidan came out and joined us watching a movie on TV and talking. I went to bed that night thinking that maybe things didn't have to change so much after all. Little did I know.

When I got home from work the next day, I found a note slipped under the door. It was from Nikki and simply said, "Dinner at six." I glanced at my watch. It was five thirty. I had stopped by my parents' house on the way home and picked up the rest of my paintings. Dad hadn't been home, so I'd only had to deal with Mom. She was fairly emotional and must have told me she missed me a half dozen times, but it wasn't as bad as it could have been.

I didn't have anything that needed my attention, so I kicked back on the couch to wait for Aidan.

I didn't have to wait long. "Lucy, I'm home," he called as he burst through the door, sounding eerily like Ricky Ricardo.

"Hey, dinner is at six."

"Cool, then I have time for a shower. Guess who I just met?"

"Uh...Fred and Ethel?"

He chuckled. "No, but you're close. Guess again."

"I give up."

"You give up too easily. I met another one of our neighbors, name of Mr. Morris. He's in the first door to the left of the elevator. He's in the hall with a trash bag when I get off the elevator, and he says, and I quote, 'I hope you two boys aren't fucking faggots. This is a respectable building.'"

"Oh, my God! What did you say?"

"I said, 'Hello, nice to meet you, too. My name is Aidan Scott.' And he goes, 'Morris, Jim Morris. You can call me Mr. Morris.' So I said, 'All right, Mr. Morris, it was nice meeting you. Have a nice day, and oh, by the way, we prefer the phrase fucking queers.'"

I felt my mouth drop open as Aidan collapsed into a chair, quite pleased with himself.

"You didn't really say that, did you," I asked, when I finally found my voice.

"Yes! You should have seen his face!"

"I can't believe you actually said that."

"Oh, loosen up, Will. It felt great. You should try it sometime."

"I don't think I will."

"Suit yourself. You don't know what you're missing. I'm gonna go take that shower now."

He was back out shortly, freshly showered and wearing a tropical print shirt and khakis.

"That is one ugly shirt," I couldn't help but say.

Aidan grinned. "You're just jealous, cuz you don't got cool clothes like me. Is my client ready for his first business dinner?"

"As ready as I'll ever be."

"Good, let's go."

We walked across the hall and tapped on Nikki's door. She answered it almost immediately wearing a brightly colored sarong with a matching scarf wrapped around her head like a turban. She looked like a white Erykah Badu.

"Aidan, I love your shirt!" she said. "Come on in."

The first thing we saw as we stepped in was the life-sized statue of a mermaid and merman wrapped around each other with their heads thrown back in apparent ecstasy. It was sitting in the middle of what should have been the living room, but Nikki apparently used as her studio. I guess we now knew who the sex-crazed artist was.

Nikki followed our gaze. "Like it? I just finished it last night. I haven't gotten it out of here yet. You'll have to excuse the mess."

"It's very lifelike," Aidan said carefully.

"I use live models for the initial sittings. I do a small clay model and some sketches that I then use to create the statues."

"Where do you find fresh mer-people this time of year?" Aidan asked.

Nikki laughed. "I have my sources. This piece is most likely already sold. I just have to get it to the gallery so they can see it."

"How do you get it out of here?" I asked.

"The elevator."

"Isn't it too heavy?"

"It's nowhere near as heavy as it looks. It's hollow for one thing. More importantly, though, it isn't really bronze. It's recycled aluminum that I paint with a metallic paint and then age and oxidize it."

"Cool."

"While we're talking shop, are those your paintings?"

"Yeah." I held out the stack.

She took them and began to look through them carefully. She went through the stack of about fifteen paintings twice, then pulled out four, stood them on the couch, and stepped back. After a few more minutes of scrutinizing, she put one back in the pile and handed the rejected pieces back to me.

"These," she said. She had chosen three of my most unusual pieces, a study of a door on an abandoned house, a window of another abandoned house, and an architectural detail of an old country church.

"Are you sure?" I asked. I was somewhat dubious.

"Yes, I'm sure."

"We went to the gallery yesterday," I told her. "Are you sure these will...fit in?"

"Oh, God, you must have met Derrick."

"Would that be the guy with the stick up his butt and wearing an Armani suit?" Aidan asked.

"That would be him." Nikki sighed. "Derrick is my brother and part owner of Avant Guard. We have somewhat differing ideas about how the place should be run. And the very reason I like these pieces is because they aren't like the other things we have. You don't want to blend in, Will. You want to stand out."

Considering how I'd spent most of my life trying desperately to blend in and not stand out, I was still somewhat unconvinced. She must have been able to tell by my expression.

"Have you ever seen one of your paintings framed and matted?"

"No."

"Do you mind if I have these done?"

"No."

"Good, then come by the gallery...um...Saturday and see what you think then."

"Ok," I agreed.

"Dinner's ready," a voice called from the kitchen.

Aidan and I turned confused looks toward the strange voice and then to Nikki.

"That's my boyfriend, Sam. He cooks. I hope you like vegetable lasagna."

"I guess we're about to find out," Aidan quipped.

It turned out to be delicious, and Sam was just as interesting as Nikki was. He had long curly brown hair, which he had pulled back into a ponytail, intense blue eyes, a goatee, and two silver hoop earrings in each ear. He looked a lot younger than Nikki, not much older than Aidan and I, in fact, but after my miscalculation with Nikki's age, I wasn't making any assumptions. Turned out I was right, though. He was only two years older than Aidan, and he was a senior at Pemberton. He and Nikki had met when he answered her ad in the paper for a live model. I couldn't help but wonder if he was the model who was "hung like a horse" as Asher had so elegantly put it. I kept taking what I hoped were surreptitious glances at his crotch whenever he stood up, but it was impossible to tell with his baggy jeans.

We also learned that Nikki specialized in erotic art and was beginning to gain an international name for herself. Her father, Giovanni Avanti, had been a world-renowned art expert and critic. He had retired to the Eastern Shore, where his wife was originally from, and opened the gallery in his later years. It had been building to a very successful international business when he died of a heart attack. Nikki and her brother, Derrick, had inherited the business jointly. She struck me as a slightly spoiled young woman, but very likeable nonetheless.

The rest of the evening passed by enjoyably, and we left around nine having made two new friends.

The week went by uneventfully, other than a Monday-morning lecture from Dad letting me know how disappointed he was that I'd missed church. There were no more run-ins with our neighbor, Mr. Morris, although we did meet a few of our other neighbors without incident. Joey, Shelley, Laura, and Gabe came over one night and watched rented movies, and that, too, went over well. I was careful to pay more attention than usual about my feelings and reactions to Joey, and it gave me food for thought. Aidan and I continued to grow closer, and I was fast coming to think of him as one of my best friends. I wondered what effect if any it would have on my friendship with Joey, which despite the movie night, continued to grow ever more distant.

Saturday finally arrived. I dressed in a button-down shirt and nice jeans and drove downtown once again, this time without anyone else.

Today, loud Celtic music flowed out of the open door of Avant Guard and drifted down the brick plaza. When I walked in, I spotted Nikki right away; she was hard to miss. Her hair was a purplish-red color, and she was wearing a matching T-shirt dress that was cinched at the waist with a length of chain with a padlock on one hip. Clunky black grandma shoes and dangly silver earrings completed the outfit. She was busy hanging a painting as I approached and didn't notice me. I looked over her shoulder and gasped when I saw what she was hanging. It was one of mine.

She spun around at my gasp, knocking the painting crooked on its hanger. "Oh, Will! You startled me. I didn't hear you come in. What do you think? Looks different huh?"

Did it ever! I hardly recognized it. I couldn't believe the difference a mat and frame could make. "Wow!" was all I could manage.

"You know you done good when you impress yourself," she said with a chuckle.

"It's not that—" I said quickly, but she cut me off.

"Of course it is. Every artist feels the same way the first time they see their work displayed properly. There's a bit of vanity in it, sure, but that's only natural. Call it pride of ownership or something like that."

"It just looks so different. Did you do anything to it?"

"I would never tamper with someone else's work. It's all yours, kiddo. All I did was stick a mat and frame on it. There's your other two," she said, pointing them out.

Once again, I found myself in awe at the way they had turned out. Nikki seemed to be enjoying every second of my reaction.

"Nikki!" A male voice bellowed, "Why are there mermaids having sex in my office? Oh, excuse me. Mr. Keegan, wasn't it?" It was Derrick.

"They're not mermaids; it's one mermaid and one merman. And they're in your office because a potential buyer is on the way here, and your office is bigger than mine. It's what you get for claiming the bigger office. I understand you two have met."

Derrick glared first at Nikki, then at me as if this were somehow my fault. "Yes, Mr. Keegan came in last week with his agent. I'm assuming from your presence here today that we are in fact representing you in this region?"

"Oh, for God's sake, Derrick!" Nikki said in an exasperated tone. "Get that damn stick out of your ass. Will is my neighbor and a friend, and yes, we are representing his work."

Derrick looked pissed for a moment, then spun on the heel of his expensive Italian leather shoe and stormed off in the direction he had come from.

"Sorry about that," Nikki said with a little sigh. "We should never be working together, but those were the terms of Father's will. We have to run it together for five years at which time one of us can buy the other out if we are so inclined. I think he thought it would force us to get along. So far it hasn't worked. We have two more years left, assuming we both survive."

I laughed.

"Come on back to my office. I'll have you fill out the paperwork, there isn't much, and then I need to get you to write on the back of each painting."

"Write what?"

"The title of the piece and any personal comments about it. Then you write Original Watercolor by Will Keegan."

I nodded and followed her behind a dividing wall and into her office. It turned out to be just as cluttered as I would have imagined. She shifted a stack of catalogs onto the floor to clear a space for me to sit and handed me a pen and some forms. It was mostly personal information for something called an artist's bio. While I was filling them out, Nikki asked, "Can I ask you a personal question? Feel free to tell me to mind my own business."

I looked up nervously. I didn't like the way this was sounding, but I said, "Uh...yeah, sure. I guess."

"Are you and Aidan a couple?"

I blushed. "No!" It came out a little more emphatically than I intended.

"I didn't mean any offense. As you can see from my art, it wouldn't bother me. I was just curious. The main reason I asked was that I'm always looking for subjects, and I thought you two would be great."

The very thought of my posing nude with Aidan for Nikki caused my blush to deepen.

Nikki laughed. "You know, not all my art is erotic." She handed me a binder with glossy full-sheet photos of her past work. More than half were erotic, often mythical beings in the throes of passion, but the rest were simply beautiful expressions of love and affection, suggestive but not explicitly sexual.

"Think about it, and let me know if you change your mind."

I still didn't think there was much chance of that happening, but I nodded anyway. "Is Derrick an artist, too?" I asked to change the subject.

"He thinks so," she said with a most unlady-like snort. "His stuff is that modern expressionist crap in the gallery. I wouldn't have it here if it weren't for him. Of course he says the same thing about my 'pornography'." She shrugged.

I finished the paperwork, which she took and filed in a folder with my name on it, and we returned to the gallery floor. I wrote the requested information on the back of each painting with a felt tipped marker and after admiring my paintings once more, we shook hands and I left.

It all seemed a little much to believe. In just two weeks my entire life had changed; I had a whole new set of friends, my paintings were hanging in a gallery, I had moved out into my own apartment, and I had found out that I might be gay. What next? I wondered. If someone had answered my question at that moment I would have never believed them.

Chapter 6

It was Sunday night, and Aidan and I were in the middle of a Daytona USA tournament when the phone rang. It was Joey asking if he could come over. He sounded serious so I quickly agreed. He was at the door in twenty minutes.

"Can we talk somewhere private?" he asked right away, with a meaningful glance in Aidan's direction.

Thinking about my last serious conversation, I led Joey out onto the fire escape. Once we were settled, Joey didn't waste any time.

"I just thought you should know that there are rumors going around campus that Aidan is gay and he's not done anything to deny them."

I sat for a moment trying to decide what to say. I wondered why Aidan hadn't mentioned it. I decided to be honest with Joey.

"He's probably not denying it because it's true," I said finally.

Joey looked stunned. "Oh, man, Will, I'm really sorry about getting you into this...wait a minute, you knew this?"

"Yeah."

"For how long?"

"Since the night I moved in."

"And you didn't say anything?"

"It wasn't something I just go around telling everyone. It's Aidan's life. He only told me because we were going to be living together. He said he wasn't ready to tell other people, and I respected that."

Joey looked out over the river. After a few minutes of heavy silence, I took a deep breath.

"Hey, Joey? As long as we're getting things out in the open I have something I need to tell you."

Joey looked over nervously at me, almost as if he knew what was coming and didn't want to hear it. For a second I thought he was going to get up and leave, but with an almost visible effort, he stayed seated.

"A few weeks ago, when I broke up with Beth, she said something that really upset me."

"I remember, you wouldn't tell me about it in the car. I asked, but you said you didn't want to talk about it."

"Right. Part of what she said involved Laura, so I asked her about it."

"That was when you were down by the river."

"Yeah. I...well...it upset Laura, but she was honest with me, and she backed up what Beth had said. Then she went on to ask me something that has been bugging me ever since, and I finally realized what she was trying to tell me."

Joey looked away again, and I wondered if Laura had talked to him or if he just suspected. Or maybe I was just being overly sensitive and reading things into it that weren't there. "I thought she looked like she was crying," he said, "but Laura never cries so I just thought it was reflections off the water."

"It wasn't the water; she was crying. Joey, Laura asked me if I was in love with you."

"WHAT? I can't believe Laura would ask something like that! Don't worry about it, Will. I'll straighten things out."

"Joey..."

"I mean that's the craziest thing I've ever heard..."

"Joey..."

"She must have lost her fucking mind!"

"JOEY! Listen to me. She's not crazy; I am in love with you."

He froze and stared at me wild-eyed.

"Joey?"

He just stared.

"Joey, say something."

"You're a fag?"

This was not going well. "It's not like that. I don't even know if I'm gay or not..."

"You don't know?"

"No, I mean maybe I'm just bi..."

"Just bi?"

"Or maybe it's nothing. I mean, I know I'm in love with you but that doesn't mean anything, right? We're still buds. Hey, it took me two weeks just to admit that. It's not like I'm going to hit on you or something..."

"Hit on me?" He stood up and moved to the railing. I stood up too and moved next to him. He pulled back sharply.

"Joey? I..."

"Look, Will, I don't know what this is about. I mean we've been best friends forever, but I don't know...this is...I just...if you like guys then you're not the same guy I've known for all these years."

"Joey, I'm the same guy I always was. Nothing's changed."

"Everything's changed. Introducing you to Aidan was a huge mistake."

"This doesn't have anything to do with Aidan. It started a long time before he came on the scene. Laura's known forever."

"Well, I didn't know." He ran his hands through his hair. "Look, Will, I don't think I can handle this. I don't know what you want..."

"I don't want anything." I reached out toward his arm, but Joey jumped back as if my hand would burn him if it made contact with his skin.

"Don't touch me!" He shook his head as if to clear it. "Look, there's no way I can be friends with a fag. I'm sorry...but I just can't. So you get yourself straightened out, and then let me know, until then, don't call me."

"You can't be serious..."

"I am serious. I'm not gonna be associated with a fag; I have my reputation..."

I couldn't believe what I was hearing. My head was spinning, and a dull roar had begun in my ears so that I almost missed what he said next.

"I mean it, Will, stay away from me. Don't call me. Just get help." He turned to crawl back through the window, and without thinking, I grabbed his arm. He shook me off violently and backed up against the rail. "Don't touch me!"

"Joey...I'm the same..."

"No, nothing is the same."

"Joey..."

He spun around, kicked the ladder down to the next floor with a clang, and started climbing down.

"Joey!" I screamed after him. He didn't even look up. He jumped to the ground and started walking away, never once looking back. "Joey...please!" I choked.

"Will?" Aidan called from the window behind me. "What happened? Are you ok?"

"No, I'm not ok!" I managed before collapsing into a sobbing heap on the metal grill of the fire escape.

Aidan was through the window in a flash and kneeling down next to me. He wrapped his arms around me and began to slowly rock back and forth while I sobbed on his shoulder. I somehow managed to tell him what had happened, which only started me crying all the harder. He never said anything, just held me while I cried. Eventually, when I had cried myself out, my seemingly endless flow of tears exhausted along with the rest of me, Aidan pulled me to my feet and helped me back through the window. He led me to the bed and tucked me in, pulling the blankets up to my chin, then sat next to me until I had calmed down. Then, with a light kiss on my forehead, he turned out the light and left the room.

I didn't go to work the next day; I had Aidan call in sick for me before he went to school. I spent the whole day sinking deeper and deeper into depression. I knew what was happening, but I just didn't care anymore. It seemed so hopeless.

By the time Aidan got home from school, my eyes were almost swollen shut from crying on and off all day. He didn't say anything, just made me a bowl of chicken soup, comfort food he said, and sat next to me on the couch.

When there was no change by Wednesday, he began to get concerned. By Friday, he'd called in the big guns. When I saw Laura sweeping in on me, I thought I would really get it now, but to her credit she didn't say I told you so, she didn't even hint it. She simply wrapped me in a big hug and said it was ok, she understood, but it was time to get back to living.

"Joey will come around. You know he will. It was just a shock; you know how clueless he is. Just give him some time."

I thought for a minute, then nodded, stood up and walked down the hall to take a shower.

"How come he didn't listen when I said that?" I heard Aidan wail.

"Sometimes it just takes a woman to do the job right," she said smugly.

The rest of the weekend went by slowly. I wouldn't say I was back to normal, but at least I was functioning again. Laura checked in often to see how I was doing. I skipped church yet again; it had been weeks since I'd been, but I just didn't feel like going. Maybe it was guilt at thinking I might be gay, but whatever it was it wasn't going over well with Dad. When I went back to work Monday morning, he was waiting in my office. My stomach sank as soon as I saw him.

"Son," he said, "I need to ask you something."

I felt my knees buckle, so I quickly sat down. "Ok," I managed to squeak.

"I received a letter yesterday afternoon, an anonymous letter," he said, and immediately the room began to spin. I gripped the edge of the desk and tried to keep my breathing regular. "It said that you are involved with a homosexual. Is that true?"

I fought the urge to stick my head between my knees. It seemed like it would be bad form. He laid a letter on the desk in front of me, and I scanned it without touching it.

> Dear Rev. Keegan,
> I think you should know that your son is gay and he's in love with another man.
> A friend.

Some friend. Should I deny it? An anonymous letter wasn't exactly proof and I wasn't even sure myself if I was gay or not. But I was in love with Joey, that much I knew, and I was so sick and tired of lying. Maybe it would be better to just get it out in the open and just let whatever happened happen. I managed to nod.

Dad sighed. "I had hoped it wasn't true. I didn't want to believe it even though I've suspected it myself a number of times."

My eyes widened. He'd thought I was gay, too? It seemed like everyone had known but me. Why hadn't anyone ever said anything to me?

"Son, if this is true then we have a decision to make." I tried to focus on what he was saying, but it suddenly seemed like he was far away and I was listening through a tunnel, watching from a distance. My body was still there, clutching for dear life to the edge of the desk, but the rest of me had withdrawn to a safer place. "If you continue to pursue this lifestyle," he continued, "then you will have to be removed from your position here at the church. We just cannot accept that lifestyle."

From my distant vantage point, I wondered what lifestyle he kept referring to. As far as I knew my lifestyle wasn't any different then it had always been. And Aidan seemed to have a pretty decent lifestyle from all I had seen. I decided not to ask, though, that would require going back.

Dad waited for a moment, then stood up. "Will, you are my son and I love you. I will always love you, no matter what. But as the pastor of this church, I cannot accept homosexuality. If that is what you choose, I will be very disappointed and as I said, I will be forced to take action." With that, he turned and walked away, his shoulders bent over as if he were carrying a great weight. I wanted to scream after him that it wasn't a choice. No one had bothered to ask me if I wanted to fall in love with Joey. No one had asked me if I wanted to be gay!

My mind froze.

I'd just said I was gay. Not out loud, granted, but in my head. That still counted for something, right? Was I? If I thought I was gay, then I must be. I mean, I should know, right? The room was spinning again. This time I didn't resist the urge to stick my head between my knees and take deep breaths. Once I had regained some modicum of control, my course of action suddenly seemed crystal clear. I switched on my computer and quickly typed up a letter of resignation. I left it on my desk, picked up the anonymous letter Dad had left, and left the church without another word.

I was sitting in the recliner at home, staring at the TV when Aidan got home.

"Hey, Will," he called as he came in. "How come the TV's not on?"

I turned my head slowly to face him. "I quit my job today."

"What? Why?"

"I'm gay."

"You're...but...I mean..." He took a breath and collapsed onto the couch. "Ok. What does that have to do with quitting your job?"

"Someone wrote a letter to my dad and told him I was gay."

"What? Who? What did your dad do?"

"I don't know who wrote it. It wasn't signed. Dad asked me if it was true."

"And you told him..."

"I didn't tell him anything. I couldn't even talk. But he knows."

Aidan stood up and began to pace in an agitated manner. "I'm moving out. I can't let this happen. I won't ruin your life, too."

"You're not going anywhere. This isn't your fault. Sit down, you're making me dizzy."

He sat down heavily. "I mean this wouldn't have happened if you hadn't moved in with me."

"Oh, please, I was in love with Joey long before I met you. It was just a matter of time. By the way, you don't seem surprised that I'm gay."

"I'm not. Well, I mean...I figured. I thought it would take you longer to deal with it, though, you know, with all your religious stuff to work through."

"I don't know if I have dealt with it yet."

"What are you going to do?"

"I don't know."

The phone rang, saving me from trying to answer a question for which I didn't have an answer. Aidan picked it up quickly.

"It's for you," he said with an unreadable expression as he handed me the phone.

"Yes?" I said woodenly into the handset.

"Will?" It was my mom. She sounded like she'd been crying.

"Yes."

"Will, your father said you quit today."

"Yes."

"Will, why?"

"It was either that or get fired."

"He said it was because you think you're gay."

"Yes."

"Oh, Will! You can't be!" she cried.

"Mom, I'm sorry, there's nothing I can do about it."

"There's counseling, I heard about it on the radio..."

"I don't think so, Mom."

A strangled sob filled my ear, "You know we can't accept this; we can't condone it."

"I know," I said quietly. I felt a tear escape the corner of my eye and slide down my cheek.

"I'll always love you, Willie."

"I know, Mom."

"Your father says you're not welcome back here unless you get counseling." She burst into sobs. "He says to read Hosea 8:7," she managed to choke out before I heard the click of the phone as she hung up. The line went dead, but I held the phone numbly in my hand until a recorded voice came on and informed me that if I wanted to make a call I needed to hang up and try again.

I stood up and handed the phone back to Aidan, who was watching me with a worried expression. I walked down the hall to my room and picked up my worn Bible. I turned to Hosea and found the indicated verse. "For they have sown the wind, and they shall reap the whirlwind."

The following days saw me plunge back into depression, this time even deeper than the first time. Nothing Aidan said could lift me out the dark miasma of despair that I sunk deeper into with every passing day. Even Laura's commands fell on deaf ears.

For the first time in my life, I found myself thinking about suicide, but worse, the idea wasn't at all as repugnant as I'd always imagined it would be. It held a certain alluring charm, a promise of escape, of no more pain and confusion. I didn't dare mention it to anyone, but as each day passed, I grew more and more obsessed with the idea of killing myself. I'd never asked to be gay, and I damn well didn't want to be gay. My family hated me, my best friend hated me, I didn't have a job — what did I have to live for? It seemed like the perfect solution.

I even drew pictures of the various methods I was considering. One showed me seemingly asleep on the bed...until you noticed the empty pill bottles lying next to me. Another showed me hanging from a noose from the fire escape. My personal favorite, though, was of me in a pool of blood with my wrists laid open.

Friday morning dawned gray and miserable. I decided it was a perfect day to bring one of those sketches to life. Who would even miss me? I pulled the sketches out from under my bed where I'd been hiding them and tried to decide which I liked the most. I immediately discarded the hanging one for purely practical reasons. I didn't know how to tie a noose. Besides, I'd heard it was a horrible way to die. After checking the medicine cabinet, I had to forget the OD method, too. The strongest thing we had was two cough drops and some mouthwash. I somehow doubted they could do the job. On the other hand, I would have nice breath when they found me. Ah, gallows humor...gotta love it.

That left me with slashing my wrists. I was morbidly pleased, since a bloody death appealed to that dark romantic side of me. I waited until Aidan was gone before slipping out of bed and into the kitchen. I sorted through our knives, disappointed to realize we didn't have many to choose from and what we did have wouldn't cut through hot butter. I needed a sharp knife so it would be quick, before I lost my nerve. I finally chose one that was marginally sharper than the rest. Now, where to do the deed? I went through several ideas before deciding the kitchen was as good a place as any; it would definitely be the easiest place to clean up.

The thought of a note went through my head, but considering the circumstances, I didn't think one was necessary. Those involved would know why, and no one else needed to know. Besides who would I address it to? To whom it may concern? Then I thought about writing up a will, but I didn't have anything worth leaving to anyone. I also wasn't at all sure I was of sound mind and body at the moment, and I was pretty sure that was a requirement.

Finally, I ran out of stall tactics. It was now or never. I took a deep breath, placed the edge of the blade against my wrist, and froze. I couldn't seem to make myself do it. Just then, I heard a fumbling at the door, and before my befuddled mind could react, Aidan walked in.

"Hey," he said as he appeared in the kitchen door. "It's good to see you up. I forgot my..." he stopped suddenly when he saw the knife in my hand. "Oh, my God, Will...what are you doing?"

I gripped the knife harder and pressed so hard against my skin that a thin cut sliced through and a small trickle of blood ran down my wrist. I gasped from the pain, and Aidan's eyes bulged. "Don't!" he shouted.

"Why?" I asked in a barely audible voice. "Why shouldn't I kill myself? What do I have to live for?"

"Will, you have your whole life ahead of you. You're only eighteen. I know things are hard right now, but this isn't the answer." As he spoke, he inched slowly closer to me.

"Then what is the answer?"

"I don't know, Will, but I promise this isn't it. I'll help you find it, though; I know someone who can help. He's my professor, a really nice guy. I want you to talk to him."

"A shrink?"

"He's a psychiatrist, a good one. I think he can help."

"You think I need to be fixed, too."

"No, I just think..."

"No!"

"Please think of all the people you would be hurting."

"Like who? My parents? I'm not even welcome in their home anymore. My best friend? He doesn't want anything to do with me."

"How about Laura? And Asher? And what about me? I care about you, Will." He had gradually crept closer until he was now within arm's reach. He stretched out his hand and looked at me pleadingly. "Please Will, don't do this. Give me the knife. Right now, all you can see is the darkness, but there is light, I promise. I promise you, Will."

Suddenly it was as if everything drained out of me. The knife slipped from my fingers with a clatter as it struck the tiles. I crumpled slowly after it, my body wracked with enormous sobs that seemed to originate from the depths of my soul and shudder their way through my whole being. Aidan was at my side with his arms around me before I even hit the floor. We sat on the kitchen floor with his arms around me while he gently rocked me and I sobbed into his shoulder. I felt his tears mixing with my own, and I knew he was hurting with me, sharing my pain. It somehow made the pain that much more bearable.

"I'm getting blood on your shirt," I blubbered.

"I don't care," he said gently, then lifted me up like a small child and carried me to the sofa where he carefully laid me down. He ducked into the kitchen long enough to grab a dishtowel which he wrapped tightly around my wrist.

"It's not deep. I'll get a bandage, and you'll be fine," he said.

Then, keeping a concerned eye on me, he flipped through his address book and made a phone call. He spoke in low tones that I couldn't quite make out, not that I tried all that hard. After he hung up, he picked me up again and carried me down the hall.

In the bathroom, he began pulling my clothes off. I didn't even protest I was so wiped out. I felt as if I had been turned inside out, beaten, and then turned right side out again. When he had me stripped to my boxers, he turned the shower on and placed me under the spray. The cold water hit me like a slap in the face. Even with the bracing coolness, Aidan still had to practically hold me up and by the time the water was turned off, he was as soaked as I was.

He wrapped a thick, fluffy towel around my shivering body and once more lifted me up and carried me into the bedroom. He set me on the bed, then turned to pull some clothes out of the dresser. He laid them next to me.

"Think you can get dressed while I change?" he asked gently.

I nodded and he left. I obediently started pulling on the clothes he had set out, feeling like a little kid, but not minding all that much. He was back much quicker than I would have thought possible and helped me finish getting dressed.

"Let's go," he said when I was once more clothed.

"Go where?" I asked meekly.

"Do you trust me?" he asked.

I nodded.

"Then let's go."

Chapter 7

Aidan's car pulled to a stop in an area clearly marked No Parking in front of one of the less prominent buildings on his campus. The university was a small but respected liberal arts school, built in a historic district of town around the turn of the century as an alternative to the stuffier, business-oriented college on the other side of town. Most of the buildings were red brick with white trim, and this one was no different, but it was obviously an afterthought and not part of the original layout.

Aidan jumped out of the car and came around to open my door. "Come on," he said.

"Why are we here?" I protested weakly.

"Follow me" was all he said. I climbed out and followed through the front door and down a short hall to a door marked with the name Dr. E. H. Wohler in simple gold lettering. We entered a room so small that if you sat on the provided sofa your knees almost touched the wall in front of you. It looked like they had commandeered a supply closet for their waiting room. A pleasant looking, slightly plump middle-aged woman sat at a desk behind a half-wall that served as a counter. She looked up as we entered.

"I'm Aidan Scott," Aidan said. "I called Dr. Wohler earlier; he's expecting us."

"Yes, go right in," she said. She had a pleasant voice to match her pleasant look.

I balked slightly at that point, but Aidan took me gently but firmly by the arm and pulled me along. When we stepped into the office, it actually took me by surprise, even in the shape I was in. The difference between the sad, cramped lobby and this large but cozy room was like night and day. The harsh fluorescent lighting had been replaced with warm incandescent lamps. Thick oriental rugs had covered up the industrial grade carpet, and instead of a worn institutional couch, there were two inviting armchairs facing a large wooden desk. A man was standing behind the desk waiting expectantly for us. He was on the short side, not much taller than I was, with a receding hairline and glasses. He was wearing a tailored gray suit that spoke his success as clearly as if he'd hung a sign around his neck that read, "I'm rich."

"Hello, Aidan, it's good to see you," the man, I presumed him to be Dr. Wohler, said. "And you must be Will?"

I looked uncertainly at Aidan. What exactly had he told him? Aidan and the doctor shook hands.

"Thanks for seeing us on such short notice, Doc," Aidan said as he gently pushed me into one of the two chairs. He sat down in the other, and the doctor settled into his plush executive chair.

"No problem, I always try to make time for my most promising student, and besides I just happened to have a cancellation on my schedule," he said the last with a small smile that showed he was kidding. "I just hope I can be of assistance. You said on the phone that it was an emergency?"

I turned a glare on Aidan, but he didn't even glance in my direction. "Dr. Wohler, can we have your complete confidentiality about what we are going to say?"

For a moment, the doctor looked somewhat insulted, then he looked at me, and an unspoken message seemed to pass between him and Aidan. He nodded, "Of course, as you know, any information that should come out while we are talking is held in complete confidence."

Aidan turned to me now. "Can I tell Dr. Wohler what's going on?" I thought for a moment, then nodded my consent. He quickly and succinctly outlined the events leading up to my depression and my attempted suicide that morning. When he had finished, Dr. Wohler sat for a minute tapping his chin with one index finger, his expression unreadable. Then he pulled a legal pad out of a desk drawer and asked me a few questions. He scribbled on the pad the whole time while I talked. A mental picture of him drawing nudie pictures while I rattled on popped into my head, almost making me giggle out loud. I decided I was definitely in the right place since I was apparently going "nucking futs", as the T-shirt said.

When he'd used up his questions, he looked up and asked Aidan to excuse us. After he had slipped quietly from the room, Dr. Wohler turned his full attention on me.

"Well, Will," he said after a few seconds of carefully studying my face, "as you probably already know, you're in a pretty deep depression. That's the bad news. The good news is that depression is very treatable. Since your depression seems to be mainly because of your situation right now and maybe some residual issues that you need to deal with regarding your upbringing, we could just work through it in some sessions. What I think is the better course is for us to set you up on some mild anti-depressants, get you out of this funk, get you so you're thinking a little clearer, and then we can really tackle those problems. You'll be able to handle a little poking at sore spots once your depression is under control. What do you think?"

I nodded hesitantly.

"Do you understand what causes depression?" he asked.

"Not really."

"Ok, to oversimplify it, there are lots of little cells in your brain, but they don't touch. To get information from one cell to another they need a conductor. That conductor is called serotonin. When your body isn't producing enough serotonin it can cause all sorts of problems, but the main one is depression. What we need to do is increase your serotonin level. Are you following me?"

I nodded.

"Ok, great!" He pulled open another desk drawer and pulled out some small boxes. "I'm going to give you some samples of a medicine that I think will do the trick. It's a very mild drug that has very few, very mild side effects, and it's not habit-forming. You won't feel an immediate difference; it takes a few weeks to get into your system. If this doesn't seem to be working for you, then I want you to tell me that. This may not be the right drug for you, but I promise there is a right one. This isn't an exact science, though, and we may have to try a couple before we hit the right one. I'm betting this one will be the ticket, however."

He slid the boxes across the desk to me, and I picked them up.

"These are on the house. Take two of those a day to start with. I gave you a two-week supply; that's the earliest that you would see some effect although it takes others longer sometimes. Is it ok if I bring Aidan back in now and tell him what we've decided?"

I nodded again, and he pressed a button on his phone and spoke into the receiver, "Linda, could you send Aidan back in please?"

Aidan was back beside me in no time. Dr. Wohler directed his comments to him, "You were right to bring Will here, Aidan. He was definitely in need of a doctor's care. He is depressed, but we are going to treat it aggressively with medication." He turned back to me. "Will, do you trust Aidan?"

I thought for a moment, then nodded slowly. "Yes."

"Good. I think you know that not too many roommates would go to this length for someone they've only known for a month. I'm going to give Aidan the medicine to administer for now until you are in a better frame of mind." Aidan took the boxes, and we both sat looking expectantly at the doctor. "There's one more thing I want you to do for me before you go, Will. I would like you to make a covenant with Aidan that you will not hurt yourself before talking to him. Can you do that, Will?"

I looked down at my lap and nodded somewhat hesitantly.

"Say it."

I looked up, startled.

"Look at Aidan and say it. Tell him that you promise not to hurt yourself without talking to him first."

I slowly turned my head until I was looking into Aidan's piercing green eyes. I saw myself mirrored in them, looking like a deer caught in headlights. I focused on the twin images of myself and forced the words from my mouth. "I promise I won't hurt myself without talking to you first," I whispered hoarsely.

"Good!" said Dr. Wohler. "Now remember, you made that promise in front of a witness and a man is only as good as his word. Aidan, take care of him, keep an eye on him, and call me if anything comes up that you can't handle. He probably shouldn't be left alone for a few days. Do you have some friends to help out?"

"We'll be ok," Aidan said confidently. I was glad someone was confident.

"Good, ok then. Will, I'll see you in two weeks."

The next few days went by in a blur. Aidan was almost always with me, and when he wasn't Laura was. Once, Gabe even spent a tortured hour trying to make conversation while I stared dumbly at the television. But most of the time it was Aidan who watched over me; he even started sleeping in my bed, chastely, of course. As far as I could tell, he never strayed from his side of the bed. At first, I thought the constant attention would be suffocating, but in reality, I found it very comforting. It was nice to know someone cared that deeply.

When the next week began, Aidan stayed home from school. When I protested, he said that everything was already arranged with his professors and for me not to worry about it.

Things settled into a nice, comfortable environment in which I slowly but surely began to feel better. The black curtain of depression began to lift, and I began to feel hopeful once again. But as my spirits began to rise, so did my restlessness. I was working at my drawing table one day with Aidan sitting nearby as usual. He was supposedly reading, but he was at my elbow if I so much as farted crooked. I got up to go look for a notebook that I was pretty sure was in my closet, but Aidan insisted on getting it for me. After some bickering, I gave in with a sigh and went back to my drawing. When he still wasn't back after several minutes, I called back without looking up, "Did you find it? I told you I should just get it myself. I'm not an invalid you know."

"What are these?" he asked quietly from directly behind me. The closeness of his voice caused me to jump. I turned to see what he was talking about. He was holding one of my sketchbooks, the one in which I had drawn my suicide fantasies.

"They were...from before," I said softly. Looking at them now, I felt a strange horror, as if someone else had drawn them. It seemed impossible that they had come from my mind and my hand.

Aidan ripped the pages from the book with such a sudden, savage motion that I jumped again. He angrily shredded them one by one, then gathered all the tiny pieces of paper and tossed them into the sink where he burned the whole lot. A strange shudder went down my spine as I watched the flames lick at the shreds of paper, eventually consuming them completely, leaving only a black mess that Aidan washed down the drain. The whole episode bothered me more than it should have. We ended up going to bed earlier than usual, and I was extra glad for Aidan's presence in my bed that night.

I awoke suddenly with the acrid smell of smoke still in my nostrils. I pushed myself into a sitting position and felt a sticky wetness on my hands. I looked down to see they were covered in blood. Whose? Mine? A knife lay on my pillow, glinting in the semi-darkness. I looked for Aidan, but he wasn't next to me in the bed. I was alone. Suddenly fire was all around my bed, jumping and leaping closer and closer like a living thing. I opened my mouth to scream, but nothing came out. The flames crept closer, and I squeezed my eyes closed so I wouldn't have to watch my skin burn away like the edges of the paper.

"Will! Will!" It was Aidan's voice. My eyes flew open to see his face, wide-eyed and frightened above me. "It was just a bad dream, Will. You're ok. I'm right here."

My heart felt like it would beat right out of my chest, and my breathing came in ragged gasps. Could it have been just a dream? But it must have been;

there was no fire, no smoke, no blood. I was in my bed and Aidan was holding me, but the terror still clung to me like stubborn fog in weak sunlight.

"It's ok, Will," Aidan whispered as he wrapped his arms around me. I felt my body slowly begin to relax into his, and I snuggled closer. I hadn't felt so comforted since I was a little kid being held by my parents after a bad dream. I slowly drifted off to sleep.

The nightmare stayed away for the rest of the night, and I awoke the next morning with Aidan's arm still around me. I sat up suddenly, waking him in the process.

"Mornin'," he mumbled sleepily.

I looked around the room for signs of a fire. It was silly, I knew, but the nightmare images were still so vivid in my mind.

"Whatcha lookin' for?" Aidan asked.

I lay back down without answering. Aidan raised himself up on one elbow to look into my face. "Are you ok?" he asked. Before I could answer, the phone began to ring. Aidan looked around for it. It was on my side, and since I hadn't made any move to answer it, he leaned over me to grab it up. His face was just a fraction of an inch from mine, so close I could feel his breath on my lips. Our eyes locked, and he froze, the ringing phone momentarily forgotten. It stopped abruptly, and the sudden silence brought us back to ourselves. Aidan quickly rolled back to his side of the bed. We carefully avoided looking at each other for an awkward moment before the phone began to ring again.

"I'll get it," I said quickly. "Hello?"

"Will! Just who I was looking for! Did I wake you up?" It was Nikki.

"No, I was awake."

"Oh, because I just called, and the phone rang and rang and no one answered so I thought...well anyway, I've got some good news. How soon can you get to the gallery?"

"Um...how soon can I get to the gallery?" I repeated to Aidan.

"An hour?" Aidan suggested with a shrug.

"An hour," I relayed.

"Perfect! See you then! Ciao!"

"See you then," I said to a dead line. "Nikki wants me to come to the gallery; she said she has good news. Have you ever noticed how you can hear the exclamation points when she talks?"

Aidan laughed as he sat up. "Do you think she sold one of your paintings?"

"That would be so cool!" I exclaimed as I jumped up out of the bed. For the first time since my depression had set in I felt really excited.

Aidan got up and started out of the room. "You take your shower first. I'll cook us breakfast. This calls for a celebration!"

"We don't even know what we're celebrating," I called after him.

"Who cares? I'm just glad we've got some good news for a change."

After we had both showered and enjoyed a delicious omelet that Aidan had whipped up, we arrived at Avant Guard slightly ahead of schedule. Today, the Dixie Chicks were serenading walkers-by on the plaza from the open door of the gallery. They were belting out a good-bye to Earl as we walked into the seemingly empty showroom. As we were standing there trying to decide what to do next, Derrick pulled his appearing trick. I made a mental note to ask Nikki how he did that. When he saw who we were, he dropped his poise and yelled over his shoulder, "Nikolia, it's your latest find, the next big thing."

Nikki swept past him with a wide grin on her face, "Guess what?"

"I sold a painting?" I guessed.

Nikki frowned. "No, I'm sorry Will; you didn't sell a painting..." I felt my face drop before she went on, "...you sold all three!"

"What?" Aidan and I chorused, then I added, "You're kidding!"

Nikki laughed. "I stirred things up a bit, called a few people to come see them, told them you were a newly discovered talent and boom...they sold themselves."

"I can't believe this!" I said.

"I can!" Aidan laughed.

"Now before you get your hopes up, I priced them on the low side since you are an unknown at this point, but now we have a benchmark. They only go up from here. We never really discussed prices so I hope you aren't disappointed."

I was surprised to realize I hadn't even thought about money. Just the fact that someone thought my art was good enough that they wanted it was enough for me at the moment. "How much?" I asked.

"Three hundred."

I blinked. "Dollars?"

"No, pesos. Of course dollars."

"For all three? But that's great!"

"No, not for all three. Each."

"Th-th-three hundred dollars each?"

"That's nine hundred dollars," Aidan said helpfully in a somewhat awed voice.

"Minus my commission of course," Nikki said with a wink. I felt like I needed to sit down, but there was nowhere to sit. I swayed a bit as Nikki went on, "How do you feel about doing a one-man show? I'd like to strike while the iron is hot, so to speak. These people that bought your paintings are the types who like to brag about their latest acquisitions to all their rich friends, so you can be sure your name will be circulating right now. I'd rather not wait more than, say, a month or so."

I was still reeling from the last blow, so it took me a while to catch up with her and realize what she was saying. Things always seemed to happen faster than I could keep up with when Nikki was around. "One-man show? Are you serious? When?" I finally managed.

"Very serious. As for when, well, it's the beginning of October now, and I'd really like to get it in before Thanksgiving, so let's say mid-November. That would give you about a month. You wouldn't have to do anything but paint; I'll take care of everything else. Think you can pull it off?"

"Do I have a choice?" I said. "I suspect that this is the kind of thing that doesn't happen twice. I'll manage somehow. It's not like I have a job to worry about."

"Speaking of that, just tell me if it's none of my business, but Aidan mentioned the other day that you'd quit your job, and I talked it over with Derrick, and we could use some extra help here at the gallery. We can't pay a lot but it's better than nothing, and we could work around your painting schedule. Interested?"

"I'd say! What would I be doing?"

"Some office work, watching the floor for us if one of us can't do it, helping with sales, manual labor, you know, the usual."

"And Derrick was ok with this?"

"He wasn't at first, but I can be pretty persuasive when I need to be, and anything that means less work for him will usually win out in the end."

"Will you teach me that trick of Derrick's?"

"You mean his poof-here-I-am trick?"

"Yeah, that one."

Nikki laughed. "Sorry, that's top-secret, but I can tell you that he practiced it for hours when we were kids."

"I did not!" yelled Derrick from somewhere unseen.

"So does this mean you want the job?"

"Hell, yeah!"

"Great! You're hired! You can start next Monday."

We shook hands, and Aidan and I left. We talked excitedly about selling the paintings and my new job all the way home. I started right to work on planning out what I wanted to do for the one-man show and even started on a sketch. Nothing more was mentioned for the rest of the day about that strange moment that morning in bed.

Aidan returned to his own bed that night, saying that he thought I was ok now by myself. I lay awake that night wondering what it would have been like if he had kissed me that morning. I knew that was what had been going through his mind when our eyes had locked. Suddenly it seemed of the utmost importance to know what Aidan's lips felt like against mine. Almost without even thinking, I got up and walked across the hall to Aidan's door. I rapped lightly.

"Come in," he answered right away, so I knew he was having as much trouble sleeping as I was.

I opened the door and then just stood there stupidly, suddenly unsure of what exactly I was doing. What was I hoping would happen?

Aidan was sitting up in his bed, his bare chest glowing in the moonlight which poured in from his window. He was looking at me with a confused expression. "Is something wrong?" he asked.

"No, I just...I missed you," I said awkwardly in a voice that was barely above a whisper.

For what seemed like an eternity, he just stared back at me. I could see his mind turning my words every which way, seeking out every implication of my appearing in his bedroom after midnight. I felt like a little kid waking up his daddy after he's had a bad dream. Just as I turned to go back to my room with a mumbled apology, he called my name. I turned back to see him toss the sheets aside and pat the bed next to him. I slowly shut the door and walked to the side of the bed before hesitating again. My heart was racing, and I couldn't keep my hands from shaking. In the near darkness, I could see Aidan searching my face, his eyes seeking mine out. Then he reached out and tentatively took my hand, pulling me gently onto the bed.

The kiss was so soft, so quick that I almost thought I was still imagining it. The second one, though, was much more decisive, as if we both now knew what we wanted. He pulled back and searched my eyes once more. I reached around his neck and pulled him back to me for another kiss, this one much longer and more passionate.

I don't know how long we stayed like that, kissing as if our lives depended on it. I was lost in the moment. It was like my first kiss all over again, but so much better. I remember the first time I kissed Beth I had wondered where all the fireworks were. Now I knew.

I felt his hand slide over my shoulder, across my chest, and down my stomach as his kisses moved down my neck. He left a trail of angel kisses down my chest and stomach where his hand had passed just moments before. His mouth lingered over my navel, and he tickled it with his tongue. I felt my breath rush out as my stomach did somersaults. His mouth moved back up to meet mine, but his hand slid under my boxers. I almost jumped out of the bed when he found his target. Then, in a blur of motion, he broke away, and before I could even think, our boxers were off and he was on top of me, kissing me once again with a passion that caught me off guard. Our bodies began to move in synchronicity as the fireworks turned into an all out explosion.

Afterwards, as I lay wrapped tightly in his arms listening to his regular breathing, I began to question what had just happened. Did I love Aidan, or had I just gone to him because I missed the security of having someone next to me? I didn't have the energy to pursue that line of thinking right then. I pushed the thoughts from my head and fell into a deep sleep.

They were back with a vengeance as soon as I opened my eyes the next morning, though. My first coherent thought was, "Oh my God! What did we do?" But of course, I had all the evidence I needed spooned into my back. My mind raced. Did I love Aidan? I wasn't sure. I was hurting from Joey's and my family's rejections; maybe I just needed to feel loved for one night. But that would make me one hell of a horrible person, using Aidan like that. Of course, I hadn't gone expecting all that to happen...had I? Aidan was without a doubt the most caring guy I had ever met. I knew I could love him, but I also knew I still had a lot of unresolved feelings for Joey.

I felt Aidan stir behind me. His lips brushed my shoulder, then my ear. "I love you, Will," he whispered.

I sat up with a jolt.

"Will?"

"Aidan, last night..."

"Was incredible. You can't imagine how long I've wanted to do that, to hold you in my arms. It was so hard lying next to you all those nights, so close and yet..."

"Aidan..."

"I've wanted so badly to tell you that I loved you, but I knew I had to wait, that you had to make the first move."

"Aidan, last night was a mistake."

Punching him in the stomach wouldn't have created the effect those words had on him. He seemed to cave in as his face fell. "What?" he whispered.

"We shouldn't have...done what we did."

"Make love? Say it, Will. We shouldn't have made love? Why? What do you mean? You came to me. I thought you wanted me."

"I don't know what I wanted. That's the problem. I still love Joey, and right now I can't separate what I feel for him and what happened last night. Maybe I did want you, but what if I really only went to you because I need to feel loved, because I couldn't have Joey?"

"I don't understand this." Aidan ran his hands through his hair. "Do you love me?"

"I...I don't know."

Aidan stood up abruptly, realized he was still naked, and grabbed the sheet to cover himself, clutching it like a security blanket.

"Aidan, I do love you," I said hurriedly. "You've become my best friend these past few weeks. I don't know anyone else who would have done what you've done for me. I'm just so confused right now. I don't know if I love you the way you want me to love you."

"You didn't seem confused last night."

"I...it's just...I still have all these feelings for Joey."

"Joey's straight. No, he's not just straight; he's homophobic. I'm here, right now. And I'm telling you I love you with everything I am. Isn't that enough for you? Aren't I enough for you?"

"It's not that you're not enough. These feelings I have for Joey, I've had them for years. I can't just make them go away. I don't have an on-and-off switch. I wish I did. And maybe...maybe once he gets used to the idea, maybe he'll be ok with it. Maybe he'll even realize he loves me, too."

"Oh, God! Wake up, Will! It's not going to happen. The guy's an asshole. I hadn't told you because I didn't want to hurt you and I thought you had enough to deal with, but ever since you broke the big news to your old pal Joey, he's been hell-bent on proving his heterosexual masculinity. Shelley dumped him weeks ago when she found out he was cheating on her, and he's been screwing everything with tits ever since. He's become the campus sleaze over night."

"Not Joey. He wouldn't do that."

"Guess what? He is. He's also managed to maintain an almost constant state of stone-assed drunkenness at every party that's been held since school began, whether he was invited or not. His trademark phrase is 'Can you believe I used to be friends with a fag?'"

The last statement hit me like a blow. Aidan saw it written all over my face. "Oh, God, Will, I'm sorry."

I stood up and staggered to the door.

"Will, please, I'm sorry."

I walked across the hall to my room and shut the door behind me. Immediately, Aidan was knocking and talking through the door. I quickly turned the lock.

"Will, please open the door. Talk to me. Don't shut me out."

I walked to the window and threw it up with a bang.

"Will! I shouldn't have said that; it was wrong. I was hurt. Please open the door."

I climbed out the window and onto the fire escape with a strange sense of detachment. It would all be over soon. Aidan sounded like he was crying now; he'd stopped banging on the door. "Will, please forgive me..." he sobbed.

I didn't feel anything anymore, but I felt I owed him at least that much so I turned back to the window. "I forgive you," I tried to say but it came out as a kind of croak, so I cleared my throat and said it again only louder. Then I turned and climbed onto the rail. I stood for a second, balancing precariously on the top rung. The ground looked so far away. I heard a key fumbling in the lock of my door, and I thought it was strange that I didn't know he had a key to my room.

"Will...NO!"

I jumped.

For a brief moment I felt like I was flying; all my troubles were gone. Then the ground started rushing toward me.

"Noooooo!"

Blackness.

Chapter 8

Beep Beep Beep Beep Beep

I've always been especially sensitive to repetitive noises. They annoy me in a way that very few things do. The first thing I remember thinking is how much I wanted that damn noise to stop.

Beep Beep Beep

I had to make it stop. But that meant I had to wake up.

Beep Beep Beep

Oh, but I didn't want to wake up. It was so nice just floating in this darkness, not having to deal with life's problems.

Beep Beep Beep

But the infernal beeping wouldn't stop. I tried to open my eyes. No, really, I did; but I couldn't seem to lift my lids.

Beep Beep Beep

I tried to move my hand, thinking I could find the source without the effort of opening my eyes, but it wouldn't move either.

Beep Beep Beep

I tried to speak, but even that proved to take more effort that I could seem to pull together.

Beep Beep Beep

I couldn't stand it. Putting forth an extreme effort, I parted my lips and forced the words past them.

"Make it stop," I rasped.

"Will? Will!" I heard a voice; it sounded like Aidan.

"Is he awake?" Another voice, this one sounding suspiciously like my mother.

"I think he said something," said the first voice.

"What did he say?"

"I don't know; I couldn't understand him. Will! Will, can you hear me?"

I mustered up some more energy. I felt I was fast depleting my meager supplies and said again, "Make it stop."

"Oh, my God! He's awake!" Aidan screamed.

"Nurse! Nurse! He's awake!" Mom yelled. She continued yelling this as her voice faded away.

The beeping was still there so I tried again, but this time I decided to be a little more specific, "Make the beeping stop."

"Oh, my God! Will, we've been so scared!" Aidan babbled on as if I hadn't just asked, quite reasonably, I thought, that he turn off the beeping. "You're in the hospital," which explained the beeping, "and you've been in a coma. You broke your arm and banged up your head pretty bad, but they said it's a miracle you're even alive. I'm so glad you're awake. You were in the coma for two weeks. They were even starting to talk about what to do if you didn't wake up."

I seriously considered sinking back into the beckoning darkness at this point, but that incredibly irritating beeping was still droning on in the background of Aidan's relieved prattle. I decided to try one last time, "Please make it stop."

"Make what stop? The pain?"

"The beeping."

"Beeping? What...oh, the heart monitor. I can't. It's what lets us know you're alive."

"I wanted to die."

"I...I know. But it wasn't your time. You've still got so much living to do."

I would have retched right about then but it was all I could do to talk; and while the effect would have been quite dramatic, I didn't think it was worth the effort. I heard my mother's voice coming closer again. She was talking to someone whose voice I didn't recognize.

"I'd really like to have a look at him before I can say, Mrs. Keegan. Let me talk to him then we'll see," he was saying. His voice stopped above me. "Will? I'm Dr. Cherrix. I'm your doctor. Can you hear me?"

"Yes. Can you make the beeping stop?"

"Yes, but right now we have more important things to tend to. We'll get to that in a minute, but only if you can stay with me long enough to answer some questions." Ah, nothing like blackmail while you are lying half-dead in a hospital bed. "Can you open your eyes?"

"No."

"Can you try for me?"

"No."

"If you play by my rules, I'll make the beeping stop."

He was playing dirty, but what choice did I have, really? I tried to open my eyes again, but my lids felt like lead weights. Suddenly the beeping seemed to grow louder, giving me the extra push that I needed. I managed to get my eyes open a tiny bit, but the light was so bright they immediately snapped shut again. I wondered if the effort would count for anything.

"That was good, Will. Now try again." Apparently not.

I sighed. Or I would have if I wasn't busy fighting a battle of wills with my leaden eyelids. I finally forced them open again and, after much blinking and adjusting to the bright light, somehow managed to keep them open this time. As the dancing spots slowly faded, I saw Aidan, Mom, and a man I assumed to be Dr. Cherrix hovering over my bed. All were wearing concerned, earnest expressions. Dr. Cherrix looked as if this were his usual expression. He was a serious looking middle-aged man, with graying ginger hair, pale blue eyes, and a ruddy complexion.

"Hi," I said.

They all broke into smiles.

"Hello! Welcome back to the land of the living," Dr. Cherrix said. "Now that I've got your attention I want you to try a few more things for me. Can you tell me your full name?"

"William Spencer Keegan."

"Good! Do you know what month it is?"

"Is it the same month that it was when I jumped?"

"No, you were unconscious for two weeks."

"Then I guess it must be November."

"Great! How many fingers am I holding up?"

I was starting to feel like a trained monkey. "Three."

"And now?"

"Still three."

"And now?"

"One."

"Fantastic!" He made some notes on a clipboard.

"Do I get a banana now?"

He looked up with confusion. "Hmm? A banana?"

"Never mind, can you just make the beeping stop?"

"I'll make you a deal. You don't go back to that secret place in your mind again, and I'll make the beeping stop. Do we have a deal?"

Anything to make the beeping stop. "Deal."

"Good answer," he said and punched some buttons on one of the several machines that appeared to have sprouted from my body while I was asleep. At last, the beeping stopped.

"Thank you," I said sincerely.

"You're welcome."

"Did you make the beeping louder before I opened my eyes?"

"I sure did," he grinned. "We do what we have to do to get the job done. I figured if that beeping was enough to pull you out of your coma we were going to milk it for all it was worth. Apparently it worked. It may be a little early to say, there are some more tests I'd like to do, but I'm going to go out on a limb here and say that there appears to be no permanent damage from your failed attempt at flying."

When no one even made an attempt to laugh at his weak stab at humor, he hurried on, "Well, I'll give you a chance to talk to these people here. They haven't left your side since you came in, you know."

He turned to Mom and Aidan. "Don't keep him up too long, though. I know he just woke up, but rest is still a high priority. I'll send the person we spoke about down to check on him later."

"Send who down?" I asked as he was leaving. He either didn't hear me or pretended not to, so I asked again, this time directing the question to Mom and Aidan. They looked at each other for a moment and then Mom answered.

"Will, do you know why you're in here?"

"I jumped off the fire escape." She seemed taken aback by my matter-of-fact tone, so I elaborated, "I wanted to die."

"Well...um...that's what we need to talk about. Not right now, of course, but sometime soon. They won't release you until they do a psychiatric evaluation. Not that you would be leaving today anyway. And when you do leave, you'll be coming home with us, of course."

"No."

"What?"

"I'll go back home with Aidan."

"What?" they both said.

I closed my eyes. "I want to go back to the apartment."

"Are you sure that would be for the best, Will?" Aidan asked as Mom said, "I don't think that's such a good idea."

I opened my eyes again even though it was the last thing I wanted to do. I looked at Aidan, "Do you want me to come back?" It was a loaded question, and we both knew it. How much Mom knew or guessed I don't know.

"If you want to come back, of course it's ok with me," he said quietly.

"Then I'm going home with Aidan," I said with as much finality as I could muster. "I'm really tired now." And I was. I felt like I had just completed a cross-country marathon.

Mom looked upset, as if she wanted to say more, but she just patted my hand, the one on my unbroken arm, and said, "Ok, Will, you get some rest. We'll talk more when you wake up."

That, of course, was exactly what I was afraid of. Just before my eyes slammed shut, I saw her shoot Aidan a look that clearly said, "We need to talk."

When I woke up next, the sun was slanting low across the floor with a warm glow that told me it was late afternoon. The overhead lights were out, and Aidan sat slumped over in the room's one chair, asleep. Mom was nowhere to be seen.

I lay there watching Aidan sleep. It occurred to me how much he had given up for me, first to stay home with me while I was depressed and then sitting here in the hospital waiting for me to wake up. I knew without any doubt that he loved me. And I knew that logically, I should love him, too. He was everything anyone in their right mind would want in a guy — loyal, kind, honest, loving, patient, forgiving, persistent, and funny to boot! But then, people in their right mind didn't jump off fire escapes, did they? And I did love him; I just couldn't shake my feelings for Joey. My mind couldn't accept this new Joey. I had to see it with my own eyes.

Aidan stirred, and his eyes flickered open. "You're awake," he said.

"Thank you, Captain Obvious," I said, but my voice came out in a raspy croak so it lost some of its zing in the process. Aidan grinned.

"A bit grouchy, aren't we?"

"In the past month I found out I was gay, I lost my best friend, my dad disowned me, I lost my job, and I can't even kill myself properly. I think I have a right to be grouchy." That little snit took a lot out of me, leaving me almost gasping.

"Ok, granted you've had a rough time. So get over it." I blinked in surprise. Where were the sickeningly sweet and equally empty platitudes I was so used to? He went on; he seemed to be building up steam. "It's time to stop feeling so damn sorry for yourself. So what if you're gay? So are 10% of the population, and you don't see them jumping off fire escapes! They're throwing parades, for God's sake! And so what if your best friend dumped you? If he can't accept you for who you are, what kind of friend was he to begin with? And so what if you lost your job? You already have a great job at Avant Guard — which is still waiting for you, by the way. And so what if your dad says you aren't welcome in his home anymore? You are welcome in mine, and that's where you live, so that's all that matters. You'd think after all this that I'd at least count for something." His chest was heaving as he slumped back in his chair. I had a feeling this had been building for quite some time now.

I sat in stunned silence for several minutes while Aidan pulled himself back together. Then he stood up. "I was supposed to let them know when you woke up," he said tersely. He started for the door, and then paused.

"You know, I've been beating myself up for the past two weeks, blaming myself for your attempted suicide. Everyone kept telling me it wasn't my fault, but I wouldn't believe them...until just now. Now I see that it was your own selfishness that made you jump. I'm not going anywhere. I'll be here for you as much as I can, but I'm not going to feel guilty anymore."

"Hello, Will," I reluctantly opened my eyes to see Dr. Wohler standing next to my bed. "How are you feeling?"

I eyed him warily. "Physically or emotionally?"

"Let's start with physically."

"My arm hurts, and my head is killing me."

"You're very fortunate that's all that's hurting. That wasn't a very smart thing to do."

"I know."

"Do you? I'm not really sure you grasp exactly what happened. Will, you've let yourself become controlled by your circumstances. These things that are happening to you that seem so incredibly overwhelming are here today and gone tomorrow, to be replaced by new problems. Suicide is a permanent solution to a temporary problem. It's an old cliché, I know, but it's still around because it's so true. Life isn't like a computer game where you say 'oops, I didn't really mean to do that' and click undo. There are no extra men. Your life is a precious gift, and you almost threw that away. It was spared this time, but who knows what might happen next time? I don't believe that things happen randomly. By all accounts, you should be dead, and yet here you are."

"Aidan said I was selfish."

"And what do you think?"

"I think...maybe he was right."

"Suicide is the ultimate selfish act. You are thinking only about what *you* want. *You* want the pain to stop. *You* want to escape. *You* don't want to face your problems anymore. It's the people left behind that have to deal with the repercussions of your selfishness."

"I never thought of it like that," I said softly.

"Of course not. You were too busy thinking about yourself. You know, the doctors told me that Aidan hasn't left this room except to eat and shower. They were worried about him. Worried he was going to collapse. I'd say that's some friend. I suspect that there might even be some feelings there that go beyond simple friendship. Have you thought about that?"

I nodded.

"You broke a promise you made to Aidan. You promised you wouldn't hurt yourself without talking to him first. That's a pretty big breach of trust."

You don't even know the half of it, I thought as I remembered the argument that precipitated my jump.

"Will," he went on, "I'm going to switch your medication to something a little stronger. I'm going to check on you when they say you are physically ready to go home and I'll probably make a recommendation that they release you. But I really want to encourage you to come see me again as soon as you are ready. There are a lot of issues that you haven't even begun to deal with. Will you do that?"

I nodded again.

"I'm going to trust you on that. For now, just concentrate on getting better. Get some rest." He patted my leg and then left me alone with my thoughts.

I had betrayed Aidan twice over, and he was still willing to sit by my side. I owed him so much...and yet Joey still had first place in my heart. If I ever wanted to move on, I knew I would have to find out if everything was lost with Joey or if there was any hope of salvaging at least our friendship. I had to talk to Joey.

When I woke up again, Mom was in the chair that had last held Aidan. It was completely dark outside. Mom woke up as soon as I stirred, if she'd really been asleep at all. She stood up and moved to my side quickly.

"How are you?" she asked.

"I'm ok. Does Dad know you're here?"

"Yes."

"What does he say?"

"It doesn't matter what he says. You're hurt and I'm here, that's all that matters."

"I'll be ok."

She was quiet for a minute, then said, "Will, I want you to know that I don't approve of the way your father has just cut you off."

I smiled at her; I knew this was her way of apologizing. "But you don't dare go against his wishes, huh?"

"I'm here, aren't I?" She was right, that said a lot. I nodded. "That doesn't mean I understand or approve of...well, you know, but I do still and always will love you with all my heart. We don't need to talk about all that now, just know that I love you."

I nodded since it was too hard to talk around the lump in my throat.

She stayed for quite a while. We talked about my art, about my new job at the gallery, how I liked the apartment and about Nikki, but we carefully avoided any more mention about my sexuality or Dad. It was nice, but after a while I began to get drowsy from the pain medicine so Mom told me to go back to sleep.

As she stood up to leave, she said, "I spent a lot of time with Aidan these last two weeks." I wasn't sure what to say, so I said nothing. After a minute, she gave me a small smile. "He's a nice boy, Will." She patted my hand and left, leaving me wondering if that meant what I thought it did.

I spent the next few days in the hospital undergoing every test imaginable before they finally pronounced me fit to go home. The highlight was when I got a visit from a well-meaning but ignorant pastor that Dad sent over to try and talk me into turning my back on my sinful ways. If I would only repent, he insisted, I would be freed from my unnatural desires. Uh huh. Unnatural for whom? They seemed plenty natural to me. Dad himself never showed up, although Mom made several more visits.

The final damage report said that besides my broken arm and quite a bit of nasty bruising that was already beginning to fade, you would never know I had done a belly flop from three stories up. I was still quite stiff, but they assured me that would go away as I moved around more. I had a fiberglass cast on my left arm that was a whole heck of a lot lighter than the plaster one I'd had when I broke my arm as a kid.

Aidan drove me home and helped me inside. When he opened the door to our apartment, a loud roar greeted us, "Welcome home!"

The apartment seemed to be full of people. I suppose there really weren't that many; it just seemed like more because they were all crowded into our small entryway. I saw Laura, Gabe, Nikki, Sam, Asher, and Killian, even Derrick, although he didn't seem especially thrilled to be there. I was most surprised to see Mom. Dad was once again nowhere in sight. Everyone stayed for cake and ice cream. Someone had thought themselves quite clever, I'm sure, in ordering a cake with a dive-bombing icing plane on top of it. No one stayed too late, though, since I still tired quickly. Everyone signed my cast on the way out.

As soon as they were gone, Aidan gave me a pain pill, then helped me down the hall and into bed. When he started out of the room, I called him back.

"Aidan," I began awkwardly, "I'm really sorry...about...about everything. I'm sorry I came to you like that before I was ready. I'm sorry I broke my promise to you. I'm sorry I was so selfish. But most of all, I'm sorry I hurt you."

He stood for a moment, then quietly said, "You're forgiven, Will," then turned to leave.

"Forgiven but not forgotten?" I asked.

He paused but didn't turn around. "No, not forgotten." And he was gone.

As I fell asleep with the aid of the pain pill, I wondered if the damage I had done to our friendship was going to prove more permanent than the damage I had done to my body.

Chapter 9

I hatched a plan over the next several days that I was sure would either exorcise Joey from my life forever or let me know conclusively whether there was any hope for us. My plan would go into effect that Friday night. Aidan had said that Joey had become a party animal, and there was never any shortage of parties on a Friday night in a college town. All I had to do was find the one he was at and get him alone. Easy, huh? I would have to wing it from there since I had no clue how he would react, but I felt confident that I knew Joey well enough to handle it.

The only hitch was that I had to get out of the apartment without arousing Aidan's suspicion. He was back in school now and not keeping the eagle eye on me that he had been before everything happened, so I decided to slip out before he got home. I'd leave a note or something so he wouldn't worry.

Friday afternoon finally rolled around. I had spent all morning fretting over what to wear. I wanted to look my best. Finally, I had settled on a flashy club shirt that Joey had given me for my last birthday and a nice pair of jeans. I had only worn the shirt a few times, flashy wasn't my usual style, but I thought it was a nice touch. I took one last look in the mirror and decided it would have to do. The cast didn't exactly scream suave and sophisticated, but there wasn't much I could do about that.

I had called Laura earlier in the day and managed to find out where the major parties were that night without her getting too suspicious. There were three that I really wanted to hit, but as near as I could figure, I had at least three hours to kill before I could start my rounds. I decided to take some pictures while the light was still good. My camera was in the car, and all I had to do was stop at Wal-Mart and pick up some film. Then it was just a matter of driving around waiting for inspiration.

It wasn't too hard to find. While I often made fun of the Eastern Shore of Maryland, where I had grown up, and the insulated life we lived, it is without a doubt an incredibly beautiful place to live. Bordered by the Atlantic Ocean on one side and the Chesapeake Bay on the other, the isthmus is made up of the southern half of Delaware, ten counties of Maryland, and two counties of Virginia. The state names were combined to get the name Delmarva Peninsula, by which it is often called. The region is rich in history and natural treasures. Much of the area is still rural and even the more urban areas, like the small city I live in, are surrounded by the flat farmland that is so typical of the Shore. Drive a few minutes outside the city limits in any direction and you're just as likely to see a white-tailed deer as a human being.

I wanted to drive to Assateague Island, but I knew I didn't have enough time to drive there tonight, so I contented myself with the wooded countryside that weaves itself around the picturesque Wicomico River. I stopped often to snap some photos of an abandoned house here, a forgotten graveyard there. I caught the sun in a spectacular display of color that would make a great backdrop for the paintings. By the time the sun dropped below the tree line, I had taken up three rolls of film. I was confident that at least some of the photos I had taken would produce a great composition for a painting.

I glanced at my car clock as I drove down the darkening roads. It was show time. The first party I hit was just getting started and no one even knew Joey, so I quickly moved on. At the next party, several people knew Joey, although no one looked impressed, but none of them had any reason to think he was coming there. One guy thought he would probably be at the last party on my list since that was where all the booze would be. I left my cell phone number with the guy just in case and moved on to crash my next party.

Turned out that the third time was a charm. I wasn't there very long at all before some girl said she'd heard Joey say that he was coming to this particular party tonight. I crossed my fingers and settled in to wait for Joey to make his appearance. While I waited, I looked around. This was apparently the party to be at this weekend. The house was filling up quickly. There was a large fenced-in back yard with an in-ground pool, but so far, no one was making any move in that direction. The damp, chilly weather probably had something to do with that. Loud music pumped from somewhere, and beer was in abundance. I had never been a party animal by any stretch, but even to my untrained eye, it appeared that at least half the partiers present were stoned already. I noticed several girls eying me hungrily; I felt like fresh meat in the lion cage at the zoo. A flirtatious redhead pressed a cold bottle into my hand, and I passed it on to the first empty-handed person I encountered. I figured I'd need all my wits about me for my mission that night.

"So how'd you get that cast? You don't look like the rough and tumble type." I turned to find a petite, attractive girl with shoulder-length honey blonde hair and light blue eyes looking me over.

"I, uh...fell three stories off a fire escape," I stuttered as I blushed furiously.

She cocked an eyebrow. "Must have been some party!" She took a drag off a cigarette and blew smoke in my direction.

"Something like that," I muttered, already trying to figure out how to gracefully disentangle myself.

"My name is Caitlin," she said.

"I'm Will."

"Nice to meet you, Will." She flashed me a quick smile that revealed an even row of white teeth. She was really quite pretty. Too bad I wasn't straight. "Do you go to school here? I don't think I recognize you."

"No, I'm meeting a friend here, actually."

"Oh, really? Too bad. What's her name? Maybe I know her."

"Him, my friend's a guy. His name is Joey Taylor."

Her expression changed in the blink of an eye. "You're friends with Joey Taylor? You should really choose your friends more carefully."

"We've been friends our entire lives. He's my best friend, but I...lost touch with him a few months ago, and I was hoping to run into him here."

"Well, I hope you don't. You seem like too nice a guy for slime like him."

"Why do you say that? What's he done?"

"For starters he's screwed two of my friends, then dumped them the next day. He promises he's in love with you and is ready to change his ways because you're 'the one', gets you in bed and then it's wham-bam without so much as a thank-you-ma'am."

"Joey?" I asked incredulously. Even after Aidan had told me almost the same thing, it was hard to picture my best friend doing these things.

"Yes, Joey. Plus he's almost never sober anymore. I've heard that he's shown up for one of his classes completely trashed a few times. The professor threw him out." She lowered her voice and leaned toward me, "I've even heard he got some poor girl pregnant, then told her he'd pay for the abortion. That he didn't want anything to do with a kid."

I shook my head in disbelief. How could this person she was describing be the same person I had grown up with?

Caitlin laid her hand gently on my good arm. "I'm sorry to be the one to tell you your old friend is such a loser, but really, you're better off without him."

"If you're trying to get in his pants, Caty-baby, I gotta tell ya it's a lost cause...ya don't havva dick," a familiar voice slurred from behind me. I spun around but not before seeing a look of disgust mar Caitlin's pretty face.

"Joey!" I said.

"Hey, fag, what are you doing here? Shouldn't you be at some gay bar in Rehomo?" he said, referring to a nearby gay friendly town by its unfriendly nickname. The smell of alcohol almost knocked me over.

I blinked rapidly as I felt my face heat up. "Joey, I came to see you. Can we talk?"

"What's to talk about? You're a fucking fag, and I'm not. End of discussion."

"Joey, please, just a few minutes?" I was embarrassed to be begging in front of Caitlin, but it was as if I couldn't help myself.

A foreign smile spread slowly across Joey's face, cruel and ugly. "Ok," he said, "I'll do you a favor if you do one for me. Follow me." He turned and started weaving through the crowd and up the stairs to the second floor as if he knew where he was going. I followed wordlessly. Apparently, he did know where he was going; he walked confidently to a closed door, opened it, and entered. He shut the door as soon as I followed him in. He immediately started unbuttoning his pants, letting them drop to the floor.

"What are you doing?" I asked although I had an awful feeling that I knew.

He pushed his boxers down, and his erection sprung up. "It's what you wanted, isn't it, Willie? A quick suck off your old pal, Joey? Well, here it is; come on, I don't have all night."

"Joey, pull your pants up. I just want to talk to you."

"Suck first, talk later. Come on, get on your knees."

"No! Joey..." He grabbed his dick and started jerking off, hard and fast. "Will you stop that?" I yelled.

"You know you want it, Will," he taunted. "Better hurry, I'm almost there already."

"No, I do not want it. What's happened to you? I thought I knew you, but I don't know who this person is. What happened to the old Joey?"

"He's gone, Wee Willie Winkle," he sneered, using my despised childhood nickname. "This is the new improved Joe Cool. I'm a chick-magnet; they can't get enough of my dick. I can have any girl I want whenever I want. Do you really wanna pass up your one chance at a piece of this?"

"You've become a sleaze who everybody either hates or pities."

"What's wrong, Will? Can't have me, so now you're jealous?" His hand hadn't slowed down the whole time and now his body suddenly tensed and he began to shoot onto the floor. "Look at all that going to waste. It could have been yours, Will."

I'd had enough. I spun around in disgust and yanked the door open. But Joey was always quicker than I was. He was on me before I even got the door halfway open, slamming me against it, and pressing his body against mine. Pain shot up my arm, and I gasped in agony. I felt Joey's still hard erection press into my buttocks and smelled his foul breath in my face.

"Where ya goin', Willie?" he rasped. "We were just gettin' started."

"Get off me, Joey," I gasped.

Ignoring my plea, he reached down, grabbed my broken arm, and spun me around, slamming my back against the door. While I was still off balance, he pressed his mouth against mine so hard I felt my teeth cut into my lips as his hand grabbed my crotch painfully. I reacted without thought, bringing my knee up sharply into his groin and slamming him in the face with my cast at the same time. He bent double and stumbled back. I was through the door before he even knew what had hit him.

Ignoring the pain in my arm, I took the stairs two at a time and plunged into the crowd at the bottom. I grabbed a bottle out of someone's hand and gulped it down, frantically trying to get rid of the sour taste of Joey's mouth. My arm was throbbing. I wanted to curl up in a ball and just cry, but there was hardly room to move. I found myself being moved around the throng like a leaf caught in the current of a fast-moving river.

A sudden wave of nausea swept over me, and I began to push and shove my way in the direction of the hallway. I managed to find a bathroom, which was mercifully empty, and slammed the door shut just in time to get violently sick. I splashed some cold water on my face and looked up at myself in the mirror as what had just happened began to sink in. A pair of haunted eyes stared back at me. Everyone had tried to tell me, but I wouldn't listen. Joey was no longer the same person I grew up with. I knew now that Joey was gone. I began to shake, and I slowly slid to the floor where I began to sob. I stayed in there awhile, crying, mourning the loss of my best friend. I was grateful for the lock on the door but eventually the banging on the door got to me and I reluctantly gave up my sanctuary.

I was ready to leave this party. I started weaving my way for the front door. By the time I got there, I was fighting another bout of nausea. Between the traumatic events upstairs and whatever it was I'd drank out of that bottle, my stomach was in full revolt. I barely cleared the front steps before upchucking the last of my stomach's contents into the shrubbery.

"Being with Joey always affects me that way, too," a feminine voice said from the shadows. I wiped my mouth with the back of my hand as I peered into the darkness. The glow of a cigarette butt drew my eyes to the dark form of someone sitting under the low hanging branches of an enormous magnolia tree that took up most of the front yard.

"Caitlin?" I hazarded a guess.

"Yup. Come on in. It's quiet, and Joey isn't likely to find us unless he passes out and rolls under here."

I crawled into the cave-like space and leaned back against the tree trunk next to Caitlin. "What are you doing out here in the cold?"

"I had to get out of there. Besides, the fresh air is good for your lungs. Smoke?" she asked as she offered her cigarette.

"No, thanks."

"Good. Don't start. It's a nasty habit." She stubbed out the butt and looked over at me. "So, are you really gay?"

I drew in a sharp breath. "Yeah."

"Hey, it's cool with me. It just figures that the first nice guy I meet in months would be gay. You don't have a thing for Joey, do you?"

"I used to."

"But not now?"

"No, not now."

"Not after tonight?"

"Right."

"I tried to warn you."

"Some things you just have to see for yourself."

She continued to stare at my face as if she were memorizing my features. "I'm sorry," she said softly.

"For what?"

"For your loss."

"What do you mean?"

"You lost a friend tonight, right?"

"Yeah, I guess I did," I said, and suddenly there were tears rolling down my cheeks again. I swiped at them angrily.

"Don't," Caitlin said. "Don't be ashamed to cry. He made me cry, too."

"You? What did he do to you?"

She looked away. "I was one of those dumb girls who fell for all his lies and promises."

"I'm sorry. But hey, at least you can move on now and forget about him. That's what I have to try and do now I guess."

"It's not that easy. You have all those memories of him, and I have my own little reminder."

"What do you mean?"

She lit up another cigarette and took a long drag. "I'm the girl he got pregnant," she said, still not looking at me.

For a minute I was too stunned to think of anything to say, then I said the first thing that came to my mind, "You shouldn't be smoking."

She laughed, but there was no humor in the laugh. "Why not? I'm going to have an abortion."

Neither of us spoke for a while.

"You don't think I should, do you?" she said at last.

"I didn't say that," I said quickly.

"No, but you're thinking it, I can tell." I stayed quiet. "You don't know what you're talking about," she went on as if I were arguing with her. Maybe she was arguing with herself. "I can't afford to raise a kid on my own. I can't even afford a damn goldfish. I just started school. Oh, my God, if my parents found out..."

"It's not the baby's fault," I said softly.

She stared at the cigarette for a minute then in a quick violent motion, ground it out angrily. Then, just as suddenly, her mood switched again, and she began to cry.

"I don't know what to do," she whispered. "I can't believe I was so stupid. I'm so scared."

I sat in uncomfortable silence unsure of what to say. Then an idea popped into my head. I blurted it out before I even thought about it. "I...I'll help you raise the baby."

She stopped crying with a hiccup and stared at me as if I had lost my mind. Maybe I had.

"Are you crazy? You can't be serious?" she said when she'd found her voice.

"Yes...I mean no...I mean..."

"Do you have any idea what you are even saying?"

"Yes, I can help you. I'm an artist so I can watch the baby while you're at school. I don't have a lot of money, but you can get help from social services, and I'll help with what I can."

"You don't even know me."

"No, but I usually have good instincts about people, and I trust you. Besides, I know Joey and this is his baby, too. If he isn't going to take care of it, then someone has to."

"Why you?"

"I've been cleaning up Joey's messes for eighteen years, I'm used to it. And...I guess I just feel kind of responsible in a way."

"How could you possibly be responsible?"

"It's kinda my fault Joey has become like this. I drove him to it...I...I told him I loved him."

"And?"

"And what?"

"You told him you loved him and..."

"And he freaked out."

"Look, Will, you're an incredibly sweet, incredibly naïve kid. I've never met anyone like you in my entire life. I hope you find happiness and the man of your dreams. But this isn't your fault, and you don't owe me anything. It's not your fault that Joey reacted like he did. There was no way you could have known and nothing you could have done differently. Thank you for your offer, but this is my problem, and I'll deal with it. I was the one who was stupid enough to fall for his load of shit. I was the one who didn't insist he use a condom. Me. So that makes me responsible for this..." she gestured helplessly at her still flat stomach. "Me and Joey. And I don't think I can count on him for anything."

"But you can count on me. That's what I'm trying to tell you. Joey was like a brother to me. So that makes me this baby's uncle, sort of, right?"

"I guess..."

"Then let Uncle Will help."

She laughed, this time a real laugh. It was a nice laugh. "I'll give you this, Uncle Will, you're persistent."

I grinned. "Yup."

"Will you stop bugging me if I promise to at least think about it?"

"If you promise you'll really think about it."

"I promise. It's all I can think about anyway."

"Great! Let me give you my phone number and stuff."

"I'm not promising to do anything but think about it," she warned.

"I know."

"And I still think you're crazy."

"I know."

I crawled out from under the tree and scribbled my name and phone number on a scrap of paper I found in my pocket.

"I still think you're out of your mind," she said as I handed it to her and I was preparing to leave, "but you've given me something to think about. I'm still not promising you anything, though. I don't owe you anything."

"No, but maybe you do owe something to that baby you're carrying."

She gave me an odd look that was a mix of exasperation and thoughtfulness. I started down the street as a bloodcurdling scream ripped through the night. Another quickly followed it. They sounded like they were coming from the back yard. I turned back.

"Sounds like Joey struck again," Caitlin said sadly.

"Maybe I should check it out," I said uncertainly.

"Are you going to follow behind him cleaning up his messes for the rest of your life? Go home, Clark Kent, you've done enough good for one night."

I turned to go again but a sense of dread had filled me and I couldn't leave. It was as if something were physically holding me back. I was trying to force myself to walk away when someone vaulted over the high fence that separated the back yard from the front. He almost barreled into Caitlin in his haste.

"Holy shit," he panted as he pushed his sweaty dark hair out of his eyes.

"What's going on?" I asked as the feeling of dread grew.

"It's that guy...uh...Joe something..."

"Taylor?" I offered even though I already knew what his answer would be.

"Yeah, that's him."

"What's he done now?" Caitlin sighed.

"What's he done?" The guy let out a slightly hysterical giggle. "He died, that's what he did."

Chapter 10

My mind stalled. Caitlin and I both stared dumbly at this bearer of bad news. Maybe I had heard wrong. "What did you say?" I finally stammered.

"He's dead. This chick just found him in the pool, floating face down. I think somebody called the cops. This party's busted." As he said this last part, he was steadily backing away. With his last words, he spun around and joined the steady stream of guests who were exiting the premises as quickly as they could.

I looked at Caitlin. "Do you think he's serious?" I asked her.

"Listen," she said. I did and could hear sirens in the distance. I guess that answered my question. "Come on, let's go!" she said grabbing my arm.

"What? We can't just leave!" I protested, but she was already dragging me into the street.

"Yes, we can and yes, we are. I don't want to be here when the cops arrive. We were out here under the tree the whole time, so it's not like we have anything to tell them. I've been through this before and trust me, it's not fun and it takes forever."

"You've been through this before?" I asked in alarm.

"Well, not this exact thing, but I was at a party where this guy turned up dead in the river."

"Does someone always end up dead in the water at parties you attend?"

"No, just these two times. Where's your car?"

"Around the corner, why?"

"You're taking me home," she said. We ran to the car and pulled away just as two patrol cars pulled up lights flashing with an ambulance not far behind. My mind hadn't caught up with recent events, but now suddenly the full impact of what I had just heard hit me. He had said Joey was dead. But that was impossible...I'd just seen him...he couldn't be dead. Maybe it was some sort of sick joke or maybe he was wrong and it was really someone else. Or maybe he wasn't dead, just really drunk. There was an ambulance so that had to be a good sign, right? Do they send ambulances for dead people?

"Where are you going?" Caitlin asked, startling me out of my thoughts. I had forgotten she was even in the car.

"Huh?"

"Where are you going? You don't even know where I live. We're going the wrong way."

"Oh...I..." I gave up trying to form a coherent sentence and turned the car around. I followed her directions to a small slightly run-down apartment complex near the college.

"Thanks, Will," she said when I'd pulled to a stop in front of her building. "You're a sweet guy. Stop blaming yourself for the loser that Joey turned out to be. If it is him, then he deserved whatever happened. I'll be in touch." She leaned over and kissed me quickly on the cheek, and then she was gone.

I drove slowly home in a sort of numb trance. Twice I missed a turn and had to back up. When I finally got home, Aidan was sitting up waiting. "Where were you? I was worried," he said accusingly as he jumped to his feet.

"I'm sorry," I said, my mind not really on Aidan or his concern.

"Your note said you were going to take pictures; it's been dark for hours."

"I'm sorry," I said again as I sank heavily into a chair.

"I didn't know where you were, if you were ok...if you were even alive..."

Something snapped inside me. "I said I'm sorry!" I yelled. "What more do you want from me?"

Aidan looked as if I had delivered him a physical blow. "Well, excuse me for giving a damn. I guess I should know better by now." He spun around and started for his room.

"Aidan, wait!" I called wearily. This wasn't what I wanted or needed right now. He stopped but kept his back to me. "I went to talk to Joey. It...it didn't go well."

He turned around.

"He...he wanted me to..." I stopped and tried to swallow the bile that kept rising in the back of my throat. "He wanted me...to...do stuff...to him. Then he...I think he was going to rape me." I started crying but kept going; it was as if the words wouldn't stop coming. "He pinned me against the wall and tried to force himself on me. He hurt me, my arm...my lip..."

All the color had drained from Aidan's face. "Oh, my God," he whispered.

"I hit him, pushed him away...then I ran."

Aidan crossed the room and knelt down in front of me. "Are you ok?" he asked gently tipping my face up so he could check for damage.

"I think he's dead," I choked.

Aidan's eyes flew open wide. "You killed him?"

"No, at least I don't think so. He was alive when I left him. I was talking to someone when he died. Someone said they found him in the pool. I don't even know what happened. We left before the police got there."

"Who is this 'we', Will?"

"Me and Caitlin."

"Who's Caitlin?"

"I met her tonight. She was one of Joey's conquests. He...hurt her." I don't know why I didn't tell him about Caitlin's pregnancy; I just didn't feel it was the right time.

"Where is she now?"

"I took her home."

"Why did you leave before the police got there?"

"Caitlin wanted to. She said we didn't want to be around because it was an awful process that took a long time, and we didn't have anything to add anyway because we were in the front yard under the tree for the whole time."

"Under the... Never mind. How does she know it's an awful process?"

"She was at party last year when they found a body in the river. Someone had killed him and dumped him in the water. Do you think that's what happened to Joey?"

"I don't know what happened to Joey or even if anything did at this point. For all we know it could have been some kind of sick prank. And that party where the body was found in the river must have been the one that Killian and Asher were at." He looked down at his watch and jumped up to turn on the TV. The late news was just coming on.

"Details are few at this time," the female news anchor was saying, "but we have received confirmation that a student from Pemberton University died tonight at a party held off campus. No word yet on the cause of death or whether it was accidental or foul play was involved. We'll keep you posted on developments in this sad case as events unfold."

She moved on to her next story, something about hog futures. Joey's death was just another story unrolling on the teleprompter in front of her. I sat stunned for a moment as Aidan snapped off the TV.

"Have you ever wondered what they mean by hog futures?" I said finally. "What kind of future does a hog have really? Ham or bacon? Sausage or scrapple?"

"Will, are you ok?" Aidan asked, quickly coming back to my side.

"We don't know for sure it was Joey...she didn't say his name," I said halfheartedly, like a child who believes that as long as you don't say it, it isn't true. But I knew in my gut that it was true, that Joey was gone. It was almost as if a part of me were suddenly missing, leaving a gaping hole in its place.

"No, we don't know for sure," Aidan said softly. "You should go to bed. It's late and you need to rest."

I nodded, too far gone to argue. As I stood up, I realized my arm was throbbing from my tussle with Joey. I took a few Tylenol PM that Aidan produced from somewhere then went into my room. I didn't turn any lights on; I just stood in the darkness for a few minutes. Suddenly a feeling of loneliness so powerful I almost cried out overwhelmed me. I turned and crossed the hall to Aidan's door, where I knocked lightly.

"Yeah?" he called warily.

I opened the door. "Can I...can I sleep with you tonight?" I felt like I sounded, like a small child at his parents' door after a nightmare.

"What do you mean?" Aidan said cautiously.

"Just...I'm afraid to be alone," I said shakily.

He thought for a moment, then nodded slowly. "Ok."

I closed the door behind me and undressed in the darkness. I crawled into Aidan's bed, being careful to stay on my side. We lay in silence with our backs to each other. I waited until I thought he had fallen asleep before letting go. The tears came hot but silent at first and slowly built into muffled sobs as I tried not to wake Aidan. I was surprised but very grateful when I felt his strong arms circle around me. Once again, I found myself crying myself to sleep in his arms.

I got up early the next morning after a fitful night's sleep. I wanted to watch the early news to see if there was any mention of Joey. The Tragic Death of a

College Student, as they were now calling it — you could almost hear the capital letters — was the lead story.

"As reported last night, a local student from Pemberton University died while attending an off-campus party. Police have now released the name; Joseph Taylor was an eighteen-year-old freshman. His friends describe him as a fun-loving young man full of life. According to police reports, Taylor was found by another student in a swimming pool owned by the family of college senior David Kemp. Kemp was hosting the party. Police say it's still too early to say conclusively how Taylor died, but they do believe alcohol was a factor.

"Are off-campus parties a significant risk to your children? We go now to our..." I turned off the TV, cutting the anchorperson off in mid-sentence. Well, at least now I knew for sure.

"I'm sorry, Will," Aidan said softly from behind me. I hadn't even noticed him there.

The empty feeling from the night before was still there, but now it had eased into a dull ache. I didn't cry; I had done my mourning the night before.

"I...should call his mom or something..." I said.

"Not now, there'll be too much going on. Later, after things have settled down."

I nodded.

The phone rang, and Aidan answered it, then handed me the phone.

It was Caitlin.

"Did you see the news?" she asked before I could say more than hello.

"Yes...are you ok?"

"I guess. It's not like I'm his chief mourner or anything. To me he was just some bastard that knocked me up then dumped me. I was calling to check on you. You were his friend."

"I'm...ok. Well...no, I'm not ok, but I'll survive."

"Do you have someone with you?"

"Yes, my roommate..." I paused, then revised myself, "my best friend Aidan is here with me."

Aidan looked up with a strange expression in his eyes, a mix of surprise and some other emotion that I couldn't name. He looked back down quickly.

"Good, I'm glad. I didn't want you to be alone."

"Did you think about my offer?" I asked.

Aidan looked up again, this time with curiosity flashing in his eyes.

"Yes," Caitlin said, "but I'm still thinking. Don't rush me on this, Will. It's an important decision, one that could affect the rest of my life."

"It's not just your life at stake here," I responded quietly.

"God! How do you keep doing that?" she said with exasperation. I didn't say anything as she went on, "Look, I'll call you next week. I've got plenty of time to decide. You can safely abort any time in the first trimester, and it's no big deal. I'm only about a month along as I figure it."

"No big deal for you maybe."

"Stop that!"

"I'm just trying to make sure you see both sides. I'm trying to speak for the one who has no voice."

"You're just making this harder!" she sounded close to tears.

"Good. A life-and-death decision shouldn't be easy."

She sighed. "Good-bye, Will."

"Bye, Caitlin. I'll talk to you next week."

As soon as I hung up, Aidan was all over me. "What was that all about?" he demanded.

"You shouldn't have been eavesdropping," I said defensively.

"You saw me sitting right there. Besides, you just said I'm your best friend. Best friends tell each other everything."

I sighed. "Caitlin is pregnant, and she's thinking about getting an abortion."

"And that concerns you how?"

"The baby is Joey's."

Aidan blinked in surprise, then quickly recovered. "I repeat, and that concerns you how?"

"I feel responsible somehow. I know it's ridiculous," I rushed on to drown out the protest that was already forming on Aidan's lips, "but I can't help it. Besides, I really like Caitlin. She seems like a good person. I want to help her." I paused for a moment, then said the next part super fast, "I told her I'd help her raise the baby if she wouldn't have an abortion."

"YOU WHAT?"

"Shh!" I hushed him.

"Don't you shush me! Have you lost your fucking mind? You don't know anything about babies! You don't even know her. You just met her last night, for God's sake! You have no obligation to this person. You cannot get yourself involved."

"I'm already involved. Look, Joey would have never gone on this... this...whatever it was...this alcohol-induced sex binge if it hadn't been for me. Don't you see that? Now there's a little helpless life that is a part of Joey. That baby didn't ask to be created. Why should it have to pay for my mistake?"

"Why can't she just put it up for adoption? Why is aborting it or keeping it the only option?"

I paused for a moment. "I don't know. I didn't ask." I felt foolish for not thinking of that option myself. "I guess I can mention it to her, but if she doesn't want to put the baby up for adoption, I'm telling you, I'm going to help."

"Will, you've got to talk to Dr. Wohler again. You are not responsible for someone else's actions. I had to realize that when you tried to kill yourself. At first, I blamed myself, but I had to realize that I didn't make you jump off that fire escape — just like you didn't make Joey become a drunken asshole. That was his choice. You didn't make Joey have unprotected sex with Caitlin — that was their decision. You are not responsible for any of this."

"I've already given my word to Caitlin, and I'm not breaking my promise."

"You didn't have any problem breaking your word to me when you took a flying leap off the balcony!"

I froze.

"Will, I'm sorry..."

"You said you forgave me for that."

He sighed. "Forgiven but not forgotten...remember?"

"Then let's just say I learned my lesson. I'm not breaking it anymore."

He stared at me for a minute. I could read his frustration easily in his eyes. "You're serious about this, aren't you? There's no changing your mind."

"Yes, I'm serious and, no, I'm not changing my mind."

Another sigh. "Fine. I can't believe I'm even saying this, but if you're absolutely positive this is what you want to do, I'll support you in any way I can."

"What?" His sudden about face caught me off guard.

"I think you've completely lost your mind, but I'll be there for you," he said with just a hint of a smile. His smile broadened a bit as he shrugged and added, "Hey, what are best friends for?"

"Scratching backs?" I said hopefully. His smile turned into a full-fledged Aidan Special Grin, complete with dimples.

"Coming right up!"

I called Joey's mom that afternoon. She sounded as upset as one would expect. I had intended to just offer my sympathy, but she surprised me by asking me to come over. It wasn't something I was looking forward to, but I knew it was something I had to do. I drove over by myself, after convincing Aidan that I was fine going alone.

She was seated on the couch when I got there, between two older women I didn't know but assumed to be family members. For as close of friends as Joey and I had been, I realized I really didn't know any of his family. He never talked about them. I knew his mom, of course, and I knew his dad had run off when Joey was two or three, but that was it. I was introduced to the two women as Joey's oldest and dearest friend. They turned out to be Joey's aunts. The one on the left looked like a hungry bulldog, complete with hanging jowls and stubborn expression. The one on the right looked like a scared chicken, gangly, thin, and beady-eyed. Joey's mom, who I had always thought looked much too young to be a mother of someone Joey's age, suddenly looked old, although it might have been because it was the first time I think I had ever seen her without any makeup. She looked vulnerable without it. I found myself feeling very uncomfortable.

Mrs. Taylor grabbed my hand and held onto it like it was a lifeline and she was drowning. Which maybe in a way she was.

"When they called me last night...I just couldn't believe it," she said, her eyes filling with unshed tears. They were red and swollen as if she'd been crying a lot. "I kept saying that they must be wrong; that it couldn't be my Joey. But then I had to go identify him. They called him 'the body'. 'We need you to come identify the body,' they said. I said, he's not just a body, he's my son."

She almost seemed to be talking to herself. "It was Joey..." She broke off in a muffled sob but choked it down and continued, "Thank you for being such a good friend to my Joey." She dissolved in sobs, still clutching my hand while I shifted uncomfortably, wishing I were anywhere but here.

I stayed for what I thought was a decent amount of time and then made my excuses and headed for the door.

"Will?" Mrs. Taylor called just before I escaped. "You weren't at that party last night, were you?"

I felt my heart drop. "Well, actually I was, Mrs. Taylor, but just for a few minutes. I didn't stay."

She seemed surprised. "Then I think the police are looking for you."

"What?" I gasped.

"They described you and asked if I knew anyone who fit that description. I told them you did, but they said you weren't on the list of people present when they arrived. Several people said they saw someone fitting your description go upstairs with Joey and come back down in a rush. They said you might be the last person who saw him alive."

"I...I left before...he was alive when I left..." I stammered.

She nodded as if it were what she had expected to hear. "I told them you were a good boy. Tell me, Will, how was he?"

What could I say? "Honestly, Mrs. Taylor...he wasn't very good. He was drunk. He wasn't himself."

She started to cry again.

"I'm so sorry," I said helplessly. "I'm going to miss him very much."

I turned to leave once more, but she called out again. "Was he wearing his necklace?"

I knew immediately which necklace she meant. I had never seen Joey without it. It was a silver chain with a small oval charm depicting a saint of some sort hanging from it. It had been the only thing left behind of his father's, who had been a devout Catholic. Joey cherished that necklace more than any other possession he owned. As far as I knew, the only time Joey had ever been inside a church was when he was baptized as an infant, but he never took that necklace off. I tried to remember if I had seen the necklace or not. It was so much a part of him I just took it for granted that he had been wearing it, but now I tried to recall if I had actually seen it or not. I mentally walked though the painful encounter with Joey until I found what I was looking for.

"Yes, he was," I said. "Why?"

"It wasn't on him when they found him. I would have liked to have had it."

She turned back to the bulldog aunt, and I took the opportunity to finally slip out of the oppressive home which already felt empty without Joey.

Chapter 11

Joey's funeral was held graveside on a suitably dreary and dismal Monday morning. The clouds hung heavy with the unrealized threat of rain and the wind whipped through the gathered mourners like an angry spirit. Despite the inclement weather, quite a few people had shown up to remember Joey. Most of them I didn't know, family, I guess; but I saw a few familiar faces, old neighbors and people from school. Beth was there, of course. It was the first time we had seen each other since we broke up. When she gave me a hug, it was an awkward moment that only served to confirm the realizations that I had come to over the last few weeks. It struck me how much I had changed since we had dated. I felt like a completely different person.

There was one person in attendance who particularly caught my attention because of his seemingly odd behavior. He stood in the back and off to one side as if he didn't want to be seen. He cried through the whole service and left as soon as the last prayer was said.

The service itself was mercifully brief and poignant. Dad was the officiating minister, and he focused on the tragic end of a promising young life. He kept staring at me as he said that phrase. It didn't take a genius to figure out what he was trying to say.

I didn't go back to the house afterwards; instead, I drove directly from the cemetery to Avant Guard. Today was my first day at my new job.

Nikki started talking before I was even all the way through the door. "The first thing we need to talk about is the one-man show," she said. "Do we need to cancel it?"

"I...uh..."

"I mean we've lost a lot of time, and I'm assuming you didn't paint any masterpieces while you were in that coma."

"No, I mean...I..."

"Will, I'm kidding. Don't bug out on me here. But seriously, we are getting pushed for time. We need to have at least fifteen to twenty paintings for a one-man show. The show is scheduled and the invitations have been sent, so we're locked in unless we just cancel it altogether. That only gives us three weeks. That means you need to do at least a painting a day. Think you got that in you?"

"What ever happened to hi, Will, welcome to your new job? How was your weekend...something like that?" I said weakly, feeling more than a little overwhelmed.

"Hi, Will! Welcome to your new job! How was your weekend? Think you got that in you?"

I laughed. "Hi, Nikki. Thanks for the warm welcome. My weekend was horrible, and, yes, I think I have it in me."

Nikki frowned. "Why was your weekend horrible?"

"My best friend died. That's why I was late coming in this morning. It was Joey's funeral."

"Oh, my God! That was your friend on the news?"

"Yeah."

"I'm so sorry, Will."

"Well, we'd grown apart lately. Actually we had a huge fight just before he died."

"It's still hard to lose someone who was a friend. Were you friends long?"

"Since we were kids."

"Do they know what happened yet?"

"If they do, they've not told me. I know they think alcohol was involved. He was really drunk when I left him so I guess he could have fallen in and drowned."

"How sad! What a waste. Are you sure you're up to starting work today?"

"Yeah, I'm fine. It helps me to keep my mind off of things, you know?"

She nodded. "Sure thing. Then let's get to work."

We went over my responsibilities, which for the most part consisted of standing around and doing nothing while I waited for customers to wander in. She showed me how to work the cash register and how to read a potential client by asking them leading questions and then steer them toward the kind of art they would be most interested in. The only thing I didn't learn was how to do Derrick's little appearing trick. Once she was confident that I was ready, Nikki retired to her office.

It was some time later when I noticed a well-dressed couple heading for the front door. I felt my palms begin to sweat as I anticipated my first customers. I stepped forward to greet them, wishing I could pull Derrick's trick since that seemed to put the salesperson in the dominant role right from the start.

"Hello, welcome to Avant Guard," I said smoothly, or what I hoped was smoothly. "If I can be of any assistance, please let me know." I hoped I sounded more sincere than Derrick had the first time we'd come here.

"We're looking for Will Keegan," the man said while the woman looked carefully around.

Uh oh. That didn't seem like the kind of thing potential customers said, especially considering it was my first day here.

"I'm Will Keegan," I said hesitantly.

The man reached into his jacket pocket and produced a badge. "I'm Detective Grafton and this is my partner, Detective Bernhardt. We'd like to ask you a few questions if you don't mind."

I looked closer at them and wondered how I could have mistaken them for a couple. They practically screamed law enforcement. Both wore no-nonsense expressions and business attire in dark, muted tones. Detective Grafton was middle-aged, with graying brown hair and a craggy, clean-shaven face. His bushy eyebrows hooded his dark eyes, making him look slightly sinister. Detective Bernhardt was younger, in her thirties maybe, with a round face, pleasant if unremarkable. She had her light brown hair pulled back into a bun at the base of her neck. "Am I in trouble?" I asked, instinctively directing the question at Detective Bernhardt. I sounded guilty even to myself.

Detective Grafton gave me a sharp look. "I don't know, are you?"

Detective Bernhardt stepped forward. "Were you at the party held at David Kemp's house this past Friday night?"

"Briefly," I said tightly. Could I be arrested for fleeing the scene of a crime? Was I a material witness? I wasn't even sure what a material witness was. I suddenly wished I had paid more attention to the police shows my mom liked to watch on TV.

"Is there somewhere we can speak a little more privately?" Bernhardt asked.

"Nikki?" There was a note of panic in my voice. Authority figures had always scared the pants off of me. I'd been sent to the principal's office once when I was in the fifth grade for something Joey had done and I'd gotten blamed for. I cried all the way there and was so hysterical by the time I got there they had to call my mom to come pick me up. I was feeling a bit like that now.

Nikki came out with a huge smile, obviously thinking I had gotten in over my head with some customers. "These are detectives," I told her and watched the smile vanish. "They want to talk to me about Joey."

"Use my office," she said immediately.

I led the two detectives to the office where they quickly took over, telling me to have a seat and rearranging Nikki's furniture so that they were facing me.

"How do you know we want to talk to you about your friend, Joey?" Bernhardt asked as soon as we were seated.

I blinked. "Why else would you want to talk to me about the party?"

She smiled. "Fair enough. Ask a dumb question..."

"We're going to be taping this conversation if you don't mind," Grafton interrupted, "and I'll be taking some notes as well."

Detective Bernhardt produced a small tape recorder and started recording, reciting some preliminary data like my name, the date and the case they were working on.

"Did you speak to Joseph Taylor on the night in question?" Grafton asked.

"Joey...yes..."

"Do you know what time it was?"

"No."

"What did you talk about?"

"I wanted to talk to him, that's the whole reason I was there. I'm not really into parties." I knew I was giving them more information than they really needed, but I was nervous and having trouble organizing my thoughts. "He was drunk. He suggested we go upstairs, so we did."

"What happened when you got upstairs?"

"We talked."

"Where and about what?"

"Joey took me in a bedroom; he seemed to know where he was going. We talked about...our friendship."

"Was it an argument? Did you raise your voice at any time?"

"I...yeah, we had an argument."

"Over what?"

I felt my already flushed face blaze. I was getting quite dizzy. "I...I...uh...recently told Joey that I was...um...gay...and he didn't...take it well."

"Did it become physical?"

I started. "What do you mean?"

Detective Grafton looked up from his notepad. "Were any punches thrown?"

"I...uh...hit Joey."

"Why? Did you feel threatened?"

I opened and closed my mouth a few times, but nothing came out.

"Look, kid, you'd better tell us everything. We're going to find out eventually anyway, and it's better if it comes from you."

"It's not like that," I said quickly. "It's just...Joey...tried to...force himself on me," I managed to choke it out then rushed on, "He was really drunk or he never would have done anything like that..."

"Is that why you hit him?"

I nodded. "I kneed him in the balls, then hit him with my cast," I told them, indicating my broken arm as if I were presenting Exhibit A in court.

The two detectives looked at each other, exchanging meaningful glances. "And then what happened?" he asked.

"Nothing. I mean I ran out. Ran back downstairs."

"And then you left?"

"After I got sick in the bathroom."

Grafton flipped the notebook closed. "Thank you for your help, Mr. Keegan. If we have any more questions, we'll be getting in touch with you."

"That's it?" I asked in surprise.

"You were expecting more?" Bernhardt said with a sardonic smile.

"Just...I mean, why were you asking me those questions? How did Joey die?"

They exchanged glances again, this time they almost seemed to be having a discussion without words. Finally Bernhardt sighed. "When the coroner checked your friend over, there were some unexplained injuries: a slightly dislocated nose and some bruising in the groin area. Our job was to explain those injuries. You've just helped us do that. As long as he was alive when you left him..."

"He was!" I asserted firmly.

"...then the official finding will cite the cause of death to be accidental drowning. We have to write our report up, but I expect that after you left he somehow managed to get downstairs and onto the pool deck without anyone seeing him. Considering the amount of drugs seized at the party that isn't really as hard to believe as one might think, plus everyone agreed the yard was pretty much deserted for most of the night. Then in his drunken state, which is supported by other statements, by the way, he fell into the pool, maybe hit his head and drowned. The medical examiner confirms that he had enough alcohol in his system to stun a bull elephant."

Detective Grafton seemed eager to leave. "Once again, Mr. Keegan, thank you for your time and cooperation. You've helped us close this case."

I nodded uncertainly and walked them out. I returned to work with an unsettled feeling in the pit of my stomach. Something didn't feel right about this whole thing.

The next several days were uneventful except for the everyday business of living, work during the day and painting at night. Aidan and I were cautiously making an attempt to rebuild the trust I had broken and in turn, piece our friendship back together. It was a slow process. We were sleeping in our own rooms after that first night, but he would sit next to me while I painted, sometimes reading or doing homework, sometimes just watching, sometimes talking to me softly. The pictures I had taken had turned out great, so I had plenty of material to work from, and it was a welcome escape from my thoughts.

Not a day went by that I didn't think about Caitlin, but on Aidan's advice, I waited for her to call me. The next move had to be hers.

A week went by, then two, and still I hadn't heard from Caitlin. I did, however, have fifteen paintings finished that I was very pleased with. I was at home painting when she finally called. I was alone for a change; Aidan had gone out with some friends from school. I'd received a half-hearted invitation, but he'd known before he asked that I would stay home to paint. I was in a place where I couldn't stop when the phone started ringing. Eventually it stopped, then immediately started up again. With a sigh, I dropped my paintbrush in the water well and grabbed up the insistently bleating instrument, stabbing the talk button as if it were the phone's fault I was being interrupted.

"Will?" Caitlin said hesitantly to my annoyed hello.

"Caitlin!" I said, immediately brightening. "I've been hoping you would call."

"Yeah, I'm sorry I haven't called before this, but this isn't the kind of thing you decide overnight, you know?"

"Yeah, it's ok, really. I'm just glad you called now."

"Look, Will, I've been doing a lot of thinking and...well, I don't really feel like going into this over the phone. Is there any way we can meet tomorrow around noon to talk about this?"

"Yeah, sure. Um...we can meet on my lunch break. There's an outdoor café on the plaza we can meet at if you want."

"That's fine; I've been there so I know where it is."

"Great!"

"Ok, I'll see you then."

"See you tomorrow."

I hung up wondering what kind of news I'd be getting the next day. I hadn't been able to read anything from her voice, but I had a feeling whatever she decided would affect me very deeply.

I was at work the next morning when a uniformed deliveryman entered the gallery with a small box in hand.

"Will Keegan?" he said.

"That's me," I said in surprise.

"Got something for ya," he said and held out his clipboard for me to sign. I did, and we exchanged the clipboard for the box.

"Hey, wait...who's it from?" I called to his retreating back. There was no return address on the box.

The deliveryman paused at the door long enough to yell back, "I dunno, boss. I only deliver 'em."

I looked at the box again. My name was written in black magic marker in careful block letters that revealed nothing. I gingerly pried open the top spilling packing peanuts everywhere in the process. The corner of a single sheet of paper stuck out of the Styrofoam squiggles and I pulled it free and read the lone sentence written in the same black block letters.

"IT WASN'T AN ACCIDENT!"

It felt like my heart dropped to the pit of my stomach. A strange ringing started up in my ears, and I suddenly felt dizzy. It couldn't mean what I thought it did, could it? This anonymous nondescript sheet of typing paper couldn't be suggesting that Joey's death wasn't an accident, that it was something more sinister.

The box slipped from my numb fingers and bounced onto the floor, sending the packing peanuts cascading across the floor. Something else flew out of the box and skittered across the tiles and under an antique sofa that stood against one wall.

I snapped out of it and got down on my stomach to see what it was. I saw a flash of reflected light all the way against the wall. I stretched as far as I could but my fingers stopped just short of the mysterious object. I managed to drag the sofa away from the wall and stopped cold. I didn't have to pick it up to know what it was. I'd seen it a million times before, but it had always been around Joey's neck before. Lying on the floor in a small, innocuous pile of silver chain was Joey's missing necklace.

I scooped it up and managed to get the gallery put back together before Nikki came back out. The whole time my mind was racing a hundred miles a second. Why would someone send me that note and the necklace that was now burning a hole in my pocket? What was I supposed to do with it? Go to the police was the obvious answer. But how did I know it wasn't some sort of sick prank played by someone at the party. Obviously, we had been overheard fighting upstairs. It might well be a hoax, but I decided I still had to go to the police. I would go right after work. I would have gone right then, but it was time to meet Caitlin. I pulled the necklace out of my pocket and slipped it over my head, tucking it under my shirt for safekeeping.

"I'm going to lunch," I called to Nikki as I headed out the front door. I emerged into the bright sunshine and crisp November air, but my mind stayed in the uncertain shadows that I had stumbled into with the arrival of the mysterious box. I tried to steer my mind away from the necklace by thinking about how weather like this made it worth the sticky, humid days of summer on the Eastern Shore. It was the kind of weather tailor-made for sipping apple cider at an outdoor café. In a few weeks, the café would be switching to hot cocoa served in the cozy, old-fashioned storefront, but for now, the tables were still set up on the plaza.

I sipped my cider and let my mind wander while I waited for Caitlin. Who had sent me the necklace? Did someone see what had happened? And if so, then why didn't they go to the police? It had to be a sick practical joke I decided just as Caitlin sat down across from me. I smiled a welcome as I once more tried to shift my thoughts toward something besides the necklace.

"Thanks for meeting me, Will," she said.

"I told you I'd be here for you, and I meant it."

She looked down at her hands in her lap where she was busy mangling a napkin.

"I've thought a lot about what you said," she began softly. "In fact, it's all I've been able to think about. It's so hard to believe that there is a human being forming inside me as we sit here right now. It all seems so unreal. I mean it would be so much easier to believe what the nurse at the clinic told me. She said it isn't really a baby yet, that it's just a lump of tissue. She called it 'the fetus' the whole time. She never called it a baby. I'd pretty much made up my mind to have the abortion, but then I turned on the Discovery Channel a few days ago. There was a special on about in vitro fertilization and they followed the whole process, from the fertilization until the birth. They showed them doing a sonogram at about the same place I am now and...it was a baby, Will. You could see everything...its little tiny nose and little tiny ears and little tiny hands and it was sucking its thumb...and then I thought about what you said, about how it wasn't the baby's fault I slept with Joey. How it shouldn't have to pay for my mistake."

She paused while a single tear rolled down her cheek. She took a deep, shaky breath and continued, "I've never been more scared in my entire life. I don't know anything about babies. I don't know how I'm going to finish school. I don't know how any of this is going to work, but I knew then that I wasn't going to have the abortion. My appointment was today, for right now actually. I didn't go...obviously. But you know, I think I knew I wasn't going to have it before that. I stopped smoking the night we talked, the night Joey died. I just...look, Will, the reason I wanted to talk to you today was to tell you I don't expect you to help me with the baby. This is my responsibility. I know the offer was made in the heat of the moment and you didn't really mean it—"

I broke in, "What about adoption?"

She blinked in surprise. "What about it?"

"Couldn't you just put the baby up for adoption?"

She started shaking her head. "No way. I could never do that. I couldn't stand the thought of someone else raising my baby. No, if I'm going to have it, I'm going to keep it."

I nodded. "That makes sense. Okay, look, when I made you that offer, you're right, it was in the heat of the moment, but I meant it and I still mean it. I have the support of my friends, well...Aidan doesn't exactly approve, but he is supporting me. I want to help you if you'll let me."

"How do I know you're not just saying that now to relieve some sense of guilt, then once the baby arrives — boom, you're gone? All my past experience with guys has been pretty consistent. Let's just say I haven't found them to be the most reliable of all God's creations."

"I give you my word."

"No offense, but I don't even know you, really. That's not worth all that much to me."

"We could have a lawyer draw up some papers, make it legal and binding," I suggested.

She thought a moment. "That might work. I could buy that. But I can't afford a lawyer. Not with school and rent and now a baby on the way. I'm not even sure how much insurance will cover."

"If we wait until December, I should have some money. I have a show later this week..."

"A show?"

"An art show. I thought I had told you, I'm an artist."

"I think you did, but it didn't register. Your own show?"

"Something like that," I mumbled. I could feel my face heating up. "I just started working at the art gallery here on the plaza. They've already sold a few of my paintings."

"That's incredible! I'd love to see them."

"They're all at my apartment right now; I'm saving them for the show. Why don't you come for dinner one night this week? That way you can meet Aidan. You'll be seeing him a lot."

"Are you two a couple?"

"No, just friends," I said quickly, maybe a bit too quickly. Caitlin gave me a suspicious look, as if she weren't convinced.

"So just how involved are you planning on being?" she said, going back to our real purpose for being here.

I thought for a moment before answering. "Aidan and I have talked about that," I said slowly. "I want to help in any way you'll let me. Lamaze coach, expenses, actually helping with the baby — you set the boundaries, and I'll respect them."

She studied me for a second, then said, "Why are you doing this?"

I opened and closed my mouth a few times before I finally found my voice. If I kept this up, I could enter a guppy look-alike contest soon. "I...well...I guess this baby is all I have left of Joey now," I said at last. "He meant a lot to me. He was like my brother. Even though things went bad at the end, it doesn't change what we had before."

She nodded. "I'm going to have to think about all this. I have an appointment with an ObGyn later this week so I'll know better what I'm up against then. Plus I'll know what the insurance covers by then." She shook her head and smiled, "Why am I seeing shades of *Object of My Affection* here? I'm feeling like Jennifer Aniston."

"You know, you actually look a bit like her, too," I laughed. "As long as you don't fall in love with me, it's all good."

She laughed. "I'll consider myself warned. No falling in love with Will. Got it. Oh, my gosh! Wouldn't it be funny if I were named Grace? Then we'd be Will and Grace!"

"My mom's name is Grace," I told her.

"You're kidding!" She laughed and then became suddenly serious. "You know what?"

"What?"

"I'm glad I met you, Will."

"Me, too. I mean, I'm glad I met you."

She reached across the table and gave my hand a quick squeeze. Then she picked up her purse and started rummaging through it.

"Let me get it," I said, pulling out my wallet.

"Starting already, Uncle Will?" she said with a smile.

"Something like that."

"Ok, then." She stood up, but forgot to close her purse first. Her wallet and a tube of lipstick fell out onto the ground. I quickly bent to pick them up for her. As I did, Joey's necklace slipped out of my shirt and swung out in plain view. I had forgotten all about it. Caitlin's eyes were glued to the charm as I straightened up. I stuffed it back under my shirt, but it was too late.

"Joey had a necklace like that," she said softly.

"It is...was Joey's," I told her. "Someone gave it to me after he died." There. I had told her the truth, just not the whole truth.

She stared at my neck where the chain was still visible for a moment longer, then shook her head as if to clear it. "What night do you want me to come over for dinner?"

"How about Wednesday?"

"Sounds good. I'll see you then."

We hugged briefly, and I watched her while she walked off down the plaza. You would never have known she was pregnant. I wondered when you started showing. I made a mental note to stop by the library that evening and pick up some books on babies. I'd better start reading up on the subject if I was going to be a good Uncle Will.

Chapter 12

When I left work that afternoon I headed straight to the police station. I didn't know what to expect since I'd never been to the police station before, but I guess I had some sort of mental picture of a dark, dingy looking hole in the wall straight out of *NYPD Blue*. What I found couldn't have been farther from what I had envisioned. The police station was housed in a modern, square brick building with lots of tinted windows and not much character. I entered a lobby that looked more like a doctor's waiting room, complete with sofas, tables, and magazines, and approached the glass window.

"I'm looking for Detective Grafton or Bernhardt," I told the lady behind the glass. She was wearing a uniform but looked like the only thing she would ever be running for was maybe the last doughnut.

"Can I tell them what this is concerning?" she asked with polite disinterest.

"It's concerning the death of Joey Taylor," I told her. Her eyes flicked up at me but quickly decided I still wasn't interesting.

"Have a seat," she ordered. I did.

Twenty minutes later, I was just about to leave when an interior door opened and Detective Grafton popped his head into the room. He seemed to be surprised to see me. He waved me back, and I followed him down a short, carpeted hall and into a cramped office that from the looks of things he must have shared with Detective Bernhardt. There were coffee rings on the top layer of the papers that covered both desks and crumpled balls of fast food wrappers cluttered the floor near the trash can.

"So what's up, kid?" he said as he sat down behind his desk. He didn't offer but I sat down in one of the chairs that were set facing him.

"Someone sent this to me today," I said as I pulled the letter out of my pocket. It was a little worse for wear after spending the better part of the day in there, but I smoothed it out best I could and handed it to him. Then I took off the necklace and handed it over as well.

Grafton looked at the paper disdainfully, then back at me with a raised eyebrow. I unfolded the letter and laid it back in front of him.

"What wasn't an accident?" he said finally.

"I think they mean Joey's death," I said, feeling more than a little uncomfortable having to explain what seemed plain as day to me to the detective. "The necklace is Joey's. He never took it off. and his mom told me it wasn't with his things when she...after she..."

"Look, son." I hate it when people who aren't my father call me son. Actually, I hate it when my father calls me son. "We investigated this death backwards and forwards. We had some questions, but you were the one that wrapped things up. Your friend was drunk; no, he was pickled. He was way over the legal limit. No one saw anything out of the ordinary and trust me, we talked to everybody there *and* tracked down those like yourself who chose to

leave before the real party got started. In fact, nobody saw Mr. Taylor or anything even remotely suspicious in the time between when you two disappeared
upstairs together and before he was found floating face down in the pool. For
the record, if there *were* any suspicion of foul play, you'd be suspect Numero
Uno. As it is, it's an open-and-shut case. Drunken college kid falls into pool
and drowns. Sad story, but not a new one. I'm sorry someone played a sick
joke like this on you."

"So that's it? You just think it's some kind of joke?"

"Honestly? Yeah, that's what I think it is. But I'll tell you what; if it'll
make you feel any better, I'll make a note on the case file and keep a copy of
the letter. If anything like this happens again, we'll look into filing some sort
of harassment charges."

"What would make me feel better is if you took me seriously. He never
took this necklace off. Never. Not once in the entire time I knew him."

"Look, he was so drunk it could have fallen off, and he wouldn't have
even noticed. Maybe even in your little tussle. Somebody finds it, recognizes
it, knows you're his best friend, and decides to send it to you with this note.
Typical college prank."

"I've been wearing the necklace all afternoon, and it's been fine; the clasp
works and nothing is broken."

"What is it exactly that you think I can do? You've handled the necklace,
heck, you've worn it! This note looks like you ran it through a food processor.
What are we supposed to do with it? Do you have the box it came in?"

"There was no return address, so I threw it away," I said weakly.

"Then there you go. There's nothing I can do even if I thought there was
something to do, which I don't."

I knew there was no point in arguing further; I would just be beating a
dead horse. "Can I keep the necklace?" I asked.

The detective shrugged. "I don't even have any reason to believe it was
the kid's except you said so. It's between you and the mom."

I picked up the necklace and fastened it around my neck once again.
Then I stood and started to leave. "Sorry for taking up your time."

"Look, kid, I'm sorry," he said when I was at the door. "It's a shitty deal
all around."

"Yeah," I agreed, "it is."

As hard as I tried to forget the note and concentrate on my painting, my mind
refused to let go. The detective had dismissed the idea of Joey's death being
anything but an accident so easily, but the necklace was really bothering me.
Together with the note, it was just more than I could pass off. Finally, I
couldn't stand it anymore, and I went to look for Aidan. I found him in his
bedroom busily typing away on his computer.

"Aidan, can I talk to you for a minute?" I asked tentatively.

He immediately pushed back from the computer. "Of course," he said.

I sat down on the edge of the bed and filled him in on the events of the
day. When I was finished, he thought for a moment.

"As far as the package goes," he said, "you might try checking with the delivery company. They may have records or something. It's a long shot but worth a try. As for Caitlin, I just hope you know what you are getting yourself into, but either way, I told you I would support you and I will."

It wasn't exactly what I had hoped for but checking with the delivery company sounded like a good idea and having something concrete to do made me feel better. I was able to go back to my painting. I finished off the evening with a few chapters of *So You're Having a Baby*.

I ran by the delivery company on my way to work the next morning but the young man working wasn't very helpful. In fact, he was downright surly. All I could get out of him was that the person who had been working on Saturday only worked on weekends. I decided it would be easier to just wait until then and try to talk to them.

Wednesday, Aidan and I spent the afternoon cooking spaghetti, which was pretty much the only thing we were sure we could pull off. I divided my time between painting and making the sauce from scratch, I used my mom's recipe, and, even though by the time I was finished I looked like I had been slaughtering hogs, I was quite proud of the results.

Caitlin arrived promptly at six, and we all sat down to eat. Conversation at the table was polite and mostly generalities. After the dishes had been cleared, we all settled into the living room for some real conversation.

"Well, I've thought about everything," Caitlin began. "The baby, your offer, you know. And I decided that I'd be crazy not to accept your offer, especially if we make it legal and all. I'm going to need all the help I can get."

"What about your parents?" Aidan asked.

"I haven't told them yet," she said with a frown. "I don't know if I even want to. They're going to totally freak out. My stepdad will anyway. He's a really strict Mormon. My mom won't be sober long enough to care one way or the other. I haven't seen my real dad since I was twelve."

"How old are you now?"

"I'll be nineteen in January."

"Do you work?"

"I'm a full-time student."

"What's your major?"

"I haven't decided yet. Hey, I feel like I'm being interviewed for something here."

I was getting the same impression, so I quickly stepped in and changed the subject. "How'd the doctor's appointment go?"

She broke into a grin. "Great! I got to see the baby on the sonogram. It's too early yet to know what it is though. The doctor said the baby was doing fine, right where it should be for how far along I am. I also found out that my insurance will cover almost everything. I just have to pay like a small amount at each visit."

"That's great!" I said. "When do you go back again?"

"In two weeks. I'll be nine weeks then."

"Can I go with you?"

Caitlin and Aidan both looked at me as if I had suddenly sprouted anten-
nae and ordered them to take me to their leader.

"What?" I said defensively.

"You want to go with me to see the doctor?" Caitlin asked.

"Yeah, I've been reading all these baby books and I'd really like to be
involved as much as possible; well, as much as you feel comfortable with anyway."

"Well, I guess if you are sure you want to..."

"I'm sure; as long as you're sure you don't mind."

"I guess not." She didn't sound too sure.

We all sat in an uncomfortable silence for what seemed like an eternity.
Finally, Aidan broke the moment. "So, uh, what are you doing for Thanksgiving?" he said to Caitlin.

The sudden shift in subject seemed to catch her off guard as if she had
been thinking about something else. I was a little surprised myself, but mostly
because I had forgotten that Thanksgiving was the very next day! I was glad
he'd reminded me. I'd been invited to dinner at Killian's house along with
Aidan. Apparently, they had some kind of tradition of inviting lost souls to
Thanksgiving dinner, and I fit the bill.

"I don't really have any plans," she said. "I don't really feel up to dealing
with my family right now. I think our ties that bind have all been cut, and I
don't know anyone else. I'll probably just settle on some Stouffer's turkey and
dressing."

"Hey, Aidan," I said suddenly. "Do you think Killian's dad would mind if
Caitlin came too?"

"No, I couldn't! I don't want to intrude," Caitlin insisted.

"Actually," Aidan said thoughtfully, "I seriously doubt they would mind
at all. Their motto seems to be the more the merrier. I mean none of them
even knew me last year except Aunt Meg, and I was completely welcome. Why
don't I call and find out at least?" He left the room to make the call.

"So you're reading baby books now, huh?" Caitlin said with a grin. "I
haven't even started reading baby books yet. It still doesn't seem real somehow."

"Well, it is real and you better get your rear in gear, missy," I teased. I
picked up the book I had just finished reading the night before and handed it
to her. "Let me recommend a book."

"*So You're Having a Baby,*" she read aloud, then looked at me with
raised eyebrow.

"It was very informative," I said defensively.

"I bet." She laughed. "Seriously though, I will read it if you don't mind."

"Help yourself. That was the whole idea."

"So when do you lose that cast?" she asked, pointing to my arm.

"Not for a few more weeks." I sighed. "I can't wait. It itches like hell."

"Ok, I talked to Adam," announced Aidan as he came back into the room.
"He says to bring anyone we want; they're cooking for a small army."

"Great, then it's settled," I said.

"I suppose," Caitlin said doubtfully, then brightened. "How about those paintings?"

I showed her what I had finished, and she was gratifyingly impressed.

"Wait until you see them all framed and matted. You wouldn't believe the difference it makes," I told her. "I have to have them all dropped off by Friday morning so that Nikki can get them done. She's calling in some favors with her framer to get them done last minute like this. Hey, why don't you come to the show Friday night?"

"That would be fun. Is it formal?"

"Yeah, technically it's by invitation only, but I think I can wangle you one."

"After all, you are the star," she teased. And of course, I blushed.

Since Killian only lived about half an hour away, we didn't leave until late afternoon. Aidan and I spent a lazy morning watching the Macy's Thanksgiving Day Parade, and I even managed to paint a little. Caitlin met us at the apartment, and we all drove down together.

We arrived at Killian's house, a two-story cedar-shingled beach house in a resort town about half an hour away, a little early, but an enthusiastic Killian and Asher met us at the door. We were ushered in and introduced to the others already there. Well, Caitlin and I were introduced; Aidan already knew pretty much everyone. First, I met Adam and Steve, Killian's legal guardians. They were the first gay couple I'd ever met besides Asher and Killian. Adam was tall and trim, with reddish blond hair that was beginning to silver at the temples and blue eyes. Steve looked amazingly like Tom Selleck from his Magnum PI days. Also early were friends of Adam and Steve named Ilana and Lysander with their new baby daughter, Melody.

While Caitlin and I were still cooing over Melody, Killian's mom and little brother got back from a last-minute trip to the grocery store. Killian's mom, Meg, was beautiful and looked much too young to have a son Killian's age. She was petite with shoulder-length blonde hair and the same brilliant blue eyes as Killian. Kane looked like an adorable little elf with bright green eyes and spiky blond hair.

The last of the guests arrived soon after. They turned out to be another gay couple, Bryant and Calvin. Bryant was the picture of health, with smooth skin tanned to a warm glow, wavy dark hair, and muscles that rippled under his ribbed turtleneck sweater. Calvin, on the other hand, looked as if he were a walking corpse. He was wraith thin and so pale I got the impression if I looked away he might have disappeared before I looked back. His wispy hair was almost white, and his eyes were such a pale shade of blue they too looked almost colorless.

Once everyone was ready, we gathered around two large tables that had been set up and Adam stood up to give the blessing.

"Before we get started," he said, "I want to say how honored Steve and I are that each of you could join us today as we celebrate Thanksgiving. Some of you are familiar faces, it's good to see you again, and some are new faces. And then some, like Will, are a new but familiar face." Everyone laughed and I turned red as everyone looked from me to Asher. "We started a tradition last year, and it was such a smashing success that we purposefully planned it the same way this year. We invited just enough people so that we could have thirteen guests, not counting Melody. Well, last night Aidan called and asked if he and Will could bring along a friend. I never turn anyone down, so I said the heck with tradition; bring it on. Well, lo and behold, who should call this morning but Killian and Asher's friend, Jake. He was supposed to be flying in this morning and spending a few days with us but had decided to stay in California with his new family for his first Thanksgiving with them. While I was disappointed, I have to say that I think he made the right choice. The bright side is that the tradition continues, and once again it's proven that God does have a sense of humor." He finished up his speech and gave the blessing, and everyone dove into the food with gusto.

Dinner was incredible. I'd never seen so much food. The turkey was so big I thought someone must have shot Big Bird; plus there was ham, candied yams, green beans, mountains of fluffy mashed potatoes, gallons of gravy, stuffing, warm yeast rolls, coleslaw, artichokes, and six different kinds of homemade pies for dessert. Steve and Adam must have been cooking for days. The atmosphere was festive as food was passed around and conversation flowed back and forth like the tide. When everyone had eaten their fill, and then some, Adam and Steve went around the table with an after-dinner wine and coffee. Even Kane was allowed a small glass of the sweet red wine. Only Caitlin refused, covering her glass with her hand and smiling with a shake of the head.

Eventually we managed to waddle into the living room for phase two of the tradition, as Adam put it. We sat in a loose circle on chairs, the sofa, and the floor. Once everyone was settled, Adam once again spoke up.

"Last year Aidan came up with this little gem, and we're going to continue the practice if everyone is game. What we'll do is we'll go around the room, one person at a time, and say one thing that you are thankful for. If you absolutely can't keep it to one thing, a panel of judges will evaluate the merit of each request on an individual basis."

Everyone laughed and looked at Bryant, who put on an innocent expression.

"Who'd like to go first?" Adam asked.

"I will," said Lysander. "I'm thankful that we now have a happy, healthy baby girl. For those of you who were here last year, you'll remember that it was one year ago tonight that we made the big announcement."

Ilana smiled down at the sleeping bundle in her arms. "What can I add to that?" she said.

"That's it?" Adam said.

"Sandy said it all," Ilana said tranquilly.

"Ok, new rule," Adam said. "You have to come up with your own thing to be thankful for."

Calvin was next. He waited for the laughter to die down, took a deep breath, and then smiled shakily. "I'm thankful to be alive for one more Thanksgiving." The room was deadly quiet for a few beats before the silence was broken by a choked off sob from Bryant. No one knew what to say and after a moment, Calvin went on. "We found out a few months ago that I'm HIV positive." There was a chorus of gasps from around the room. "I've been having health problems for about a year now, and they tested for HIV early on and nothing showed up. They tested me again later on and it came back positive. So far...so far Bryant has tested negative."

By now, Bryant had pulled himself together enough to take his turn. "I'm thankful for whatever time we have left. We're going to make the most of it."

No one said anything for several minutes as the clock ticked noisily on the wall. Finally, Bryant gave a slightly hysterical giggle. "Well, wasn't that quite the show stopper? Next year we'll go last." Everyone laughed, and the tension seemed to be broken. Some questions were asked about treatment; Calvin had opted for an aggressive action, but it was too soon to tell how effective it would be.

"Well," Adam said some time later, "I guess we'd better get back to our thanksgiving. It's my turn and, well, I'm thankful that it's been almost a year since anyone in my family has been threatened, held at knifepoint, or almost blown up. In fact, no one has had anything worse than a cold. It's been very peaceful and deliciously dull. And for that I am very thankful."

Steve nodded. "Me, too." Adam shot him a pointed look, and he hurried on, "I have my own, don't worry. I was just saying that I wholeheartedly agreed with yours, too. I'm thankful that I have been blessed enough to not only find my soul mate, but to also truly love his family as my own and be accepted by them. I am truly content and happy in my life. Your turn, Meg."

"Well, I'm thankful most of all to get to see my handsome son again and see how happy and well adjusted he is these days. As an extension of that, so I'm still on my first thing, Adam, I'm also thankful for my second son, Asher." Asher blushed, and for once, I was glad to see someone else turn red besides me. "Now, I would like to ask for a second thing if I may."

Adam gave an exaggerated sigh. "You're really pushing the limits, Meg, but I suppose we'll allow it."

"Thanks, you're a dear. I'm also thankful that things have been going well for me up in PA. The divorce is now final, and I've managed to get back into school. I'm really excited about my future for the first time in a long time. Now I'm done. You're next, Kane."

"Um..." Kane thought a moment. "I'm thankful that my mom is talking to me again, and things are better between us now, so now I get to see my mom and my dad, which, of course, means more presents at Christmas." He waggled his eyebrows, and everyone chuckled.

I made a mental note to ask Aidan what that was about later.

"My turn," announced Killian. "I'm thankful for two things. Is that ok?"

"Go ahead; we set a precedent with your mother."

"'K, well, I'm thankful that my real dad is behind bars where he belongs and where he can't hurt anyone else."

"Here, here," muttered Meg under her breath.

"I'm also thankful that I found my soul mate, too, but to make mine different from Steve's, I'm glad my soul mate found me."

Asher smiled goofily at Killian while the chorus of aw's died down. "I'm thankful that Killian and I were both accepted at Pemberton," he said. "Next year, we'll be going to school with you, Aidan."

After a round of congratulations, it was Aidan's turn. "Mine is a multiple part thanks but it's really all one. I'm thankful that Aunt Meg brought me down here with her last year because out of that one trip has come so much good. One, I was able to accept that I was gay with a little help from my not-so-little cousin, Killian. Two, I made a successful move from PA to the Shore. And three is the part I'm most thankful for, I made the best friend I've ever had in my whole life, and he's my roommate, Will."

I flushed crimson and stared down at my feet, but it was my turn and every eye in the room was on me. I cleared my throat and spoke up, "I guess it's my turn, huh? I know most of you don't know me, but I'm Asher's cousin. No one knows this but Aidan, not even you, Ash, but about a month ago I tried to kill myself because I'm gay."

Everyone's mouth dropped open at once. I almost giggled out loud they looked so comical. Not even Asher had been told what had really happened; we'd just simply said that I fell off the fire escape. "There were a lot of other factors, but what it boils down to is that I was a selfish coward and I tried to run from my problems instead of dealing with them. Aidan helped me to see that and ever since then, even though I've still had a lot of stuff going on, I've known that I had to face my problems head on. So I guess all of that was to say that I'm thankful that God didn't take the life that I tried to throw away. Instead, He gave me a second chance." After that somewhat lengthy speech, I suddenly realized I was still the center of attention and began to blush again. Luckily, Caitlin spoke up and shifted the focus off me, or so I thought.

"I'm new here, too," she began softly. "I really don't know any of you that well. I've even only known Will a few weeks, but you've all made me feel so welcome, like I was part of a family. I'm really glad Will asked me to come, but that's not what I'm most thankful for. I'm most thankful for Will, himself. He kept me from making a horrible mistake that would have probably haunted me for the rest of my life. You see, I'm pregnant and I'm not married and the father just died. Even before he died though, he told me that he didn't want to have anything to do with the baby. He told me to have an abortion and that's what I decided I would do." She stopped for a moment to blink back tears. "Then I met Will, and he forced me to see what I didn't want to see; that this was an innocent life that I created as a result of my bad decisions. And that life shouldn't have to pay for my mistakes. Then he went beyond just offering advice, he offered himself. He's going to help me raise my baby so that I can have it and keep it."

For the third time that night, a stunned silence fell over the room as I tried to shrink into the sofa. Finally Adam spoke in a somewhat awed voice, "Wow...well...that certainly gives us all something to work toward."

I couldn't stand it any longer. "I'm nothing special," I protested. "It was just something that I knew I had to do. Haven't you ever just known that you had to do something even though you weren't quite sure why? You just know you have to."

"But that's exactly what makes it all the more special," Meg said. "I'm sure that all of us have experienced what you just described, but how many of us can say that we actually acted on that urging? Most people just ignore that compelling, pass it off as insensible or unrealizable. Or maybe they just don't have the faith to step out and take that kind of risk. Besides, true heroes never know they are heroes. They just simply are."

"I'm definitely not a hero," I argued, my face blazing away. "I'm so screwed up, I've tried to kill myself not just once, but twice in the last two months. Aidan is the real hero. He saved my life both times."

Aidan opened his mouth to argue, but Steve cut him off, "The mark of a true hero, or true bravery, is this — not a lack of fear, that's just foolishness, but rather to be afraid and do what you know you must do anyway."

Everyone thought that over quietly for a few minutes.

"Ok, enough philosophical wanderings," Adam said suddenly. "This night is supposed to be about a celebration of life, so let's start living! Who's up for a board game?"

We all played some party games for a while, and then the guests began to say their good-byes. Lysander and Ilana were the first to leave, saying they needed to get Melody to bed. Bryant and Calvin left shortly after, since Calvin was visibly tiring. Aidan, Caitlin and I prepared to leave too, since we had the drive home still ahead of us.

"You guys are coming to my show tomorrow night, aren't you?" I asked before we left.

"Are you kidding? We wouldn't miss it for anything!" Killian exclaimed.

"Great," I said. "Why don't you two plan on staying for a little while after? I have something I need to talk to you about."

"Sure, that shouldn't be a problem. It's not a school night," he said.

"What was that about?" Aidan asked once we were in the car.

"What was what about?" I asked innocently.

"What do you need to talk to Killian and Asher about?"

"That matter we were discussing the other night; you know, the note?"

"Oh...I don't understand."

"We'll talk about it later," I said meaningfully.

"What Will is trying to say is drop it while Caitlin's around," Caitlin said with amusement in her voice. I laughed as she gracefully changed the subject. "Will, thanks for inviting me. It was great."

"It was, wasn't it?" I agreed. "I'm glad you could come. You're still coming tomorrow night, too, aren't you?"

"I wouldn't miss it for the world. I just hope I can still fit into the dress I was planning on wearing."

"Are you gaining weight with the baby?"

She laughed. "Not yet! I was talking about that huge meal we just had. I don't think I'll be able to eat for a week."

We all laughed.

"It was great, wasn't it?" I asked. "I think it was the best Thanksgiving ever and I'm not just talking about the food."

I settled back into the seat in contentment. If I could just make it through tomorrow night, I thought, I would be home free. If I had only known how wrong I was.

Chapter 13

Friday was a whirlwind of activity as final preparations were made for that evening's show. All the art on display had to be moved out of the gallery and carefully stored in the back room to make room for my work. Then, my pictures were picked up from the framing shop and hung, often being moved two or three times before we decided it was perfect. Tables were set up that would hold the hors d'oeuvres and beverage. Since I was still underage, Nikki had bought sparkling cider instead of champagne. Finally, everything was just the way we wanted it, and we raced back to the apartment building to change.

As I rushed into our apartment, Aidan met me at the door. Grinning like the Cheshire cat, he held up a pair of black leather pants and a rich maroon crushed velvet shirt with flowing sleeves. I skidded to a halt.

"What is that?" I demanded. "That's not what you're wearing, is it?"

"No, it's what you're wearing," he said brightly. My mouth fell open. "It's a surprise," he added.

"You're damn right it's a surprise. Here's another one, I'll be damned if I'm wearing leather pants," I said firmly.

"Yes, you are," Aidan said equally firmly. "Nikki and I bought these just for you the other night when I went out without you. You're a hot new artist, and you have to look the part."

"You've got to be kidding! I'll look like some Ricky Martin wannabe."

"We don't have time to argue. Shut up and take off your clothes."

"Oh, baby!" I teased. "I love it when you talk dirty."

"If you don't start getting undressed, you're going really gonna hear me talk dirty."

I laughed but decided it would be easier for everyone involved if I just went along with him. We both knew I would end up doing as he said in the end anyway. I did as he ordered and started getting undressed. He helped me into the unfamiliar clothes, then dragged me down the hall to the full-length mirror in the bathroom.

"Wait! You're missing something," he said.

"Yeah, my dignity. I think I left it in the living room with my real clothes."

"Oh, quit bitching. What size shoe do you wear?"

"Ten."

"Good, I wear 10 ½, that's close enough." He raced out of the bathroom and was back in no time carrying a pair of heavy black shoes. Once they were on, I had to admit that the whole ensemble looked better than I had feared, although I still felt like a kid playing dress-up. The pants, though, were much more comfortable than I would have ever imagined.

"See, I told you!" Aidan said with his famous grin. And then we were off again. This time he dragged me out the door and across the hall to Nikki's apartment where he knocked on her door. The door swung open to reveal

Nikki hopping on one foot while she tried to put in a dangly carved jet earring in the shape of a multi-armed deity. She was wearing a tight bright yellow top that looked like it was made of rubber and an extremely short black leather skirt. She wore a clunky yellow high-heeled shoe on one foot; its mate lay on its side a few feet away next to a pile of black leather. Her hair had turned bright yellow since I had seen her last and I wondered how it had been possible to dye it that quickly. She managed to get the earring in, slip on the other shoe, and scoop up the pile of leather in one smooth motion. The pile of leather turned out to be an ankle-length fitted coat, which she now pulled on.

"You look fah-bulous, dahling," she said, calmly eying me, as if seconds before she hadn't been hopping around on one foot like a demented stork.

"I think we killed a cow between us," I said dryly.

"It's worth it when you look this good."

"Tell that to PETA. How did you get away without wearing a dead animal?" I asked Aidan, as I eyed his khakis and white oxford shirt enviously.

"Because he's not the star," Nikki said. "Now come here, you need a few finishing touches."

I stepped reluctantly forward, and she suddenly pounced on me and mussed up my hair with both hands.

"Hey!" I yelled.

"Oh, hush," she chided as she unbuttoned the top two buttons of my shirt. "Oh, the necklace is a nice touch."

My hand went immediately to Joey's charm. I had forgotten I was even wearing it. I hadn't taken it off in weeks. I felt my jangled nerves calm just a bit. It made me feel good to know that in a way, Joey would be with me tonight — the old Joey, who had been my best friend for eighteen years, not the shadow that he had become at the end.

Nikki stepped back and gave me a final once-over, then nodded as if she were satisfied with what she saw. "Let's blow this popsicle stand."

Nikki gave me some last-minute instructions on the elevator ride down.

"Everyone is going to want to meet you. Shake their hands and be polite, but don't let any one person monopolize you for too long. Circulate. And whatever you do, do not allow yourself to be cornered by one of the Polyester Posse."

"Huh?"

"You'll know them when you see them, a group of widows who all wear these horribly tacky polyester pant suits. If someone asks you for your inspiration for a particular painting, ask them what they think of it, then tell them how amazingly perceptive they are and how impressed you are that they nailed it so perfectly on their first try. If they want to know how much, send them to me. Be careful what you say, and remember if you can't bedazzle them with brilliance baffle them with bullshit."

I nodded although I strongly suspected I had just been baffled rather than bedazzled.

Aidan and I drove to the gallery in his truck, and Nikki drove her own car. We didn't talk much. I was too nervous and, after a few monosyllabic responses, Aidan gave up any effort on his part. Derrick had the gallery open when we got there, but thankfully, no one else had arrived except the classical guitarist Nikki had hired.

Aidan was stationed at the door to check invitations. It had been Nikki's suggestion to make this an invitation only event. She said it made it seem more exclusive, and it made the "right people" more likely to attend. By "right people", I assume she meant those with fat bank accounts.

People started arriving shortly after. Everyone made a point of coming up to me after they had made a preliminary sweep of the gallery. It wasn't long before the gallery was filled with well-dressed people sipping champagne and speaking in hushed tones. Adam, Asher, and Killian arrived and waved from the door. Laura and Gabe followed on their heels. As busy as I was, I had been keeping an eye on the door for Caitlin. As it got later and later, it became more and more obvious that she hadn't showed up. I was just about to give up on her when she appeared at my side, as if out of nowhere. I wondered if she had been taking lessons from Derrick. She was wearing a form-fitting, ankle-length black dress with a black satin wrap and strappy black shoes. Her blonde hair had been pulled up into a sophisticated chignon and her gold jewelry was simple and elegant. Without a word, she slipped her hand into the crook of my arm and smiled as if she had been attending high society social functions all her life.

A camera flashed from somewhere, but by the time I turned around, I couldn't tell where it had come from. Before I could think about it anymore, though, someone caught me by the other arm and asked me about a painting I had done of an old shack in Worcester County. They were sure that the shack was on their grandfather's property on the Eastern Shore of Virginia. I told them how impressed I was that they could recognize it from my painting. I felt a little guilty for lying...for at least two seconds.

The evening wore on, and by the time people began to leave, my arm was sore from all the handshaking and my face ached from all the smiling. I took a good look around and was surprised to see that all the paintings were still here. I couldn't believe that I hadn't sold a single painting. As soon as I saw an opening, I pulled Nikki aside. Before I could say a word, though, she cut me off.

"Can you believe this night? It's been more successful than I dared hope for."

"But...all the paintings are still on the wall," I said in confusion.

Nikki laughed. "Of course they are. Didn't I explain that to you? They don't take the paintings home tonight. They put their name down for the pieces they want, and then we deliver them later, after they are paid for."

"Oh..." I said, feeling about as bright as a burned out light bulb. "How many did we sell then?"

"Oh, Will, I hate to disappoint you, but you know tonight was more about exposure than sales," she said with a concerned expression on her face. "We sold...ALL OF THEM!"

"Wha? All?" was my witty comeback.

"Every last one is spoken for," she said with a huge grin. "Gone! And the critics were impressed, too."

"Critics?" I said weakly.

"I didn't tell you because I didn't want you to be more self-conscious than you already were. There were critics from the local paper, plus the DC and Baltimore papers, and at least two major art magazines. They came because they all knew my father and they respect the gallery very highly. I can't guarantee what they will write, but we should know something I'd say at least by next week's Sunday edition."

"Review?" I repeated dumbly. I was starting to feel like I had just stepped off one of the centrifugal rides at the carnival.

"You're starting to sound like a parrot, Will," Nikki said. She spun me around and pointed me toward a corner of the room where Aidan, Adam, Killian, Asher, Laura, Gabe, and Caitlin were talking in a small group. "Now be a good bird, and go tell your little friends the good news." She sent me off with a pat on my leather-clad bottom.

I walked over to the group in a kind of daze. They jumped toward me as one person, all of them chattering and jabbering at once.

"We sold all the paintings," I said.

All the chatter stopped for a second, then they erupted into a chorus of cheers, congratulations, high-fives, and back thumping. I was glad everyone else had left.

"You're a star for sure now!" Asher exclaimed.

"You sure look the part anyway," Killian said, with an appreciative glance at my outfit. Asher delivered a sharp elbow jab to Killian's side.

"Yeah, Will," Caitlin chimed in, "I didn't get a chance to tell you earlier, but you really do look great."

"You're the one who looks great," I said. "I guess that's why you waited so late, so you could make an entrance."

"Not to break up your little mutual appreciation party," Adam interrupted, "but I need to get home. Before I leave, though, I wanted you to know that at least one of your paintings is going to a good home and you are more than welcome to come visit it any time you want."

"You bought one?" I asked in surprise.

"Of course! I thought I'd better buy a Will Keegan original before your prices went through the roof."

"I would have painted you one anytime."

"Well, then I couldn't say that I bought one at your very first show, could I?" he said and left after telling Killian not to be home too late.

Laura suggested the rest of us go somewhere for a celebration. Nikki overheard and shooed us out before I could protest. We walked down the plaza to an ice cream parlor that kept late hours.

"So," Laura began once we were all crowded into a corner booth with our ice cream, "I don't think I know everyone here really."

"I'm Killian, and this is my boyfriend, Asher," Killian spoke up. "I'm Aidan's cousin, and Asher is Will's cousin."

"I've heard of you guys," Laura said. "I'm Laura, one of Will's oldest friends, and this is my boyfriend, Gabriel."

"Call me Gabe," Gabe said as he shook Killian's and Asher's hands.

"And this is Caitlin," I said to Laura. Laura looked confused, not an expression one usually sees on Laura's face.

"And Caitlin is..." she said.

"I...I knew Joey," Caitlin said, choosing her words carefully.

Laura looked even more confused. "You must not have known him long," she said bluntly. "I know I'm out of the loop here, but this is ridiculous, Will. Are you two dating?"

"No, we're not dating," I said. "We're just friends; we met at a party and found out we have a lot in common."

Laura gave me a look that let me know that she knew there was more to this story and she expected to be filled in completely later. I nodded almost imperceptibly.

"Not to change the subject," I said to change the subject, "but since everyone is here that I wanted to talk to I might as well get it all over with at once. I have something I need to tell you all." That got everyone's attention. Everyone watched me now as they ate their ice cream. "Last week I got a package in the mail. Inside the package was Joey's necklace and a note that said 'It wasn't an accident.'"

Five spoons stopped in mid-air. Only Aidan kept eating since he knew the whole story already.

Laura was the first to snap out of it. She dropped her spoon with a clatter as she leaned toward me over the table. I thought she was going to grab me by my shirt and drag me across the table, but instead she planted her hands palm down and said in a deadly calm voice, "What?"

"Is this some kind of sick joke?" Caitlin asked, looking very pale all of a sudden.

"Who sent it?" Gabe asked.

"What wasn't an accident?" Killian asked, looking very lost.

Asher didn't say anything. He just looked like he knew what was coming and didn't like it one bit.

"I don't know who sent it; there was no return address," I told Gabe, then I turned to Killian. "I think whoever sent me this note was trying to tell me that Joey's death wasn't an accident."

"You mean that he was murdered," Laura said in a tight voice.

"Oh, my God," Caitlin whispered.

"Did you go to the police?" Gabe asked.

"Yeah, and they just passed it off as some college prank. I haven't been able to dismiss it so easily."

"So you're taking this seriously then?" Laura said sounding a little more like her usual self.

"I just can't stop thinking about it. The person that Joey had become these last few weeks wasn't the real Joey. If someone killed him, then I can't just let the murderer walk away. No matter what happened between us, he was still my best friend for eighteen years and I can't just write that off."

Laura nodded. I knew she of all people would understand.

"So what are you suggesting? That we try to catch the killer ourselves?" Gabe asked.

"Wait," Asher interrupted before I could answer. "I don't mean to be insensitive or anything, but what does this have to do with Killian and me? We didn't even know Joey. I mean, I'm sorry for your loss and all, but..."

"Well, Aidan told me about how you caught that killer in your town, the one that killed your friend. Since you're the only people I know who have actually had any kind of experience in this area, I was hoping you'd help me out," I said, feeling kind of silly. Killian's eyes lit up immediately. Asher blanched a whiter shade of pale.

"No way, Kill," he said quickly. "You remember what it was like last time. We almost got killed. Besides, there's no way Adam would let us get involved in something like that again."

But Killian was already hooked. "Who said Adam would have to know? And besides, this wouldn't be like last time. We don't really know any of the people involved so we won't really be at risk."

Asher let out a low moan and pushed his ice cream away, as if he'd lost his appetite.

"You know, Will," Laura said softly, "I've been meaning to call you because I knew you were probably blaming yourself for Joey's death." I started to deny it, but decided that there was no point, Laura knew me too well. She went on, "I don't think Joey ever really told you about his dad?" I shook my head. "As close as you guys were that seemed to be the one thing he could never talk to you about. I think he was jealous of your family."

I opened my mouth to argue, but she held up a hand and I stopped. "No matter how bad your family may have seemed to you, you know Joey idolized your dad and part of him always wanted his dad to come back so they could be a family like yours. His dad was an alcoholic, a bad one. He didn't just disappear as Joey always said; his mom kicked him out and told him to never come back. Joey was four at the time and saw the whole thing. As far as I know, he never came back. You know Joey always drank too much at parties, but it got worse when he started college. You didn't drive him to drink, Will. He's always been looking for an excuse to do just what he did, become his father."

I was quiet for a moment while I thought about what Laura had said. "Thank you for telling me that," I said finally, "but that just makes me want to find the person who did this to him all the more, because now he'll never be able to prove to himself that he wasn't his father."

"I want to help," Laura said firmly.

"Where Laura goes, I go," Gabe said.

"You know I'm behind you," Aidan said, laying his hand gently on the back of my neck.

"I'm in," Killian said cheerily.

Asher's head thumped as it landed on the table. A muffled "Count me in too" emerged from him in the form of a resigned sigh.

Everyone except Asher turned to Caitlin.

"The only reason I'd want to find Joey's killer is to congratulate them on a job well done," Caitlin spat out.

Laura's eyes grew wide, and her head swiveled toward me, "Ok," she said carefully. I could tell she was fighting not to deck Caitlin right there in the ice cream parlor. "I'm ready for the rest of the story now."

I sighed. "Caitlin is pregnant."

"Wonderful," Laura bit off. "I'll buy the cigars. Go on."

"The baby is Joey's," Caitlin said defiantly. "When I told him, he told me to get an abortion. And I would have too, if it hadn't been for Will."

"I see," said Laura. "And how exactly is Will involved?"

"I told you, we met at a party," I jumped in before things got out of hand.

"The night Joey was killed," Caitlin filled in helpfully.

Laura's eyebrows jumped. "And what were you doing at the party?"

"I went to see Joey. We had an argument. Caitlin and I started talking and...well...I offered to help."

"Help how?" Laura's eyes flashed between Caitlin and me. Caitlin finally seemed to grasp how dangerous Laura could be and had fallen silent, leaving me to answer her question. Aidan had suddenly found searching for Reese's Pieces in the bottom of his sundae completely engrossing. Killian was hanging on every word while Asher's head was still resting on the table. I wondered if he had fallen asleep and, if so, I was terribly envious. Gabe just looked as if someone had dropped him onto the set of a soap opera and failed to give him a script.

I knew I had to answer carefully or Laura would fly off the handle. Despite that knowledge I opened my mouth and horrified myself by saying, "I'm going to help raise the baby."

For an eternity no one around the table moved. Then in a flash Laura was on her feet and leaning across the table, "You're what?" she yelled.

The few other customers in the place looked over at us as if we were on drugs or something, and the owner looked at us suspiciously.

"Laura, sit down," Gabe hissed.

She sat, but it was obvious that what she really wanted to do involved beating me senseless with the napkin dispenser. "William Spencer Keegan," she seethed. Uh-oh, she was pulling out the full name. "What do you know about raising a baby?"

Suddenly I was mad, too. I leaned in toward her intensely, catching everyone by surprise, including myself. "I know just as much as any first-time father. I'm reading books so I can be prepared. I'm even going to go to Lamaze class with Caitlin, so do not give me a hard time about this, Laura. I've made up my mind, and it's really none of your damn business. I want to do this more

...in my entire life. Do you have any idea ... have left of Joey; this baby is a part ... e's become my friend, and I gave her ... g to be a part of this baby's life, and if ... t of mine."

lps. No one moved or even seemed to ... poke first, "You're right. It's your life, ... that even though I haven't been there ... d and I love you. For what it's worth, I ... ill be here for you, and I'll support you ... one..." Her voice broke, and she started ... ink I could bear to lose you, too."

... k Laura's hand. "It's worth a lot and I'm ... , and that makes it your business. Your

... . "I've never had any close friends, not ... ays there for each other, it really makes

Laura said with only a slight edge to her ... Vhen you get one of us, you get all of us.

... nd Asher even sat up, proving he was still ... ison.

... e we scared off any of the poor proprietor's

... ura asked as we walked onto the moonlit

... Joey's killer, we have to have some sort of plan," she said, sounding ... eacher explaining something to a particularly slow pupil.

"We don't know anything about finding a killer," Gabe said reasonably.

"No, but Killian and Asher caught a killer last year," I reminded them.

"We didn't exactly catch a killer," Asher said in a pained voice. "He more or less caught us and Killian just kinda blew him away."

"Oh," I said in a small voice. "We'll have to keep that in mind..."

"But we did do an investigation first," Killian said with a withering glance at Asher, who snorted.

"At least you've had some experience with this kind of thing," Laura said. "But that brings us back to my question, where do we start?"

"Well," said Killian slowly, "the obvious place to start would be to find out who would want to kill Joey."

"Everyone who knew him?" Caitlin said.

"He wasn't exactly Mr. Popularity the last month or so," I explained. "He was drinking a lot and sleeping around. Apparently he hurt a lot of people."

"We'll have to make a list and start talking to people. The more people you talk to the better. What about the necklace? Who could have sent it to Will?"

"I'm going to the delivery place tomorrow to see if I can find out," I volunteered.

"Oh, well, if that works, everything would be all tied up in a neat package, but I don't think we should count on that happening," Killian said. "The next logical thing would be to talk to people who were at the party when it happened. Like, who found him?"

"I don't know," I said, feeling incredibly stupid that I hadn't thought to ask that.

"I heard it was Blake Hammond," Gabe said.

"She's in one of my classes," Laura said. "I'll talk to her on Monday."

"Whose house was it at?" Killian asked next.

"David Kemp's," I answered quickly. I knew that one.

"He's in a couple of my classes. I can talk to him," Aidan suggested. "What do I ask him?"

"Ask if he saw anyone who shouldn't have been there," Laura said.

"Or if he saw anyone acting suspiciously," Gabe said.

"Half the people there were on E; everyone was acting suspiciously," Caitlin said.

"Ask if anyone knows about the necklace," I said. "Maybe he found it cleaning up."

"Also ask if he saw Joey go out to the pool," Gabe threw in.

"The police already asked everyone that. Nobody saw anything," I said.

"Somebody saw something," Gabe said meaningfully and pointed to the necklace around my neck.

"What if the killer sent you the necklace?" Killian said suddenly.

"Why would the killer send me the necklace?" I asked. "With a note that said it wasn't an accident? He was getting away scot-free; why draw attention to it?"

"Some killers want the attention. They secretly want to get caught. They hate the idea that they might not get credit for what they did," Aidan offered.

"But isn't that usually serial killers?" Gabe argued. "Killers who kill for the thrill?"

"How do you know that's not what we're dealing with?" Aidan countered.

"The MO doesn't fit the profile," Gabe shot back. I felt as if I were watching a tennis match. "Joey was drowned right?"

"As far as I know," I answered.

"We need to know for sure. You've got a contact at the police department, right?"

"I guess you could call it that," I said hesitantly, thinking of my last visit with Detective Grafton. I was beginning to feel like I had started something which I was quickly losing control of. Kind of like paddling a canoe into calm waters and suddenly finding yourself being sucked into white-water rapids.

"See if you can get a copy of the autopsy report," Gabe ordered.

"Can just anyone get one of those?" Aidan asked.

"I guess I'll find out," I said when no one seemed to know the answer.

Gabe shrugged. "If not, let me know. My cousin is a dispatcher there, but I'd rather not get her involved if I can help it."

"What about Shelley?" Laura asked suddenly.

"What about her?" I said.

"Shouldn't someone talk to her? I heard she was pretty pissed when Joey broke up with her."

"I can do that," Caitlin said brightly. "You know, one jilted ex to another. Hell hath no fury, et cetera, et cetera. We both share a common bond; we both hate Joey."

"Are there any other ex's?" Killian asked.

"I'll check," said Caitlin.

"Have we forgotten anything?" Gabe asked.

"Our good sense?" Asher offered.

"There is one more person," I said slowly.

"Who?" Killian and Gabe asked at the same time.

"Joey's mom," I said. "She may know something we don't."

"I'll talk to her," Laura said, and I released a breath I hadn't realized I'd been holding. I didn't think I could handle facing her grief again. "But do you think you could go with me, Will?"

I sighed. I knew it was too good to be true. "I guess."

"Do you think you could search Joey's room while you are there?" Killian asked.

"We can try," Laura said. "If all else fails, we can just offer to help pack up his stuff."

"I think that's enough to start with," Killian said.

"More than enough," Asher grumbled.

"Why doesn't everyone talk to the people you mentioned and we'll get back together in one week and share reports," Killian suggested, carefully ignoring Asher.

"Good idea," Gabe agreed. The two of them seemed to be sharing director duties. I figured it was only a matter of time before an argument broke out, but I would deal with that when and if the situation arose.

Killian stopped walking suddenly and held his hand out in front of him, palm down. Laura realized what he was doing first and placed her hand on top of his. I smiled and added mine to the growing pile. Then Gabe, Aidan, and Caitlin added theirs. After a moment's hesitation, Asher heaved a monumental sigh and slapped his hand on top on the pile.

"Remember," Killian said, "we're a team, and teams work together. No hot-dogging or taking unnecessary risks. We're not necessarily going after the killer. The first proof that we get that Joey was killed we go straight to the police, agreed?"

"Agreed," we all said together.

"Then let's get this son-of-a-bitch!"

Our huddle dissolved into a round of hugs and good-byes as we slowly and reluctantly went our separate ways. No one seemed to want to leave the comfort and protection of our little group. I suddenly understood the pack mentality, the allure of gangs. There was an instinctive internal feeling of safety in numbers and alone we felt vulnerable. Joey had been alone when he went out to the pool that night. I wondered if he had felt vulnerable. I hoped he never even knew what hit him, literally.

Chapter 14

Having a real plan and knowing my friends were behind me filled me with a sense of purpose and renewed energy. Now that the show was out of the way, I felt like I could really focus on the feeling that I had nagging me ever since the necklace arrived. Something wasn't right about Joey's death, and I was determined to find out what.

The first thing I did the next morning was run by the delivery service again. An older lady with bright blue eyes and a cloud of snowy white hair was working behind the counter.

"Hello, can I help you?" she said with a cheery smile. Her nametag read "Edna".

"I hope so, Edna," I said, with a smile of my own. I had intended to shoot straight and hope for the best, but now that I stood before this grandmotherly woman, I decided a more tactful approach might work better. I decided to improvise. "An old friend sent me a present last Saturday, and I'd like to send her a thank you card, but the thing is, we've lost track of each other and I don't even know her married name now. She only signed her first name on the card. Do you think you could help me?"

"Well, I'm really sorry, but I'm not sure how I could possibly help," she said with a very phony look of disappointment. She could really stand a few acting classes if she was going to try that look often. I wasn't at all convinced that she was sorry. "We don't release that kind of information."

"Oh, well...thanks anyway," I said as I turned to leave. My look of disappointment was not feigned.

"Unless..." she said slowly.

I forced myself to slowly turn back around. I didn't want to appear too eager. I was beginning to get the impression I was dealing with a very sadistic grandma. "Unless?"

"I suppose if I just happened to have the information pulled up on the screen and had to go into the back room for a few minutes I couldn't help it if you looked at the screen."

I blinked in surprise. This was one weird old lady.

"What's your name?" she asked me.

"Will Keegan," I told her.

She hit a few keys on the keyboard, then looked up at me slyly and...was I mistaken or did she just wink at me? She turned and walked into the back room without another word. I stared after her for a second trying to decide if this was real or if it was possible that I was on Candid Camera. I shook my head with a sigh and leaned over the counter so I could see the computer screen. I was at the wrong angle, hampered by a glare from the overhead lighting. I leaned farther onto the counter.

"Caught you!" the old bat hollered as she jumped back through the door. I jumped back with a yelp, almost falling backwards onto my bottom, as she cackled merrily. "I'm just kidding. This job gets pretty boring, you know?"

I decided I was dealing with an escapee from the insane asylum and started edging my way toward the door. I didn't want to turn my back on her again.

"Did you get what you needed?" she asked me.

"No, but don't worry about it," I said in a soothing voice.

"Nonsense, you've gone to this much trouble you can't stop now. Here, the name is Joey Taylor. Does that sound right?"

I froze. No, it didn't sound right at all. "That's impossible. Joey died a week before that was sent," I said when I found my voice.

Edna's eyes widened. "Well, someone used his name to order the delivery."

"Do you remember what they looked like?"

"No, I'm sorry; I really don't."

"Was it a man or a woman?" I asked desperately.

"I don't remember; after a while they all just blur together. Sorry I couldn't be more help."

"Me, too," I mumbled under my breath as I left. I hoped the others would make out better with their assignments.

It was Monday before I got to my next assignment, trying to get the medical examiner's report from Detective Grafton. After waiting in the lobby for so long that I was beginning to get afraid that I'd be drawing Social Security before I left, the detective finally made time to see me.

"Back again?" he said in way of greeting after I'd been let into his office by the dispatcher. Once again, Detective Bernhardt was not in the office. I sat down without being invited.

"Um, yeah. How is Detective Bernhardt?" Small talk did not seem like the best course of action when dealing with Grafton, but I wasn't sure exactly how to ask for the report. Was there a protocol involved?

Grafton's eyebrows inverted themselves into a "V" as he frowned intensely at me. I started to point out that he was going to give himself even more wrinkles, but wisely refrained.

"Detective Bernhardt is fine, thank you for asking," he said shortly.

"It's just that she hasn't been here the last couple times I've come."

"I'm sure if you called ahead she'd drop all her work and wait here for you."

I blinked, not sure what to say to that. I didn't have to worry; he took the reins of the conversation.

"What exactly are you doing here, kid? If you came to chitchat, I've got more important things to do. If you have a point, which I somehow doubt, then let's get to it."

I bristled under his rudeness, but decided to ask for what I'd come for. "Can I get a copy of the medical examiner's report for Joey Taylor's death?"

That seemed to catch him by surprise.

"What?"

"Can I get a copy of..."

"I heard what you said. Why in God's name would you want that?"

I didn't have an answer ready for that either, but again, he didn't really seem to expect one.

"Never mind, it doesn't really matter why you want it, and besides, I can guess. You still think the Taylor kid was murdered, and you've decided to play detective. Look, kid, this isn't a game of let's-make-pretend. We've told you, your friend had too much to drink, fell into the pool, and drowned. A tragic accident, but that's all it was. You have to move on. This isn't healthy."

It was thoughtful of him to be so concerned for my well-being, but he hadn't really answered my question. "About that report..."

"Didn't you just hear me?" He waved away any response. I had a feeling he wouldn't have heard me anyway. "Look, ME's reports aren't public knowledge, kid. You can't just waltz in and ask for a copy." He heaved a gigantic sigh. "I'm going to tell you one more time, and I hope you listen this time; it was an accident. Go back to your life. Forget about this little fantasy of yours."

"I wish I could forget about it, but I can't. I don't think it was just an accident, and I intend to find out who killed him, with or without your help."

I stood up, turned on my heel, and stalked angrily out of the room. So far, I was 0 for 2. I wasn't getting very far with my investigation.

Laura called me later that night and said that Joey's mom had gone home with one of her sisters for the week and we'd have to put off our visit until she got back. I wasn't too broken-hearted.

All in all, I had precious little to offer at our meeting Friday night. It was a small comfort to learn that I wasn't the only one. Everyone gathered in our apartment around a couple of extra-large pizzas. Killian and Asher were there, although I sensed some tension between the two of them. I had a feeling that their presence was not exactly a mutual decision. After everyone had scarfed down their first slice of pizza, Killian called the meeting to order.

"We've had a week to start looking into things," he said around a mouthful of hot cheese and pepperoni. "Has anybody come up with anything?"

Nobody jumped to answer.

"Will?" he asked. I told them about my disappointing run-ins with the psycho at the delivery office and Detective Grafton.

With my failures out in the open, it seemed to break the ice for everyone else to share theirs. Aidan reported that David Kemp had been so high he didn't even remember the police arriving, let alone if there had been anyone suspicious hanging around. A bull elephant could have gone on a rampage in his living room and he wouldn't have noticed. Needless to say, he didn't know anything about the necklace either.

Caitlin said that all Joey's exes had said pretty much the same thing: he was a jerk, and they weren't exactly choked up over his death. Only Shelley had been at the party, though, and she claimed she had an alibi; she had been with her new boyfriend, David Kemp. Since we had already established that

David didn't even know if he'd been at the party, the alibi wasn't really all that strong so we didn't cross her off the list. Then again, that may also have had something to do with the fact that we didn't really have a list.

Laura hadn't had a chance to talk to Blake yet. Since none of us was having much success with our interviews, Killian suggested we team up for future assignations. The idea was that if one person froze up or didn't know what to ask, hopefully the other person could step in and pick up the slack.

"It's important that we talk to this Blake as soon as possible," Killian said. "Now that we know the package is a dead end, she's our main hope. If she saw something, anything, then we've got somewhere to head toward; otherwise, we've got nothing."

"If you ask me, that's exactly what we've got," Asher said. It was the first thing he'd said since he and Killian had arrived, and it earned him a warning look from Killian.

"It's early yet," Gabe said. "We've barely gotten started."

"We've barely gotten started, and it's already almost a month since he was killed," Caitlin pointed out. "Talk about a cold trail. Why are we even doing this?"

"Because he was our friend and we loved him," Laura snapped. "Maybe you don't give a damn about him, but we do. What are you even doing here?"

"I thought I was one of the gang now. Isn't that what you said?"

Laura's eyes flashed, and I could tell a major catfight was brewing, but before I could step in to dispel it, Killian did the job for me.

"Gabe's right, it's too early to know how things are going to go just yet. There are still several avenues to explore. What about Joey's mom?"

"She's out of town," Laura grudgingly. "Will and I will see her as soon as she gets back."

"So what do we do next?" I asked dejectedly. "It seems like we keep hitting a brick wall."

"Give up?" Asher said hopefully.

"It's way too early to give up," Gabe said. "Didn't you just hear us? We haven't talked to Blake yet or Joey's mom...and we still don't have the medical examiner's report. Let me try to get it; it seems to me it should be a matter of public record. Maybe that detective just didn't want you to be playing cops and robbers."

"You mean like we are doing?" Asher asked innocently.

Killian shot him another dirty look.

"Why is this report so important?" Caitlin asked.

"It might...tell us...something we don't know," Gabe finished lamely.

"That wouldn't be hard," Aidan said, which gained him a dirty look from Laura this time.

"I mean, it might show if he had head trauma," Gabe said defensively.

"What would that tell us?" I asked.

"That maybe someone hit Joey over the head before he fell in the pool."

"But wouldn't the cops have noticed that?" Aidan argued.

"They might have assumed it happened when he fell in."

"And how would we know it didn't?"

"We wouldn't," Gabe said through clenched teeth, "but it would at least be a possibility."

"Why don't I go with Laura when she goes to talk to Blake?" I asked, as much to change the subject as anything. "We can ask her about the necklace, too."

"How about if I take a look at David's back yard while I'm at it? You know, to get a feel for the layout of things," Gabe offered. "I know him pretty well. He's a major pothead, so I'll just act like I'm trying to score a little weed."

"Good idea!" Killian enthused. "It sounds like everyone knows what they are doing; let's meet back here again one week from tonight."

With all the tension in the air, everyone quickly cleared out of the apartment. Killian and Asher were the last to leave, and on their way out, I overheard Killian say to Asher, "Are you happy? I'm letting them do all the footwork and we're staying out of it."

To which Asher replied, "I'd be happy if we weren't involved at all."

I hoped my asking them to get involved wouldn't develop into a major rift in their relationship. I would never forgive myself if that happened.

When I arrived at work the next morning, Nikki was waiting. "The reviews come out tomorrow," she announced.

"Don't you ever say hello?" I said grouchily. I hadn't slept very well the night before.

"It's a waste of time and breath. Why not just go right to the important stuff?"

"Did you get any advance copies of the reviews?" I asked her.

"You know," she said absently, as if I hadn't even asked her a question, "you'd better get some more paintings done pronto so we can get them up in here."

I wondered if she was purposefully avoiding my question and, if so, what that meant. Were the reviews so bad she didn't want to tell me?

"You know, you've never even asked me how much money you made," she said suddenly.

I blushed. I'd thought about it, of course, but felt it would be rude to ask. Nikki laughed when I told her that.

"You're going to have to get over that attitude fast, buster. Pushy has to be an artist's middle name, or you'll get walked all over. People are sharks in this business. Do you want to know now?"

"Yes, please."

"Pushy!"

"Uh...yes, tell me."

"Pushier!"

"Er...um...tell me now, wench!"

She burst into laughter. "Ok, that was a little much. You definitely need some assertiveness training. Now, about the sales...maybe you'd better sit down."

"Why? Is the news that bad?"

"You decide. I priced your paintings between $300 and $500. After my commission that means you pulled down about $6,000."

Maybe I should have sat down. I stood staring dumbly with my mouth hanging open.

"Better shut that thing before you swallow a fly," she said with a grin. "Not bad for a month's work, huh? Of course, you can't do that every month. You can only pull off a show like that once or twice a year. The good news, though, is that at your next show your prices will start at $500 and go up from there. We've set a benchmark, and it only goes up."

"I've never had that much money at one time before," I managed finally.

"Don't go buy yourself a mansion just yet, Richie Rich. It's not as much as it sounds like, especially if that was all you had to live on. The term starving artist was coined for a reason, you know. If, and it's a big if, you become well-known and your prices soar, you might become rich being an artist, but those cases are few and far between. The reviews will have a lot to do with your immediate future, but even if they aren't favorable don't get discouraged. Many successful artists had terrible critical reviews when they were first starting out. Even a bad review can be good if it stirs enough interest."

I again wondered if she was subtly trying to tell me to expect bad reviews. I didn't get a chance to ask her, though, because an older couple came in at that moment looking for a painting for their living room. Something preferably with green and gold in it, the lady said. By the time Nikki had wound down from her lecture on how art should not be bought to complement the décor, the whole matter of the reviews had slipped my mind. The couple left eventually with slightly stunned expressions and a painting tucked carefully under the gentleman's arm.

Just before closing, Laura swept through the door.

"What are you doing here?" I asked.

"Nice to see you, too," she said dryly. "I came to pick you up. Mrs. Taylor is home and she feels up for a visit."

"I don't know if I feel up for a visit," I said weakly, but I knew it was futile to argue with Laura. I went and told Nikki that I was leaving, and we set off for Joey's house in Laura's little red Camry.

"Let me do the talking," Laura said as we pulled into the driveway.

"Great, how about if I just stay in the car then?"

"Oh, for God's sake, Will! Get some balls! Why are you so scared about seeing Mrs. Taylor again?"

"I just don't like dealing with other people's grief," I said. "It's too...real. It almost overwhelms me."

Laura sighed and opened her door. "Come on, Dionne, and bring your psychic friends with you."

"Very funny," I grumbled as I followed her up to the front door.

Mrs. Taylor answered looking about ten years older than the last time I had seen her. Her hair was a mess and dark circles surrounded her eyes, making her look rather like a rumpled raccoon.

"Come on in," she said. "I'm sorry the house is such a mess. I was out of town, and then, well I just haven't felt like doing anything since I got back."

"It's fine, Mrs. Taylor," Laura said soothingly. "We're not worried about the house."

We settled in the living room, which still had plastic cups and saucers scattered about the room from the day of the funeral. After some initial small talk and general remembrances, Laura brought up the purpose of our visit.

"Mrs. Taylor, we're trying to get a better picture of what was going on in Joey's life just before this happened. He seemed...different, somehow, and we feel we need to know why so we can move on."

Mrs. Taylor nodded. "He was different, that's for sure. I don't really know what was going on with him."

"Did anything unusual happen in the last few months?"

"No, not really. Well...except...he did get very interested in his father. He wanted to find him."

Laura could barely contain her excitement. "And did he?"

"Not that I know of. I discouraged him, of course. He dropped it after a while."

"Mrs. Taylor, would you mind if we took a look around Joey's room?"

She thought for a moment. "Well, I don't guess it matters much now, does it?" she said at last. "Go ahead."

She followed us to the door but didn't come into the room. Laura and I stood awkwardly in the middle of the room. Neither of us had much experience searching a room, let alone with someone watching us. After a few seconds, Mrs. Taylor turned and walked away, taking with her the weight of her sadness. I almost gasped with relief. As soon as she was gone, Laura pounced on the small desk that sat by the bed.

"I feel weird going through Joey's stuff," I said.

"It's not like he's going to care," Laura said as she sifted through a pile of papers.

"Still...it just feels weird."

"We're his best friends. You know he wouldn't care."

"Maybe there was a time when he wouldn't have cared, but toward the end..."

"Oh! What's this?" she said suddenly as she straightened up.

"What's what?"

"It looks like a letter."

"Lemme see."

Laura held it behind her back. "No, you feel weird going through Joey's stuff, remember?"

"Oh, grow up, Laura," I growled. She grinned and produced the page. I read over her shoulder as we both scanned the sprawling handwriting.

"I think we just hit the jackpot," she breathed.

It was a letter from Joey's dad.

> *Dear Son,*
> *How's my little slugger? Not so little anymore, huh? I can't tell you how much it meant to get a letter from you after all these years. I know I've missed so much. I would very much like to make it up to you if you would give me a chance. How about if you meet me at my boat at the marina this weekend and we can catch up? Hope to see you then.*
> *Your Old Man.*

"Do you think he went?" I asked.

"I don't know. It's dated October 28th. That would have been the weekend before he was killed."

"What's his name? Is there an envelope?"

"I didn't see one."

We searched the rest of the desk's contents and the rest of the room as well, but didn't find anything more.

"Should we ask Mrs. Taylor what her husband's name was?" I asked.

"I don't know," Laura said thoughtfully. "It might just upset her to know that Joey went behind her back and found his dad against her wishes."

"So how do we find him? I guess we can assume he's a Mr. Taylor, but that's a pretty common last name. That doesn't exactly narrow it down."

"But how many own boats docked at the marina?"

"Good point," I said. "We can go down there and ask around."

"I can't do it now," Laura said. "This took longer than I thought it would, and I'm meeting Gabe for dinner. Maybe you and Aidan can do it tomorrow."

"I can go by myself."

"I don't think you should go by yourself; you don't know what this guy is like. Maybe he's the one who killed Joey. Besides, Killian said we should do things in pairs." Her eyes narrowed with an evil glint, and I knew she was getting ready to say something she thought would irk me. "Why don't you want to go with Aidan? He is your boyfriend, isn't he?"

Even though I knew she was trying to draw me in, I couldn't help myself. "He's not my boyfriend!" I exclaimed. "We're just friends."

"Uh huh, if you say so."

"I do say so! We're friends and that's it."

"Ok, whatever you say."

"Laura, we are not boyfriends!"

"I'm not arguing. Who exactly are you trying to convince?"

I sputtered impotently for a few seconds as a small, satisfied smile played at Laura's lips. "Are we done here?" she asked, nonchalantly.

"Yes, I think we are definitely done here." I was steaming.

I followed Laura out of Joey's old room and back into the living room, where we thanked Mrs. Taylor and left. I seethed over Laura's crack about Aidan and me all the way back to my car. I wasn't interested in Aidan in that way...was I? I pushed it out of my mind; I couldn't even think about that right now. I had more important things to worry about, like who killed Joey.

"Do you really think Joey's dad might have killed him?" I said when she pulled up next to my car in the plaza parking lot. "I mean killing your own son?"

"It's happened before. We don't know anything about this guy. For all we know he's been in prison for murder for the past fifteen years. We'll know more after you and Aidan track him down. For now, I'd definitely say he's a suspect."

"Ok, I guess you're right. I'll see you later, Laurie-bell," I said, using her childhood nickname as I got out of the car. "Oh...and I'm not interested in Aidan in that way."

She grinned knowingly. "Methinks thou dost protest too much." And with that, she reached over, slammed the door, and drove quickly away, leaving me fuming in the parking lot.

Chapter 15

The next morning I awoke to the sound of pounding coming from the front door. I stumbled out of my room and into the hall where I met a sleepy Aidan, looking as startled as I felt.

"Who would be knocking on our door at six a.m.?" he asked accusingly, as if it were somehow my fault.

"Knocking? I think it would be more accurately described as banging...no pounding, or maybe beating..." I grumbled as I padded off down the hall barefoot. To my surprise and embarrassment, since I was still in nothing but my boxers that I was sleeping in, I found Nikki on the other side of the door. She looked disgustingly chipper for that ungodly hour. She swept by waving something in her hand.

"Oh, good!" she said when she spied Aidan blinking in confusion at finding her in our apartment with no apparent emergency. "You're up, too! Great! Come on out."

"I wasn't up until someone woke me out of a very nice dream," he said acidly.

Nikki narrowed her eyes at me. "You woke Aidan up?"

I sighed and decided it was too early to even attempt to answer that. I tried to focus my sleep-clouded eyes on the object she was still waving around. It looked like a rolled newspaper or maybe a magazine. "I'm going to go put some clothes on," I said.

"Take a look at this first," she said, and then to Aidan, "And while you're up, you look, too. The reviews are in!" She tossed the bundle onto the table with a flourish. The newspaper unrolled sending a magazine sliding off the table where it landed at my feet.

"We need a new paperboy," Aidan said as he came over to the table.

I snatched the magazine up. It was the *Mid-Atlantic Monthly Art Journal*. The glossy cover featured an idyllic scene of a lighthouse.

"Turn to page forty-eight," Nikki ordered me as she began flipping through the newspaper.

I did as she had said and scanned the text for my name. It jumped out at me from the second column under the heading New Talent. I began to read out loud.

"'Promising New Artist Debuts in Maryland,'" I read. "'Avant Guard, the internationally renowned art gallery founded by Giovanni Avanti and now managed by his sole heirs, Derrick and Nikolia Avanti, recently played host to a delightful new artist by the name of Will Keegan.' That's me!"

"Duh! Keep reading," Aidan said.

"'Keegan, only eighteen and still very obviously in the early stages of his career, shows great promise for the art world. His watercolor paintings of old buildings are reminiscent of Andrew Wyeth, though without much of the soul and depth that is so evident in Wyeth's work.' I'm soulless?" I asked with a frown.

"It comes with age and experience. Keep reading," Nikki said.

"'It's his more interpretive pieces, some bordering on surrealism, which truly capture the imagination, however. They show a complex and sometimes tortured inner being. Over all, the twenty paintings on display were an impressive first showing for a talented and charming young man.' I'm charming?"

"Keep reading!" Nikki and Aidan said in unison.

"Jeez! 'With his candid and unique views of the world around him, Keegan is a welcome addition to the art community. Look for great things to come from this artist's brush.'"

"Is that it?" Aidan asked. I was beginning to think he wasn't a morning person.

"It? That's wonderful!" Nikki crowed. "They gave you a glowing review! And they mentioned the gallery. We couldn't have bought that kind of publicity."

"They said I was soulless," I whined.

"Who cares? It's a critic; they have to say things like that. Look, your picture is in the paper."

Aidan and I both bent over the table to see where her finger was pointing, bonking noggins in the process. Rubbing our heads, we moved in more carefully a second time. Sure enough, there I was, in all my flashy leather glory with Caitlin hanging on my arm looking for all the world like a Hollywood starlet. Aidan looked at it for a moment, then walked away and turned on the TV. I decided not to let his attitude ruin this moment for me. I read the short article that accompanied the photo, but it didn't really say anything; it was just a blurb in the Lifestyle section, but it was still exciting. I couldn't help but be a little disappointed that Aidan wasn't sharing this moment with me.

"Well, I'd better get back to the apartment," Nikki said. "I left Sam asleep in bed. I don't want him to wake up and find me missing. Will, take the day off and celebrate the good reviews." I got the impression that she was picking up on Aidan's strange behavior and was tactfully giving us a chance to talk. She waggled her fingers in our direction and let herself out.

"Sure, she let him sleep," Aidan said as he pushed himself up off the sofa. "I'm going back to bed."

"Aren't you even the slightest bit happy for me?" I asked. I sounded peevish, even to myself, but I just didn't understand his attitude.

He sighed. "Oh yeah, I'm thrilled for you and your fiancée."

"My what? What are you talking about?"

"Your fiancée? Caitlin?" he said.

"Caitlin?"

"They spilled the beans in the caption there, lover boy," he called as he disappeared down the hall.

"What caption?" I yelled, but his door had closed, cutting off any further attempt on my part to find out what was eating him.

I bent over the newspaper article again and found the caption under the photo of Caitlin and me. I had missed it earlier in my rush to read the article. "Keegan and fiancée Caitlin Stewart talk to Mr. & Mrs. Edward Curran of Baltimore," it read. It was so ridiculous I almost laughed out loud. Obviously, Aidan hadn't found it so amusing. I hurried down the hall to his room and knocked. No answer, so I pushed it open. He was lying on the bed with his back toward me, on top of the blankets.

"Aidan, you don't actually think Caitlin and I are getting married, do you?"

"Why not?" he asked without moving. "You're raising the baby, the other night you called yourself a first-time father, you're always talking about Caitlin this and Caitlin that...why not get married? You're so obsessed with this baby that I think you'd do whatever you had to do to make sure you're a part of its life."

I stared at him in slack-jawed amazement. Where was all this coming from? "I...I thought you supported me."

"I tried, Will. I really did. It's just..." He sounded like he was crying. Suddenly things fell into place.

"You're jealous of Caitlin and the baby," I said aloud as the realization jolted through my brain.

"Of course I'm jealous, you idiot!" he yelled as he rolled over to face me. "I'm in love with you! Can't you see that?"

"I...you're...wha?"

"I told you that, the night we made love. I told you I loved you. That wasn't just pillow talk. I meant it." He stood up and walked to the window. "I've done everything I can think of, tried every way I could think of to show you that I loved you. I've been there for you every time you've needed me — when you needed someone to talk to or a shoulder to cry on because Joey had hurt you in some way. I was there when Joey died. I was there when you decided to go ahead with this crazy idea to raise Joey's baby. I was there when you came up with this even crazier idea to catch Joey's killer. I'm always there. And what have I accomplished? Nothing. I'm still just good ol' buddy, Aidan."

He stopped and took a shaky breath and turned to face me. I was speechless. "And you know what?" he went on after a moment. "I'd do it all again; I'd have my heart broken again, because I love you. But just once...just once, I'd like...no, I need — I need to know it matters. That I'm not just pissing in the wind here."

He collapsed onto the edge of the bed and buried his face in his hands. I walked over to him and knelt down in front of him. I reached up and gently took his hands in mine.

"It does matter," I said softly. "Aidan, I'm so, so very sorry. I don't know what I would do without you. I'd be dead if it wasn't for you. I...I've taken you for granted, and I'm sorry. You always seem so strong. You're always the rock I lean on, and sometimes cling to, and it just never even occurred to me that maybe you needed someone to lean on, too. I owe you so much; I owe you my life. You're my best friend."

"But you don't love me." It was a statement, not a question, but I answered it anyway.

"I...I don't know..."

Aidan pulled his hands from mine. "Then that says everything, doesn't it?"

"Aidan..."

"Save it, Will," he said without anger, just resignation. "I'll be ok. I always am." He walked out of the room and into the bathroom, shutting the door behind him. It wasn't long before I heard the shower come on.

I sat down wearily on the edge of the bed, where Aidan had been moments before. I *had* taken Aidan for granted; that was very clear now. I was so busy chasing after Joey and then memories of Joey that I had never taken the time to see what was happening right under my nose. How many times had I thoughtlessly slipped a knife into Aidan's heart and not even noticed? I didn't even want to think about it; it was too many by far.

And now...was it too late? I still wasn't sure how I felt about him, but I knew I had grown to love him very deeply. I had just taken it for granted that he'd be there when I got home. I'd taken it for granted that he'd be there when I needed a pair of strong arms to comfort and hold me while I cried. I'd taken it for granted that he'd always be there to support and encourage me with no support and encouragement from me. I'd taken so much for granted. Had I lost him now because of my neglect? The very thought filled me with such a sense of loss and grief that it felt as if my heart would explode.

I was still sitting on the bed when Aidan came back in, water dripping from his hair and a towel gripped around his waist. He seemed surprised to find me still in his room.

I looked up at him and suddenly felt the tears that had been threatening to spill over and roll down my cheeks. "I do love you," I whispered.

Aidan squeezed his eyes shut for a moment and then opened them again. The pain in his eyes was so raw, so naked, that it almost took my breath away.

"Not again, Will," he pleaded hoarsely. "Don't do this to me again."

"Do what?"

"Don't make me open up my heart like this only to have it slammed in my face. I can't keep doing this."

"I won't...I...I love you."

Tears streamed down his face, and he didn't even bother to wipe them. "No, it'll always be something: Joey, Caitlin, the baby. They'll always come first."

"No!" I cried, desperate to make him understand what I suddenly knew with all my heart. "Listen to me. Maybe I'll always love Joey, some part of me. And yes, I have made a commitment to Caitlin and this baby, but now I want to make a commitment to you."

"And what if Joey walked through the door right now and said he loved you?" Anguish filled his voice, making it sound foreign, as if it didn't really belong to him.

"Joey's dead," I sobbed.

"WHAT IF?" he screamed. Then he began to sob, too. "What if?"

I cried for a moment, then managed to find my voice long enough to say, "If Joey was here right now I'd tell him...I'd tell him that...that it's too late now. I'd tell him that I gave him my heart once, totally and completely. And he took it and smashed it to a thousand pieces. But someone else came along, and he started piecing all the little parts back together. And even when it seemed like the pieces would never fit together and that some pieces must have been lost forever, he didn't give up. And when it was as good as it would ever be, he gave it back to me, even though he longed to keep it. It was only when I got it back that I realized that it really did belong to that person after all, and I very much wanted him to have it. Will you take it back, Aidan? Can I give you my heart?"

He stood deathly still for an eternity. Not a muscle twitched; he looked as if he had been turned into a statue. Then slowly his lips began to move, although no sound escaped them. Then finally, "Do you mean that?"

I held my hand out to him and nodded, "I love you, Aidan."

He took a hesitant step forward, then another. I reached my arms around his waist and pulled him close, resting my face against his stomach. I slowly ran my hands up his back and then back down again. I kissed his chest and then his belly. He let out a low whimper as I loosened the towel, and it fell to the floor. Then I slowly lay back, pulling him down with me.

The first time hadn't been a fluke...the fireworks were still there.

I awoke a few hours later, his arms around me, my legs tangled with his. There were no misgivings this time, only a sense that everything was just as it was supposed to be. I inhaled deeply, savoring the sweet, musky scent that was left from our lovemaking. I twisted around so I could see his face. My stirring woke him, and his eyes fluttered open. I smiled and kissed him softly on the lips.

"It wasn't a dream," he whispered in an awed voice.

"No, it's for real," I said softly. "I love you, Aidan Scott."

A patented Aidan original grin spread slowly across his face and I realized how long it had been since I'd seen one. "And I love you, Will Keegan."

We kissed again; this time neither of us was in any hurry to end it. We were working our way toward another fireworks display when the phone started ringing.

"Mmm...let it ring," Aidan said.

"It might be important," I said. I never could ignore a ringing phone.

"Then they'll call back," his lips started down my neck, and I forgot what I was arguing about.

The ringing stopped, only to start again a few seconds later. I sat up. "It must be important."

Aidan sighed. "Fine, but I'll answer it. You don't move." He stood up, then bent over me for one more quick kiss before running off to find the phone.

Aidan walked back in while he talked on the phone. I took the opportunity to drink him in. His body was so perfect it was almost too beautiful. He
looked like Michelangelo's David come to life. His gently curling dark blond
hair framed a chiseled face and those beautiful, intensely green eyes. Under
them was a straight, even nose that led directly to those full, incredibly kiss-
able lips. His chest and arms were muscled without being huge and his stomach was hard and smooth. All that working out had obviously paid off. I was
suddenly filled with two warring emotions — a sense of love and desire like I
had never felt before and a deep shame at the way I had treated the one person
who had loved me through the hardest times of my life.

Aidan held out the phone, interrupting my thoughts. I hadn't been paying attention to his side of the conversation, so I really had no idea who he was
talking to or why they had called. Aidan read the confusion on my face.

"It's Laura," he said. "She wants to go talk to Blake."

I took the phone. "Hello?"

"Will?" Laura said. "What's going on? I didn't think you were ever going
to answer. I called the gallery, and Nikki said you had the day off. You weren't
still asleep, were you?"

"No, we weren't asleep," I said carefully.

"Well, anyway, I was going to see if you wanted to talk to Blake after
work, but since you're off how about going now?"

"Now?"

"Yes, as in right now."

"I can't go now."

"Why not? You have the day off, what do you have to do that so important?"

"Nothing, it's just..."

"Great, then we can go."

"Now isn't a good time."

"Then when?"

"I don't know."

"For God's sake, Will! Do you want to do this or not? I thought you
wanted to find Joey's killer."

"I do!"

"Then act like it. You know we need to talk to Blake. Killian even said it
could be really important."

"You should go," Aidan said softly into my ear. He'd been lying next to
me the whole time, lazily trailing his fingers across my chest.

I covered the mouthpiece of the phone with my hand. "What about us?"

"We're great, don't you think?" he said with a grin. "Besides, I'll go with
you. I'm free; I slept through my only class I had today. I'll follow wherever
you lead, oh, fearless leader."

I stuck my tongue out at him and sighed. It was obvious the water was
moving too fast for me to swim upstream; I might as well go with the flow. If
Aidan was offering to go with me, there was no point in arguing. I spoke back
into the phone, "Ok, let's do it."

"Great! How soon can you meet me at the dorms?"

"I don't even know where the dorms are."

"I do," said Aidan.

"Give us a couple hours," I said.

"Great." I could hear the triumph in her voice. "I'll see you then. Oh, and Will...are you and Aidan..."

She left the question unasked, but I knew what she was after. With a malicious smile playing on my lips, I said, "Bye Laura," and hit the end button disconnecting the line. Revenge was sweet, and I knew the best torture for Laura was unsatisfied curiosity.

I dropped the phone off the side of the bed and turned toward Aidan. His arms wrapped around me.

"A couple hours, huh? That should be enough time. Shall we pick up where we left off?"

He didn't have to ask twice.

Chapter 16

We were late meeting Laura. She was sitting on the curb waiting for us when we got there. She eyed Aidan with suspicion as we approached.

"He came along to help," I said before she could ask.

"At least you're here," she said grumpily. "What took you so long?"

"We were, uh...in the middle of something when you called," Aidan said with a wide grin. I couldn't hold back one of my own even as I felt my face flush. Laura looked back and forth between us for a second, then her eyes slowly grew wide.

"Oh, my God!" she exclaimed. "You two are together, aren't you?"

I blushed even harder, and Aidan just nodded happily.

"When did this happen?"

"This morning," I mumbled.

"And again this afternoon," Aidan added with a snicker. My face became even hotter, and I briefly feared it might burst into flame.

"Oh, God! I did not need to know that," Laura said with a slightly stunned expression on her face. For a moment, I wondered if Aidan had gone too far, but suddenly she grabbed us both in a ferocious hug that removed all doubt. "I'm so happy for you guys." Her voice left no doubt that she meant what she was saying.

I got a little misty eyed for a second as she pulled back. Aidan just kept on grinning.

"Ok, enough mush," Laura said briskly. "Wipe that grin off your face, Aidan. As long as you're here we might as well get to work."

"Yes, sir!" Aidan said, snapping to attention.

I giggled, and Laura rewarded me with a scathing glare. The emotional moment was over. I made an effort to become more serious. "So what's the plan?" I asked, trying to redeem myself.

"Why do we need a plan? We're just going to talk to Blake."

"All three of us?"

"Well, I didn't know Aidan was coming, did I?"

"If we all show up, she might feel as if we're ganging up on her."

"Good point."

"And do we know for a fact that she's in her room?"

"No," Laura admitted reluctantly.

"I think we need a plan," Aidan said, earning him a glare of his very own.

"Then come up with one," she growled.

"Ok, well, first we need to know if she's in her room. Why don't you call up and see?"

I could tell Laura resented Aidan taking over as the unspoken leader of the group, but the logic of his suggestion was obvious, so without a word she stalked over to the call box. She found Blake's room code and dialed it in. A female voice quickly answered.

"Is Blake there?" Laura asked.

"No, she's in class," the girl responded.

Laura looked at us questioningly. I shrugged.

"Um, ok, thanks," Laura said awkwardly.

"You want to leave a message?" Blake's roommate asked.

"No, that's ok. Thanks anyway."

"No problem."

"Ok, now what?" Laura said after she had disconnected.

We stood for a minute, staring at each other in silence.

"I'm fresh out of ideas," Aidan admitted at last.

"We could search her room," I suggested.

They both stared at me as if I'd just grown a second head.

"Search her room?" Laura repeated.

"Yeah, to see if..."

"If what? To see if she spray-painted a confession on the wall?"

"Maybe we should search her room," Aidan said, coming to my rescue. "It can't hurt. Maybe we'll get lucky."

"What would we even be looking for?" Laura continued to argue.

"Well, like when we searched Joey's room, you said to look for anything out of the ordinary."

"How do I know what's ordinary for this girl? I hardly even know her. At least I knew Joey."

She had a point.

"Maybe her roommate can help," Aidan suggested. "She sounded nice."

"We could talk to her," Laura conceded. "Blake might have confided in her."

"So do we just march up and knock on the door?" I asked.

"We need a plan," Aidan said with spirit.

"Here's a plan, you dork," Laura said. "You distract the roommate with questions, and Will and I'll look around discreetly."

"I thought you didn't want to search the room," he pointed out.

"Will you quit making everything so difficult?" she snapped.

"Why am I distracting her? Why can't Will?"

"Because I said so, and that's the plan."

"How am I supposed to distract her?"

"You're a cute guy, she's a female...you'll think of something. Improvise."

"I'm not exactly an expert on guy/girl dynamics."

"Wing it, Romeo."

"If he's Romeo, does that make me Juliet?" I asked. "I want to be Romeo."

"You're the one with a thing for balconies."

"Ouch," I swung my cast at her head, and she ducked.

"So I'm the distraction while you two get to do the fun part. What would you have done if I hadn't come? After all I wasn't even invited to this party to begin with."

"I would have made do with what we had. A good leader makes use of the resources available to her."

"Ok, that's what a good leader does, but what do you do?"

"Ha-ha. Are we going to stand here trading snappy one-liners, or are we going to do what we came here to do? Now come on, we don't have all day."

We took the stairs up to the floor Blake lived on and found her room number.

"Ok," Laura whispered, once again taking charge. "Aidan, you knock on the door, we'll be around the corner."

"Why will you be around the corner?" he hissed. I was beginning to think that Laura was making stuff up just to be bossy.

"We just will. Stop arguing."

"I'm not arguing..."

Laura cut him off by knocking on the door and quickly dragging me off by the wrist. Aidan took a few steps after us as the door swung open. From my vantage point of just at the edge of the corner, I could see Aidan but not the person who had answered the door. I watched as Aidan straightened suddenly to face Blake's roommate, looking like a kid caught with his hand in the cookie jar.

"I...uh...hi..." Aidan stammered. I stifled a giggle.

"Hey, Aidan," the roommate said. "What's up?"

"Keisha! Hi!" Relief flooded his voice. Obviously, Aidan knew Blake's roommate.

No one said anything for a second, so Keisha tried again, "So, what are you doing here? Did you miss an assignment in class?"

"Assignment? Oh, no. I, uh..."

"Aidan, boy, I know you're not trying to hit on me!" Her voice was filled with laughter.

"What? No! I mean, yes?" Poor Aidan sounded so flustered I couldn't stand it anymore. I let loose with a loud snort of pure amusement.

Laura jabbed with an elbow to my side, and Aidan looked aghast.

"Is someone with you?" Keisha asked, suddenly sounding suspicious.

"Um, yes?"

With a sigh, Laura pushed past me and went to stand next to Aidan. I followed still trying to keep from laughing. This was not going as planned.

"Hi, I'm Laura," she said introducing herself to the young black woman standing in the doorway.

"I'm Will," I volunteered.

"What's going on?" Keisha asked. She had a wary expression now, as if she thought we were trying to pull something over on her. She was tall and a little on the heavy side, but not in an unattractive way. She wore the extra pounds well, as most African-American women seem to do. She had huge dark brown eyes and a short afro.

"We were friends of Joey Taylor," Laura said. Keisha gave her a blank stare, and she went on. "The guy who died at the party about a month ago?"

"Oh yeah," Keisha said, still looking confused. "So why are you here?"

"Well, Blake is the one who found him."

"Yeah? Oh, you're here to see Blake. She's at class."

"I know. We're the ones who called up. We were hoping she might have said something to you about what happened that night. None of us was there, and we were just trying to figure out what happened. You know, so we can move on."

"Sure, I know what you mean. Sorry to burst your bubble, but Blake and I aren't exactly bosom buddies. She doesn't tell me much, and I don't tell her anything. To be honest, I can't stand her. The girl's like the fucking Energizer bunny. You know how bunnies mate? They got nothing on Blake. She just keeps going and going and going. Guys in here all hours of the day and night. I hafta do all my studying either in my girlfriend's room or in the library."

I was the first to grasp the possibilities here.

"You and Blake don't get along?" I asked to clarify.

"Nope. Oil and vinegar."

"Would you care if we looked around her stuff real quick?"

"Help yourself; it's no skin off my nose. I don't know what you're looking for, but as far as I'm concerned, you can take whatever you want. The less of her shit in here the better. She'd probably not even notice it was missing. Not that she has anything worth taking unless you want a lifetime supply of condoms."

"We're not going to take anything..." I started, but Keisha waved me off as she turned back into the room, disappearing briefly from view. I didn't know whether I was supposed to follow her or not.

"I don't care what you do, baby," she said as she quickly reappeared carrying a canvas backpack. "I'm off to class. The room is all yours. Just leave my stuff alone, and nobody will get hurt."

She slipped past me and sashayed off down the hall to the elevator. We watched her go with slack jaws until the elevator door closed after her.

"We have a class together," Aidan said unnecessarily.

"You are such an imbecile," Laura growled.

"What? I got us in, didn't I?"

"No, Will and I got us in. You almost got a date."

"We can stand out here and argue, or we can take a look inside," I said as I started into the room. Laura and Aidan followed. It was immediately obvious which side of the room was whose. You didn't even have to be a detective to figure it out. Keisha's side was meticulously neat with everything in its designated place and a few pictures of what must have been her family set up on the desk. In contrast, Blake's side looked like a dump truck had backed up and dumped a load of trash on it. Wadded balls of fast-food wrappers were tossed haphazardly about the floor and almost every surface was covered with discarded clothing, makeup products, and papers.

"Dear Lord in heaven," Laura breathed. She nudged the closest pile cautiously with her foot, as if afraid that something alive might be hiding in it.

"Where do we start?" I asked.

"With a shovel?" Aidan suggested.

"We'll never find anything, even if we did know what we were looking for," Laura lamented.

I picked up a pile of papers and flipped through them. They were all school assignments. I dropped them back in their place and picked up another pile which turned out to be the same thing. With a matching pair of sighs, Laura and Aidan started pawing through piles of their own. We worked for a few minutes, trying to keep things pretty much where they were just in case Blake did have some sort of order to the chaos.

"Hey," Aidan called just as we heard someone at the door. We all jumped guiltily to our feet and clumped together in the center of the room. The door swung open to reveal a rather startled-looking girl with shoulder length dirty-blonde hair. She had on just a little too much makeup and was wearing skin-tight jeans and an equally tight shirt that made the most of her considerable assets.

"Who the hell are you, and what are you doing in my room?"

"Hi, Blake. Keisha let us in," Laura said quickly. "I'm in one of your classes. Laura Duvier?"

"Yeah, ok," Blake said looking confused. "So what are you doing in my room? And who are they?" She gestured toward Aidan and me.

"These are my friends, Will and Aidan. We came to talk to you."

At our names, Blake's eyes flickered over us uncertainly, but then came back to rest on Laura. "Why do you want to talk to me?"

"You're the one who found Joey Taylor at David Kemp's party, right?"

Her eyes slid back toward Aidan and me. "Yeah," she said cagily. "So?"

"We were friends of Joey. We wanted to ask you some questions."

"What did you say your names were?"

"I'm Laura Duvier and this is Aidan Scott and Will Keegan."

Something was definitely going on inside Blake's head, but what it was I couldn't begin to guess. She seemed to become agitated at the mention of our names.

"Look, I have a lot of stuff to do," Blake said, edging past us into the room. "This isn't a good time to talk."

"It'll only take a second," Laura tried.

"I can't help you." She clutched her books close to her chest, as if they were a shield she had to keep between her and us.

"But you don't even know what we want to ask."

"I only found him."

"Blake, please. At least listen to us."

"Fine. You have one minute."

"How'd you find him?"

"I, uh, I needed air so I stepped outside, and there he was, floating face down in the pool, just under the surface. It was horrible. I...I screamed." Her eyes had become unfocused, as if she were seeing that night again.

"Was anyone with you?" Laura asked gently.

She snapped back into focus. "What? No! Why would you ask that?"

"So you were alone?"

"That's what I just said, isn't it?"

"Did you see anyone before you went out there?" I asked. "There was nobody in the back yard when I was inside."

"You were there?" Blake asked, her eyes narrowing.

"For a little while."

She thought for a moment, as if deciding how much she wanted to say. "There was nobody else around when I found him. The back yard was empty."

It looked like things were going to be over before they even got started. I turned to leave, but then I noticed the expression on Laura's face. I'd seen it before. It usually meant she thought I wasn't telling her the whole story and she wasn't about to give up before she got it.

"Who else was with you?" Laura asked ever so casually.

"What? I already said there was nobody else there. It was just me."

"Who's the guy?"

"For Christ's sake, are you saying I'm a liar?"

"Who was it, Blake?"

"Get out. Leave me alone."

"Not until you tell me his name. If you didn't see anything, maybe he did."

"Nobody saw anything. Just please leave me alone."

"What are you scared of, Blake?"

"I...I'm not scared."

"You know it wasn't an accident, don't you? What do you know?"

"I don't know anything. I'm calling Security." She snatched up the phone. I was getting nervous. It seemed like Laura was pushing too hard.

"Just tell us who he was, and we'll go."

Blake slammed down the phone and spun around angrily. "I don't know, ok? I never even got his name. I was high. I'd done some E. He was cute and sweet. He suggested we go somewhere quieter so we went out to the pool house in the back yard. Like he said, there was no one out there."

"What happened? How'd you find Joey?"

"He wasn't there when we went out. We went into the pool house and we were...you know, and all of a sudden, he says he hears voices. I wasn't exactly paying attention, you know? I tell him to ignore them. I guess he does because he kept on. And then, after we're done, we go back outside and there he is, like I told you, floating in the water."

"And what happened then? Where'd your friend go?"

"I told you, I screamed. That's when he took off. He just took one look at...at him in the water like that and he just took off running. Jumped right over the fence. He just left me there with a dead body."

"Poor baby," Laura said with undisguised disgust.

"You think I'm some kind of slut, don't you?"

"I didn't say that."

"You do. I can tell. Your type always thinks you're so much better than me."

"My type? What type is that exactly?"

This was quickly degenerating into a catfight. We'd gotten what we came for; I thought it would be wise to get all of us out of there. Apparently, Aidan had the same idea. We each grabbed one of Laura's elbows and started pulling her toward the door, which Blake had left open.

"Look, thanks for talking to us," I was saying, as if Laura had given her much choice.

"Just get out and stay the hell away from me," Blake snapped.

We managed to get a sputtering Laura into the hall before Blake slammed the door. A couple other doors on the hall opened, and a few heads popped out to see what all the fuss was about, reminding me of the prairie dogs at the zoo.

I smiled reassuringly. "It's ok." The heads retreated back into their rooms.

"Ok, I don't think getting into a fight with the person you are questioning is an approved interrogation method," I said.

"She started it," Laura sniffed. "Skank."

"At least we found out what we were looking for," Aidan said helpfully.

"Not really," Laura said.

"We know there was someone else with Joey."

"Do we? All we know is that Blake's lover boy thought he heard some voices. We don't even know his name or what he looks like."

"Actually, we might know what he looks like," I said thoughtfully.

"We do?" Aidan and Laura asked in unison.

"Caitlin and I were in the front yard when Blake screamed. We heard her and wondered what was going on. We were still there when the guy came over the fence. It has to be the same guy. I think I would know him if I saw him again."

"Great, so now what do we do? Ask for a line-up of all the guys who were at the party?"

"I don't know," I admitted. "Maybe Killian will have some ideas."

"In the meantime, we can all think about it and maybe we'll come up with something," Aidan suggested reasonably. "More importantly, though, we know that Blake is the one who sent you the necklace and the note." His voice took on a smug sound with this last statement.

"Oh, really?" Laura said archly. "And just how do we know that?"

"It's elementary, my dear Watson."

"If you think you're Sherlock Holmes, you got another think coming," Laura growled warningly.

"Look, just before Blake came in, I found this." He produced a crumpled sheet of paper with four words written on it in bold block letters, just like ones I'd seen before.

"IT WASN'T A ACCIDENT," it read.

I gasped.

"Rough draft?" Aidan asked. "See how she used 'a' instead of 'an'? She wrote another one, correcting her grammar mistake, the one she sent to you."

"How considerate," Laura said dryly.

"Should we go back in and confront her with it?" I asked.

"I don't think now would be the best time," Aidan said, with a meaningful look in Laura's direction.

"Oh, so now it's my fault, is that it?" she snapped.

"I didn't say that," Aidan placated. "I just don't think this would be the best time. For now, we should just go."

Laura waved us away irritably. I wondered what exactly her problem was. Aidan and I started toward the elevator, but Laura didn't move.

"You coming?" I called back to her.

"I'll take the stairs," she said.

The elevator arrived at that moment, so I just shrugged and stepped in. When the doors opened on the ground floor, I stepped out, almost running right into Caitlin.

"Caitlin!" I exclaimed in surprise. "What are you doing here?"

"I have a friend in the building," she said after an almost imperceptible pause. "What are you doing here?"

"We just came from talking to Blake."

"Oh, you talked to her? Did you find anything out?"

"Yes and no," Aidan said.

"We think she was probably in the pool house when Joey was being killed," I explained, "but she was, um, otherwise occupied."

Caitlin's blank look quickly changed to understanding as my meaning sunk in. "Does she know anything?"

"The guy she was with may have heard voices, she's not sure. I think he may have been the guy we saw, the one who jumped over the fence and told us Joey was dead."

"Really? What's his name?"

"We don't know. That's what we have to figure out next."

She nodded thoughtfully. "Well, if I think of anything, I'll call you. I'd better get going. My friend is waiting."

"Ok, see you, Caitlin."

"Bye, Will. Bye, Aidan."

I woke up the next morning, and for a few disoriented moments, I couldn't remember where I was. Then I felt Aidan's arms around me, and it all came back to me. The night before I had started into my room out of habit before Aidan had caught my hand and drawn me into his. It made sense that I would move into his room since it was bigger, but I would miss my view of the river — though not the balcony and all its associated memories.

I lay for a while just watching him sleep. I could lie like this forever, I thought, but the morning was wearing on and I had to get to work. I carefully slipped out of bed, and I succeeded in doing so without waking him. I started the shower, then went into my old bedroom to get my clothes. When I went back into the bathroom, I was startled to find Aidan waiting for me in the shower. Before I could say a word, he pulled me under the hot spray, boxers and all. He cut off my protest with a passionate kiss.

"Why didn't you wake me?" he asked while I caught my breath. He took the bar of soap and started to wash my back.

"I was going to after I took my shower."

"I woke up, and you weren't there."

"I'm sorry," I said with another kiss. "I won't let it happen again."

"Good," he said as his soapy hands slid down my sides.

"Aidan, I have to go to work," I protested faintly.

"I'll drive you."

"How does that make a difference? I still have to be there at the same...ooohhh," the rest of my case was cut off by Aidan's convincing counter-argument. That morning I learned that fireworks go off even in the shower.

Since Aiden did end up driving me to work, he had to pick me up, too. After we left downtown, to my surprise, we didn't head back to the apartment.

"Where are we going?" I asked.

"To the marina. We might as well look for Joey's dad. I'm really starting to get into this whole detective thing. It sounded like in the letter that his dad has a boat at the marina. I thought we could nose around."

"Nose around? Where'd you get that? What, are we rooting for truffles?"

"Don't be a smart ass."

We parked and walked around the marina for a few minutes looking for someone. The place seemed pretty deserted, and most of the boats were covered in canvas for the winter. Finally, we found someone struggling to pull his canvas boat cover down far enough to snap it on.

"Excuse me," I called. "Do you know a Mr. Taylor who has a boat in this marina?"

The man turned and eyed us suspiciously. He was an older man, rough and weathered by years in the elements. I began to feel vaguely guilty under his gaze; for what, I didn't know.

"Nope, sorry," he said finally. Then as we started away, "Could you guys give me a hand here, mebbe?"

"Sure," we quickly agreed. We stepped onto his boat, named the Mildred Belle, and for the next few minutes helped him pull the cover taut enough to snap in place.

"Thanks, I appreciate the help," he said when we'd finished. "She's named after my wife."

It took me a minute to realize he meant the boat. "She must have been very flattered," I said uncertainly. I wasn't sure how I'd feel having a boat named after me. I suppose it would be an honor.

"She died two years ago, a year before I got this girl."

"Oh, I'm sorry."

"She'd suffered for a long time. Cancer."

I didn't know what to say. Luckily, Aidan stepped in. "My dad died of cancer, too," he said. The two men stood in a companionable silence for a few moments, sharing a common grief.

"You wouldn't happen to mean Jack Taylor, would you?" he said finally.

"Jack Taylor?" I said cautiously. I didn't know if that was who I meant or not.

"Yeah."

"I don't know, maybe..."

He looked at me with renewed suspicion. "Why are you looking for him?"

"He's my best friend's father."

"Well, now, Jack's boy jus' died a few weeks back."

"That was him, Joey."

He nodded as if I'd spoken the secret password. "Jack was right broke up over that. I was here the day he heard tell about it. On the radio, no less! Helluva way to hear your boy is dead."

"Yes, sir, it is. I wanted to find him to tell him how sorry I was."

"Well, I'm sure he ain't here today, it being winter and all."

"Well, if you should happen to see him, could you tell him Will Keegan was trying to get in touch with him?"

"Will Keegan, you say? I'll do that."

"Thank you."

He watched as we walked away. He was still standing on the dock staring after us as Aidan backed out of our parking space and drove away.

"Another dead end," I sighed.

"Maybe not. Let's wait and see."

"The longer we wait the longer the killer has to get away with murder."

"The killer hasn't gotten away with anything yet. We still have a chance here, Will. Don't give up."

"I'm not giving up. I just hate this feeling that we're spinning our wheels while something awful is getting ready to happen."

"Nothing awful is going to happen. We're going to get this guy."

"I hope you're right."

I left work early the next day to go with Caitlin to the doctor. It seemed like we sat in the waiting room forever while we waited to be called. Eventually a nurse called Caitlin back, leaving me adrift in a sea of very large, very pregnant women. I could feel what little testosterone I had being leached out of me as I sat. Just as I was about to break down and read *Martha Stewart Living*, the nurse stuck her head back into the waiting room.

"Mr. Keegan?" she said. "Caitlin has asked if you would come back. The doctor said it's ok."

"Me? Come back there?" I squeaked.

Several of the other mothers grinned, and I heard one say, "He sounds just like my husband the first time I asked him to come back."

The nurse nodded encouragingly, and I reluctantly followed her back. She led me into an examining room where Caitlin lay on a table, her stomach exposed and covered in what looked to me like Vaseline. Her doctor was sitting next to her holding a small device to Caitlin's stomach. They were both staring intently at a monitor. They turned toward me as I came in, and I immediately felt myself begin to blush. The doctor was a woman, and judging by her dark complexion and the red dot in the middle of her forehead, I guessed she was from India.

"You are jes' in time to see de baby," the doctor said with a warm smile.

"See the baby?" I repeated.

"Yes, on the little TV here," she pointed to the monitor.

I looked at the screen but all I could see was static and undefined shapes and shadows. "Where is it?" I asked.

"Right dere. Dat's de head," she said pointing, "and dat's de arm. Oh, look, he's waving!"

"He?" Caitlin asked, while I stared hard at the screen.

"It's too early to tell, I jes' said he. It could be a she."

Slowly, while they talked, a tiny alien-like form began to appear before my eyes. It reminded me of those puzzles that were so popular when I was a kid, those geometric designs that if you stared at them long enough hidden 3-D images slowly formed.

A sense of awe swept over me as I stared at the image on the monitor. I was looking at a person that hadn't even drawn its first breath yet. This tiny life was still being formed even while I watched. Its tiny organs were being shaped, its mind developing, and yet the gene patterns that would determine if it was right-handed or left-handed, blonde or brunette, blue-eyed or brown were already established. Wonder and amazement filled me, and a verse I remembered hearing in church ran through my mind: "For you have created my inmost being. You knit me together in my mother's womb. I praise you for I am fearfully and wonderfully made."

Caitlin and the doctor both stopped talking and turned to stare at me. I realized I had spoken the words aloud.

"It's from the Bible, Psalms," I said self-consciously as I blushed once again.

"Listen to dis," the doctor said. I was grateful for the distraction. She twisted a knob on the monitor and suddenly a sound filled the room. It was a fast-paced, wet-sounding rhythmic beating.

"The heartbeat?" Caitlin asked.

The doctor nodded.

I stood for a moment as the sound washed over me. Then suddenly I couldn't breathe. It was as if all the oxygen had been sucked from the examining room. I needed air; I needed out of that tiny room.

"Excuse me," I gasped and quickly let myself out of the room. Forcing myself not to run, I made my way outside where I stood gulping in the cold air. An overwhelming feeling of responsibility had come over me in the examining room like I had never felt before. Somehow, none of this had seemed real until that moment. Even with the baby books, it had seemed distant, almost imaginary, like I was playing let's pretend.

But it wasn't pretend. Now I had seen the baby with my own eyes, heard its heartbeat with my own ears. The baby was real. And I had committed myself to raising that child. And in just a matter of months, it would be born, and I'd be holding it in my arms. Would it be a girl or a boy? What would it call me? Daddy? The very thought took my breath away. But I'm not the father, I reminded myself. Joey is. And then a small voice whispered, but Joey's dead.

And then a new fear crept into my mind, closing my throat and filling me with a sense of loss like I had never known. What if Caitlin met someone else and fell in love? What if she got married? I'd be out of the picture for good. As scared as I was, I knew I wanted more than ever to be a part of this baby's life.

While I was still thinking about that, Caitlin came out.

"Ready to go?" she asked.

"Yeah," I said slowly.

"What happened in there? One minute you're fine, the next you're spouting Bible verses and going all pale."

"It just kinda hit me all at once. I mean, this is really happening. That's a real baby in there, and I'm going to be at least partly responsible for it."

"Do you want to back out? Nothing is official yet. If you want out, now is the time."

"No, I don't want out. In fact, I want to do this more than ever now. I'll try to find a lawyer tonight, so we can start the legal stuff."

We walked to the car and got in.

"You're quite a guy, Mr. Keegan," she said once we were out on the road. "One of a kind in fact. Are you sure you're not straight? We could run off to Vegas right now, get married by an Elvis impersonator."

I laughed. "I don't think Aidan would be too happy about that."

Her head snapped around, and her eyes grew wide. "I thought you and Aidan were just friends."

"We were. Now...we're more than just friends."

"Oh. Well..."

"Does that bother you?"

"No," she said quickly. A bit too quickly? "It just...surprised me."

We drove the rest of the way to her apartment in silence. I couldn't tell what if anything that meant.

Chapter 17

As soon as I walked through the door of our apartment, I stopped dead in my tracks. Obviously, Aidan had beaten me home. Curtains had been drawn over the windows to block out any light, and candles flickered on every possible surface. The smell of Italian food and the soulful crooning of Billie Holiday filled the air.

"Aidan?" I called.

He appeared out of the kitchen with a shy smile. "Surprise?"

I'd never seen him like this; he seemed almost timid, as if everything depended on my reaction. He was dressed in jeans and a jade green silk shirt. It was obvious that he'd gone to great lengths to make this a special night. I frantically searched my memory trying to figure out what I had forgotten. Was I missing an anniversary? A birthday? I couldn't think of anything.

"What...I mean...did I miss something?" I said finally.

"No. I just wanted to surprise you, to show you how much I love you. There's been so much going on..."

I crossed the room quickly and wrapped my arms tightly around him. We kissed for a few minutes before he suddenly pulled back.

"The bread!" he gasped as he ran back into the kitchen. I followed him.

"You baked bread?" I said.

"Well, I cheated. It's the frozen kind. But I made manicotti."

"The frozen kind?"

"No, I really made it. I found a recipe on-line. I don't know how it turned out. I haven't tasted it yet."

"Well, if it tastes anything like it smells, it's going to be delicious," I said as I slid my arms around his waist again.

This time all I got was a quick peck on the lips.

"Save it for dessert," he said with a grin. "We can't let the food get cold."

We ate dinner, which turned out even better than it smelled, in the living room on a blanket Aidan had spread out on the floor. Afterwards we made love, slow and relaxed, just enjoying each other's bodies. As we lay content in the afterglow of our lovemaking, I told Aidan about how seeing the baby had affected me.

"This is really important to you, isn't it?" he asked softly.

"Yeah, it is. I've never wanted anything as much as I want to be a part of this baby's life, even though it scares the living shit out of me at the same time. Now I'm just worried that something will happen and I'll lose this chance. I need to find a lawyer."

"Ilana is a lawyer," Aidan said. "In fact, I think she handled the custody battle between Adam and his ex over Kane. And I know she handled all the legal stuff with Killian."

"Do you think I could call her?"

"I don't see why not. I'll call Adam in the morning and get her number for you."

I kissed him. "Thanks. So what's the story on Kane?"

"What do you mean?"

"Well, at Thanksgiving he said something about his mom talking to him again and just now you mentioned a custody battle."

"Oh, I don't really know the whole story. Killian could give you the scoop better than me. I think it all started back when she and Adam split up. She couldn't handle that he was gay; she wouldn't let Seth and Kane see him at all. When Seth told her he was gay, she kicked him out and wouldn't let Kane have anything to do with either of them. There was a big fight over Kane being able to live where he wanted. I think she finally just wrote him off, too."

"That's awful!" I said. "Seth was the one who was murdered, wasn't he?"

"Yeah."

"God! That family has been through hell."

"But they got through it by sticking together. Killian is like another son to Adam, and I know Killian thinks of Kane as his brother. And from what Kane said at Thanksgiving, I guess his mom has finally come around and she's talking to him again."

"So it all worked out in the end?"

"Yeah, I guess it did. You don't get to see many happy endings in real life; it's nice to see one every now and then."

I tipped my head back so I could see his face in the candlelight. "We're a happy ending, aren't we?"

We were so close I could feel his heart beating while I waited for him to say something. Finally, he said, "I'd like to think we aren't any kind of ending. We're just beginning. We've got a lot of living left to do before we can have a happy ending."

"What does that mean? You don't think we're going to make it?"

"I didn't say that."

"Then what are you saying?"

"Just...I don't feel as secure in our relationship as I'd like."

"What do you mean? I thought we settled that whole thing with Joey."

"It's not Joey."

"Then who? Not Caitlin still?"

"I...Will, are you sure you're gay? I mean, are you sure you're not going to fall in love with Caitlin and leave me? You're so into this baby..."

"Aidan."

"I'm afraid to give you all of me..."

"Aidan."

"I'm so scared of getting hurt again..."

"Aidan! I'm here, with you. I'm making love to you. I live with you. I love you. Not Caitlin. I only want you. What can I do to convince you of that?"

"Marry me."

"What?"

He sat up, keeping his eyes on mine. "Marry me. I was going to wait until I had a ring and do this right, but I just can't wait. I want to spend the rest of life with you, Will. I want to grow old with you. I'm willing to accept whatever that means; raising this baby, always living in Joey's shadow...but I need some sense of security. I need commitment."

"You're serious," I said in amazement as I sat up next to him. "But it's not legal in Maryland."

"We don't need a sheet of paper from the State of Maryland to validate our commitment," he said. "It can just be me and you, maybe our friends, but mainly just you and me, declaring our love and our promise to each other."

I couldn't believe we were even talking about this. Marriage? I hadn't even thought about it. I hadn't thought of anything except finding Joey's killer and the baby. Did I want to spend the rest of my life with Aidan? Did I want to marry him?

"Yes," I whispered aloud.

"What? Do you mean..."

I turned to face him. "Yes, I will marry you, Aidan Scott. Yes, I want to spend the rest of my life with you. Yes, I want..."

He grabbed me and kissed me passionately, cutting off any further proclamations. I could feel his tears warm against my cheeks.

"Does this mean I have to change my name to Will Scott?" I asked when we came up for air.

He laughed and cried at the same time. "I don't want you to change a thing, Will Keegan. I love you just the way you are."

When we got up the next morning, we found a blanket of snow had fallen during the night. The world had been covered with a soft layer of white purity. It was magical and beautiful and seemed perfect. I took it as a sign that I had made the right decision about marrying Aidan.

I was staring out the window when he came up behind me and wrapped his strong arms around me. I melted into his embrace with a contented sigh. After I spent a few minutes just enjoying his embrace, my mind wandered to thoughts of Caitlin and the baby.

"Did you say you could get Ilana's phone number?" I asked him.

"Sure. You want me to call Adam?"

"Please."

His arms slipped reluctantly from around my waist as he went in search of the phone. I followed him out to the living room after a minute. He was talking on the phone, I assumed, to Adam. He jotted a number down on the paper and handed it to me after hanging up.

"There ya go," he said. "I'm going to go take a shower while you call her."

I picked up the phone and held it in my hand without dialing. I noticed my hand was shaking. I took a deep breath and quickly dialed the number before I could panic.

The phone rang once, twice, three times. I was just beginning to think that maybe her office was closed when a soft, cultured voice answered.

"Ilana Constantino's office, Jennie speaking. How can I help you?"

I almost hung up, but I caught myself just in time. "Hello?" Jennie asked into the line.

"Um, yes," I said quickly. "I'm calling for Ms. Constantino, please."

"May I ask who is calling?"

"My name is Will Keegan. We met at Thanksgiving, at Adam Connelly's house."

"Hold just a minute."

I sat listening to soft Muzak while I waited nervously. Would she even remember me? I got my answer a moment later when her warm voice came on the line.

"Will, it's Ilana. How are you?"

"I'm good. I wasn't sure if you'd remember me."

She laughed. "How could I forget a guy like you? What can I do for you?"

"Well, uh, I need to talk to you in person. Can I make an appointment?"

"Of course. Let me look at my schedule." The line was silent for a few seconds except for the sound of rustling paper. "Is this afternoon too soon? I have an opening at four thirty."

"That would be wonderful," I said with relief.

"Good, I'll see you then."

We said goodbye and hung up. I was sitting in the living room still holding the phone when Aidan came back out from his shower. One look at the man I was now engaged to and all thoughts of nervousness about the baby flew right out of my head.

We decided to wait and tell everyone about our engagement at our next meeting on Friday night. Keeping quiet was the hardest thing I've ever done. I felt like I would explode from my good news. I couldn't stop grinning that day at work. Nikki kept asking what I was so happy about, but I just kept shaking my head and grinning until my cheeks ached.

When I came back from lunch, Nikki met me at the door.

"There's someone here to see you," she hissed loud enough to be heard all over the plaza.

I looked around but didn't see anyone in the gallery.

"He's in my office," she explained. "He looks a little shady to me."

My heart started racing. "Did he say who he was?"

"No. All he would say was that he needed to speak to you and you only."

It had never occurred to me before that moment that I might be in danger myself. Now suddenly my mind was filled with terrifying questions. What if the killer decided I was a threat? What if he thought I knew more than I did? We hadn't been subtle in our investigation so far. More often than not, we'd used a sledgehammer when a fly swatter would have sufficed.

"Stay by the door," I said to Nikki. "If you hear anything suspicious, get out and get help."

Her eyes grew wide, and she grabbed my wrist.

"Will, are you involved with the Mafia?"

The tension broke as I tried not to laugh in her face. I almost succeeded.

"What Mafia? This is the Eastern Shore. The most organized crime family we have are redneck moonshiners."

"That's what they want you to believe," she said ominously.

"I'm not involved with Al Capone or any other gangsters," I assured her.

I left Nikki standing anxiously by the door and walked back to her office. I knocked lightly as I opened the door. I figured I didn't want to surprise whoever was waiting for me. I found a slightly familiar middle-aged man with a full beard and worn, but clean clothes waiting for me. Where had I seen him before?

"Hello?" I said uncertainly. "I'm Will Keegan. Are you looking for me?"

"Yes, yes, I am. Your parents said I could find you here. I hope you don't mind me barging in like this, interrupting your workday..."

"Wait...my parents?"

"Yes. I didn't know how else to find you."

"Who are you?" I blurted out.

"I'm sorry. My name is John Taylor; folks call me Jack. You talked to Mr. Dennis at the marina. You told him you wanted to talk to me about my son, Joey. He went to the marina office and got my number and called me." He wound to a sudden stop as if he had run out of words.

"You were at the funeral, in the back," I said, suddenly remembering where I had seen him before.

"Yes," he said in a broken voice. "I was there. I stayed in the back so Olivia, Joey's mother, wouldn't see me. He didn't want her to know that we were seeing each other again."

"Why all the secrecy? Joey was eighteen; he could see whoever he wanted."

"Olivia hates me, with good reason. I was a lousy husband and an even worse father. I...I was a different man then. I drank. All the time. I'm an alcoholic. I haven't touched the stuff for three years, but once an addict always an addict. When Joey contacted me...I can't tell you how happy I was. When I left them all those years ago, I thought I'd lost my son forever. I can't tell you how thrilled I was to get his letter. I thought...I thought that maybe I was being offered a second chance with Joey. He's the only child I ever had.

"I was living in Norfolk then, in Virginia. I quit my job and left the next day on my boat. We met a few times; I thought it was going well. Then, the last time I saw him, he was drunk, drunk out of his skull. I don't know, something snapped inside me. I lost it. I yelled at him, told him didn't he know how poisonous that stuff was? Didn't he remember how it had torn his family apart?

"He got mad right back. Inherited his temper along with his weakness for the bottle from me, I guess. Told me I had no right to tell him what to do. Said I'd given up that right years ago when I walked out on him and his mother." He choked up, fought back tears and won. "He was right. What could I say? He left, and a few days later, I heard on the radio that he was gone. So much for second chances."

I didn't know what to say. His pain was almost palpable; the office suddenly seemed too small, too stuffy.

"Joey wasn't himself those last weeks, Mr. Taylor," I said at last. "When he started drinking, it changed him. He was my best friend for eighteen years, and I didn't even know him at the end."

"Tell me about him. Tell me about my boy, the boy I never got the chance to know."

So I did. I took the rest of the afternoon off with Nikki's blessing. Mr. Taylor, or Jack as he insisted on being called, and I sat in a café, drinking hot chocolate for me and coffee for him, as I told him everything I could think of about Joey. As I did, I began to get a clearer picture of Joey than I ever had before. How selfish he was and had always been, and how the drinking had just exacerbated an inherent trait. I tried to cover over as much of that as I could, only telling the positive side. I could tell how much it meant to him. I felt sorry for this sad, broken man. I knew in my gut that he hadn't killed Joey, at least not in cold blood. He may have started the slow process of self-destruction that Joey had been in, and he would live with that for the rest of his life. I felt confident that we could cross him off our list of suspects.

When I finally left Mr. Taylor, I had to drive straight to the upscale modern office building that housed Ilana Constantino's law practice. I took the elevator to her floor and found the door with her name stenciled in gold lettering on frosted glass over the words "Family Law". The foyer area screamed elegance and style, much like Ilana herself. She was standing behind the receptionist's desk talking to her when I came in. Immediately her face lit up in a warm smile, and she stepped out from behind the desk.

"Will, it's good to see you again," she said as she offered her hand. "Come on back to my office. Hold my calls please, Jennie."

"Thanks so much for taking the time to see me so quickly, Ms. Constantino," I said as she led me into a well-appointed office.

"Call me Ilana. And you sounded like it was important."

"It is," I said and quickly outlined the situation as succinctly as I could. She already knew a little about it since she had been at the Thanksgiving dinner. When I finished I sat back and waited for her response.

She thought for a minute, tapping one long manicured nail against her lips. "Let me see if I have this right," she said. "You would like me to draw up some documents that give you legal rights to this baby, that isn't yours, to make sure that Caitlin doesn't skip out on you and take the baby with her."

"Something like that," I said halfheartedly.

"Well, I have to say that it's just a bit unusual. Are you sure this is what you want to do? You understand that once it's done you will be held just as responsible for this baby as if it were your own."

"I know. It's what I want to do."

"Then essentially what I'll be doing is an adoption with a joint custody kind of thing. It will ensure that you will support the baby and, in turn, you will have access to the baby. Is Caitlin agreeable to this?"

"Yes, I think so."

"And what about the paternal grandparents?"

"You mean Joey's mom? What about her?"

"His father isn't in the picture?"

I shook my head no. "Just his mom."

"How does she feel about all this?"

"I...I don't know. I don't think she even knows about the baby."

Ilana sat back in surprise. "Don't you think someone should tell her?"

I shifted uncomfortably. "Wouldn't that be Caitlin's responsibility?"

"I suppose, although you are getting yourself involved pretty deeply here."

"Could she...cause problems?"

"Well, she does have some rights — for visitation, at the very least. And she could have some claim to the baby if anything happened to the mother or if the mother was deemed unfit."

"I would never want to keep the baby away from its grandmother. I can't imagine Caitlin would either."

"Then as long as nothing happens to Caitlin, it should be fine. As the biological mother, she has every right to make this...arrangement with you if she chooses. Although I have to say it is rather unconventional."

"How much is all this going to cost?"

"Well, since you're a friend I'm not going to charge you for my time. You'll have to pay the various legal fees and so on, but I'll let you know what that is when it's all done. It won't be outrageously expensive."

"Ok. How long will it take?"

"I'll get right to work on it. I'll call you in a few days. You and Caitlin will have to come in and sign the paperwork."

"Ok, I'll call her and fill her in."

"Good. You do that, and I'll be in touch."

I left with a sense that everything was falling into place at last. Aidan and I were engaged and now the legal work for Caitlin and me was on the way. All we needed to do was find something concrete to take to the police and everything would be perfect. Well, except for my family. I hadn't thought much about them lately. I tended to avoid thinking about things that were too painful, but Mr. Taylor's mention of them earlier had brought them back into my mind full force. We'd always been a fairly close family even if my dad hadn't been around that much. And though I'd tried not to think about it or let it show, I really missed them. Maybe it was time to try and mend that broken relationship, I thought. I decided I would talk to Aidan about it the first chance I got.

When I arrived home, however, the thought completely slipped my mind. Once again, the curtains were drawn and candles were lit. No enticing aromas filled the air tonight, though. Instead I found a trail of rose petals scattered on the floor leading to my old bedroom. They continued to the window that opened onto the fire escape. There I found Aidan waiting, looking out over the river with his back to me. The red rose petals stood out brilliantly against the background of white snow, broken only by Aidan's footprints.

"You're going to spoil me," I said, and he spun around.

"That's the idea," he said with a grin. "But this is a special occasion."

"And why is that?"

"We're celebrating our engagement."

"I thought we did that last night," I said with a grin. "Several times."

He answered with a grin of his own. "Why don't you join me out here on the fire escape? It's time we replace the bad memories with some good ones."

I took a deep breath and climbed out with him. It was the first time I had been out here since I had jumped.

Aidan took my hand and gave it a squeeze. Then to my surprise, he went down on one knee in the snow, still holding onto my hand.

"I know I asked you this last night, but I want to do it right this time," he said. He reached into his coat pocket and pulled out a ring box.

"Oh, my God," I whispered.

He opened the box and took the ring out. It was a beautiful silver ring, with an intricate gold design around it.

"William Spencer Keegan, will you marry me?" he said.

I felt a tear roll down my cheek. "You know I will. Yes, I'll marry you."

He slipped the ring onto my finger. It was a little big, but it didn't matter. I noticed a matching ring on Aidan's hand, and I drew him up for a lingering kiss.

"Let's do it now," he said in a husky voice.

"What? Right now?"

"No, not right this minute, but before Christmas, next week."

"That's crazy," I laughed.

"Why? I don't want to wait. I want to do this now."

"Why not?" I said, feeling exhilarated. "But who will perform the ceremony?"

"Well, since it's not legally binding, it doesn't really have to be a judge or a preacher. Why don't we ask Adam if he knows anyone?"

"Good idea," I said with a giggle. "I have an idea. Let's not tell anyone what's going on. Let's throw a surprise wedding!"

Aidan laughed. "And you thought my idea was crazy?"

"No seriously! I read about it in a magazine once, some celebrities did that. I thought it sounded so cool at the time. We can have everything arranged, tell them we're having a party, and then when they show up we tell them."

"What if they have other plans?"

"We tell them it's really important to us that they come."

Aidan laughed again. "I think it's the craziest thing I've ever heard, but I love it! Let's do it!"

"Adam will have to be in on it if we're asking him to find someone to do the ceremony," I pointed out.

"Well, that's good. He can help us plan it. After all, I've never planned a wedding before, let alone a gay wedding."

"Let's go back inside," I said, suddenly realizing how cold it was out here. We crawled back in and shut the window.

We went and called Adam right away. He was as excited as we were. He said he knew a gay minister nearby who led a mostly gay congregation and who would be thrilled to do the wedding. And he had a ton of ideas for the wedding itself, from flowers to reception favors.

"Whoa, slow down," Aidan said. "We don't want to go overboard. We just want something simple and meaningful. It's just going to be a few close friends."

"Simple doesn't mean it can't be special," Adam said.

We settled on the Friday after next, in the evening, and left the planning in Adam's capable hands.

Chapter 18

After a hectic first half of the week, the second half calmed down into routine. Not blurting out the news of the wedding turned out to be the hardest thing I had to do. Finally, Friday night rolled around, and it was time for our meeting.

Killian and Asher arrived with pizza, and Caitlin knocked on the door soon after. I had offered to pick her up, but she'd refused, saying she was borrowing a friend's car. Laura arrived not too long after, wearing a disgruntled expression.

"Gabe's going to be late. He called me a little while ago and told me I was going to have to drive myself. Something's going on over at the campus."

Gabe was the only one of those who went to the school who actually lived on-campus.

"What's going on?" Aidan asked.

"I don't know. He was going to go see if he could find out before he came."

"Should we start eating without him?" Killian asked hopefully.

She shrugged. "Why not? Who knows how long he'll be."

We were just finishing up the pizza, with the exception of a few pieces set aside for Gabe, when he finally arrived. Aidan got up to let him in. He appeared in the doorway a second later, looking pale under his dusky complexion.

"Gabe! What's wrong?" Laura asked, jumping to her feet as soon as she saw him.

"Blake is dead," he said in a slightly shaken voice.

Everyone seemed to freeze. Killian was the first to recover. "She's the one who found Joey, right?" I nodded. "How'd she die?" he asked Gabe.

"I'm not sure. There are cops everywhere. I just heard she was dead from someone on her floor. They said her roommate found her this afternoon."

I saw Aidan glance at his watch. "The news is on," he said as he started for the living room. The rest of us quickly followed him.

They were giving the weather report when we turned it on. We had to sit through commercials and the sports report before they finally mentioned what we were waiting to hear.

"We have breaking news on the latest death to rock Pemberton University," the anchorwoman said. "Police have confirmed that the death of a female student, whose name is being held until her family can be contacted, was most likely suicide. She was found in her room earlier today by her roommate. Early reports have indicated that drugs may have been involved. This is the second death of a college student attributed to illegal substance abuse in as many months. Is drug and alcohol abuse on the rise on our local campuses?"

Aidan snapped off the set, and we all sat in stunned silence. Laura broke the quiet. "Suicide my ass," she snapped.

Every head swiveled to look at her.

"What, you don't think that's just a little too convenient? She was fine the other day when we were there."

"She did seem a little scared," I pointed out.

"Scared isn't suicidal."

"Whoa, hold up!" Killian said. "You guys talked to her before she died?"

"Yes," Laura said shortly.

"We went earlier this week," I explained. I quickly told them what we had found out from our brief conversation with her and, more importantly, about the note we'd found that appeared to be the rough draft of the one I'd been sent. Everyone sat for a minute, allowing this to sink in.

"Ok," Gabe said. "So we know that Blake knew more than she wanted to let on, but now she's dead. So where does that leave us?"

"We need to find out who was with her in the pool house that night," Killian said.

I noticed Asher start to say something, but then he seemed to think better of it and sat back, arms crossed tightly across his chest. Tension oozed from his every pore. Laura spoke up, drawing my attention back to the matter at hand.

"How do we do that? Will and Caitlin might have seen him, but how are we supposed to find him? It's like looking for a needle in a haystack."

"Not really," Killian said. "There were only so many people at the party. I'm sure you have to know some of the people who were there. Just start asking around describing our mystery guy. He didn't appear out of thin air. Somebody there has to know who he was."

"And if they don't?" Aidan asked.

"Somebody has to. Eventually we'll find this guy." Everyone was looking pretty glum by now. "This isn't over, guys!" Killian exclaimed. "Think of this as a challenge. Nobody said this would be easy. Let's look at what we did find out this week. Who wants to go first?"

"I might as well go first," Gabe said. "After all, I came in with the bad news about Blake. The least I can do is give you some good news, too. When I went by David's house no one was home."

"I heard his parents sent him off to rehab," Laura interjected.

"Whatever, he wasn't there. But I went around back anyway and found that anyone could have gotten into or out of the back yard. There's a door in the fence as big as life, and it's not even locked."

"Great, so that means it could have been anyone, not just someone at the party," Aidan said.

"That really throws open the field," I added dolefully.

"Not really," Killian said thoughtfully. We all turned to face him. He thought for a moment before continuing. "Think about it. If it was an outside person, let's call him Mr. X..."

"Mr. X?" Asher laughed.

Killian shot him a dirty look but kept on speaking without comment, "How would he know Joey was going to be at this particular party? How'd he know to find him in the back yard?"

"He could have followed him," Aidan suggested.

"Or he could have done what I did and just party hopped until he found the right party," I said.

"If he party hopped, then he was still at the party; he didn't have to come in through the back yard."

"I agree with Killian," Gabe said. "I think it was someone at the party. I think the gate was an escape route, not an entrance."

Everyone started to speak at once.

"Let me explain," Gabe yelled over the din. "Nothing about this feels planned. It seems like a spur of the moment crime of passion. The killer didn't check to see if anyone was in the pool house, he left the necklace, which probably fell off in some sort of struggle, and a pool isn't exactly the most reliable murder weapon. Chances are he didn't even mean to kill Joey. I mean, what if someone had found Joey before he died? Or what if someone had just happened to look out the window and seen him bop Joey on the head?"

"Do we even know for sure that he was bopped on the head?" Killian asked.

"Oh yeah, that was the other thing I found out. The cause of death is public knowledge unless it's a continuing criminal investigation. Your detective was just being a pain. Technically, Joey died of drowning, but..." Gabe paused dramatically, "...my sources at the police station confirmed that Joey did have a pretty serious head wound, which is probably what kept him from getting out of the pool once he was in it. The medical examiner said it could have been sustained when he fell into the pool if he'd struck his head on the edge."

"Sources at the police station?" Aidan repeated.

"A good detective never reveals his sources," Gabe said smugly.

"His cousin works at the police station, remember," Killian said. "She's one of the dispatchers."

Gabe shot him an appraising, "I'm impressed you remembered that."

I was impressed, too. I'd forgotten all about Gabe's passing mention of her in a previous planning session. I wondered if his cousin was the personality-deficient woman I'd met on my visits.

Killian just grinned and picked up where Gabe had left off. "So, the head wound could have been from the pool...or it could have been from getting bopped in the head."

"Exactly," Gabe said. "While I was in the back yard, I looked around a bit. They have these rocks that surround their flowerbeds, pretty good-sized rocks. I found one that looked out of place, like it might have been moved. So I took a closer look at it, and there's something on it that may or may not be blood."

"What did you do with it?" Caitlin asked.

"I picked it up with my shirt and wrapped it up in a plastic bag. It's at my house now."

"Great!" I said excitedly. "That's solid evidence we can take to the police!"

"Not so fast," Aidan said. "We've tampered with evidence by moving it. You can bet that they are going to be exceedingly pissed."

"Not to mention," Caitlin added, "that they've already made it clear they don't think Joey was killed. What are we supposed to do? Just waltz in, plunk this chunk of rock down on their desk, and tell them that they are wrong? That we, being the seasoned professionals that we are, have solved their little mystery for them? I'm sure they'll be ever so grateful. Probably even give us the key to the city."

"And what if it's just barbecue sauce?" Laura chipped in. "Then we'd really look like idiots."

I sighed. "You're right, you're all right. They already think I'm some crack-head who's crazy with grief over the death of his best friend. Why prove them right?"

"We're not giving up," Aidan said. "We just need to find out some more facts first. Tell everybody what we found out from Joey's dad."

I filled everyone in on our trip to the marina and my ensuing visit from Mr. Taylor. "I think it's safe to assume that Mr. Taylor didn't do it," I finished.

"We don't really know that Mr. Taylor didn't do it," Killian said, "but I agree with you that it isn't all that likely. I think we can strike him off the list."

"So who does that leave? Do we even have a list?" Caitlin asked.

"Well, we were thinking that maybe it was an ex-girlfriend," Aidan said.

"But we decided it wasn't really all that likely," Laura pointed out. "After all, Shelley doesn't seem like much of a killer to me, and she was the only one that was at the party."

"That we know of," Aidan argued. "Don't forget about the door in the back yard fence; anyone could have come or gone."

"Maybe it was the boyfriend of one of the girls Joey had sex with," Gabe suggested.

"Or," Caitlin said slowly, drawing out the word as if an idea was just occurring to her, "maybe Blake killed Joey. We know she slept around; maybe she fell for Joey and he hurt her. We only have her word for it that there was someone else there with her, this mystery guy. We know she had the necklace and sent it to Will. Maybe she did commit suicide, because she was so guilty over Joey's death. Maybe your visit to her sent her over the edge. You said yourself she was scared and acted like she knew more than she was saying."

Caitlin's words chilled me. It was a solution that fit all the facts.

"That's a lot of maybes," Laura said dryly.

"Actually, it's a possible scenario," Killian said, "but we don't have any real proof that she had any sort of relationship with Joey. That's just conjecture. We'd need some evidence, and in the meantime, I don't think we should overlook the possibility that her mystery man does exist. Right now, those are our best bets. Can anyone think of anything else?"

"Well, if Blake was telling us the truth," Laura began, "or at least mostly the truth, then she didn't kill Joey. If she didn't commit suicide, which I still don't think she did, then that means someone killed her. It's a little much to believe that there are two murderers wandering around killing college students at Pemberton. I think we can assume that the same person killed both Joey and Blake."

"Why would he kill Blake?" Caitlin asked, obviously not happy that Laura was throwing a wrench into the cogs of her neat little theory.

"He or she," Gabe said, and everyone turned to look at him. "What? The killer could have been a woman."

"He, *or she*, could have thought that Blake knew who he *or she* was," Laura answered Caitlin's question, placing extra emphasis on "or she".

"Maybe another visit to Blake's roommate would be a good idea," Killian said. "What was her name?"

"Keisha," Aidan and I said at the same time, and I added, "But I don't know that she would be all that helpful. They didn't get along, and I don't think they talked all that much."

"Still, they shared a room. She would know better than most if Blake was acting any differently since your visit, if she was suicidal. She may even know more about Blake than she thinks she does."

I nodded. "Aidan and I can go see her; she knows Aidan already."

"Great," Killian said. "So what do we know? According to Blake, she was with a guy in the pool house, probably while Joey was being killed. She says the guy she was with heard voices from out by the pool. We know that Blake must have found the necklace, either before or after she found Joey, and at some point afterwards she decided that Joey's death wasn't an accident and sent the necklace to Will with the note."

"We know that Blake died today, just a couple days after Will, Aidan, and Laura talked to her," Gabe picked up.

"We know that Joey was seeing his father secretly behind his mom's back." I froze with the last word still on my tongue.

I watched Laura's eyes widen. "No way, Will!" she said quickly.

"How do you know?"

"There's no way."

"It's as likely as anything."

"What are you two talking about?" Aidan asked in exasperation.

"Joey's mom," Laura said.

"What if she found out that Joey was seeing his father behind her back?"

"Wouldn't it have made more sense for her to kill Mr. Taylor, then?" Gabe asked.

"Parents have been known to do stranger things," Aidan said.

"It's worth looking into," Killian said.

"Then I'll do it," Laura said with a sigh.

"Then the only other thing we have to do is figure out who the guy was with Blake."

"Is that all?" Laura scoffed.

"I can do that," Caitlin offered.

"I think that's something we'll all have to be involved with," Killian said, and Caitlin shrugged.

"Is that everything?" Laura asked. "Gabe and I are supposed to go out with some friends of his tonight."

"I'd almost forgotten about that!" Gabe exclaimed.

"Yeah, I think we're done, unless anyone can think of something else," Killian said, looking around. No one said anything, so he went on. "Then we'll meet one week from tonight unless someone comes up with something important."

"Actually," I said with a look in Aidan's direction, "Aidan and I have a special favor to ask everyone."

That got their attention.

Aidan took over. "Will and I want to invite you guys to a rather unusual party we're throwing next Friday night. It's kind of a surprise party, but the surprise is for you all. It's top secret, but we really want you to be here, at seven o'clock sharp."

"What's going on?" Laura said suspiciously.

"You'll find out then," I said with a grin.

I could tell she was loath to give it up that easily, but Gabe grabbed her by the elbow and started steering her toward the door. They bundled up and headed out the door. Caitlin left soon after them, after promising that she would be there next Friday night.

After they had left, Asher went to get Killian's and his coats, while Killian started helping Aidan and me clean up.

"Killian, I really want to thank you for all your help with this," I said quietly. "Even if we never find anything out for sure, at least I'll know I tried."

"You don't have to thank me, Will," he said. "I love doing this, and you're a friend. I'm just glad I can help."

"It's not caused too much stress on you and Asher, has it?" I asked as we carried some glasses into the kitchen, knowing full well it had.

Killian shrugged. "I dunno. I don't know what's going on these days."

"I can tell you what's going on," Asher snapped from the doorway. I looked up quickly and was surprised to see the undisguised anger on his face.

"Not now, Ash," Killian sighed.

"Why not? Will asked, so let's give him the whole story. I never wanted to get involved with this in the first place."

"Ash..." Killian tried, but Asher cut him off.

"I went along at first, against my better judgment, because I could see how much you wanted to be involved. Although why you'd want to get involved in another murder investigation after last time I still don't understand, but I went along. But it's different now; people are being killed. I want out. I want you out."

"We don't know that Blake was killed," Killian said. I pressed back against the counter, wishing I was anywhere but stuck in a small room while they had a fight. I was very envious of Aidan in the living room.

"What do you need?" Asher snapped. "A signed confession? You want to be next? Killian, for God's sake, we're not professionals; we don't know what we're doing. We have no business being involved in this. I'm scared, ok? I admit it. I'm scared and want us both out."

"We're getting close, though, Ash, I can feel it," Killian said. He was unable to keep the excitement out of his voice. "I've not been involved at all up to now, and that's not going to change now. We're not in any danger; this is completely different from last time."

"Aren't you even listening to me? Don't my feelings matter at all?"

"Of course they do; it's just that I can't leave Will like this." Don't drag me into this, I thought. "He needs me."

"Well, I need you, too." Asher suddenly burst into tears. He dropped the coats and spun away from the room and out the door.

Killian threw me a helpless glance and ran after him, scooping the coats up as he went. "I'm sorry," he said, pausing in the doorway.

"Don't apologize; just go after him."

He nodded and started to turn. "And Killian," I called, "if you need to drop out of this, I'll understand."

"No, somehow I don't think that would be the best idea," he said quietly. And then he was gone.

Aidan and I went to visit with Keisha as soon as I got home from work the next day. We were gambling that we'd be able to catch her in her room before she went to dinner or evening classes. When we got to her floor, though, we were stopped by yellow crime scene tape stretched across the door of the room she had shared with Blake.

"Great," I sighed. "Now what do we do?"

"I didn't know they used crime scene tape for a suicide," Aidan said thoughtfully, fingering the tape as if he hadn't even heard me.

"It's obvious Keisha isn't here," I said. "How are we going to find her?"

"Let's try the room next door," Aidan suggested as he dropped the tape, strode to the room next door, and knocked. It was quickly opened by a giggling heavy-set girl with black hair and clothing and dark Goth make-up. A wave of pot-scented air rushed over me.

"Yeah?" she said with a toss of her hair. I was almost blinded by the reflections off her ear jewelry, studded in multiple piercings all the way around the outside edge of her ear. There was enough metal there to forge a small sword.

"We're looking for Keisha. Do you know where she's staying?"

"No, I don't know. Ask the girl over there," she said and indicated the door opposite Blake and Keisha's. "She's tight with Keisha." She shut the door without further comment.

"Nice girl," Aidan mumbled as he started across the hall.

An attractive light-skinned black girl answered our knock. Her gray-green eyes took us in before she spoke. "Yes?"

"We're looking for Keisha," Aidan said again. "Do you know where she's staying?"

"Why are you looking for her?" the girl said in a challenging tone.

"It's ok, Leigh," Keisha said, appearing next to her in the doorway. "They're cool."

Leigh gave us a final once-over and must have decided we didn't look too threatening. She stepped back and allowed Keisha to take her place in the door.

"Well, well, well," Keisha said with a small, unconvincing smile. "Two visits in one week. Careful there, stud, or I might think you gots the hots for me."

Aidan smiled. "I'm really sorry about Blake," he started.

Keisha snorted. "Now I know you didn't come up here to extend your sympathy about my loss. I made it clear last time you were here that I couldn't stand the girl. Just cuz she's dead don't mean I suddenly think she was my best friend. So let's cut the crap and you can tell me why you're really here."

"We're still trying to figure out what happened to my friend Joey," I said, deciding it was time to step in.

Keisha gave me a look. "I still don't see what that has to do with me."

"Do you really think Blake killed herself?" Aidan asked suddenly.

Keisha's eyes grew wide, and she looked up and down the hall as if she were afraid someone was listening. "What the hell are you doing, Aidan? Get in here, before you get us all in trouble."

We followed her into Leigh's room, and Keisha shut the door behind us. Leigh was studiously reading a book, giving us the illusion of privacy.

"You can't go around just saying stuff like that in the middle of the hall," she said tensely. "What's wrong with you?"

"You don't think it was a suicide, do you?" Aidan pressed.

"I don't know what to think," Keisha said with a sigh.

"What happened? How did you find her?"

"I came back from a class, and when I opened the door, there she was, on the floor face down, not moving at all with a little puddle of blood under her. I've seen dead people before, and I knew she was dead as soon as I saw her. There were empty pill bottles on the floor near her with some pills spilled out and a gun in her hand. It didn't look like it had been a peaceful death, if you know what I mean. I pulled the door shut and ran over to Leigh's room and called the cops and an ambulance from here."

"Pill bottles? Do you think that's what killed her, an overdose? Or was it the gun? Did she shoot herself?"

"I don't know. See, that's what's confusing me. Blake wasn't really a doper, especially not sitting in our room all alone. Maybe at a party or something she'd pop some E, but she wasn't a druggie. I never saw her doing anything stronger than that. I don't know what the pills were about. And she sure as hell didn't have a gun. I'd have known about that."

"Then where'd they come from?" Aidan asked.

"You got me."

"Had she been acting any differently the last few days, maybe since we came by the other day?" I asked.

"Not really. Although she was really pissed that I'd let you guys in the room. She went off on me as soon as I got back that night. I just yelled right back and told her it wasn't my problem. She backed down real quick. She wasn't a fighter."

"What happened when the cops arrived?"

"I don't know for sure. They kept everybody away. Then later, these two cops, a man and woman, came and told me they thought it was suicide and that I couldn't go in the room. If I needed anything out of it, I was supposed to give somebody a list and they'd get it for me. Seemed a lot of trouble to go to if a girl had just committed suicide. I asked if she'd left a note, and they looked at each other and then the woman said no. I asked them if they were sure it was suicide. The man got kind of snotty and said they knew what they were doing and that it was in everyone's best interest if I didn't suggest it was anything but a suicide."

"The two cops weren't named Grafton and Bernhardt by any chance, were they?" I asked with the feeling I already knew the answer.

Keisha look surprised. "Yeah, they were. You know them?"

"We've met," I said wryly. The question now was what were Grafton and Bernhardt doing on this case? Did they think there might be a connection between Blake's death and Joey? Or was it just a coincidence? And why were they so intent on passing this off as a suicide? It had seemed fishy even to Keisha. Were they covering something up? What was going on?

"You and Blake never talked about her finding Joey?" Aidan asked while I was thinking.

"I told you before; we never talked about anything really. I knew she'd found some guy dead in a pool cuz everybody on campus knew she'd found him."

"Did you ever see this?" I asked on a sudden inspiration as I pulled Joey's necklace out from my shirt.

Keisha took a closer look, "Maybe."

"Did Blake have it?"

"If it's the same one I'm thinking of, yeah. She asked me who was on it. As far as I know, the girl had never set foot in a church, but she knew I went every week. I guess she thought I'd know who the saint was. I tried to explain that there's a big difference between Catholics and Baptists, but she didn't get it. I swear, talking to her was like talking to a wall sometimes."

"So Blake did have this necklace then?"

"Well, I can't say for sure, but I think so."

I looked at Aidan and an unspoken message passed between us. We were done here. Aidan thanked Keisha for talking to us, and we left with more questions than we'd started with.

Chapter 19

All the way home, we discussed the different possible scenarios that the new information we had just gleaned from Keisha could mean. And we came up with nothing. The things Keisha had told us just didn't make sense. Did Blake commit suicide or not? And if not, why were the police so set on making us think she did? The whole situation made me very uneasy. Maybe an emergency meeting was in order.

As soon as we got home, I called Killian. He couldn't come over until the next night so we chose a time and I called Laura, Gabe, and Caitlin. There was nothing left to do now but wait.

Adam called twice the next day with questions about the wedding, but other than that, it was a quiet Sunday. I was afraid to do anything until we talked to the rest of the gang and got their take on the situation with Blake.

Aidan was working out while I tried to distract myself with painting when he suddenly dropped his weights with a thump and turned to face me.

"Will, I have a question, and I think it's something we need to talk about before the wedding."

That didn't sound good. I put my paintbrush down and gave him my full attention. "Is something wrong?" I asked nervously.

"No, at least I hope not. It's just... Well, we haven't talked much about this whole wedding thing. I asked and you said yes and that was it. I'm not pushing you too fast, am I? Do you really want to do this?"

"Are you having second thoughts?" I asked in surprise.

"No! I mean, I know I want to do this, but I want to be sure you do, too. I don't want you to just because you think I want it or out of some sort of guilt. It has to be because you want it, too."

"Well, it's all happened pretty fast. I mean, two weeks ago we weren't even a couple. But yeah, I'm pretty sure I want to do this. I know I love you and I know without a doubt that you love me." I smiled at him. "Besides, this is really exciting, isn't it? Getting married and surprising everyone, starting a real life together, putting all the past behind us and looking only to the future — our future."

Aidan smiled back. "Yeah, it is pretty exciting. I guess I just want to be sure that you're sure. With your background and all, I know this can't be easy for you."

"My background?"

"Well, you were raised in the church and all, and your parents won't even talk to you. I know that early on you thought that God would hate you because you were gay. We talked about it once, on the balcony, remember? Do you still think that? Or what?"

"It's funny you should bring up my parents. I've been thinking about them a lot lately. I feel like that's unfinished business, you know?" He nodded. "But as far as the other stuff, I think I made my peace with that a while ago. I don't think God hates me just because I love you. That just doesn't fit what I've been taught all my life about God. I thought about what you told me, about how some of the Bible was translated incorrectly from the original language, and I decided that what I felt inside was more important than what I was taught as a child. It's kind of freeing, really, to realize that you can think for yourself and you don't have to blindly accept what you're told. There were always so many things that I didn't agree with, but I didn't have the courage to look into them for myself. I think I'd like to do that sometime."

Aidan sat and grinned at me.

"What?" I asked self-consciously.

"You are so amazing," he said.

"What do you mean?"

"Most people who have been through what you have would have either driven themselves crazy with guilt or turned their backs on God altogether. Instead, you make your peace with God himself and then want to do research."

I frowned. "What would turning my back on God have accomplished? It's not His fault people have twisted His words so badly."

"I think I can stop worrying about you," he laughed.

I stuck my tongue out at him. "Who asked you to worry in the first place? Just lift your weights so I can get back to my painting."

We went back to working in companionable silence.

Killian, sans Asher, was the first to arrive for the emergency meeting I called that night.

"Where's Asher?" I asked him as I let him in.

"Don't ask," he grumbled.

"Did you have another fight?" Aidan asked.

"Another? We're still having the first one. I didn't even tell him about this meeting. I knew he'd just flip out."

"What if he calls?"

"Kane knows to cover for me, and you can bet he'll be the one that answers the phone. Every time it rings, he pounces on it like a hungry tiger on a sick antelope. Nine times out of ten, it's one of his girlfriends, too, so nobody else bothers to race him for it anymore."

I laughed as another knock came at the door. This time is was Caitlin.

As I took her coat, she leaned in and whispered into my ear. "Can I talk to you after the meeting?"

"Yeah, sure. Is anything wrong?"

"We'll talk later."

I was still trying to figure that out when Laura and Gabe arrived. I couldn't help but notice that Gabe looked an awful lot like the proverbial cat that ate the canary. He couldn't hide a smug smirk, and I wondered what it was that was going on. Laura looked a little cross, so whatever it was he knew, I was willing to bet he hadn't shared it with her yet. I hoped that whatever news he had would be good and that it would help untangle some of the mysteries we were left with after our meeting with Keisha.

Since I was the one who had called the emergency meeting, I started things off. "I asked you all to come here tonight because Aidan and I talked to Keisha yesterday, and I thought it raised more questions than we got answered. We thought it was significant enough that we all needed to talk about it together."

With Aidan's help, we gave them a detailed rundown of what we had learned from Keisha.

"So was it a suicide or not? That's the question, right?" Gabe asked when we'd finished.

"That and if it wasn't a suicide and it was murder, why did the police want Keisha to think it was a suicide? Wouldn't it be better to have the campus warned if a killer was running around?" I added.

Killian sat forward. "The police may not want to panic the campus."

"I think it's obvious that she killed herself," Caitlin said. "Her roommate even said that she was acting strange, as if she weren't looking forward to something. She was probably planning her suicide."

"Then why wasn't there a note?" Laura asked.

I looked down at my lap. "Not every suicide leaves a note," I said softly.

Everyone suddenly looked horrified at their faux pas. No one seemed to know what to say. I was trying to think of a way to deflect the attention off of myself and back onto our investigation when Aidan saved the day. "Will's right. We learned that in our psychology class."

"So what's the consensus?" Killian asked, picking up on Aidan's cue. "Did she commit suicide or was she murdered like Joey?"

"Do we even know for sure that Joey was murdered?" Caitlin asked before anyone could speak. "I mean, it looks like this Blake chick wasn't exactly wrapped real tight. Maybe she found the necklace and made the rest up."

"What did she have to gain?" Aidan argued. "Besides, she didn't strike me as bright enough to come up with all this on her own. No, I think she either knew something or someone thought she knew something and she was taken out of the picture."

"I agree with Aidan. It was murder," I said.

"I think it was a suicide, but I don't think that necessarily means Joey wasn't murdered," Gabe said. "If Blake was murdered, then we're no longer dealing with someone who acts in the heat of the moment, as it appeared happened with Joey. They've moved into carefully planned and carried out premeditated murder."

"So, do you really think Blake killed herself, or would you just prefer that to dealing with a cold-blooded killer?" Killian asked.

Gabe grimaced. "Maybe a little of both," he admitted.

"Well, I have to agree that, while I hate coincidences, it sounds an awful lot like a suicide to me," Laura said. "I know I originally said it was too convenient to not be a murder, but why would the police lie?"

"We know that Caitlin thinks it was a suicide." Caitlin nodded. "So that makes it three to two, in favor of suicide," Killian said as if he was announcing the score to a game. "I'm afraid I'm going to tie things up. I have to side with Aidan and Will. I think it was murder. Just because the first murder was unplanned doesn't mean the killer couldn't feel trapped and think he had to kill again to protect himself."

"So we're split evenly," Laura said. "Where do we go from here? How do we proceed?"

"Well," Gabe said dramatically, his self-satisfied expression from earlier returning, "I have some information that isn't affected by whether or not Blake committed suicide. And it definitely gives us a direction to head in."

That got everyone's full attention.

"What information do you have?" Killian asked.

"I know who Blake's mystery man is."

Everyone began talking at once.

"Wait, wait, wait," he called, grinning the whole time. It was obvious he was enjoying the attention. "One at a time."

"Who is it?" we all yelled at once.

"His name is Robbie Meade," Gabe said, chuckling. "He doesn't go to Pemberton; he's from the tech school, but apparently he came with a friend who does go."

"How did you find this out?" I asked.

"And why didn't you tell me?" Laura demanded.

"I wanted it to be a surprise when I told everyone at once," he explained, answering Laura's question first. "I just found out today. I just happened to mention that I was trying to find this guy to someone in one of my classes. Someone else overheard and said that it sounded like his friend, Robbie. He wanted to know why I was looking for him. I asked him what his last name was, and he told me. Then he asked me again why I was looking for him. I told him someone had seen him with my girlfriend, and the guy just laughed and said it sounded like Robbie to him. When I asked for his phone number, though, the guy clammed up. Said he wasn't about to get his friend in trouble."

"Well, at least we have a name now," Killian said. "That's a lot more than we had before. Now all we have to do is find this guy and that should just be a matter of checking the phone book. If that doesn't work one of us can call the office at the tech school and weasel it out of someone there."

"Should we do it now?" I asked. I was ready for this to be over, and it seemed like Robbie Meade was our last chance.

"I can't," Laura said quickly. "I have to go."

"You do?" Gabe asked in surprise.

"Yes, I have a project due, and I have to get home and get started."

Gabe looked a little put out. "Well, it's a good thing we drove separately," he sulked.

"Is the meeting over?" Laura asked.

Killian looked as surprised by Laura's sudden rush as I felt. "Will called it. Are we done, Will?"

"I guess," I said, wondering what Laura was up to.

"Great," she said, bouncing to her feet. "Then I'll see everyone Friday night at Will and Aidan's surprise...whatever the hell it is. Oh, and I think we should all wait to call Robbie until we can do it together. Ok?"

She shrugged on her coat and started for the door.

Gabe grabbed his jacket and rushed after her with a shrug and a wave to the rest of us.

"That was a bit odd," Aidan said with a frown.

"If you ask me, she's a bit odd." Caitlin sniffed. "Can we talk now?" she asked me.

"Sure," I answered.

"In private?"

"Oh, right. We'll go in my bedroom."

As we left the room, I could feel Aidan and Killian's curious stares on my back.

"What's up?" I asked once we were in my room.

"I need to talk to you about something," she said. I couldn't read her voice, and her expression was guarded.

"Is something wrong?"

"You tell me," she shot back.

"What are you talking about?"

"I've been thinking about this whole thing with you and Aidan dating. I don't know that I'm comfortable with it."

"What?" I gasped. "You mean you aren't comfortable with me being gay? But you knew that from the beginning."

"It doesn't have anything to do with you being gay. I just can't help but wonder where this leaves me and the baby now that you're with him."

"I'm not following."

"How does this affect our arrangement about the baby?"

"It doesn't affect it at all. Why would it? I told you I've talked to a lawyer, and she's working on the paperwork now. She'll probably have it ready for us to sign in a couple days. Once that's done, it'll all be final."

"How does Aidan feel about all this?"

"He supports me one hundred percent."

"Does he? Maybe I'll feel better once the papers are signed, and it's all official. You have to understand that this baby means more to me than anything else in the world. When I decided to have this baby, I decided that I was going to do this right. I want what's best for him and that means I have to do whatever it takes to protect him. I won't let anything or anyone hurt my baby. And that includes you, Will."

I felt a chill run up my spine at her words. Was she threatening me or just trying to make me understand how much the baby meant to her?

"The baby means a lot to me, too, Caitlin," I assured her. "I want what's best for him or her, too. If that's what this is all about, then understand that I'm not going anywhere. I want to be a part of this child's life, and I'm certainly not going to do anything to intentionally hurt it."

She smiled. "Thank you, Will. I feel better now." She patted me on the cheek and slipped past me back into the hall. I got her coat for her, and I let her out.

Killian and Aidan were still in the living room. They sat close together on the sofa with their heads bent toward each other, speaking in soft voices. They stopped talking abruptly as I approached.

"What were you guys talking about?" I asked as I sat down on the other side of Aidan.

"Nothing," Aidan said, slipping his arm around me.

"If you were talking about nothing, then why'd you stop when I came over?"

They exchanged glances.

"What's going on?" I pressed.

"Maybe we should try calling this Robbie person," Killian suggested.

His attempt to change the subject wasn't even subtle. But I suspected my chances of getting anything out of either of them was slim to none, so with a sigh to let them know I knew what was going on, I gave in, "Ok, but what about Laura? She wanted us to wait."

"I don't think it's a good idea to wait," Killian said. "What if the same thing happens to him that happened to Blake? Then we would never get the chance to talk to him, and we'd never know what, if anything, he saw that night."

"Good point," I agreed. I slid out from underneath Aidan's arm and went to find the phone book. When I came back, I wiggled my way in-between the two cousins so we could all look at the pages.

We quickly discovered that we didn't know which spelling Robbie used on his last name. There were two Robert Meads, one Rob Mead, three Robert Meades, one R Meade, and no guarantee that any of them was the Robbie we were looking for. We decided that there was no way of finding out except to just call them all until we found the right one. We took turns calling, striking out on the first five tries. Although all the Roberts were perfectly nice, they weren't the guy we were looking for. I dialed the next number.

"Are you Robbie Meade?" I asked. By now this was our standard question.

"Yeah," said a male voice cautiously.

"Do you go to the tech school here in town?"

A pause, then, "Yeah."

For a second I didn't know what to say. I'd gotten used to all of us receiving negative answers to that question, after which we'd politely tell whomever we were talking to that we had the wrong number. I felt my pulse quicken. "Were you at the party the night Joey Taylor died?"

The line was perfectly quiet. For a panic-stricken moment I was afraid he'd hung up. "Hello?" I said.

"I'm still here," Robbie said quietly. "Who are you, and what do you want?"

"My name is Will Keegan; I was there too. Joey was my best friend. Please don't hang up."

"What do you want?"

"I don't think it was an accident. I think someone was with Joey right before he died, and I think they killed him."

"What does that have to do with me?"

"We talked to Blake," I said, and I heard a sharp intake of breath.

"Look, I'm sorry about your friend but there's nothing I can do to help you," he said with finality.

"Wait!" I called. "Please, just answer a few questions. Please! What can it hurt?"

"Ask Blake that question, why don't you? Oh wait, you can't. She's dead. And that's what I'll be if I get involved."

"You're already involved. You were in the pool house with Blake that night. What you know could help catch a killer."

"I don't know anything. I'm telling you, I can't help you. I've been hiding in my apartment ever since Blake wound up dead in her dorm room. Then a friend of mine called and said some guy was asking around about me at the school he goes to. I'm not dumb; I can see what's going on. I'm next on this homicidal maniac's hit list. I'm leaving town tomorrow for good. I'm moving to Maine to live with my dad."

"If you're leaving, then it can't hurt to tell us what you saw."

"You're not listening to me. I didn't see anything."

"Then you heard something. Blake told us you said you heard voices. What did you hear?"

"For God's sake, why can't you just leave me alone?"

"Because I need to know."

"Shit! If I tell you what I do know, will you leave me alone?"

"Yes, I promise," I said.

He sighed heavily into the receiver. "I heard something — well, someone — talking to the guy who ended up dead. At least, I assume it was the same guy. I wasn't paying attention at first, except to hope they stayed out of the pool house until we were done. Then they got louder, like they were mad or upset."

"Did you recognize the voices?"

He let out a short burst of nervous laughter. "Hell, no. That's why this is all so fucking messed up. I don't even know anybody at Pemberton except my friend. He's the one that invited me that night. Damn, I wish I'd never gone. Look, all I know is that they sounded like they were arguing. The guy sounded...I don't know, pissed off. He was loud, sounded kinda drunk. The girl was quieter, but if I had to say, she sounded more upset than he did."

"A girl?" I latched onto the word.

"Yeah."

My heart was pounding. "What were they saying? Could you hear anything they were saying?"

"I don't know. I wasn't listening, and I was kinda busy, you know?"

"But you're positive it was a girl?"

"Look, I'm not sure of anything. It coulda been a couple of fags for all I know. Ok? Now I've told you all I know. I gotta go; I have another call beeping in."

"Wait..." I tried, but I heard the click of the phone as he hung up, and then the line went dead.

I hit the end button on the phone and then stood staring dumbly at it for several seconds.

"It was a girl?" Aidan asked.

"That's what he said. He said they sounded like they were arguing, but he didn't hear what they were saying because he wasn't paying attention."

"A girl..." Killian said thoughtfully.

"What are you thinking?" I asked him.

"Nothing," he said, but he exchanged a meaningful look at Aidan, who nodded ever so slightly.

"Ok, that's it. What the hell is going on? What were you guys talking about earlier, and what was that just all about?"

"Calm down," Aidan soothed.

"Not until you tell me what is going on."

He sighed. "Killian and I were talking while you were in the back with Caitlin. He pointed out that the way things have been happening with this case it almost seemed like the killer knew what we were doing every step of the way."

"Well, we've not been very secretive," I pointed out.

"Still, it does seem to be just a little too coincidental."

"So what are you suggesting? You think the killer is one of us?"

"Not just any of us," Killian pointed out. "According to Robbie, it was a girl."

"There are only two girls in our group," I said. "And I know it isn't Laura or Caitlin."

"How do you know?" Aidan asked gently.

"What? You can't be serious! I've known Laura forever. Just because you two haven't hit it off doesn't make her a murderer. And Caitlin was with me when Joey was killed, so it couldn't have been her. Besides, what did she have to gain with Joey dead?"

They exchanged another look.

"Will you stop that!" I yelled.

"Will, think about it," Aidan tried again. "You'd known Joey forever, too, but his behavior took you completely by surprise. So much so, in fact, that you didn't even believe me when I first told you about it. You had to see it for yourself. You have to admit that Laura's been acting strangely. What about the way she left here so suddenly tonight, as soon as Gabe told us Robbie's name?"

"That's why I thought it was important that we call him right away," Killian explained.

"And you remember she stayed in the hallway the day we talked to Blake after we left. Maybe she went back in there as soon as we were gone. There's just too much that doesn't fit."

"So you're convinced that Laura is the killer?"

"No, not convinced. It's just a possibility that we have to look at. To be honest, Caitlin is just as good a suspect except that she was with you. She didn't have to have anything to gain from Joey's death. We've already decided that it was a crime of passion, committed in the heat of the moment, not planned out like Blake's murder."

"Well, I don't believe it. I don't believe it was either one of them. Caitlin just isn't a killer and, for all we know, there could be a perfectly reasonable explanation for the way Laura's been acting."

Aidan and Killian exchanged one more glance.

"I hope you're right, Will," Aidan said with a sigh. "I really do."

Chapter 20

The next morning at work, I was busy in the back room, trying in vain to force some sort of organization on the mess that had accumulated back there over the years. Hearing a noise, I looked up to find Nikki in the doorway with a worried expression on her face.

"Will?" she said. "There's a Detective Grafton here to see you."

"What?" I asked. The clipboard I had been taking notes on slipped unnoticed from my hand.

Grafton's unpleasant face appeared over Nikki's shoulder.

"I'll talk to Mr. Keegan right here if that's alright with you, Ms. Avanti," he said in a manner that made it clear that he was going to whether it was ok with her or not.

Nikki looked to me, and I gave her a curt nod. She turned and walked stiffly back to the gallery. Detective Grafton stepped in, letting the door shut behind him.

"Mr. Keegan," he said conversationally, "since we last spoke, some very interesting things have been happening. Your name keeps popping up everywhere I turn."

"Oh?" I asked carefully. I had decided that the less I said the better.

"Yes, oh. Do you have anything you'd like to tell me?"

"Maybe. What things are we talking about?"

"I think you already know the answer to that. Miss Hammond's untimely death? You probably heard about that on the news. What you don't know is that while we officially released a report of suicide, we were still investigating the whole incident. As you well know, Miss Hammond was the person who reportedly found your friend, Mr. Taylor. There were many things about her death that didn't wash. I couldn't help but remember our conversation about your suspicions concerning the death of your friend. We took a second look at Mr. Taylor's death and we found a few things that took on a different shade in the light of Miss Hammond's death."

"Why are you telling me all this now?"

"Two reasons. Number one, you and your junior detective club have been royally fucking up our investigation. You're blundering through this whole thing like the infamous bull in the china shop. You're destroying evidence everywhere and where you've not destroyed it you've outright stolen it."

"I...we..."

"We know all about the rock Mr. Maza so kindly kept for us. We swung by and picked it up on the way here."

I was starting to get nervous. Was I in trouble? "What's reason number two?" I asked, even though I didn't really want to know.

"Number two is simple. For your own protection, you need to stop this stupidity now. This is not a game. You kids are in way over your heads. You're playing with a cold-blooded killer. This whacko has already killed three people; I don't want you to end up number four."

"Three?" My blood ran cold as his words sank in. "Joey, Blake, and...who?"

"It happened last night. It's not even hit the news yet. We're trying to keep a lid on it as long as possible."

"Who?" I insisted, fighting a rising feeling of panic. "Who was it?"

"Robert Meade, age nineteen, student at the tech school, attended the party the night Mr. Taylor died, was with Miss Hammond when she found Mr. Taylor. But you already knew all that. You talked to him on the phone last night."

"What? How..."

"We checked his phone records."

"When was he killed?"

"Most likely very shortly after you hung up from talking to him. His friends found him less than half an hour after your phone call was logged in."

"He got another phone call while we were talking."

"We know. It was another of your cronies, a Ms. Duvier I believe."

My mind whirled. Laura had called Robbie? Why? And then he'd been killed shortly after.

"You might be interested to know that our killer is getting sloppy...or cocky...or desperate. Of the three that last one is the most dangerous. Desperate people do stupid things."

"What do you mean?"

"He gave up all pretense of making it look like a suicide. Put six holes in him and left him on the doorstep."

"He was shot?"

"Yep, five more times than was needed to kill him."

"Oh, my God," I whispered.

"Are you scared, Mr. Keegan?"

I nodded numbly.

"Good. You should be. You've been poking a beehive, and if you don't stop you're going to get stung. I hope you're scared out of your mind. It's the only thing that's going to save you. Now, I want you to get out of police business and stay out."

A wave of anger suddenly burned through me. "If you'd done your job in the first place. I wouldn't be in police business," I snarled.

He stopped on his way to the door and turned slowly back to face me.

"Maybe you're right, but I'm telling you we're on it now and I want you out of it." He turned to leave again.

"Do you even know that it was a girl with Joey that night?" I called out.

He stopped again and turned sharply on his heel. "What did you say?"

"It was a girl, with Joey, right before he died. They were arguing..."

"How do you know that?"

"Robbie told me, on the phone last night. You mean the junior detectives found something out the big bad policemen didn't know?"

He crossed the room in two strides, grabbed the front of my shirt, and slammed me back against the wall.

"Listen, kid," he snarled, "I've tried to be nice up to now, but I've just about had it with you and your little friends. You're damn lucky I'm not bringing you up on obstruction charges, and you're even luckier that you aren't dead yet. It's because of your fucking around in police business that that kid is even dead now. Did you think about that? And for that matter probably the girl, too. And if you keep it up, you can bet your sweet ass that you'll be joining them. Then they can thank you in person for getting them killed."

He stared down at me for a few seconds before letting go of me. I slid to the floor where I started shaking. He stalked to the door, then paused before leaving. "Stay out of this, kid. I mean it." And he was gone.

When Nikki found me a few minutes later, I was crying so hard I couldn't talk. I was still crying when Aidan arrived to take me home. By the time we got to the apartment, I had pulled myself together enough to tell Aidan what had happened. He was as shaken up about the news of Robbie Meade's death as I had been. He had already received word about the police visit to Gabe's house; Gabe had called him as soon as they left.

"Grafton was way out of line," Aidan said. We were sitting on the couch, Aidan with his arms around me, holding me close. "He can't know that Robbie died because of us. He should have never said that."

"He's right," I sniffled. "We're as much to blame for his and Blake's death as if we'd killed them ourselves."

"That's insane," he argued. "The killer would have found them herself eventually. What were we supposed to do, just let her get away with Joey's death?"

"At least no one else would have died."

"You can't know that. We did what we thought was best at the time, and I still think it was best. If someone is crazy enough to kill once, chances are they'll kill again. Especially if they got away with it the first time."

"It's just that this killer always seems to be one step ahead of us."

"Or one step behind us. Actually, if anything, she seems to be right in step with us."

I sat up and pulled away.

"I'm sorry, Will. I didn't mean to bring that up again."

"Laura called Robbie last night."

"What?"

"While I was talking to him. That's why he hung up on me; he had another call coming in."

"Why would Laura call him?"

"To get his address?"

"Will, don't go jumping to conclusions."

"You and Killian are the ones that suspected her."

"We didn't say we suspected her; it was just a possibility. Look, we'll just look into it and figure out for sure..."

"No. We won't."

"What do you mean?"

"We're out of it."

"What? We can't just…"

"Aidan, we're done, finished. I told you what Grafton said; it's up to the police now. Too many people have died. I can't lose anyone else. I…I can't risk losing you."

He pulled me into his chest again, and I cuddled into him gratefully.

"You're right," he said, rubbing his hands over my back. "I just wish I could be there when they bring this bitch in. After all she's put you through…"

"I'm so lucky to have you," I whispered.

By some sort of silent mutual agreement, the topic of Joey, his killer, or any of the murders didn't come up the rest of the night. We watched some TV and went to bed early. The next morning though, it seemed Aidan assumed it was open season again.

"What happened after Joey attacked you and you ran away?" he said over breakfast.

I stared at my bowl of cereal for a second, then pushed it away. I seemed to have suddenly lost my appetite.

"Do we have to talk about this now?" I asked plaintively.

"I'm just trying to settle all the loose ends in my mind."

I sighed. "I ran downstairs and then I went outside."

"Right away?"

"Huh?"

"You went straight outside after you came downstairs?"

"No, I got sick so I ran to the bathroom and locked myself in. Why?"

"I'm just trying to create a timetable between when you last saw Joey and when Blake and Robbie found him in the pool."

"We're out of this, remember? It's up to the police now."

"For my peace of mind, Will. How long were you in the bathroom?"

"I don't know. I forgot my stopwatch."

"Five minutes? Ten?"

"More like fifteen or twenty."

"That long to blow chunks?"

"No, once I was in there I didn't want to come out. It was like my own private sanctuary for a little while. I just sat there and cried until someone pounding on the door became too much. Then I went outside."

"And Caitlin was there? Under the tree?"

"Yeah."

"Ok."

"Ok? That's it?"

"Yeah. That's all."

"Aidan, what's going on? What was that all about?"

He got up, walked around the table to my side, and bent over for a kiss.

"Don't worry about it," he said. "I've got to get to school now, and you've got to get to work. I'll see you this evening."

The next couple of days passed without incident. Everyone was shaken up by the news of Robbie's death, and no one was eager to go on playing detective. It was obvious that we'd been playing out of our league.

Neither Aidan nor I was in exactly a party-planning mood, so we left all the wedding plans to Adam. We were going to be almost as surprised as our guests.

On Wednesday, Ilana called and said that the papers were ready. After talking to Caitlin, I called Ilana back and made an appointment for the two of us to look over and sign them the next day.

Caitlin was strangely quiet on the ride over to Ilana's office Thursday afternoon.

"Are you ok?" I asked her in the elevator.

"Yeah, why?"

"You just seem kinda distant."

"I guess this is just a big step. I'm glad we're doing this, but in some ways I feel like I'm giving up my baby."

"You're not giving up your baby. No matter what, you'll always be its mother."

She smiled. "I know. You're right. I'm just being silly."

The explanation of the papers was long and somewhat boring, filled with legalese and formal phrases that didn't make much sense. After that, the actual signing of the papers was surprisingly quick and more than a little anticlimactic. It seemed hard to believe that simply signing my name on a few lines could make such a huge difference to so many lives, including one that was yet to be born.

I shared my feelings with Caitlin on the elevator ride down.

"It does seem unreal," she agreed. "If I wasn't starting to show, I almost wouldn't believe any of it."

"You're starting to show?" I asked in surprise. I hadn't noticed at all.

Caitlin proudly pulled her shirt tight across her belly, and sure enough, the beginning of a very slight potbelly could be seen.

I grinned at her with a slightly giddy feeling.

"We should do something to celebrate," I said.

"What? The signing of the papers or me showing?"

"Both." I laughed.

We went to a nice Chinese restaurant since Caitlin said she was craving egg drop soup and had a celebratory lunch.

After I dropped her off at her apartment, I found myself driving in the direction of my parents' home instead of our apartment. It took me a while to realize what I was doing, and when I did, I decided that it was a sign. They had been on my mind more and more of late, and I found myself wanting to at least make an effort to include them in my life once again, especially now, when I was about to become a parent of sort. I could really use the advice. No book, no matter how many times I read it, could ever take the place of good solid experience. And besides, there's just something about becoming a parent that makes you connect to your parents in some strange way.

I pulled into the driveway and was surprised to see Dad's car there in the mid-afternoon. He was almost never home during the day; he practically lived at the church. I walked slowly up to the door and stood there a minute without knocking. Now that I was there, I was suddenly less sure of what I was doing. Was I expecting a warm greeting with open arms? If so, I suspected I was at the wrong address. I remembered Mom's voice on the phone the day they found out I was gay. *"Your father says you're not welcome back here..."* Just as I was about to turn and leave the door swung open to reveal my mother.

"Will?" she said with a confused expression on her careworn face. She looked older than the last time I had seen her. "I...I thought I heard a car pull up."

"Mom," I said in surprise. I couldn't think of anything to say, so we stood there awkwardly, looking at each other for what seemed like an eternity. Finally I said, "I don't know what I'm doing here. I shouldn't have come." I turned to leave.

"Will," she called softly, "come in. Please?"

I turned to see she was holding the door open. I hesitated just a second before stepping inside. I hadn't been in the house in months, but nothing had changed. Everything was right where it always was. Mom started for the kitchen, and I followed her.

"Where is Dad? Why is his car here?" I asked her as we walked.

She didn't answer until we were in the kitchen. She sat in one of the chairs that had been around longer than I had and let out a deep sigh.

"Your father is sick, Will."

"What? Sick how?"

"We don't know exactly. He had some kind of attack. The doctors think it's his heart."

"When? Why didn't I know?"

"Last month, right before Thanksgiving. I didn't call, because he didn't want you to know. It's...it's been hard. He's not recovering like he should be. The doctors say it's just one of those things they can't explain. For all their technology and miracle cures, some things are still beyond their understanding. So all we can do is watch and wait."

"Can I...will he see me?"

She thought for a moment. "Probably, yes. A lot has changed since his attack. He's changed. Let me go in first and make sure; he's so weak now."

She stood up slowly and walked out of the room. I noticed that she moved like an old woman, as if every movement were an effort. She wasn't gone too long before she was back.

She nodded. "No surprises, though, Will. He's really very weak. And don't be too shocked when you see him. He probably should be in the hospital, but he insisted, and since there wasn't really anything they could do they let him come home."

I nodded numbly and followed her upstairs to their bedroom. The first thing I noticed was how much like a hospital room it looked. Dad was lying slightly elevated in a hospital bed that must have been brought in just for him.

Machines stood all around him, like malevolent guards. Most of the room's furnishings had been moved out to make room for all the new paraphernalia. I put off focusing on Dad until last. If Mom hadn't told me that it was Dad, I would have never recognized him. He was a pale shadow of his former self, gray and faded.

"Will, I didn't want you to see me like this," he said weakly.

"Like what, Dad?" I asked, trying to keep my voice light and knowing there was a slight quiver in it anyway. "You look great."

"No, I look like death warmed over. I won't be here much longer. I...I'm glad you came."

"Don't say that, Dad." I moved closer to the bed and sat down in the chair that was there.

"Why not? It's the truth. I feel it. I see it in the doctors' faces, although they are scared to say it. I see it in your mother's face, although she's terrified to even think it. I'm not afraid to die, Will. I've been preparing for it all my life. I have a peace about death. What I didn't have a peace about was how I'd left things with you. And here you are. God brought you to me so I could make my peace with you before I go."

"Dad, stop talking like this. You're not going anywhere."

"Son, I know I handled things badly. I know I hurt you."

"Don't worry about that; I'm ok now."

"No thanks to me. You almost died; if that had happened I don't think I could have ever forgiven myself." He took my hand that was lying on the bed and gripped it tightly.

I was amazed at the difference that had come over him. Could this be the same man who had practically disowned me just a few months before?

"I handled things badly," he went on. "I should have known that you're my son and above all else, that comes first. I messed up. I thought with my head instead of my heart. I thought I was doing what was right, as far as the church was concerned. I never stopped to think about whether or not it was right for you, for our family. I don't know...if you ever have children, don't ever turn them away, no matter what they do. Promise me, Will."

"I...I promise. You know...I'm still gay, you know," I said uncertainly. I wasn't sure if that was too much or what.

"I know, Will," he said. His eyes closed, and for a second I was afraid he had passed out or worse. But then they opened again. "I can't say that I accept it still. I don't understand. Everything I've ever been taught says one thing, and my heart says another. I don't know if I will ever be able to accept it, but I love you and that's all I can offer right now."

"It's enough, Dad," I said around a lump in my throat.

"I'm a bit tired now," he said. And he did look even worse than he had when I'd come in, if that were possible.

"I'll let you rest," I said softly.

"Will you be here when I wake up?" he asked feebly.

"Yes," I promised.

I turned to find Mom crying, slumped against the doorway. She shook her head, signaling me not to speak, then she turned and walked back to the kitchen. I followed.

"That's what he's been waiting for," she said once we were there. "He'll go now."

"What do you mean?"

"He's been hanging on; I wasn't sure why. Now I know."

"For me?"

"Yes, he needed to know you forgave him."

"I'm getting married tomorrow, Mom," I blurted out suddenly.

"You're what? To who?"

"To Aidan."

She pulled out a chair and sat down heavily.

"I don't expect you to be happy," I said quickly. "I just wanted you to know. It seemed like you should know."

"Don't tell your father."

"I won't. I wasn't..."

"How can you get married?"

"It's not a legal wedding. It's just a commitment ceremony between Aidan and me. I don't even know all the details. A friend of ours is doing all the planning. We're just showing up."

"When is it?"

"Tomorrow night at six. And there's more."

"More?" she repeated in a voice that made me wonder if she could handle more.

"This is complicated. I'm going to be raising a baby. Legally I guess I'm the baby's father now."

She stared at me dumbstruck for several minutes before she spoke.

"How in the world... I thought you were gay. You're marrying a boy. Where'd the baby come from?"

"It's not really mine. The baby is Joey's."

She shook her head in confusion. "But Joey is dead, and you just said you were the father."

"Caitlin got pregnant before Joey died; she's the mother. And I said I'm the legal father, not the biological father. We signed papers."

"What? Why would you do something like that?"

"Joey was my best friend, Mom. I loved him. This baby is all I have left of him. And this baby deserves a father. I wanted to do this. I can't explain it. It's just something I knew I had to do."

"I don't understand."

"I'm not asking you to understand. I just...I'm going to need some help, some advice. And you're the person I respect most in the world when it comes to raising a child."

Fresh tears rolled down her cheeks as she buried her head in her hands.

"I need to call Aidan, let him know where I am," I said as I walked over to the phone.

"I'm going to go check on your father," she said as she fled from the room.

I dialed our number and was relieved when Aidan answered on the second ring.

"Hey, the papers are all signed," I told him.

"Good. Where are you? I expected you back a long time ago."

"I'm at Mom and Dad's."

"You're where?" he asked in disbelief.

"At my parents. I know. It was a whim. I don't know why I did it. I just ended up here somehow. Dad had some sort of attack last month, a bad one. They don't know how he's lived this long. Mom said it was just because he wanted to see me again, but he was too stubborn to make the first move. Aidan...it was like he was a different man."

"Did you tell him about you and me?"

"No, but I told Mom."

"How'd she take it?"

"I'm not sure. She was kind of stunned, I think. My news about the baby kind of took precedence, though."

"Jeez, Will, you really know how to dump it on someone, don't you?"

"It just kept coming out. I think I'll stay here awhile. I'm sure she'll have a lot of questions once it all sinks in."

"Ok. If you need me, call me."

"I will. I love you, Aidan."

"I love you too, Will."

I hung up just as Mom rushed back into the kitchen.

"I can't wake your father. Call 911."

I snatched the phone back up without even thinking and dialed 911.

"Is he alive?" I asked as the operator answered on the other end.

"Yes, I think so," Mom said, sounding slightly hysterical. I couldn't blame her. She clasped her hands in front of her face as if she were praying. She probably was.

"Hello?" the 911 operator said for the second time.

"Yes, we need an ambulance. My father had a heart attack last month, and now we can't get him to wake up."

"Ok, an ambulance is being sent out now. I need your name and address, sir," the operator said.

I gave her the information and answered some more questions. She had me stay on the line while we waited for the ambulance. Mom went back to stay with Dad.

The next half hour was a blur. The ambulance arrived, and soon the house seemed full of technicians as they ran back and forth between my dad's bedside and the emergency vehicle. They ended up taking him to the hospital. I called Aidan and drove Mom there. Aidan was waiting for us when we arrived. After that, things settled into a long, tedious wait.

After some time had passed, a doctor came out to tell us that Dad had slipped into a coma, and they didn't really expect him to come out of it. Medically, they still couldn't explain it, but it didn't look good. It could be hours, it could be days, but it was just a matter of time now.

"What do you want to do?" he asked Mom.

"I think he'd want to be at home," she said softly.

"Are you sure?" he asked.

"Yes, his sister will come and stay with me."

And so that's what we did. We arranged for Dad to be transported back home, and Aidan and I stayed with mom until my aunt, Asher's mom, arrived to spend the night. Aidan and I drove our separate cars back home where I collapsed into a fitful sleep filled with nightmares about Joey, Blake, Robbie, and my father, all dead, and all demanding something of me that I felt I couldn't give.

Chapter 21

I called Mom first thing the next morning. She said that there had been no change since the night before.

While I was on the phone, a polite knock came at the door.

"Who could that be? Can you get that?" I asked Aidan.

"Well, we know it isn't Nikki, or she'd be beating the door down by now," he said as he started for the door.

When he opened it, Adam swept in with his arms loaded with shopping bags, which were brimming over with flowers, ribbon, and Christmas lights. In all the confusion of Dad's crisis, the wedding had completely slipped my mind.

"Oh, my gosh!" I gasped.

"What is it?" Mom asked on the other end of the line.

"I forgot all about the wedding! We'll have to cancel it."

Both Adam's and Aidan's faces fell so quickly it would have been comical if I wasn't so upset.

"What's going on?" Adam asked Aidan, who proceeded to bring him quickly up to date.

Meanwhile, Mom was talking to me. "No, you can't cancel your wedding. Your father — well, I can't say he would have wanted you to go ahead with this, but he would want you to be happy, and if this is what will make you happy, then...at any rate, don't cancel it. Please. You heard the doctors. It could be today; it could be next week. They just don't know."

"It doesn't seem right..."

"Will, you've been living your life separately from us for months now by your father's choice and my silent agreement. You shouldn't stop living your life now simply because his is coming to an end. I want you to do this. Celebrate life. Please."

"If...if you're sure."

"I am. I love you, Will."

"I love you, Mom. I'll try to get by the house sometime today before the wedding."

"Ok. Tell Aidan I said hello and thank him for being there last night."

"Aidan's been there for me many nights. He knows how grateful I am."

"Well, now he needs to know how grateful I am."

"I'll tell him."

I hung up and turned to face Adam and Aidan.

"The wedding is still on," I said.

"Woohoo!" Adam and Aidan yelled together. Adam quickly grew serious again. "I'm sorry about your father, Will."

"Well, like Mom said, I've been living without him for months now..."

"It doesn't make it any easier."

"I've got to get ready for work," I said as I felt tears building. I fled to the bathroom where I turned on the shower to cover the sound of my muffled sobs.

I should have known I couldn't fool Aidan. He followed me right in and wrapped me in his arms.

"Are you sure you want to go ahead with this?" he asked me when I had calmed down.

"No, but I feel like we should anyway. I feel like if we don't do it now we might never do it."

He squeezed me tight. "Why don't you call and tell Nikki you won't be in today. You've got too much going on, your dad, the wedding, all this with Joey's killer."

"No, I need the distraction. I'll go in for at least part of the day. I want to go see Dad this afternoon, too."

"Do you want me to go with you?"

I sighed. "Yes, but I don't think it would be such a good idea. Are we supposed to wear anything special for tonight? Like am I supposed to pick up a tux or something?"

"I hope not. I'll go ask Adam."

He left me to my shower and reappeared as I was getting dressed.

"Adam says we're to dress casual. Since everything else about this has been unconventional he decided we shouldn't have to dress in monkey suits, which is perfectly fine with me."

"Me, too," I agreed.

By the time I came back out the entire entryway was filled with bags full of decorations.

"Oh, my God, Martha Stewart died and left us all her shit," I moaned.

Adam laughed as he appeared from behind a seven-foot undecorated live tree that had miraculously sprouted in the middle of our living room. "Get in the spirit, Will!" he said. "You guys should have been decorated by now. What kind of self-respecting gay couple are you?"

I started to answer that we were the type of gay couple who until recently had been trying to find who killed their best friend, but I stopped myself just in time. Aidan stepped in to fill the awkward pause left by my second thought.

"We're still trying to get the hang of this whole couple thing. Give us a little time and we'll figure it all out."

"I've got to get to work," I said and made my exit.

How am I ever going to get through this day? I wondered as I drove to work. Work did prove to be a distraction, however. There were lots of people out looking for unique Christmas presents. Not too many bought anything, though. For the most part, when they got a look at the prices, people's reactions ranged from shock to abject horror. Finally, though, the façade of geniality just proved more than I could keep up, and I asked Nikki for the rest of the day off.

"No problem, *bello niño*," she said with a soft caress to my cheek. "I will see you tonight. Take care."

I drove straight to Mom and Dad's house. I found Mom dozing in a chair next to Dad's bed. As for Dad, I had to look closely to see the movement of his chest before I was even sure if he was breathing. I had only been to one funeral, besides Joey's, in my entire life. It had been for a great uncle on my father's side. I had thought then that he looked like a wax dummy, as if there had never been any breath of life in him. As I stood looking at my dad now, that image came back to me. It was how Dad looked now. As if his spirit had already left. I wondered if Mom could see it, too, or the nurses. Maybe it was just my imagination.

I stepped into the room and touched Mom lightly on the hand. She jumped and looked wildly about for a second before she focused on me. Her tired face lit up when she saw who it was.

"Will, you made it."

"I told you I'd be by sometime today."

"I didn't think you would with everything going on."

I gave her a hug and then stood by Dad's side, looking down on him.

"Can he hear us?" I asked.

"They think so. They said to talk to him. The doctor said that many times he's seen people who hold on until their families tell them it's ok to go, and then they just slip quietly away."

I looked over at her. The unspoken words had been as loud as the spoken. "Is that what you want me to do?" I whispered.

She looked at me as tears filled her eyes. She gave a jerky nod and then stood up and walked out quickly.

I looked helplessly after her for a moment, then turned slowly back to my father.

"Dad?" I began in a raspy voice. I cleared my throat and began again. "Dad, it's Will. I...I don't know what to say really." I cast about desperately for something to say. How do you tell someone it's ok to die? Then it occurred to me that you simply make it so that there is nothing holding them here.

"Dad, I want you to know that I forgive you." I choked up, and it was a while before I could continue without crying. "I know I disappointed you. I wasn't what you hoped I would be. I'm sorry. I'm doing the best I know how. And I'm doing all right now; I'm going to be ok. Don't worry about me. I've got my friends. I've got...Aidan. He loves me. And I love him. He's good to me, Dad. And I've got Mom. Don't worry about her either; I'll take care of her. So I guess what I'm trying to say is, it's ok to let go. You don't have to stay here and suffer any more. Dad...I...I love you."

I broke down and cried at his side for a few minutes. When my tears had run their course, I backed slowly away. At the door, I turned to find Mom waiting for me, tears rolling silently down her cheeks. She took me in her arms, and we cried together.

I wasn't in much of a celebratory mood when I arrived back at the apartment later that afternoon. I tried to shake the heavy mood as I rode the elevator up, but it wasn't easily dislodged.

As I came through the door, I received my first glimpse of the magic Adam had created in the relatively short time I'd been gone. It was so spectacular that I stopped dead and just gaped.

The entryway had been made into a tunnel of fairy lights and pine garlands. It ended at the living room, which had been transformed into a beautiful sanctuary. All the furniture had been removed and folding chairs had been set up in a semi-circle facing the huge windows. In the center of the windows a Christmas tree had been set up and decorated completely in gold and white. All the other decorations in the room carried on the simple, elegant theme: gold and white bows were fixed here and there with sprays of pure white lilies; white pillars held gold candles that had been set up inside frosted glass globes with wreaths for bases. The result was stunning.

Adam was putting some finishing touches on the tree and didn't hear me come in.

"Adam, this is...incredible." I gasped.

He spun around and a wide grin quickly spread across his face. "Do you like it, then?" he asked eagerly.

"Like it? Are you kidding? I love it! It's absolutely perfect."

"Good, I was hoping you'd approve. Aidan hasn't even seen the finished results yet. You're the first."

"I'm honored. Where is Aidan?"

"He's in his room, working on his vows."

"His what?" I asked in panic. "We were supposed to write our own vows? Why didn't anyone tell me?"

"Aidan just decided a little while ago. But don't worry, I'm sure Bryan will have some vows for you to use. Bryan is the minister I told you about; he's at the local Metropolitan Community Church."

"If Aidan's writing his own, I have to write my own," I wailed. "I'd better get to work."

I dashed back to my old room and threw open the door to find it packed full with the furniture from the living room.

"Whoa!" I exclaimed.

Aidan opened the door to our bedroom across the hall. "You're home!" he said with a grin.

I closed the door and gave him a kiss on the lips. "I can't believe you decided to write your own vows without telling me!" I whined. "Now I have to hurry up and write mine."

"You don't have to," he said. "I just had so much that I wanted to say I decided to write my own."

"Well, I want to do it, too."

"Then you'd better get to work. Time's running out, and it isn't as easy as you'd think."

"No kidding! I never thought it would be easy; you started this," I said as I slipped by him. He followed me in and quickly scooped up a notepad that was lying open on the desk. He ripped off the top page and tossed the notebook to me.

"Get to work. I'll go see if Adam needs any help."

He left, shutting the door behind himself, and I set to work.

Several hours later, the door opened again. A small pile of crumpled false starts and frustrated attempts surrounded me. I turned expecting to see Aidan, but it was Adam. He was holding a white bundle in his arms.

"Sorry to interrupt," he said, "but it's almost time to start. Your guests will be arriving soon, and I have a surprise for you. I know I told Aidan to just dress casually, but I thought of this today and got your sizes out of your closet and well...here."

He held out his bundle, and I saw now that it was clothing. White chinos and a white chamois button-up shirt that was as soft as velvet. I accepted with a hug.

"Consider them a wedding present," he said. "Now get dressed and get ready. Bryan is here already. I'll send him back with Aidan in a minute."

I quickly pulled on the clothes Adam had bought me and found that they fit perfectly. I was reading over my completed vows when a soft knock came on the door.

"Come in," I called.

It opened to reveal Aidan and a young man who appeared to be not much older than Aidan and I.

"Will, this is Rev. Cairbre," Aidan said.

"Please, call me Bryan," the minister said as he held out his hand for me to shake. He was a stocky guy with brown hair and eyes and an athletic build. He looked like he would be more at home on a football field than in a pulpit. He was wearing a simple black suit and tie.

"Thank you so much for doing this on such short notice," I said.

"Oh please, thank you for the privilege," he said with a warm smile. "I don't get to do nearly as many of these as I would like. Besides, I owed Adam a favor. He designed our church's website and wouldn't let us pay him for it."

"I'd like to come to your church sometime," I said. "I haven't been to church in months, since I admitted that I was gay. My dad's a minister..." I choked up and couldn't go on. Aidan was by my side in a flash with his arm around my waist.

"Hey, say no more," Bryan said sympathetically, misunderstanding my emotion, "so was my dad. It leaves its share of scars. If you want, after the wedding and all the excitement has settled down, get up with me and I can give you some material on recovering from Bible abuse."

"Bible abuse?"

"Yeah, that's the term for how religion has twisted and used the Bible to hurt people like us and others. Come in with an open mind, and you may just find some healing. I know you'll find God's love."

I nodded uncertainly, but I already knew I wanted to know more. Now wasn't the time, though, our wedding was getting ready to start in fifteen minutes.

He asked for our rings — we were using the rings Aidan had bought — and then quickly ran over the order of the ceremony. It was short, simple, and very elegant. I loved it. I found myself getting truly excited about what we were about to do. There had been so much going on that I hadn't really had time to think about it. But now my heart was racing, and I felt a growing anticipation.

After that, it was just a matter of waiting. Adam was greeting the guests as they arrived and making the big announcement. Steve, who had been in on it all from the first, was filming everyone's reactions so we could watch it later.

Finally, after enough time had gone by for me to develop a severe case of butterflies, a soft rap came at the door. Adam popped his head in.

"Bryan?" he said. "We're ready."

Bryan slipped out, and Adam stayed in the doorway.

We could easily hear Bryan as he addressed our small group of friends. "Friends, we are here this day to share with Aidan and Will a most important moment in their lives. They have learned to know and love each other, and now they have decided to live their lives together. I would like to thank each of you on their behalf for being here. You have each been invited because you are important to them and they wanted you to share in this moment with them. I would like to start by reading a passage of scripture that I find very appropriate for such a time as this. It's from 1 Corinthians 13: 4-13.

"Love is patient and kind; love is not jealous or boastful; it is not arrogant or rude. Love does not insist on its own way; it is not irritable or resentful; it does not rejoice at wrong, but rejoices in the right. Love bears all things, believes all things, hopes all things, endures all things. Love never ends; as for prophecy, it will pass away; as for tongues, they will cease; as for knowledge, it will pass away. For our knowledge is imperfect and our prophecy is imperfect; but when the perfect comes, the imperfect will pass away. When I was a child, I spoke like a child, I thought like a child, I reasoned like a child; when I became a man, I gave up childish ways. For now we see in a mirror dimly, but then face to face. Now I know in part; then I shall understand fully, even as I have been fully understood. So faith, hope, love abide, these three; but the greatest of these is love."

As his last words faded away, music started as if on cue. I quickly recognized the opening of *NSYNC's "This I Promise You". Adam signaled to us to come. Aidan offered his arm, which I took, and together we walked down the hall and into the living room. As we entered, everyone stood up and I got my first glimpse of who had come.

There, beaming back at us was everyone in my life who mattered to me. Killian and Asher were the first faces I focused on. To their right stood Kane and beyond him, Caitlin, wearing a slightly stunned expression. Behind them stood Ilana and Lysander. Gabe and Laura were there, and Nikki with her boyfriend, Sam. Steve was across the room aiming a camcorder in our direction. Bryan was standing in front of the Christmas tree. To my surprise, I noticed it was snowing outside the windows. It couldn't have been more perfect.

Then I noticed the final touch. Mom stood at the back of the room, just inside the door. She looked worn out, tired beyond measure, but she was there and she was smiling with tears in her eyes. Aidan squeezed my hand, and I realized that he must have had something to do with her being there.

We turned finally to face Bryan as the last notes of the song faded away. Adam took a seat next to Kane as everyone sat down and looked at us expectantly.

Bryan spoke again. "Will and Aidan, all of us know that you are deeply in love. But beyond the warmth and glow, the excitement and romance, what is love, really? Real love is caring as much about the welfare and happiness of your partner as about your own. Real love is not possessive or jealous; it is liberating; it sets you free to become your best self. Real love is not total absorption in each other; it is looking outward in the same direction together. Love makes burdens lighter, because you divide them. It makes joys more intense, because you share them. It makes you stronger, so that you can reach out and become involved with life in ways you dared not risk alone.

"Aidan, do you find within you a love that united you and Will?"

"I do," said Aidan.

"Do you find within you the courage to resist the many deaths by which love can die? Are you willing to love Will into his unique fullness, and to take the risk and the vulnerability of love again and again?"

"I am."

"Will, do you find within you a love that united you and Aidan?"

"I do."

"Do you find within you the courage to resist the many deaths by which love can die? Are you willing to love Aidan into his unique fullness, and to take the risk and the vulnerability of love again and again?"

"I am."

"Aidan and Will, as you have affirmed your willingness to join together, I now invite you to make the promises of your covenant together. Aidan?"

"Will, these past few months have been so difficult for both of us. There were many times when, if you'd told me this day would ever come, I would have laughed in your face or cried because I wanted it so much. But here we are, and I can't even find words to say how happy I am. I have been so blessed to find you. I now join you to share all of life with you, its responsibilities and freedoms, its joys and sorrows, to love and care for you. As we continue to grow in our love for each other, I will always love you, and listen to you, and speak the truth to you, and try to be the best person I can be for you. I look forward to spending the rest of my life with you, as long as God gives us together."

I took a deep breath and tried not to cry. "Aidan," I started and then realized I was going to have to read my vows if I ever hoped to get through them. I pulled them out of my pocket and tried to ignore the sniffling coming from the rest of the room. "Aidan, when I met you a few months ago, I never in my wildest dreams thought I would be standing here now, doing what I am doing. I didn't even know I was gay then. And in reality, my love for you goes so far beyond labels or gender. It doesn't have anything to do with being gay or straight; it just has to do with the fact that you are a beautiful person and I love you. I love you with all my heart and with all my soul. You've been there for me so many times, even to the point of saving my life more than once. Now I give to you that life that you saved. I look forward to living that life with you, sharing all that life brings, and celebrating each day as a gift from God, as long as we both shall live."

Bryan reached into his pocket and pulled out the two rings. He held one up for everyone to see. "These rings are the symbol of the vows just taken, a circle of wholeness; an unbroken, never-ending, perfect form. These rings mark the beginning of a long journey together filled with wonder, surprises, tears, laughter, celebrations, grief, and joy. May these rings glow in reflection of the warmth and the life which flow through the wearers today."

He handed the ring to Aidan. "Aidan, place this ring on Will's hand and repeat after me, 'I give you this ring as I give you my love and faithfulness.'"

We repeated the process with me placing the ring on Aidan's hand.

"Let us pray. Our Father, we rejoice with Aidan and Will. We thank you for their families and friends who have helped to shape their lives. We thank you for the opportunities and events which challenge them to their life's work. We thank you for their ever-deepening relationship and their decision to share the future together. We pray that we may be responsible witnesses to them, enabling them to share their lives for the sake of all people.

"Aidan and Will, go into the world and fulfill your lives. Hold fast to your ideals. Give one another new experiences of joy. Challenge one another that you might grow together. May this love now sealed with your mutual covenant mature and enrich the experiences of you both. May your home be a happy one and your lives fulfilled. Amen.

"Aidan and Will, why don't you seal your vows with a kiss?"

He didn't have to ask twice. We stepped forward and kissed softly.

"Ladies and gentlemen, it is my great honor to pronounce Aidan Michael Scott and William Spencer Keegan joined before God. May your lives be blessed together."

With that, everyone rose to their feet and began to applaud as one.

Chapter 22

The small, informal reception that followed the wedding was almost as unconventional as the ceremony itself. The most traditional touch was a beautifully decorated three-tiered wedding cake, but even that had an original touch. On the top proudly stood two grooms, one with black hair, and one with brown.

Everyone stayed for the festivities, including, to my surprise, Mom, although she was looking a little pale and strained. That was understandable under the circumstances. Who could blame her, really? Dad was at home, quite possibly dying, and here she was attending her son's marriage...to another man. She'd been a pastor's wife her entire adult life; I knew this couldn't be easy for her. I was very touched that she was there at all.

She wasn't the only one who wasn't one hundred percent supportive. I could tell Laura wasn't exactly thrilled about this turn of events. I wasn't looking forward to our next conversation. And then there was Caitlin. I'd noticed that she'd had a strange expression on her face throughout the ceremony, and now she seemed to be positively glaring in our direction every time I looked her way. Whenever she noticed that I was looking at her, though, she would quickly rearrange her features into a poor imitation of a smile. It came out as more of a grimace, though, as if she were experiencing some sort of sudden attack of gastrointestinal pain.

Eventually I disengaged myself from Aidan, no easy task since he seemed to have become so attached to my arm that I thought I might have to be surgically removed, and made my way over to her.

Once there, however, I didn't know what to say. She didn't make it easy on me. She stared at me with her arms crossed and an unreadable expression on her face.

"Um, hey. You ok?" I said after an awkward pause.

"Why wouldn't I be?" she said icily.

"I don't know, but your body language is speaking pretty clearly," I said in what I hoped was a lighthearted manner.

"And what is it saying?"

"Um...I just wanted to make sure you were ok."

"Oh, I'm grand. That was some surprise you guys pulled here tonight. I sure as hell didn't see it coming. God, I wish I had a drink."

I blinked in surprise at the venom in her voice.

"We didn't want to make a big deal out of it. We wanted it to be a surprise."

"Well, you succeeded. It makes me wonder what else you've been keeping from me."

"What are you talking about?"

"I can see the writing on the wall, Will. You've got your perfect little family now, newlyweds with a baby on the way. Only one little problem: me. Once the baby's here, I'll be out of the picture."

"Caitlin! That's crazy!"

"Oh, so now I'm crazy?"

"No, I mean...Caitlin, you're the mother. I'd never try to cut you out of the baby's life. I'm just going to help you, that's all."

"Sure, that's what you say now. I'll bet you're already planning ways to get rid of me."

"Where is this coming from?" I looked around to see if anyone was close enough to bail me out of this bizarre encounter. Everyone seemed to be involved in their own conversations, completely oblivious to the parallel universe that I seemed to have slipped into.

With a sudden intensity that took me off guard, Caitlin leaned in and grabbed me tightly by the wrist. Instinctively, I pulled back, but her grip was like iron.

"Don't think I don't know," she hissed furiously.

"Don't know what?" I asked helplessly. I felt like I was in a play in which someone had switched the scripts halfway through and no one had thought to provide me a copy.

"Don't play games with me, Will."

"Caitlin, I'm not playing games with you. I'm not playing games with anybody. I swear that I have no clue what you are talking about."

Just then, the phone rang, providing me with the perfect escape from this unreal exchange.

"I'd better get that," I said and went off in search of the phone.

Killian found it before I did and answered it. I watched him listen for a few seconds then motion to Aidan. Aidan took the phone, and after listening for a few seconds himself, looked around the room. When his eyes met mine, he quickly looked away and disappeared down the hall. Was it my imagination, or was he acting a bit guilty? What was going on? Had somebody slipped something in the punch? First Caitlin and now Aidan.

Thinking of Caitlin again, I turned around to see if she was still there, but she was just slipping out the door with her coat on. Everyone else was still deep in conversation, so I made my way over to Killian.

"Who was that on the phone?" I asked casually. Or at least I was going for casual. It probably came out sounding desperately nosy.

"Oh, uh...I dunno. You should ask Aidan. I, uh, hafta pee. Excuse me."

I sighed. So much for casual. Another glance around the room told me everyone was still engrossed in their conversations, so I started off down the hall to find Aidan.

He was in our bedroom, talking in a hushed tone. When he noticed me in the doorway, his eyes widened for a split second, then he smiled and covered up the mouthpiece.

"Hey, babe, you need something?" he asked cheerily. Curiouser and curiouser, I thought, especially considering that he never calls me babe.

"I was wondering where you'd disappeared to," I said.

"I have to take this call, and then I'll be right out. You go on back to the party."

"Who is it?"

"Who is...uh...who?"

I sighed again. "On the phone, Aidan, who is it on the phone?"

His mouth opened and closed soundlessly several times.

"Ok, look, never mind. Forget I asked. You look like a freakin' goldfish. I'll get back to our guests."

"Will," he called, and I stopped, "I...I'll tell you later, ok?"

"Whatever," I said with a disgusted wave. "I think there must be a full moon."

"Huh? Full moon?" he called after me, but I was gone.

I grabbed my coat and slipped out of the apartment. I was a little disappointed that no one even seemed to notice my departure. So much for being the guest of honor.

There was no sign of Caitlin anywhere, so I wandered into the back yard of the apartment building. I was standing by the river with my head thrown back, staring into the sky when Asher found me.

"Hey, cuz, how come you're out here? The party's inside."

"I know. That's why I'm out here."

"Not much of a party person, huh?"

I shrugged. "I was right. The moon is full."

"Is that why you're out here, to admire the moon? What are you now, an astronomer? It's your wedding night, for Pete's sake! Come on back in."

"Everybody's acting weird. It must be because of the full moon."

"I don't know about everybody else, but you sure are acting weird."

"Caitlin flipped out on me, accused me of playing some sort of game with her, and then Aidan was acting all secretive. Even Killian's acting weird."

"Ok, first off, Killian always acts weird. Second, Caitlin is pregnant. Aren't pregnant women supposed to act weird? You know, hormones and all? And as for Aidan, I don't know, maybe he's planning a surprise wedding present. You guys seem to be really into surprises."

"What am I doing, Ash?"

"Um, right now? You're staring into the sky. Your neck is going to get stiff, by the way. What do you mean?"

"I mean, what am I doing with my life? Getting married? I'm eighteen! And to a guy? I mean, three months ago I didn't even know I was gay! And a baby?" I gave a short bark of edgy laughter. "What do I know about raising a baby? Absolutely nothing. I've been messing around with a killer, I may have gotten two people killed, I could have been killed myself, or one of my friends...I've lost my fucking mind!"

"Will, take a deep breath. You've got to calm down," Asher said calmly. "I'm no expert or anything, but I'm pretty sure you're supposed to have cold feet *before* the wedding."

"Who had time?" I laughed again. I was definitely teetering on the edge of hysteria.

"Maybe that's what this is, you're moving too fast. Do you love Aidan?"

"Yes, of course."

"You know he loves you. What more do you need? No one's saying it'll be easy, but if you love each other, you can make it through anything. Like the baby. Nobody really knows how to raise a child at first. They don't come with instruction manuals. You just do your best and give them lots of love and support. Listen to me, like I know what I'm talking about! I don't even have kids!"

"You're right, though," I was starting to calm down; my panic was subsiding. "I should have listened to you to begin with. You're the one who didn't want to get involved with this killer."

He sighed. "I didn't want anything to do with this whole thing, but if you'd listened to me the police wouldn't be investigating now."

"If I'd listened to you, Blake and Robbie would still be alive."

"You can't know that, Will. The killer would have found them eventually if he was determined enough."

"She."

"Huh?"

"The killer is a she. You said he."

"You know that for sure now?"

"Robbie told me, before he was killed. He said he thought that the person with Joey when he died was a female."

"Oh." He didn't seem to know what to say.

"You really think Aidan and I can make it?"

He looked over at me. "Yeah, I do. I think if anybody has a chance you guys do."

"What about you and Killian? Do you guys still have a chance, or did I screw everything up?"

He was quiet for a minute. "I don't know. I hope we still have a chance. I love him, and I know he loves me, but I just don't know. I do know one thing; if things are screwed up, it's not your fault. It's something that we have to deal with between us."

"I hope it's not too late."

"Me, too. You ready to go back in?"

"In a minute. You go ahead."

"'K," he said and started away.

"Hey, Asher, did you know Seth?" I asked suddenly.

"What?"

"Did you know Seth? Adam's son?"

"Whoa, where did that come from?"

"I don't know. I've just been thinking about him lately."

"Did you know him?"

"No, Aidan told me a little about him, about what happened with you and Killian and all. And then Adam was here all day today working his butt off putting together our wedding. And I couldn't help but think that he had to be thinking about Seth and how he would never get the chance to get married."

"You know I never even thought of that. Killian must have, though; he's been staying kind of close to him all night. Steve, too, of course. I did know Seth a little. Not like Killian, though; he was Seth's only real friend. Killian took it really hard when he died, but it brought us together. You know, this really isn't what you should be thinking about tonight."

"Why not? Death has been all I've thought about for the last few months. It seems fitting somehow to think about death on my wedding night. And I have a feeling I haven't seen the last of it yet."

"You mean your dad?"

"Yeah...and I don't know. I just have a feeling that we haven't seen the last of Joey's killer."

"God, Will! You're freaking me out."

I forced a laugh. "Sorry, Ash. Come on; let's go back in. I don't know what's wrong with me. I should be deliriously happy, but I just can't shake this feeling that something is going to go wrong, that it won't last."

"Will, you're still grieving for Joey and your dad could be dying; no one expects you to be delirious, but it is your wedding night, so try to enjoy it, huh?"

"Yeah, ok."

We walked back inside in a companionable silence. I was glad to have a friend and cousin as grounded as Asher. Everyone cheered as we re-entered the apartment.

"There you are," Aidan said. "Nobody knew where you had gotten to."

"You seemed busy, so I went out for some air," I mumbled through a deep blush. It felt like every eye in the room was on me, which of course it was. Mom made her way over to me and said that she wanted to get home to Dad. I gave her a kiss and thanked her for coming. I think she knew how much it meant to me.

The party went on until late into the night. I noticed that Killian and Steve did seem to be hovering a bit around Adam, but to all appearances, he seemed fine.

Things came crashing to a halt a little after midnight. The phone rang, and this time I got to it first.

"Will?" It was Mom, and she sounded as if she were crying.

"Dad?" The single word was all I could manage to squeeze past the sudden lump that had formed in my throat.

"He took a turn for the worst, Will. Deb had to call the ambulance again. I came home to find a note saying they were at the hospital. That's where I am now. The doctor just came. He said...he said I should call the family together. You're the only family..."

"I'm on my way, Ma."

I looked up to find the whole room had gone deathly quiet, apprehension was clearly written all over every face.

"It's my dad," I said hoarsely.

"I'll drive," Aidan said as he swept into action, scooping up the car keys and my coat.

"We'll come, too," Killian said, and Asher nodded.

"Me, too," Laura said immediately.

"We'll stay and clean up the apartment," Adam assured me, and everyone else was quick to agree. "Don't worry about anything here. Just go."

We were out the door in record time and speeding to the hospital. We traveled in separate cars, Aidan, Asher, Killian, and me in one car, Gabe and Laura in another. Once there, we went directly to Dad's room, stopping just outside the door.

"You go on in," Aidan said gently. "We'll be right out here in the waiting room."

I nodded, but I didn't move. With all the death that had surrounded me over the last several months, I had never actually seen anyone die. I wasn't looking forward to my own father being the first. Even with everything that had happened between us, he was still my father and I loved him. And now I was about to lose him forever.

As I stood there, immobile, I felt a hand slip into mine and pull me gently forward. It was Killian.

"Come on," he said softly, "I'll go with you."

I guess it made sense that Killian would be the least affected by the idea of seeing someone die. He had been witness to more death in his short life than most people ever saw; he'd lost several friends and had almost been killed himself. He had faced death and survived. Somehow, his courage and his presence gave me the strength I needed. I stepped forward.

Mom looked up as we came in. She was sitting next to Dad's bed, his pale, limp hand in hers. Her hair was disarranged, and there were dark circles under her red-rimmed eyes. Aunt Deb, Asher's mom, stood behind her with her hands on Mom's shoulders. She seemed surprised to see Killian but didn't say anything.

Mom gave me a shaky smile, then turned back to Dad's still form.

"Will's here," she said to him. "We're all here now."

There was no response from Dad. He looked like he was already dead. Wires and tubes came from every direction and were connected to various machines. They all attested to the fact that, despite appearances, he was still alive, at least for now.

"Now that Will is here, you can let go, Lowell," she said, her voice thick with emotion. I clutched Killian's hand tighter. "He knows you love him. I know you love me. And we both love you. It's ok; we'll be ok. You don't have to stay here for our sake any more."

She broke down and began to weep silently. I felt like I was watching a movie with the volume turned off. Her body was wracked with huge, shuddering sobs, but not a sound was heard. It was the most disturbing sight I had ever seen. I quickly knelt down next to her and hugged her. Aunt Deb bent over us in an awkward embrace.

Suddenly a nurse ran into the room, followed closely by a second. We were quickly and efficiently herded from the room.

"What's going on?" Mom demanded.

"Ma'am, you and your family will need to wait out here. A silent alarm went off, and we need you to wait here until the doctor can talk to you."

"What alarm? Please tell me what's going on."

Just then a doctor in a white coat came rushing past us and into the room.

"Excuse me," the nurse said, "I need to get back in there."

She left us alone in the hall. Aidan, Asher, Laura, and Gabe quickly joined us, and I saw Asher and his mom having a whispered conversation. We stood awkwardly in the hall, waiting. I paced and Mom sat on a bench rocking back and forth. After several minutes, the doctor came back out. Mom quickly stood up and positioned herself in front of him.

"Doctor?" she said.

"Mrs. Keegan," he began. He looked very tired, as if it had been a long night and it wasn't about to get any better. I knew what was coming. "I'm very sorry. Your husband suffered another severe heart attack. The damage was so extensive that there was nothing we could do. He passed away. I'm so sorry."

He continued talking, but I didn't hear him anymore. It was as if the world were slowly spinning away. The last thing I remember hearing was a horrible inhuman keening coming from my mother, and then everything went black.

When I came to, I was lying in the hallway with a nurse waving smelling salts under my nose.

When she saw my eyes flutter open, she asked, "Are you ok?"

I thought that was an incredibly stupid thing to ask someone whose father had just died, but I somehow refrained from saying so. I simply nodded and sat up. Aidan was at my side in a flash to help me up. Killian and Asher were now occupying the bench, and Mom was crying on Aunt Deb's shoulder. Laura and Gabe had moved away, I guess to give us some space.

There were a few formalities, papers to be signed, arrangements to be made, but Aunt Deb took care of most of those and it didn't take very long. We left the hospital and went back to Mom and Dad's house, or I guess it was just Mom's now. Laura and Gabe just went on home after expressing their condolences. Once we arrived at the house, there really wasn't anything to do. Mom took some sleeping pills that the doctor had given Aunt Deb, and she fell asleep within minutes. Finally, Aidan insisted we go home so I could get some rest, too. Killian and Asher decided to go home with Aunt Deb and come back to pick their car up tomorrow.

We arrived back at the apartment building just after two a.m. Nikki's door flew open as soon as we stepped off the elevator. As soon as she saw our faces, she threw her arms around me in a tight hug.

"I'm sorry, sweetie," she murmured in my ear, "as if you haven't been through enough already, now this. I couldn't sleep I was so worried. Every time the elevator came up, I was out the door. Caitlin came by; I told her what was going on, and she said she'd be back tomorrow, or well...I guess later this morning. Listen to me babbling on, as if you care about all this right now. You need to rest. Don't even think about coming in to work tomorrow. You take some time off. We'll get by without you."

She gave me a quick peck on the forehead, and then she was gone, her door shut. I stood for a minute, feeling rather like Dorothy must have felt after the tornado had dropped her off in Oz.

"Caitlin," Aidan said under his breath, a frown pulling down the corners of his mouth.

"What about her?" I asked.

"Never mind," he said and went to our door. As he slipped the key into the lock, the door swung open at his touch, it wasn't even shut all the way.

"They must have forgotten to lock it," he muttered as we stepped in.

My mind was so numb that it took a minute for it to register that all the wedding decorations were gone and the furniture had been replaced. The tree had been left up but other than that, you would have never known a wedding had taken place in this very room only hours before. My mind kept going back to the name Aidan had uttered in the hall, Caitlin.

Aidan came up behind me and began to massage my shoulders. Then he kissed the side of my neck.

"Why don't you go get in bed?" he said softly. "I'm going to get myself a drink, and I'll be right there."

"Why did you say Caitlin's name just now, in the hall?" I asked.

He sighed. "It'll wait till morning."

"No, it won't. I want to know now. Is this something to do with that phone call tonight?"

"Yeah, it is. Look, you know Killian and I had our doubts about Caitlin. Something just didn't ring true. So we've done some checking around."

"You what?" I asked as I turned around to face him. "I thought you suspected Laura?"

"We did; we checked up on both of them. Laura was the easiest. I called her and confronted her. She admitted to it right away. She was really shaken up. She said she called Robbie that night because she was mad at Gabe for not telling her about him and she wanted to be the first to talk to him. He wouldn't talk to her, since he'd just talked to you. He hung up saying someone was at the door, and he had to go. It was probably the killer."

A shiver ran up my spine.

"Caitlin was more of a challenge," he went on. "We made some phone calls. Killian found out she deliberately told the reporter at your big show that night that she was your fiancée. So then we wondered what else she was lying about. I managed to find out what her home address was from a friend in admissions at school and I called her parents. It turns out they're just fine, they're still together, and they aren't strict at all. Definitely not Mormon. They had no idea that she was pregnant. There's more, but there's no point going into it now."

"But why—"

"Would she lie? I've been trying to figure out the same thing."

"Do you think she's the killer?"

"I don't know, Will. It's possible. She had time while you were in the bathroom to have killed him and then gone to the front yard. Or maybe she's just nuts. But one thing's for sure, there's nothing we can do about it tonight. Let's go to bed, ok?"

I nodded and stumbled off down the hall, my mind reeling. I pushed open our bedroom door and stopped abruptly just outside. The hairs on the back of my neck suddenly stood on end and a deep sense of foreboding filled me. I'm not sure what it was, whether my subconscious noticed something and sent me an inner warning or whether it was something on a deeper level, but whatever it was, I knew with perfect certainty that something horrible waited in the darkness of that room.

"Who's there?" I called out.

"What?" Aidan answered from the kitchen.

I took a step backwards, away from the room, as a voice snaked out of the shadows.

"Stop," a seemingly disembodied voice ordered.

I froze.

"Will?" Aidan called. "Do you need something?"

"Don't speak," the voice hissed. "Go across the hall to the other bedroom."

At first, I didn't move, but then a hint of movement in the gloom caught my eye and slowly a gun materialized. It was followed by an arm and at last, the rest of the killer.

My heart stopped. Everything stopped. It seemed like time itself simply ceased to move forward. And then everything made a horrible kind of sense.

"Caitlin," I said sadly.

She cocked her head to one side.

"You don't seem surprised," she said.

"Somehow I'm not."

"You're not as smart as you think you are," she growled. "You never even suspected me. I even tried to warn you, but you wouldn't listen. I told you I would do anything to protect my baby, and I meant it. I don't want to do this. You're different from the others. I like you, maybe I even love you, but I don't have a choice."

"Yes, you do have a choice. You don't have to do...whatever it is you're thinking about doing." I couldn't bring myself to say the words.

"I'm going to kill you, Will, you and Aidan. And you're wrong. I don't have a choice. I have to protect my baby."

"There's always a choice. How is killing me going to protect your baby? I'm going to help..."

"Enough with the lies already, Will!" she interrupted angrily. "I already told you I figured out your little scam. You're not getting my baby."

"I don't want to take the baby away from you, Caitlin. I just want to help." I desperately wanted to look and see where Aidan was, but I couldn't tear my eyes off of that gun.

"Get in the bedroom, now. I'm tired of playing games."

I backed up until I felt the door at my back and opened it without turning around.

"Come on out, Aidan," she yelled suddenly. "There'll be no last minute heroics from you unless you want me to kill Will right now."

Aidan stepped calmly out of the kitchen but stayed at that end of the hall.

"I know the truth, Caitlin," he said in a reasonable tone, as if he was commenting on the weather or mentioning that night's TV schedule.

"What truth?" Caitlin said. It was obvious his attitude was unnerving her.

"I talked to your dad earlier tonight, nice guy."

"You're lying."

"He told me the whole story. You see, some things didn't add up to me, I got suspicious. So I called him."

"You're a lying bastard."

"Really? Then how would I know that you've been in and out of mental hospitals all your life. Emotionally unstable is the phrase I believe he used. He told me about the time you killed the family dog when you were ten because you said he kept chewing your dolls up. And the time you attacked your friend at school because she cheated with your boyfriend. That one was pretty serious; she could have died. You were in the hospital for quite a while that time. He also told me how the doctors had finally said you were stable enough to be released and how he and your mother fought it, but they released you anyway. They haven't heard from you since...until now. Are you even enrolled at Pemberton?"

"I'm going to kill you, and I'm going to kill Will, and then I'll go away and start over somewhere where nobody can hurt me or my baby."

"You're not going anywhere, Caitlin. I'm not the only one who knows this. They'll find you, and the very thing you've been afraid of all along will come true; you'll lose the baby."

"Oh, sure, what am I supposed to do then? Stay here and wait for the police? I don't think so. This is all Joey's fault. He's the one that kept telling me to kill our baby. Kill it! Can you believe it? I never intended to have an abortion. I would never kill my baby. I didn't mean to kill Joey. It was a mistake. I'm not sorry, though. I'm glad he's dead."

"What about Blake and Robbie?"

"They had to die. They knew about me. If they had told anyone, I would have lost my baby. Everything I've done has been for the baby. I have to protect my baby. That's what I'm doing now. That's why you both have to die. Get in the room, now."

"No," he said flatly.

What was he doing? I let my eyes dart his way for a second. He was standing at the end of the hallway, leaning against the kitchen doorway, backlit by the bright light from the kitchen since I hadn't turned on the hall light. He looked almost angelic, as if he were glowing from within.

"Don't play games with me, Aidan!" Her voice was getting shrill. It was obvious she was losing what little control she had. Why didn't Aidan just do what she said, before he got us both killed? If he were closer maybe we could both rush her at once.

"I'm not the one playing games. You've played us all along, lied to us, manipulated us, and all the while you were a killer."

She shook her head. "Shut up!"

"And now the very thing you're most afraid of is about to happen."

"Shut up!"

"You're going to lose your baby because you're an insane murderer."

"Shut up, shut up, shut up!"

"You'll never see your baby again."

"Shut up, damn you!"

The blast was deafening. My body reacted without thought. At the sound of the explosion, I launched myself at Caitlin full force, slamming into her and taking us both down in a pile just inside the doorway to the dark bedroom.

I lunged for the gun in her hand, and we grappled for control of the weapon. With what seemed like almost superhuman strength she wrenched the gun from my grasp and whipped me across the face with it. I tasted the metallic bite of blood in my mouth, but I was beyond pain. I blindly threw punch after punch, some connected and some didn't, but I kept on swinging. She struck me in the face again, this time connecting more solidly, and I reeled back from the blow.

I was blinded by the pain and blinked frantically to clear my vision. I found myself with the muzzle of the gun only inches from my face. I scrambled backwards until I came against something solid, the dresser. I groped frantically behind me and grabbed the first thing I felt.

"Say hello to Joey for me," she said with a frightening smile.

I swung my hand forward, yanking the cord I had grabbed with it.

To this day I don't know if the swinging lamp distracted her or if at the last moment she hesitated for one second too long, but for whatever reason, the shot went wild, shattering the mirror across the room as the heavy pottery lamp caught her full in the face.

I didn't waste a second. While she was still stunned from the blow, I sprung on her. Grasping the lamp like a club, I brought it down over her head, once, twice...then I felt her go limp beneath me.

I snatched up the gun and shoved away as quickly as I could. I held the gun trained on her even though I had never held a gun before in my life. She didn't move a muscle, though. I struggled to my feet and backed into the hall, still keeping a careful eye on her.

"Aidan?" I called. There was no answer. "Aidan?"

I tore my eyes away from her inert body and looked for Aidan. His feet lay splayed out in the middle of the hallway; the rest of him lay out of sight in the kitchen.

"Aidan?" I screamed, and then I was running down the short hall. I came up short at the door.

"Oh, my God," I whimpered. He was still all in white, wearing the clothes that Adam had given us for our wedding, but now the front of his chest was soaked bright red. A slow growing pool of blood surrounded him. His eyes were closed.

With a wordless cry, I fell to my knees next to him and cradled his head in my lap.

His eyes fluttered open, and I felt a tiny glimmer of hope stir inside me. "Oh, my God, Aidan," I cried. "It's going to be ok, right? You're going to be ok. We're going to be ok."

"I'm sorry..." he whispered as his eyes slipped shut.

"There's nothing to be sorry about. It's going to be fine. I know it."

"...tried to draw it out...keep her talking..."

"Shh, Aidan. Don't talk, honey. Just hang on, ok? Just hang on. Don't leave me."

"...called the police..."

"Don't leave me, Aidan."

"...I love you, Will..." he breathed, his voice so soft now I might have imagined it.

"Don't go, Aidan," I sobbed. "Please don't leave me."

"...I'll love you forever, Will..."

"Oh, God, I love you, too, Aidan. I love you."

His eyes fluttered open again, and he looked into mine, past my eyes and into my soul. And then they closed for the last time. I knew he was gone. I felt him leave. I felt a part of my soul leave with him.

"I love you. I love you. I love you," I sobbed. I kissed his lips and rocked his body back and forth. I was still rocking and crying when the police burst in minutes later. They swarmed around me and down the hall, but they were too late. Too late for Aidan. Too late for me.

Epilogue

"Looking back, it's clear. I should have seen it, should have known."

"Known what?" Doctor Wohler asked. "That your new friend was a very sick young woman? Not physically but mentally unbalanced? That she ruthlessly killed your best friend and two others? That she would try to kill you and your lover? How could you have known any of those things, Will? It's useless to blame yourself, although it's a natural response. We've talked a lot about how we can never be responsible for someone else's actions, and it holds true here. What a person does is fully their own choice, no matter what the circumstances."

"But..."

"But what? You should have known? How? You're not a psychic. No one knew."

"I should have done something, done more..."

"You did all you could. What you did saved your life."

"But not Aidan's, and maybe my life isn't worth living without him."

"You have your whole life ahead of you, Will. Your mother is still alive, and I imagine she'll need you in the weeks ahead."

"I've moved back in with her. I couldn't bear to go back to the apartment."

"That's probably for the best. And you've got a promising career in the arts ahead of you." I shook my head as he continued, "And you've got a baby on the way. That agreement still stands, I suppose."

"Yes," I said slowly. "It's legally binding, which is just as well now since Caitlin's been arrested and all. I don't know what would have happened to the baby otherwise; I don't think her parents wanted it. She's awaiting trial now. I don't know what will happen to her, and to be honest, I don't really care. They could give her the death penalty for all I care, but I get the baby. Although, she hasn't been doing very well lately. The doctors say it looks like it may be a difficult pregnancy, so I suppose there's a chance the baby might not make it."

"You've been surrounded by so much death in the last few months I guess it's natural for you to expect it around every corner, but with modern medicine the way it is now, the baby has a very good chance of surviving even a difficult pregnancy."

"I guess we'll see," I said disconsolately.

"Yes, we will. At least we will as long as you don't do anything to hurt yourself."

"I won't," I said firmly. "Not that I haven't thought about it, but...I guess I feel I owe it to Aidan to not give up again. He taught me that..."

"Then his life was not lived in vain."

"No, it wasn't in vain," I agreed softly. "I should go. I've taken too much of your time as it is."

"Nonsense, it's quite alright. That's why I'm here."

"Still, I need to go, to get home."

"Will you come see me again? Soon perhaps?"

"I think I will."

"Good."

"Thank you, Dr. Wohler," I stood to leave but paused by the door and turned around, my hand on the knob. "You know, Dad once told me to look up a Bible verse, right after he found out I was gay. It was Hosea 8:1. Do you know it?"

"No, I'm afraid I'm not very familiar with the Bible. Can you quote it?"

"Oh, yes. I can't get it out of my head these days. It says, 'For you have sown the wind, and you shall reap the whirlwind...' I've thought about that a lot. Do you think that he could have been right? Maybe I'm just reaping the whirlwind."

"No, Will, I may not be much of a Bible scholar, but I don't think that's how God works. I don't think you are being punished. You're not reaping the whirlwind. In fact, I think you've weathered the storm, Will, and you're stronger because of it."

I thought for a moment about what he had said, and suddenly the painting I had done so many months ago popped into my head. It had fit my situation so perfectly then, and it still fit. I saw the tiny frog clinging doggedly to that thin blade of grass while a raging storm whipped furiously around him. He might bend but he wouldn't break. He was a survivor. Like me.

A small smile turned up the corners of my mouth. I looked to find Dr. Wohler smiling back at me. "Thank you." I slipped out, closed the door behind me, and maybe, just maybe, closed the door on my past.

Josh Aterovis has been writing fiction for over six years. His first two books, *Bleeding Hearts* and a spin-off mystery *Reap the Whirlwind*, were published in 2001 and 2003, respectively. The first book, *Bleeding Hearts*, introduced gay teen sleuth Killian Kendall, and won several awards, including the 2002 Whodunit Award from the Stone Wall Society. He followed up by winning the Whodunit Award again the following year for *Reap the Whirlwind*. In addition to novels, Aterovis also writes for AfterElton.com, an entertainment news website for and about gay and bisexual men, doing articles, interviews, and reviews.

Aterovis was born and bred on the Eastern Shore of Maryland and lives there with his husband, Jon. Aterovis is a Latin pseudonym meaning "black sheep". He has won numerous awards for his writing and for his website — www.joshaterovis.com — which also features his well-received art gallery.

Other works by Josh Aterovis:

Bleeding Hearts

ISBN: 978 - 1 - 933720 - 34 - 0 (1-933720-34-4)

Killian Kendall is used to being overlooked, even in his own family. That's about to change. With the arrival of a new kid at school, Killian's whole world is about to be turned upside down. The new guy is openly gay and, for reasons he can't really understand, Killian finds himself drawn to him. When the boy is killed in a brutal attack, and Killian is injured in the process, Killian begins to questions everything around him.

The police seem eager to write the attack off as a random mugging, but Killian was there and he knows better. With the help of the murdered boy's father and his friends, Killian starts his own investigation. His search turns up hatred in small town America, and before it's over, more people will be dead, and Killian's life will be on the line again.

Available at your favorite bookstore.

ATERO   HMNTV
Aterovis, Josh.
Reap the whirlwind /

MONTROSE
12/11

CPSIA information can be obtained at www.ICGtesting.com
Printed in the USA
BVOW050814291011

274803BV00001B/246/A